MURDER
AT
DARESWICK HALL

by Margaret Addison

A Rose Simpson Mystery

Rose Simpson Mysteries in order

Murder at Ashgrove House
Murder at Dareswick Hall
Murder at Sedgwick Court
Murder at Renard's

Chapter One

'Are you sure about this?' asked Mrs Simpson, perched on the edge of her daughter's bed, watching as Rose packed her suitcase. Her daughter had her mind set on the task at hand, going backwards and forwards laden with clothes, first from her wardrobe, and then to her pale green-glazed chintz covered bed, where her suitcase lay open invitingly. As she looked on, it seemed to Mrs Simpson that a great many items were being packed for just a weekend in the country.

'What do you mean, Mother?' enquired Rose, her mind only half listening to what her parent was saying, being more concerned in packing her case as quickly as possible, so that she would be ready in time to catch her train. What a pity that the Simpsons' finances did not stretch to employing a servant. How much more convenient it would have been to have had a maid make sure that all her clothes were freshly ironed, and to pack her case for her.

'Well, you know what happened last time, my dear, when you attended a house party at a country house hosted by the gentry,' Mrs Simpson said, quietly.

'Oh, Mother, you mustn't worry so,' said her daughter, abandoning her task and flopping herself down on the bed next to her mother. 'It's hardly going to happen again, now is it? It was all very sad and unfortunate, but really, there's absolutely no reason to think there's going to be another murder, now is there? I mean, what are the chances of it happening again?'

'I suppose you're right,' admitted her mother, rather grudgingly. 'But that won't stop me worrying about you all the same. I know I'm just being silly, but I can't help it.'

She might have added that she was equally worried about her daughter meeting up with the new Earl of Belvedere again, but decided it was wise to refrain from comment on that matter. She reminded herself that Rose was a sensible, level-headed girl, after all, but it did not lessen the reservations she had concerning her daughter mixing with the aristocracy. Her daughter worked in a dress shop after all, as a result of the family having come down in the world. For both Rose and herself, working for a living had become an unwelcome necessity.

Mrs Simpson sighed. It was true that she wished her daughter to aspire to greater things, but surely entering the British aristocracy was beyond her reach. She had refrained from prying into her daughter's relationship with Cedric, because up until now it had consisted mainly of written correspondence. But now her daughter would be seeing him in person again, the first time since the disastrous events that had occurred at Ashgrove House some two or three months previously. She wondered whether it could be considered wise or responsible of her to allow her daughter to go unaccompanied for a visit to Dareswick Hall, although Rose had assured her that there would be at least two other young ladies present.

'Now where did I put my tea dress with the blue flowers on it?' enquired Rose, rummaging through the clothes in her wardrobe, oblivious to her mother's concerns regarding Cedric and the company she kept. 'Don't tell me that it's gone for the wash? Oh, if only Madame Renard had allowed me to take today off work so that I could have sorted out my clothes and set off earlier. As it is I'll be lucky to arrive at Dareswick Hall before dinner is served. But I suppose I should be grateful that she let me leave work early today and is allowing me to take the day off tomorrow, especially as she considers me responsible for Lavinia not going back to work in her shop. As if she really would after everything that happened.'

Rose had first met Lady Lavinia Sedgwick some seven or eight months earlier when Lavinia had taken up a bet made with her brother Cedric that she could not earn her own living for six months. Lavinia had chosen to work in the dress shop where Rose herself was employed and for a time, despite their very different backgrounds, the two girls had been inseparable.

'Will Lavinia be there this weekend?' asked Mrs Simpson, tentatively.

'You know very well she will not, Mother,' replied Rose, sadly. 'She holds me partly responsible for what happened at Ashgrove. Cedric seems to think that she will come round eventually, but I'm not at all sure that she will. And I'm not sure that I blame her. I feel some responsibility myself.'

A knock at the front door drew Mrs Simpson's attention away from the activities of her daughter and caused her to hurry back downstairs. Rose, in turn, having finished her packing, or at least given up hope of finding any more suitably clean and ironed clothes to pack, closed her case and collapsed

2

on to her bed to abandon herself to her thoughts for a few brief delicious moments, before necessity dictated that she set off to catch her train.

She had not seen Cedric since that last fateful day at Ashgrove House, when he had told her that as far as he was concerned nothing had changed and he still loved her. She remembered, her cheeks glowing red with the recollection, that she had cut his speech short by flinging herself into his arms. Then, promising to write, she had gone out into the day, a beautifully bright and sunny day if she remembered rightly, which had contrasted sharply with the sorrow in the house. And since then Cedric had been so engaged with everything, with sorting out the affairs of the estate, arranging the funerals and communicating a version of the tragedy to the world as a whole, that they had not had a chance to meet up in person, making do instead with hurriedly scribbled notes and letters to each other.

It had come as something of a pleasant surprise when Cedric had suggested that their first meeting after Ashgrove be at a house party at Dareswick Hall, hosted by Baron Atherton, an old friend of the Belvedere family. She remembered how she had felt when Lavinia had first mooted the idea of going to stay at Ashgrove House, a mixture of anticipation, apprehension and excitement. She felt something similar to it now. Then it had been because she was anxious at the prospect of being a guest of the local gentry and wondering if she would pass muster with Lady Withers and, perhaps more importantly, with her servants. Now she felt those same emotions, but this time it was due to the prospect of meeting the man she loved, the man she had been prepared to protect and keep quiet for, in order to save him from the gallows. She suddenly felt a sharp stab of sorrow to know that Lavinia would not be there. It had been her erstwhile friend who had introduced her to her brother in the first place.

She realised now, as the reality of the situation dawned on her, that she had been living in an almost fairy-tale stupor, hardly conscious of the mundane everyday activities of living, instead dwelling in her daydreams so that they became her sense of reality. And tonight she would discover if reality successfully mirrored her rose-tinted recollections.

She sighed and made her way down the stairs, her case banging awkwardly on each stair due to the weight of the clothes, accessories and toiletries within. If her daydreams were about to be dashed then so be it. After all, she was a sensible girl really, she had needed to be due to the

3

deteriorating financial situation of her family that had forced her to seek employment. If she found now that she was required to put her own personal dreams aside then she would but, and she crossed her fingers tightly, how much more wonderful would it be if she did not have to and her wishes could be realised.

The Honourable Isabella Atherton regarded her reflection in her dressing table mirror. She smiled briefly because what she saw pleased her, for there was no doubting by anyone's standards that she was a beautiful young woman.

Then her mood darkened, as swiftly as a cloud passing over the sun, and she shuddered and clutched on to the dressing table, as if to give herself courage. Suddenly she could not bring herself to study her own refection too closely. If she looked into the mirror too intently now she would be able to detect every flaw and she was afraid of what she would see. She would catch glimpses of the character of the woman behind the superficial beauty. Her eyes, she knew, would be cold, her lips thin; her mouth downturned. Above all, though, she could not bear to see the misery that would be etched on her face, for with no audience present there was no need for pretence. Her face would reveal the wretchedness of the position in which she now found herself.

Oh, how could she have been so impulsive and reckless? How could she not have thought about the consequences of her actions before she had done what she had done? And now she was trapped as surely as a bird in a cage. She would never be free, she knew that. He would never allow her to be free. And the worse thing of all was that it was all her own fault. She had no one else to blame. She had brought it all on herself. She stifled a sob. She mustn't cry. She mustn't let herself lose control and go to pieces. It would be so easy to do that and yet too dangerous. She took a deep breath. She would have to decide within the next few days whether she was capable of gritting her teeth and going through with it. If not, then she must find a way out of her predicament. Instinctively she looked down at her hands, now sitting demurely in her lap. She watched in horror as her hands slowly began to shake of their own accord, as if they knew. Of course there was only really one satisfactory way out. She studied her trembling hands and wondered whether, if the time came, she would find the courage required to see it through.

'So what did Isabella say exactly, Hallam?' asked Josephine, standing over her brother as he sat on the sofa in the music room at Dareswick Hall, idly flicking through gramophone records.

'I've told you already. She said that she would be bringing someone down with her this weekend and I just got the feeling that it would be her latest beau, that's all,' Hallam replied, somewhat irritated by her refusal to leave the subject alone. If he had realised that she was going to go on so about it, he would never have mentioned it. 'I could have got it completely wrong. She could be bringing down one of her girlfriends. I say,' he frowned suddenly as a thought struck him, 'I hope it's not Celia; I can't stand the way she laughs like a horse at simply everything as if it's all a joke. And do sit down, Josephine. It's very off putting having someone loom over you, don't you know. It's bad enough when Crabtree does it, without you doing it too. Of course, I expect it of him, I mean, it's what butlers do, isn't it? But the least you can do is to sit down if you are intent on questioning me.'

Josephine perched herself reluctantly on the arm of the sofa. She felt too agitated to sit down properly, and longed instead to pace the room. But then even her brother, who could never be accused of thinking too deeply about anything that was not directly related to his own entertainment or amusement, might guess that something was wrong. And she couldn't have that. Really, Hallam was too irritating for words. Why couldn't he remember his conversation with Isabella word for word? She would have done, she knew, but then she would have been listening carefully, which she supposed he had not been doing.

'Just tell me one more time, Hallam, there's a dear, and then I'll leave you in peace to peruse your gramophone records. Mrs Hodges will need to know so she can arrange the bedrooms. If it's a man she'll put him on your corridor. If it's one of Isabella's girlfriends, then she'll probably put her in the Pink Room next to mine.'

'It wasn't so much what she said,' admitted Hallam. 'It was more the way she said it, as if she was nervous and she'd hardly be nervous if she was just bringing down one of her girlfriends with her, would she? I say, do you think it would be quite the done thing to put on the gramophone and have dancing this weekend, what with Cedric still being in mourning and everything?'

'Probably not. Although I suggest we just play it by ear,' replied Josephine, distracted, 'you know, see what he's like.'

So Hallam really had very little basis for his impression that Isabella was going to be bringing a man with her; that was interesting. For a moment Josephine did not know whether she was disappointed or relieved. If she had been close to her sister, then no doubt Isabella would have confided in her. But they were very different in both appearance and character. Her father was always likening them to chalk and cheese; beautiful, outgoing Isabella, the belle of every ball who simply had men tripping over themselves to adore her and be entranced by her sparkling conversation; and Josephine, plain, quiet, studious and rather timid, more at home clad in a sensible tweed skirt and plain blouse, poring over books in the family library than dressed in the latest Parisian fashions attending society parties. As a consequence, Josephine had stayed at Dareswick Hall to keep home for her widowed father while Isabella resided most of the time in a service apartment in London, only deigning to come home for special occasions and house parties, declaring that she found country life dull and backward compared with the bright lights and delights London had to offer.

'I rather thought that the reason Isabella might be coming back this weekend was to see Cedric,' Josephine remarked, trying to appear nonchalant. 'I thought she might want to try and get her claws into him, what with him having come into the earldom and everything.'

'Hmm, the same thought occurred to me,' said Hallam, putting aside the gramophone records, 'You know our sis, she can be rather mercenary, especially where men are concerned. But I think he's a trifle young for her, you know how she tends to prefer the older man. Besides, he's invited the girl from the dress shop to stay, Rose Simpson I think her name is.'

'She was there at Ashgrove, wasn't she?' Josephine enquired, looking interested. 'She must know what really happened, mustn't she? I mean, not just the official version of events.'

'Well, don't you try and get it out of her,' warned her brother, suddenly becoming serious. 'I promised Cedric that we wouldn't pry. That's why he's coming to visit us. He knows that he can just be himself here. He's had an awful time of it, the newspapers have been hounding him something rotten.

He hasn't been able to step outside Sedgwick Court without being pounced on. His head gardener has even found pressmen roaming around in the grounds trampling the borders. They've had to employ a man with a couple of dogs to keep them out.'

'Poor Cedric, sounds as if he's had a rum old time of it. He must be serious about this girl though, mustn't he? I mean bringing her here. I can't imagine that went down well with his parents. They'd have wanted him to marry another member of the nobility or at least someone with money. Still, he's frightfully rich isn't he, even richer than Daddy, and I suppose he can do what he wants now.'

'There was a time when I wondered whether you might be rather sweet on him,' said her brother, watching her closely. 'You know before −' He broke off what he was going to say sharply, as he saw his sister frown and put her hand up to cover her face. 'Oh, gosh, I'm sorry, Jo. How jolly rotten of me. I didn't mean to rake it all up again. How beastly of me to remind you of it all. I know you've tried so hard to put it all behind you …'

'It's all right, Hallam,' said Josephine, patting her brother's arm affectionately. 'It's not that, really it isn't. I'm quite over Hugh. It was just a silly girlish infatuation, that's all. And as for Cedric, I was rather fond of him once when we were both very young, but really it was nothing.'

'All right, if you say so, old thing,' replied Hallam not at all convinced about her denial over her feelings for Hugh, and still feeling rather bad. It had been rather an awful time for them all, really; Cedric hadn't been the only one of them to have been subjected to scandal, gossip and speculation. The Athertons had had their fair share earlier in the year.

Brother and sister sat quietly together for a few moments, each lost in their own thoughts. At last Josephine broke through the silence, all the while looking at her brother keenly while she spoke.

'You know, Hallam, I'm awfully fond of you. You really are the best sort of brother any girl could have. Whatever happens in the future …' She faltered slightly, causing her brother to look up at her sharply. 'What I mean to say is that I hope you will always remember me fondly and know that I never meant to hurt you, not any of you, not Father, not even Isabella.'

'What a strange thing to say, Josephine. As if *you'd* ever do anything to hurt us. I can't think of anyone less likely. Dear old sis, why you are the most respectable, reliable young woman of my acquaintance. Heaven help us if you ever do anything wrong. And I'd mind very much if you ever do anything to change that. I love coming back to Dareswick and knowing that everything will be the same. You'll be here, looking after Father, the same old big sister doing the same old things. But I won't be too selfish, though. I shan't mind a jot if you marry some country doctor or even some librarian come to help you catalogue all the old books in the library, so long as you promise to stay here and always remain the same.'

'I don't think any of us can ever promise that,' said Josephine, slowly.

'You're not unhappy here, are you Jo?' asked Hallam, suddenly concerned, alarmed by her unusually serious tone. 'I always thought you were happy here, looking after Father. I know Dareswick's in the middle of nowhere and that it's very quiet and there's no society to speak of, but I always thought you rather liked that. Cocktail parties and bright lights really aren't your thing, are they? I thought tennis parties and village bazaars and suchlike were much more to your liking.'

'Yes, of course,' Josephine said, quickly. 'Oh just ignore me, I was just being silly, that's all. I didn't mean anything by it. Goodness, how very serious we've both become. Now, let's talk about something else, shall we? This weekend for instance. I'm really looking forward to it, aren't you? It will be nice to have a house party for a change, although I have to admit I'm glad that it'll only be a small gathering. And you'll be able to talk to Cedric about Oxford, won't you?'

Hallam looked relieved and happily chattered about his planned entertainment for the weekend, Josephine nodding every now and then encouragingly, appearing equally engrossed in their conversation. Had Hallam bothered to look at his sister more closely though, he would have seen how she picked nervously at a loose thread on her skirt, and fidgeted in her seat as if she could not get comfortable, and that there lingered about her a certain air of sadness, which she was trying hard to conceal.

Chapter Two

Rose was relieved. The train had arrived on time and the journey itself had been uneventful. She had sat back in her carriage, her eyes half shut as she had gone through in her mind the various items that she had just packed, reassuring herself that she had forgotten nothing, or at least nothing of great significance. It was a pity, she thought, that for dinner tonight she would be reduced to wearing again her black, silk velvet, bias-cut dress. She had worn this same dress on two occasions at Ashgrove, although she was fairly confident that Cedric would not remember. He had also assured her in his letters that the Honourable Josephine Atherton was not a girl to follow fashions, preferring instead to dress in country tweeds. Rose was therefore hopeful that Josephine might be wearing a similar outfit to her own. She would however have a new dress to wear for dinner on the Saturday night. Her mother, a skilled dressmaker, had insisted. She had set to and made one from three leftover pieces of silk satin material from the gowns of three of her more affluent customers. Three pieces of material, two of different shades of blue and the other one of silver, had been combined into a simple entwined design. The dress itself was backless, as was the rage, and was quite simply the most exquisite and daring gown Rose had ever owned. She only hoped that she would have the nerve to wear it.

Her thoughts drifted to reflect on those who would be present at the house party in addition to herself and Cedric. It was with relief that Cedric had written that it was to be a very small house party and that the Athertons were old family friends who were unlikely to ask her any awkward questions concerning the events that had occurred at Ashgrove House.

She thought it likely that she would get on well with Josephine who, by all accounts, was quiet and unassuming, content to keep house for her father and involve herself with church bazaars and other such charitable causes. The Honourable Hallam Atherton, only son of Baron Atherton and three years' Cedric's junior, had just started at Oxford whereas Cedric had just finished. Cedric spoke of him with warmth, saying he had a simple, kindly disposition and was devoted to, and teased and mollycoddled by, his two older sisters. It had been obvious from Cedric's letters, although she thought not intentionally so, that of the two sisters he preferred the older, Josephine. From what she could tell, Isabella was very similar to Lavinia, and now that she and Lavinia were estranged, she could not help but be relieved that there appeared some doubt as to whether or not Isabella would be coming to Dareswick.

When she arrived at the station, Rose considered it prudent for appearance's sake to engage a porter to carry her case to the entrance rather than try to wrestle with it herself. She was pleased she had done so, for she was greeted almost immediately at the station door by the Atherton's chauffeur, Brimshaw, a rather attractive young man, who took her luggage and put it straight into the boot of a black Rolls-Royce Barker. Rose sank back into the luxurious tan leather seats.

'Miss Josephine asks me to convey her apologies for not being here to meet you, miss,' Brimshaw said over his shoulder, as they set off, Rose leaning forward to hear his words over the noise of the engine. 'It seems Miss Isabella will be coming down this weekend after all, and that she'll be bringing a friend with her, although apparently there is some confusion as to whether it will be a young lady or a young gentleman. So Miss Josephine's with Mrs Hodges now, she's the housekeeper, miss, trying to decide which bedroom to get ready for the visitor.'

'I see, well not to worry. It's very nice being met by a chauffeur-driven car.' Secretly, Rose was more concerned at the absence of Cedric. She wondered why he wasn't there to meet her himself. She had assumed that he would have made sure that he was at Dareswick ahead of her arrival. It occurred to her then that he might have had second thoughts about seeing her again. Perhaps she would arrive at Dareswick Hall only to be sent home again. Perhaps … No, she mustn't think like that. She forced herself to put the idea at the back of her mind and engage in conversation. 'I say, is it very far to Dareswick Hall?'

'Only about five miles, miss, but we have to go along some very steep and windy country roads so it'll seem a little longer as we'll have to take some of the roads slowly like.'

Rose sat back in her seat and reflected. So Isabella was going to be there after all. She knew that she was being unreasonable to resent Isabella's presence this weekend. But she wanted as few people to be there as possible when she and Cedric met again. She wondered whether they would have a chance to snatch a few moments together before they were obliged to dress for dinner and join the others. She looked at the back of Brimshaw's head and then leaned forward in order to speak to him. The fact that she would not have to look him in the face when she asked her question, gave her the courage she needed to ask it, even so she could not help blushing.

'Has Viscount Sedg … the Earl of Belvedere arrived yet?'

'No miss, although his arrival is expected imminently. He's driving down from Sedgwick Court, I believe, and had hoped that he might be here to meet you off the train in person. But he hadn't turned up and Miss Josephine thought it better not to wait any longer. She didn't want you to be left hanging around at the station so she asked me to come and meet you.'

It seemed to Rose that, while they were talking, the roads had become very narrow and windy indeed, in some places seeming little more than tracks.

'Is Dareswick Hall very out of the way?' she asked.

'Aye, it is, miss, quite out in the sticks. On occasion, when we've had bad weather, we've been completely snowed in and not seen a soul for weeks. But it's a grand place and I wouldn't work anywhere else not for love nor money.'

In the end they came to Dareswick Hall abruptly. The car had turned a sharp corner and Rose had been fully prepared for their journey to continue when there it was, a classic redbrick Georgian mansion standing behind massive wrought iron gates with a long tree-lined driveway leading up to the house. At first glance, Dareswick Hall reminded her of Ashgrove House, and she could not help but take a sharp intake of breath. However, it seemed to be built on a grander scale, with the overall effect being one of splendour, being six-bayed to Ashgrove's five, and its eighteenth century origin from first glance appeared unspoilt by Victorian extensions and alterations. Later she was to discover in the course of her various conversations with Josephine that the only contribution made by the Victorians to the Hall had been the large and exuberantly planted rose and vegetable gardens. Like Ashgrove, she saw that Dareswick consisted of some three storeys in addition to the basement which housed the kitchen and servants' working quarters, and the attics which housed their bedrooms.

She hardly had time to take in the splendour of Dareswick Hall's façade before the car was brought to a smooth stop in front of the house by the chauffeur. Her car door was opened for her and she found herself ushered towards the front door. For one brief moment she looked back over her shoulder and saw that Brimshaw had opened the boot and a footman was gathering up her case. Almost immediately, however, her attention was diverted back to the front door due to the exclamation of welcome uttered by a woman a few years older than herself, accompanied by a rather stout butler of less than middling height.

'I say, I'm awfully sorry that I wasn't there to meet you at the station,' the girl said hurriedly, rushing over and shaking hands. 'Jolly rude and all that, but I do hope you'll forgive me. There was a bit of a bedroom crisis. My sister, Isabella, has decided to bring a friend with her this weekend and we're not sure whether it's one of her girlfriends or a gentleman. It put our housekeeper, Mrs Hodges, in rather a quandary, I can tell you. Still, I think we've sorted everything out now, although it's meant getting two bedrooms ready just to be on the safe side. Oh dear, and how very rude of me, Miss Simpson, I haven't introduced myself, have I? I'm Josephine Atherton; may I call you Rose?'

Josephine Atherton was dressed in a plain white blouse and a rather shabby tweed skirt and, unless Rose was mistaken, there was a small ladder in one of her stockings. Although she had a nice face, she could scarcely be described as beautiful let alone pretty. Rose felt that the same could very easily be said about herself and this, together with Josephine's pleasant and unassuming manner, and the informality of her greeting, helped to put her at her ease.

'Cedric's just parking his car in the old stables,' Josephine said, linking her arm through Rose's and leading her into the hall. 'He was so disappointed not to be there to greet you at the station but he was caught up in some estate business at Sedgwick, I believe, which delayed his departure. Now do let me introduce you to my little brother, Hallam. Although I expect he's gone off with Cedric; they've got loads of catching up to do and I expect he wants to tell him all about how he's finding Oxford. Cedric's graduated now, hasn't he? I say, do you fancy taking a turn around the garden, Rose, while we're waiting for the boys to join us? It's still quite warm for the time of year and not quite dusk so we should just about be able to see where we're going. And besides, I've been stuck indoors all day with this and that. Well, of course you have too, haven't you, working in your dress shop?'

It was late September when dusk seemed to range from anytime between six o'clock and seven o'clock in the evening, and although it was not far off seven, there was still sufficient daylight left for Rose to take in the formal gardens. Following the abnormal rains experienced in mid-July, Dareswick's gardeners had taken advantage of the mellow autumn to make a start on clearing away the remains of the summer flower gardens, and had commenced bulb planting in earnest. It gave the gardens a transitional air as if they were waiting for something to happen.

'We're planting British-grown bulbs for the first time,' Josephine informed Rose. 'You know, stimulating a new home industry. Tedson, our head gardener, got most of ours from the West Country. We've always bought imported bulbs before, but he assures me that British bulbs are now just as good and in many respects superior. I've yet to be fully convinced, though, because as I told him I thought the bulbs looked a jolly lot smaller. But Tedson says they are heavier and more solid than imported ones and that they'll produce a better bloom ...'

Rose found herself only half listening to what Josephine was saying, unable to prevent herself from glancing up every now and then, eager to catch her first glimpse of Cedric. She was reminded that she had first laid eyes on him when she had been strolling in a garden very like this one. It had been a summer's day then, and everything had been bright and seemed to shine. She had looked up and seen him, and in that moment everything had seemed to stand still. She had found both his looks and the unaffected way in which he had engaged with the Withers' servants mesmerising.

'... he says British bulbs are likely to flower earlier too,' continued Josephine, apparently oblivious to the fact that her words were falling on to almost deaf ears, 'than imported ones, I mean.' She lowered her voice suddenly, as if she was talking only to herself. 'Of course, I won't be here to see if he's right, what a pity...'

'You won't be here?' enquired Rose, reluctantly rousing herself from her daydreaming and trying to show some interest in what her companion was saying, although the practicalities of gardening had rarely concerned her. She had been content instead just to look at the finished effect. 'Are you going away then?'

'What? No ... of course not.' Was it her imagination or did Josephine appear unduly flustered? Certainly there had been alarm in her voice, if Rose was not mistaken. 'No, no. Why would I go away? I live here, I'm always here. Always will be, I expect.'

'It's just that you said –'

'Yes, how silly of me, just ignore me. I do talk a lot of old rot sometimes. I'm so used to talking to myself you see, when Father's in town and Hallam's at Oxford, there's often no one to talk to but the servants. Now what was I saying? Oh yes, Tedson's going to hold over planting the tulip bulbs until next month. And the hyacinths too, although we'll still import those, of course, we won't get them from the West Country ...'

Rose let her mind slip on to other things. She was beginning to feel rather sick with apprehension. What if Cedric was not as she remembered him? What if her recollections of him were flawed and unreliable? Worse, what if she was not as he remembered. What if when he looked at her she saw only disappointment in his eyes? It had been a very strange weekend after all at Ashgrove, even before the murder had taken place and they had all come under suspicion ...

It was only after a minute or two that Rose realised that Josephine had stopped talking and appeared to be as lost in her own thoughts as Rose was herself. The two girls strolled on together for a little while in silence, which seemed to get heavier with each step as Rose tried to think of something to say, fighting against the desire to be quiet and alone.

'It's awfully good of you to invite me for the weekend?' She said at last. Josephine relaxed noticeably.

'Not at all. We're delighted to have you here. Any friend of Cedric's is more than welcome any time. Poor boy, he's been through such a lot, as of course have you. Don't worry though, you won't be pressed for details while you're here. Goodness knows we've had enough scandal of our own recently, what with that awful business at the lake earlier this year ...'

Rose looked at Josephine enquiringly. Cedric had not told her in his letters about anything untoward having happened at Dareswick Hall. Surely if there had been anything like a murder or a suspicious death, she would have read about it in the newspapers. But before she had time to enquire into the matter further both girls became aware of Crabtree walking at a brisk pace across the grass towards them, the stoutness of his body rather reminding Rose of a penguin.

14

'Excuse me, madam,' the butler began, having to pause for a moment before he could continue, as he was clearly out of breath. 'But Lord Belvedere and Mr Hallam have returned from the stables and are in the drawing room, and have been enquiring as to where you and Miss Simpson were.'

'Goodness, yes, we've been out here rather a long time, haven't we? It's almost getting dark,' Josephine said leading the way, the plump butler in her wake, trying to keep up. 'Do come inside, Rose, and meet my brother. And of course you'll want to see Cedric. Oh, how very remiss of me, I've just realised that I haven't offered you any refreshment after your journey. I know that we'll be going up to dress for dinner shortly, but perhaps you could be so good, Crabtree, as to arrange for Robert to bring in some tea and perhaps a few slices of one of Mrs Gooden's very good Victoria sponges to keep us going.'

'Very good, madam.' The butler bowed briefly and departed, but not before Rose was left with the distinct impression that he considered afternoon tea at this hour not the done thing at all. Personally she was sure that she would be too nervous to eat a thing, but a nice cup of hot tea would be most welcome.

The two men stood up as soon as the women entered. Rose barely had time to take in the double drawing room formed by two good-sized rooms, the large doors between each room open; the fine Sheraton sideboard with its serpentine front; the magnificent chandelier which glittered in the light. A warm glow extended from the fireplace, the fire in which had not long been lit. She barely registered the plaster cornice that preserved the original Georgian gilding or the large marble fireplace with its early Victorian grate of polished steel and brass. She barely saw the wing chairs and sofas, richly upholstered in heavy damask, velvet or shot silk trimmed with silk fringe; or the solid parquet floor on which were a number of rich Persian rugs. She had eyes only for Cedric.

She felt herself utter a sigh of relief for at first glance he was as she remembered him. He was still tall and slender with finely chiselled features and there was still something of the matinee idol about him. But as she rushed up to him, she was aware of subtle changes too. The blond hair that was slicked back from a side parting was peppered with a few strands of grey; gone was the tanned looking skin of summer, replaced instead with pale skin tinged with grey. She noticed too that while he smiled at her in the way he had always done, there were a few fine lines around his eyes where there had been none. The events at Ashgrove had undoubtedly taken their toll, for the man that stood before her seemed to have aged more than the two or three months that had elapsed since she had last set eyes on him.

Chapter Three

'I cannot tell you how good it is to see you at last,' Cedric said, clasping her hands in his. After a quick cup of tea and slice of cake both Hallam and Josephine had made their excuses and left on the pretext of chores and tasks that needed completing before dinner, leaving Rose and Cedric alone at last. 'It is the only thing that has kept me going, knowing that you are there for me and that I should see you again before too long.'

'Was it very awful?' asked Rose, leading him to a sofa where they sat down, hands still clutched, each not taking their eyes from the other. 'I tried not to read what they said about it in the newspapers …'

'Yes, it was jolly beastly. It would have been a good deal more so though, if it hadn't been for Inspector Deacon. I have to say he was an absolute brick, that man. He did his very best to hush things up. I'm not sure that anyone has really swallowed that story of a shooting accident. But hopefully the newspapers and public will soon tire of speculating about what happened. There would be those who would argue that justice had not been done if they knew the truth; the murderer did not hang.'

'Yes, but Inspector Deacon must be satisfied with the outcome, otherwise he wouldn't have played along. Tell me, Cedric, thinking about Ashgrove, where is Lavinia now? You made scarce mention of her in your letters.'

'She's on the Continent on an extended visit. We have some relatives in Switzerland and then I think she plans to do a tour of the Italian lakes and then to stay in Paris for a while to improve her French. She's taken it all very badly, I'm afraid. She went away to escape it all. She thinks her chances of meeting a suitable husband are now ruined unless she seeks one in America. It would not surprise me very much if she never returns to England, although I suppose it's still early days and anything might happen.'

'Does she still blame me for everything?' asked Rose with a heavy heart.

'Yes, but me just as much as you. In time I'm hopeful that she'll come round. She and I were very close and she considered you a good friend once, so I think there's still hope.' There was a pause of a few minutes, as both became lost in their own thoughts.

'Anyway, enough of this, Rose,' Cedric said, sounding resolutely cheerful. 'I have done nothing but think about what happened at Ashgrove to the exclusion of all else for these past few months. I refuse to think about it anymore, at least while we are here at Dareswick. Don't you agree? We should try and put it all behind us and look to the future.'

Rose nodded slowly, looking serious; it was easier said than done.

'Right, my girl, we're going to have a jolly fine time here at Dareswick. The Athertons are old family friends and will want nothing but to wish us well. I have given Hallam very firm instructions that neither of us is to be interrogated about what happened at Ashgrove and that if we are, we'll leave immediately.' He forced a smile and tapped her knee affectionately. 'I suppose we'd better go and dress for dinner. Haven't seen any sign of Isabella and her guest, have you? I wonder if they've arrived yet. I doubt they'll hold dinner for them. Between you and me I rather wish Isabella wasn't coming. She's nice enough, of course, but there is something rather cold and aloof about her, she's not a patch on Josephine.' Rose secretly wondered whether Isabella reminded him of his sister, Lavinia, but said nothing.

When they came out into the hall they found Josephine looking agitated.

'Father's only just arrived home and has gone straight into his study. I hope that you don't mind that he didn't come into the drawing room to say hello. I thought you'd appreciate a little time together alone. But we're still waiting on Isabella and her guest to arrive. Really, it is too bad. We've pushed dinner back to a quarter to nine as it is and Father says we're not eating any later. They'll just have to make do with cold meats and leftovers from the kitchen if they don't get a move on. And we still don't know who she's bringing down with her. Well, I'm not waiting around down here any longer. I'm going up to change and I suggest you two do the same. Your room's opposite mine, Rose. Come up with me now and we can check that you have everything you need. Hopefully Pearl will have unpacked your case and hung up your clothes by now.'

Rose looked at her wristwatch. It was ten past eight. She had made particularly good time with her toilet and now stood before her kidney shaped dressing table, with its drapery of muslin over chintz, and regarded her reflection in the mirror. She had a full twenty minutes to wait before she was due to go in to dinner. She sat on her bed with its damask silk cover and wondered what to do. There had been some talk of cocktails before dinner, but she didn't want to find herself the first down, standing there awkwardly as she waited for the others to join her. Perhaps instead she ought to wait five minutes or so. She fiddled with her hair and cosmetics to while away the time. Just as she was getting ready to pluck up courage and vacate her room, she heard the doorbell followed by a commotion in the hall with doors opening and shutting, the sound of feet hurrying up and down the stairs and the general murmur of voices. Isabella and her guest must have arrived at last. She had no wish to pass them on the stairs and so decided to wait on a few more minutes before making her way down. If she was not mistaken, she had heard Isabella hurriedly making her way to her room, but she had not heard her guest. Could it be that the guest was still in the hallway being attended to by the servants? But there was no sound now from downstairs. She stole out of her room and stood in the gallery overlooking the hall, which to her relief she found empty. Without another thought she tore down the stairs and into the drawing room. This, to her dismay, she also found empty. Where was everyone?

'Mr Crabtree!' Mrs Hodges looked aghast. She could not remember the butler ever having looked so awful. His usually red face was a ghastly shade of white and he was sweating profusely. What was more, he had practically burst through the green baize door as if an army was in hot pursuit. 'Whatever is the matter?'

The man was panting so heavily that he was unable to utter a word and just bent over the table clutching the edge in an attempt to catch his breath. The housekeeper ushered him quickly into her sitting room before the junior servants could take in the spectacle the butler was making of himself. As it was the kitchen and scullery maids had lifted their eyes from their tasks, the scullery maid from peeling vegetables and the kitchen maid from standing over the stove stirring a white sauce, being careful to ensure it did not catch the bottom of the pan and burn.

'Take a grip of yourself, man,' Mrs Hodges said urgently. 'Think of the lower servants. Whatever will they think of you crashing into the kitchen looking fit to burst? You'd better take a small glass of the master's brandy to steady yourself or you'll not be in a fit state to wait at table tonight.'

'Thank you, Mrs Hodges,' said the butler, collapsing into a rather sagging wing chair and accepting the glass of brandy proffered, which he swallowed in one gulp. 'Ah, that's better. I feel more like myself again.'

'Whatever came over you, Mr Crabtree? Awful queer you looked, I must say. Why, you looked as if you'd seen a ghost,' said the housekeeper taking the empty glass from him and setting it beside him on an occasional table. 'Not like you at all, it isn't.'

'I feel as if I *have* seen a ghost, Mrs Hodges,' replied the butler, somewhat recovered. 'And I suggest that you take a seat yourself before I tell you the news.'

'Pray, what news is this?' demanded the housekeeper, perching on the edge of a chair, her hands clutching at her plain black gown in nervous anticipation. She had still not fully recovered from witnessing the butler in such a state. Usually he was an example to all as to how a good servant should conduct themselves even if he were a little too fond of his food.

'You must brace yourself for a shock, Mrs Hodges. And we must do the best we can to prepare the staff, especially young Robert. It's a pity we can't do without him at dinner tonight.'

'Mr Crabtree will you be so good as not to keep me in suspense any longer,' cried Mrs Hodges, 'and tell me, for goodness sake, what is the matter?'

'The matter, Mrs Hodges, is the friend that Miss Isabella has brought with her.'

'From that I gather it is a young gentleman?'

'It is indeed, Mrs Hodges, although I think applying the word gentleman to him may be considered by some to be a little generous. A more rude young man I cannot imagine. He practically pushed me aside in his eagerness to see the master. Didn't wait to knock at the study door or for me to announce him. Just burst in with no by your leave, he did, as if he thought the master wouldn't mind the interruption.'

'Well I never! I'm sure the master must have given him short shrift. He doesn't like being disturbed when he's in his study, does our lordship,' said Mrs Hodges, somewhat disappointed at the explanation for the butler's erratic behaviour. 'Even so, Mr Crabtree, I'm somewhat surprised it's left you so flustered. You and I are no strangers to the inconsiderate behaviour of our betters. Miss Isabella's got one or two other friends who could do with learning a lesson or two in manners.'

'It's not that, Mrs Hodges, I could have coped with that.'

'Then pray what is it, Mr Crabtree?' cried the housekeeper leaning forward in her seat looking exasperated.

'It's who the guest is, Mrs Hodges,' replied the butler sadly. 'A gentleman I never expected to set eyes on again at Dareswick. I'm awfully afraid that there's going to be trouble; I feel that something dreadful is almost bound to happen.'

'There's a bit of a queue for the bathroom in the men's corridor, I'm afraid,' said Josephine bustling into the drawing room where Rose was hovering uncomfortably by the sideboard. 'Hallam will take ages. It really is too bad of him, especially when we've got guests. Oh, I say,' she said, looking at the empty sideboard in dismay. 'Wherever are the cocktails? Robert should have had them prepared and put ready in wine glasses by now. Really, we'll have no time at all to drink them before we have to go in to dinner.'

Josephine went over to the fireplace and pressed the bell push. The two girls stood in an awkward silence, Josephine clearly agitated by both her brother not being there and the unexpected tardiness of the servants. Her mood was not improved by the inordinate amount of time it seemed to take for the bell to be answered.

'Crabtree, this really will not do. Did you not hear the bell? We've been waiting simply ages. And why did you come and not Robert? There's absolutely no sign of any cocktails, where is he?'

'I'm very sorry, madam I'm afraid Robert is indisposed at the moment. Will you be wanting me to ask Mrs Gooden to put back dinner by half an hour or so?'

'No, I don't think so, Crabtree,' Josephine said, admitting defeat. 'It doesn't look as if the men will be down any time soon, so we might as well go straight into dinner as soon as they appear. Let's not delay things further by having cocktails. You know my father doesn't like to eat late. I passed Miss Isabella on the landing and she said she'd only be a minute getting changed. I didn't see any sign of her guest, I must say. Did she not bring one with her after all?'

'Indeed, madam. The young gentleman requested an immediate audience with his lordship.'

'How strange. I doubt whether my father was too pleased. Is this guest still in with his lordship, Crabtree?'

'No, indeed not, miss. They've both gone to change for dinner. I understand it was a very brief interview.'

'What strange behaviour,' Josephine said to Rose as soon as the butler had left. 'Crabtree seemed so very vague and wasn't at all apologetic about Robert not having laid out the cocktails. It's not like him at all. He's usually very particular about everything, excessively so given that it's usually only Father and me here. I do hope nothing's wrong.'

A wave of uneasiness came over Rose. She could not put her finger on it exactly, but she felt suddenly that there was something sinister in the air, as if the arrival of Isabella's guest had brought with him something contaminated and unpleasant. Josephine had been relaxed and chatty when Rose had first arrived, now she was clearly agitated and irritable as if she had got caught up in the atmosphere which now prevailed over Dareswick Hall. Rose shivered and told herself not to be so fanciful, imagining things that were not there. But the behaviour of the servants also troubled her. Crabtree did not seem the sort of butler who would put up with dilatory behaviour from his staff. And yet it appeared to her that he had gone out of his way to protect the young footman, Robert, while at the same time not giving an adequate explanation for his absence from the drawing room.

But before Rose had time to consider the matter any further, they were joined by Cedric and Hallam, who appeared in dinner jackets and black bow-ties. Rose had been relieved to find that Josephine was dressed in a simple black silk crepe dress not that dissimilar to her own gown, except that it had cream lace work at the neckline embellished with rhinestones. It struck her now, however, that with this predominance of black amongst both men and women there was something of a funereal air about the gathering.

'Oh, Hallam, I wonder poor Cedric had time to take a bath,' said Josephine scolding her brother.

'Don't worry, old thing,' Cedric assured her. 'I say, you're looking jolly marvellous, Rose. You too, of course, Josephine.'

'And what about me, Cedric, can't you tell I've spent hours getting ready? Will I pass muster?' laughed Hallam. 'I don't see why it should be just the girls who get all the compliments on their appearance, do you?'

Cedric thumped him on the back good humouredly. 'You look jolly spiffing too, Hallam. Why, I'm surprised you haven't got women falling at your feet. Now where's that other sister of yours, is she going to keep us waiting for dinner? I've a good mind to –'

But whatever Cedric was about to say remained unspoken. For the door of the drawing room had opened and a vision of loveliness, or at least that's how Rose thought of her then, entered the room. Later she realised that Isabella's gown had had a lot to do with the illusion of perfection. Although no one could dispute that Isabella was beautiful with her slender frame, highly chiselled features and pale porcelain white skin offset by hair so black it was almost ebony in shade. By contrast her eyes were the brightest blue Rose had ever seen. But it was the dress she was wearing that made her stand out. It was of a deep crimson velvet, with a high waist, ruched sleeves and open back and was decorated with a large flower appliqué of red and purple petals. The overall effect was breath taking, not least because it contrasted so strikingly with the blackness of the dress of the others in the room. Immediately Rose felt plain and dowdy, as if she had somehow melted into the background with Isabella's entrance.

Isabella in turn surveyed them all for a moment before speaking. She smiled, but it seemed to Rose that the smile was done more to show her amusement at the reaction her entrance had caused rather than to be a greeting. She glided into the room, her hand outstretched so that she could clasp Cedric's arm.

'Cedric, how wonderful to see you,' Her voice had a light musical tone to it which, while pleasing, Rose thought appeared forced and artificial, as if it were hiding a sea of emotions. 'It's been an age since you were last at Dareswick. Anyone would think that you've been avoiding us and that really will never do. And this must be Rose.' Isabella arched an artfully painted eyebrow and gave Rose a look which she thought to be rather mocking. 'How do you do, my dear? I understand that you work in a dress shop. You must know all the tricks of the trade to dressing well. You'll have to tell me what's in fashion next season.' She turned her attention to Josephine. 'Now don't scold me big sister, I know we're frightfully late. We were held up leaving London, but really it couldn't be helped. But we're here now and have you ever known me change so quickly for dinner? Quite a record even if I say so myself. Now, where's Papa? Isn't he down yet? I thought he'd be dying to eat. I have to say that the journey has made me feel quite ravenous.'

'Your companion insisted on seeing him straightaway,' replied her sister, somewhat coldly. 'Really, Issy, couldn't he have waited until after dinner? What can have been so very important that it couldn't have waited until then?'

Isabella said nothing, but Rose noticed that a frown creased her lovely forehead for a moment before she turned her attention to her brother. 'Are you going to tell me off too, little brother?'

'No, but I'm awfully keen to know who you've brought down with you,' replied Hallam, a mischievous grin appearing on his young face.

'All in good time,' said Isabella and it seemed to Rose that she was making an effort to make light of it, although she was sure she detected a sadness in her eyes.

'Well, I really don't know why you have to be so jolly mysterious,' retorted Josephine. 'The very least you could have done was to have told us whether you were bringing a girlfriend or a young man. I am sure housekeeping arrangements never occur to you for one moment, but poor Mrs Hodges has been in quite a quandary trying to decide which room to get ready for your guest.'

It was possible that Josephine might have gone on to say more about her sister's inconsiderate behaviour, but as it was she did not get the opportunity. For at that moment the door to the drawing room opened and all eyes were diverted to study the two gentlemen who entered. The first was a middle-aged, large and heavy set man with a ruddy complexion and thinning grey hair who appeared to be in highly jovial spirits. Certainly he was beaming, his smile taking in the whole room and lighting up his eyes so that they seemed to shine in the light from the chandelier. But it was not the first man that caught everyone's attention or drew a collective gasp from all those present. It was the second. He entered the room a little behind Baron Atherton, a tall, dark and uncommonly handsome man, although his eyes betrayed his arrogance.

Rose found that she was clutching on to the sideboard as if for support; only just in time did she stop her nails from digging into the polished wood.

Of all the guests that Isabella could have brought with her, it had never occurred to her that she might be acquainted with the gentleman. And of all the people she never wished to see again, which admittedly were few, then surely this man before her must come top of her list. Hands shaking slightly, with an effort she forced herself to look up and meet the man's gaze full on. She looked Lord Sneddon squarely in the eye.

Chapter Four

Lord Sneddon's entrance had caused a collective gasp; as the moments passed it now caused complete silence as if each person in the room was unsure how to react to his sudden appearance. Rose expected Cedric to feel disappointed and agitated. Indeed, looking across at him she could clearly see the anger etched on his face. She went to stand next to him to reassure him that, from her perspective at least, it did not matter even though of course it did. But she had no intention of letting it spoil their visit. What she had not expected, however, was that the others would look so distressed at Lord Sneddon's entrance. She felt that she and Cedric had good reason to after what had happened at Ashgrove, but Hallam, if anything, looked more livid than Cedric at the identity of Isabella's guest. Josephine had gone quite pale and Rose could not help but notice how every now and then Hallam glanced over at his sister anxiously, as if he did not know how Josephine would be taking Sneddon's appearance. Indeed, he looked as if he feared that she might faint at any moment.

The moment was broken by the baron clearing his throat noisily in preparation for making an announcement, and by Isabella crossing the room to go over to Sneddon to take his arm.

'My lords, ladies and gentlemen,' began Baron Atherton pompously, 'I cannot tell you all how very honoured I am to make this announcement. This evening my dear Hugh, Lord Sneddon,' at this he turned to beam at Sneddon, 'asked, nay demanded even, so great was his mission, to see me in my study to ask permission for my youngest daughter's hand in marriage, which I gave gladly. Crabtree! Now where is that man?' A frown appeared on the baron's forehead as he surveyed the room in search of his butler. 'The man was told to get the champagne on ice and arrange for it to be brought in. Oh there you are, Crabtree, what kept you? Come on now, pour.'

There was a general shuffling of feet and fidgeting as those present waited restlessly for the butler to pour the champagne and distribute the drinks. Rose caught Cedric's eye, and saw the sadness in his face. Meanwhile, Hallam's face was getting redder and redder and he was clawing

26

at an occasional table to such an extent that there was a very distinct possibility that he might upset a crystal vase of cut flowers.

'My lords, ladies and gentlemen. I would like you to raise your glasses and toast –'

'No!' Before anyone could stop him, Hallam sprang forward and tore the champagne flute from his father's hand, upsetting the contents and hurling the glass to the ground where it smashed on the parquet floor into a hundred little pieces. 'No father, you can't. You can't possibly give your consent to such a union. Not after everything he's done and everything we've been through. I forbid it! And you,' he said turning to Isabella, 'you, darling Issy, you can't possibly want to marry him. You know what sort of a man he is.'

'Quiet!' bellowed the baron, his face quite purple with rage. 'That will do, Hallam. How dare you act so outrageously and discourteously to a guest in my house? If you can't be civil and hold your tongue then you can jolly well go up to your room and have your dinner brought up to you there on a tray.'

'But –' But Hallam did not finish his sentence. Cedric had placed a steadying hand on his arm and had shaken his head slightly to indicate that while he understood how the young man felt, this conversation should take place outside the drawing room when no women were present and preferably not just before they were all due to go into dinner. Hallam looked for a moment as if he would resist these attempts to curtail his behaviour, but then he sighed, threw up his hands in desperation and just looked miserable.

There was a tense, uncomfortable silence in the room as everyone else wondered what would happen next. Casting a glance at Crabtree, Rose found that even the butler looked ill at ease. In fact, this very moment in the drawing room he positively looked quite unwell. She wondered whether it was Hallam's outburst that had caused this, by upsetting the decorum of the house, or the unexpected identity of Isabella's guest. Certainly the inattentive service of the servants, first with the cocktails and then with the champagne, appeared out of character from what Josephine had said. Looking across at the baron, given the anger on his face and the manner in which he had admonished his son in public, Rose could not believe that he was a man who would tolerate sloppy, slatternly service from his servants.

She looked across at Josephine. The girl, she thought, looked very pale as if she had suffered something of a shock. Her hand, almost instinctively and unconsciously it seemed went to touch a spot on her forehead covered by her hair in very much the same way one might put a hand to one's mouth or heart to try to steady oneself from a fright. Rose studied Josephine's face closely. She was clearly surprised and distressed by the young man's unexpected arrival but there was something else that Rose detected in her face. It seemed to her to make no sense at all given the circumstances, but she could have sworn that she detected a look of relief, albeit fleeting, to be replaced almost at once by a look of apprehension as her eyes darted to her brother. Josephine was very obviously moved by the state Hallam was in and went to join him where she took his arm and bent forward to whisper something in his ear. Almost instinctively Rose moved closer so that she might catch the whispered words.

'It's all right, Hallam. Don't worry on my account. Really, I am quite over him now; I really am.'

It was only now that Rose looked over at Isabella to see her reaction to her siblings' somewhat negative response to the announcement of her engagement. Her face, to Rose, looked surprisingly blank and unmoved by the events that had unfolded. True, she had moved to stand beside her fiancé, but she did not appear particularly surprised or distressed by Hallam's outburst or Josephine's discomfort. If anything her face looked distinctly devoid of any emotion, as if while she was there in body, she was not there in spirit. She caught Rose watching her and met her gaze. The look she gave her was cool and Rose found herself shrinking back from such a stare, but not before she wondered at Isabella's detached reaction to everything. Certainly Isabella did not apparently see the need to give assurance to Lord Sneddon in the light of the opposition expressed by her brother to their engagement. It was almost, Rose thought, as if she did not care how he might be feeling.

Lord Sneddon himself, she saw, was clearly furious at Hallam's outburst but trying very hard not to show it. He was pretending to laugh as if he found the boy's reaction rather amusing. Oh, the ideals and emotions of youth, his look seemed to say, although his smile did not reach his eyes, Rose noticed, and when he thought no one was looking, she saw him cast Hallam a furious look.

If the baron felt minded to demand an apology from his son for his behaviour, he obviously thought better of it, and instead contented himself by leading everyone into the dining room for dinner, no doubt hopeful that good food and full stomachs might restore the mood and encourage a feeling of celebration, although it seemed to Rose that he alone believed there was anything to rejoice about.

There was a precedence for dinner, Rose knew, as to which gentlemen should take in which lady. As the only female guest, the baron as host gave her his arm and led her in to dinner. She felt that Josephine, acting as hostess, should have been taken in next by the gentleman of highest rank, which in this case would have been Lord Sneddon as heir to a dukedom. But it seemed that the baron had considered it wise to break with precedence on this occasion given the atmosphere, for he indicated that Sneddon should lead in Isabella. They in turn were followed by Cedric who led in Josephine and lastly Hallam who brought up the rear, walking in alone, partnerless and distinctly sulky. Rose reminded herself that at eighteen he was barely more than a child and that no doubt he had been spoilt and doted on by his sisters. She pitied him, for he alone had been prepared to say in public what the others surely felt in private.

Family and guests filed into the dining room, which had retained its eighteenth century panelling and had pale scrubbed floorboards, typical Georgian features of the house. The baron remained standing in order that he could indicate where each gentleman should sit, the intention being that each lady sit on the right hand of the gentleman who had taken her into dinner. However, Rose saw that on reflection the baron obviously felt, in light of what had passed in the drawing room, that it would be both wise and diplomatic to ensure that Hallam sat nowhere near to Lord Sneddon and Josephine also be seated away from him. She wondered what there had been between Lord Sneddon and Josephine for Hallam to show such concern as to how she would be taking the news of his engagement to her sister. Could it be that she had once harboured dreams herself of becoming his wife?

In the end the seating arrangements resulted in Hallam sitting at the head of the table with his father on his right and Josephine on his left. Next to Josephine sat Cedric, and next to him, on his left, sat Isabella. Opposite her sat Sneddon who, to Rose's dismay, was also sitting on her right, while the baron was on her left.

The meal started well enough for Rose with the baron engaging her in pleasant small talk about Dareswick Hall, its history and how long it had been in the ownership of the Atherton family. For a while she wondered whether the inevitable would not happen after all, that she would not be forced to engage in conversation with Lord Sneddon. For it appeared that the baron had no intention of speaking to his son. Hallam, she noticed out of the corner of her eye, seemed to barely register the existence of anyone at the table, preferring instead to study the tablecloth and pick at his napkin, although every now and then he lifted up his head to scowl at Sneddon, who seemed oblivious to his action, or to throw the odd glance at Josephine, which she met with a troubled smile.

'Mr Crabtree, if I may disturb you for a moment,' said Mrs Hodges, coming into the butler's pantry and closing the door firmly behind her.

'What can I do for you, Mrs Hodges?' enquired the butler, mopping his brow and hoping that the housekeeper had not caught sight of the empty whisky glass on the counter behind him, or indeed seen him gulp down its contents hurriedly before she entered the room.

'Pearl has just told me that Lord Sneddon has brought his own valet with him. Surely not! No one said anything about getting a servant's room ready. As if I haven't enough to do what with all the bother as to whether to arrange a room for Miss Isabella's guest to be got ready in the gentlemen's corridor or in the ladies', and then Miss Josephine deciding after all that we'd better get both ready just to be on the safe side. And jolly good it is that we did too, otherwise his lordship would be laying his head down in the Pink Room!'

'I am afraid Pearl is correct, Mrs Hodges,' said Crabtree with a sigh, 'insofar as Lord Sneddon has brought *a* servant with him. I was just on my way to tell you.'

'Were you now?' said Mrs Hodges allowing some scepticism to enter her voice as she eyed the empty whisky glass suspiciously. 'And what precisely do you mean by that, Mr Crabtree?' She continued getting more and more frustrated by the situation. 'Either he's a valet or he's not. Can't think what he can be if he isn't, unless his lordship saw fit to bring his chauffeur with him.'

'No, indeed,' agreed the butler. 'What I meant, Mrs Hodges, is that the man purports to be Lord Sneddon's valet but that he bears no resemblance to any valet that I have ever had the experience of knowing.'

'Why's that, then?' demanded the housekeeper, interested despite the threat of additional work for her already overstretched staff. 'Do you think he's a footman acting up to be a valet, or what?'

'No, not even that,' said Crabtree pausing for a moment before continuing so as to create maximum suspense. 'I would be very surprised if the man has ever set foot in a grand house such as this before, let alone ever worked as a servant in one. But don't just take my word for it, Mrs Hodges, have a look at the young man yourself and let me know what you think.'

Feeling rather apprehensive and curious in equal measure, the housekeeper marched into the servants' hall and was brought up short by the scene that unfolded before her eyes. A young man of dubious appearance was seated on a chair, his tie askew and his hair sticking up all over the place, with his arm trying to encircle the waist of Doris, the under housemaid and persuade her to sit on his knee. Doris in turn was shrieking and giggling for all she was worth as she dodged his advances.

'Stop that at once!' bellowed Mrs Hodges. 'You, my girl,' she said, pointing a finger at the unfortunate Doris, 'can get out of here and finish your dusting or whatever else you've got left to do. And as for you,' the housekeeper turned to glare at the dishevelled young man, 'you should know better. Call yourself a valet. I'd expect better behaviour from the boot boy!'

'Ah, come off it, missus,' protested the young man seemingly unfazed at being admonished by the housekeeper. 'We was only having a bit of fun. That don't harm anyone, do it? We was just having a laugh, like.'

'My goodness,' exclaimed Mrs Hodges, hands on hips. 'Wherever were you brought up? Have you never heard of speaking the King's English?'

'I talk all right, so I do,' the young man replied sulkily. 'I don't hold with all those airs and graces and bowing and scraping. That all went out with the War, so it did. I'm as good as the next man, I am.'

'Then why, pray, are you a valet by profession if you don't agree with being in service?'

''Cause it suits me, that's why.'

'Have you been in service long,' enquired Crabtree, appearing suddenly at Mrs Hodges' elbow and making her jump. 'Do you know the first thing about what the job entails?'

'No and no,' replied the young man moodily. 'But I'm a quick learner; that's why his lordship took me on. Besides,' he continued, looking at them slyly, 'I'm good at doing other things apart from valeting.'

It was inevitable, Rose supposed, that she and the baron would run out of things to say and that he would feel obliged to let her turn to speak to the gentleman on her right, unaware as he was of their history. He probably felt obliged too to have a word with his wayward son, having first made a point of deliberately ignoring him. She sighed. What a pity that it was expected in polite society that one engage in conversation with the person seated on your right as well as the one seated on your left.

Shortly there was a lull in the conversation between Lord Sneddon and Isabella, so that Sneddon turned his attention to Rose for the first time since they had been seated. She took a deep breath, aware that not even the soup had yet been served and that the dinner was likely to consist of some six or seven courses. She had hoped that she would be able to put off speaking to Lord Sneddon until the meat dish at the very least. She turned desperately to the baron to see if she could reignite their dying conversation. She found however that, while the baron was still furious with Hallam, he had resolved to take the opportunity between courses to reprimand his son for his behaviour in words whispered angrily between clenched teeth.

'Ah, Miss Simpson, this is a pleasant surprise,' began Lord Sneddon, bestowing on her an ambiguous smile. 'Although I have to confess that I didn't imagine that I'd ever be seeing you again, certainly not so soon, not that it isn't most welcome.'

'I wish I could say the same,' Rose retorted, primly. 'But I'm afraid that I can't. But believe me, it's just as much of a surprise for me to find you here.'

'Oh, don't be like that, Rose,' said Lord Sneddon, grinning. 'Of course, I know that I behaved abominably towards you at Ashgrove, but can't we just let bygones be bygones while we are both here?'

'It's not quite so easy for me to do as you ask,' replied Rose, remembering with a shiver their last encounter on the staircase at Ashgrove, 'but I suppose we must, just while we're both here.' Besides, she had no intention of giving him the satisfaction of ruining her weekend with Cedric.

'That's a girl,' beamed her dinner companion. 'Now suppose you start by giving me a friendly smile, or at the very least stop looking as if you'd like to disappear under the table. Because I have to say, if looks could kill, young Cedric over there would have finished me off three times already this evening.'

Rose looked up. Cedric was indeed glaring at Sneddon in a manner which suggested that he would like to do him harm. She felt herself panic. She must not let him make a fool of himself as Hallam had done. Whatever Cedric had to say to Lord Sneddon, and she was sure it was a great deal, she must ensure that he said it in private.

'You'd never think that young Cedric and I used to be inseparable,' continued Lord Sneddon. 'We were the absolute best of friends.'

That's before he was aware of your true character, Rose longed to say, but she held her tongue. She would not be provoked for she felt sure that that was exactly what he wanted.

'I must admit, Rose, I didn't see your little romance with Cedric lasting, touching though it was. It just proves me wrong, doesn't it? He's had a pretty rum time of it, hasn't he? The newspapers have been absolutely hounding him; fortunately they don't appear to know that I was there. I'm somewhat surprised that he didn't take a leaf out of dear Lavinia's book and head for the Continent. I assume she's planning to stay there until all the fuss has died down, that's what I'd have done.'

'Yes, but Cedric isn't you, is he?' Rose said, finding it hard to keep her temper despite her good intentions. 'He isn't the sort of man to run away from things. Besides, he had all the estate affairs to sort out and of course the funerals to arrange.'

'Mr Crabtree, is there absolutely no way you can manage at dinner without having young Robert serve?' asked the housekeeper, clasping her hands tightly together in her agitation. She had collared the butler yet again in his parlour and he was beginning to think that this, regrettably, was becoming a rather regular occurrence, particularly when he saw her eyes darting around her on the search for any sign of a hidden glass. Mrs Hodges, in turn, although never going so far as to think that the butler had a problem with drink, was of the view that in times of stress he had been known to overindulge to take the edge off his anxiety.

'I know that you said before that you couldn't, but I really don't think it a good idea. As it is we've had to keep him away from that awful manservant of Lord Sneddon's, Ricketts would you believe his name is. Mrs Gooden's banned Robert from her kitchen because she's afraid he's half a mind to take a meat cleaver to him. He's a thoroughly bad 'un that one, mark my words. Still, it's hardly surprising if he takes after his master, is it?

'Now, now, Mrs Hodges, don't let anyone else hear you say that. I'm not saying that I don't feel the same way about Lord Sneddon as you do, but we've got to set an example to the lower servants you and I, otherwise where would we be?' He took a pocket watch from his waistcoat pocket, which he consulted. 'Time to serve dinner, I believe. We don't want Mrs Gooden's fine dishes to be spoilt, now do we? And I'm afraid, as I've said before, if we could manage without Robert having to serve at dinner tonight then we would. But we are already a man down with Sidney in bed with the flu and Mr Tallow would be sure to drop a dish or two if we asked him to stand in. I'd ask that fellow Ricketts to help out, but I doubt whether he knows one end of a serving spoon from the other, even if we could tidy him up a bit and get him to pass a comb through his hair.' He bent forward to whisper to the housekeeper in a conspiratorial manner, which Mrs Hodges considered rather unnecessary since there were only the two of them there in the room. 'I'm going to be counting the silver while he's here, I can tell you, and keeping an eye on the master's best port.'

'And I'll be making sure that the attic door leading to the maid servants' bedrooms is kept securely locked at all times and all,' Mrs Hodges said firmly.

'A very wise precaution,' agreed the butler, 'particularly after what happened before.'

Rose looked about her, eager to find any distraction which meant that she would not be obliged to continue her tiresome conversation with Lord Sneddon, which she was beginning to find very tedious. It was a welcome relief when she saw the first course being carried in. It appeared to be white soup, a rich soup made of sweet almonds, poultry and cream, spiced with mace. The footman carefully put the steaming hot tureen on the sideboard to enable him to ladle the soup into the individual bowls which would be served to the guests accompanied by sherry.

Later, Rose was surprised that she had not seen at the time that it was almost inevitable that disaster would strike. For one thing, she noticed that the young footman, whose task it was to serve the soup, appeared nervous and ill at ease. Crabtree himself was looking on with trepidation, watching the footman's every movement like a hawk. As was the custom of the day, the footman began by serving the first bowl of soup to Rose as she was on the right of the host. She could not help but notice that his hands were shaking and she turned to study his face which she noticed to her alarm was deathly white. It seemed to her that there was a strong possibility that he might be about to collapse, and she wondered whether she should draw this to the attention of the butler.

Before she could make up her mind what to do, the footman had passed on to attend to the next diner which should have been the lady on the host's left, but as this position was currently occupied by Hallam, the next to be served was Josephine. Rose watched as the footman continued to serve straight round the table so that Cedric was served next and then Isabella. It seemed to Rose, scrutinising the footman's behaviour as closely as she was, that he appeared to hesitate for a moment when he came to serve Lord Sneddon. Everything then seemed to unfold in slow motion and she wondered why she had not cried out a warning, for her eyes had locked for a moment with those of the footman. All at once she knew instinctively what he was about to do for she had been shocked by the look of pure hatred lighting up the young man's face as he focused his attention on Sneddon. She put up her hand in a futile attempt to distract the footman from his chosen course. He appeared oblivious to her action for, in a moment, he had tilted the dish of hot, steaming soup so that its contents poured into Lord Sneddon's lap, like water tumbling down a waterfall.

Lord Sneddon shot up out of his seat immediately with a loud cry of pain, his trousers covered in the thick, creamy soup. The footman looked for a moment stunned as if he could not quite believe what he had done. Quickly he became apologetic, although Rose was certain that the spillage had been no accident. The footman tried to wipe off the worst of the soup from Lord Sneddon's clothes with a napkin, but his attempts were ineffectual and lacked commitment, resulting in Lord Sneddon waving him away angrily. The baron's face was purple with rage as he admonished the footman for all he was worth, advising him in no uncertain terms that his services were no longer required and that he was to pack his bags and leave on the morrow at first light. He then proceeded to turn his rage on Crabtree, as if the butler was in some way responsible for the incompetence of his staff.

Cedric, Josephine and Hallam all acted as Rose would have expected. Not having foreseen the mishap with the soup, they, not surprisingly, all looked shocked that such a thing had occurred. Hallam began pleading with his father in vain on behalf of the young footman. But this was to no avail as the baron was adamant that the footman should forfeit his job forthwith. However, it was Isabella's reaction to the events that interested Rose most, because it was unexpected. While all about her was confusion, raised voices, and garbled apologies, with the coming and going of servants as they tried to remove the worst of the mess from Lord Sneddon's clothing and the chair, Isabella alone remained calm and composed. Rose studied her face closely and, although it seemed incredible considering that the injured man was her fiancé, Rose was sure that the look on her face was one of amusement. Indeed, unless she was very much mistaken, she would even have gone so far as to believe that Isabella had smiled, as if she were laughing at some private joke. Certainly she did not trouble herself to go to Sneddon's aid. Rather she remained seated, her spoon still in her right hand as if she were debating whether or not it would be seemly for her to continue eating her soup.

'Crabtree, get this man away from me,' said the baron angrily, pointing to Robert, 'and get Lord Sneddon's valet here now to see to his master. You'd better telephone Doctor Brown as well.'

'I'll be all right,' said Sneddon, 'no need for a doctor. But I'll take your valet, mine won't be any good at dealing with this.'

'You heard his lordship. Get Tallow here, Crabtree'. The baron looked as if he were about to request Hallam's help, but thought better of it. 'Cedric, would you mind helping Lord Sneddon to his room and Crabtree you'd better have Mrs Gooden make up one of her treatments for scolds.'

Within a few minutes Sneddon was escorted from the dining room between Cedric and the baron's valet. An uncomfortable silence was left in their wake, broken at last by an outburst from Hallam. 'Well what did you expect, Father? Isabella, what –'

'Enough,' thundered the baron. 'We can talk about this later in private. In the meantime, I suggest that we finish our soup and then adjourn to the drawing room until Lord Sneddon is able to join us to resume our dinner.

You hear that, Crabtree?' The baron turned to address his butler. 'Have the cook put back dinner.'

'Yes, my lord.' The butler departed, fearing that the delay in serving the remainder of the meal was likely to result in it being ruined, which would do nothing to improve his master's temper.

Following a restless time in the drawing room where no one was quite sure what to do or say, and where Hallam insisted on standing apart from the others angry and sulky, Cedric and Lord Sneddon finally appeared, the latter in a fresh dinner jacket which looked a couple of sizes too big for him and which Rose guessed probably belonged to the baron. Lord Sneddon stared pointedly at Isabella for a moment, who averted her gaze to study a picture on the wall. He gave a shrug and they all traipsed back into the dining room, taking up their seats as if nothing untoward had happened.

Chapter Five

To Rose's relief the meal resumed without further incident and Crabtree's worry that the dinner would be spoilt proved unfounded. It was late when the meal finished and that, coupled with the baron's determination to ensure that Hallam was given no opportunity to give rant to his feeling towards Sneddon, meant that port was taken hurriedly at the table while the ladies were still present. Everyone then adjourned together as one to the drawing room for coffee and liqueurs.

'This is all very odd,' whispered Cedric when he was at last able to snatch a few words with Rose. He took her by the elbow and led her to a velvet covered settee that was located a little away from the other occupied chairs and sofas. They sat down, their heads bent towards each other so that they could not be overheard. 'Sneddon made remarkably little fuss over that soup incident, which is very out of character for him. And I've never seen Hallam be so angry. What can Sneddon possibly have done to him to cause such rage?'

'Hallam appeared very concerned about how Josephine would take Lord Sneddon's sudden appearance,' said Rose. 'Do you think it could be something to do with her? Didn't Sneddon say anything to you while you were helping him upstairs to get changed and have his wound seen to?'

'Not a thing, which again is not like him. I know we did not part on the best of terms, but I would have expected him to say something. But he hardly uttered a sound. He seemed totally engrossed in his own thoughts. I suppose he must have been in shock, not to say some pain.'

'Was he hurt? That soup was jolly hot.'

'No, at least not badly. A scold rather than a burn, I think.'

'And that's another thing, Cedric, the footman did it deliberately.'

'What!'

'The footman dropped the soup on Sneddon on purpose. I saw him do it. You should have seen the look on his face, it was pure hatred.' Rose shivered at the recollection. 'What could Sneddon possibly have done to make the servant hate him so? What's more, I think the butler half expected something of the sort to happen; he was keeping his eyes trained on the footman throughout dinner.'

'Well I never! And how jolly observant of you. Well, the poor fellow's lost his job over it now, whatever his reasons for doing what he did. And what's more, he'll have difficulty getting another position without a decent reference.'

'Yes, the baron did seem very angry about it. It's funny, isn't it, that he appeared to be the only one delighted by the news of his daughter's engagement. I suppose he's pleased that his daughter is marrying so well and will become a duchess.'

'Now you come to mention it, Isabella didn't exactly look that happy herself about it all. I'd have thought she'd have been in her element at the prospect of marrying the heir to a dukedom, even if it meant marrying old Sneddon. But she was quiet as anything at dinner. She hardly exchanged a word with me, although I noticed she and Sneddon were whispering together a lot of the time.'

'She did seem very detached from it all,' said Rose, looking over to where Isabella sat perched now on the edge of a Queen Anne chair, her hands clasped in her lap with her head bowed. She looked to Rose as if she was trying to shut out the world. Certainly her posture deterred anyone from going over to speak to her. Even Sneddon only glanced at her a couple of times before walking over to engage in conversation with the baron. She looks miserable, Rose thought, miserable and dejected. Clearly something was very wrong. Aloud to Cedric she said:

'I think Isabella was quite pleased when the soup got poured onto Sneddon's lap. I think she thought it was funny, even though he could have been quite badly hurt.'

'Yes, it's all quite strange,' said Cedric, wearily. 'But let's not get involved in it at all if we can possibly avoid it. I want us to enjoy ourselves while we're here and make the most of spending this time together. Goodness knows we deserve it after what we went through at Ashgrove. I only hope that Sneddon's arrival won't spoil everything. That man does have a tendency to put a dampener on things. At least Hallam's stormed off to bed in a mood. I didn't fancy having to spend the whole evening trying to keep those two apart, particularly if Hallam had decided to drown his sorrows in drink, which would only have worsened his temper.'

'I'm sorry, Mr Crabtree, truly I am,' said Robert, the young footman. He was sitting at the table in the servants' hall, his head in his hands, close to tears.

'I don't believe a word of it, Robert,' the butler replied harshly. 'I could see it in your face the moment we walked in the dining room that you had it in mind to do something. I never dreamed though that you'd be so irresponsible as to pour boiling hot soup onto his lordship's lap. Whatever were you thinking of, man? You could have burned him good and proper. You're jolly lucky that Lord Sneddon didn't make more of a fuss about it. Otherwise you might be seeing the inside of a prison cell rather than just losing your position.'

'That's 'cos he knew he was in the wrong. It was his guilty conscience see, he knew it was the least he deserved.'

'That's as may be, Robert, but it seems to me that the only one who has really suffered by this act of stupidity of yours is yourself. How's your mother going to manage now with no money coming into the house, what with your brothers still at school?'

'I need this job, Mr Crabtree, I can't afford to lose it,' the footman cried desperately. 'Please say you'll have a word with the master.'

'You should have thought of that before you did what you did,' replied the butler huffily. 'His lordship wants you off the premises before first light tomorrow, you heard him.'

'Oh, leave the boy alone, Mr Crabtree,' pleaded Mrs Gooden, the good-natured, rotund little cook, placing a cup of tea before the footman which he gulped down greedily, almost burning his mouth in the process. 'We're lucky Robert didn't see fit to stick a knife in Lord Sneddon after what he did. The boy's young and I daresay a bit headstrong, but he only did what we'd all have liked to have the courage to do. Why, I had half a mind to put some poison in Lord Sneddon's soup myself, if I could have been sure that he'd have drunk it and nobody else and I'd have got away with it.'

'Mrs Gooden!' Crabtree was clearly appalled.

'All I'm saying, Mr Crabtree, is that we all know why Robert did what he did and that Lord Sneddon deserved a great deal worse. He got off likely if you ask me. It ain't fair that we're expected to wait on the man. He's a murderer, that's what he is, as good as!'

'That's as maybe, Mrs Gooden, and I don't say I disagree with you morally speaking. But while we're in the employ of the master we must attend to his guests as best we can and that means not trying to maim or kill them!' He turned to Robert and took in his tearstained face and red, swollen eyes. Despite his fine words, he felt a great deal of sympathy for the young man. 'I daresay his lordship spoke rather hasty. Who's to say that, when he's had a chance to calm down and think it over, he might not be encouraged to change his mind, particularly if we can persuade him that it was a genuine accident? In the meantime, Robert, keep to the kitchen and servants' quarters. I'm sure that Mrs Gooden and I can find you some jobs to keep you busy and out of mischief. But don't you go causing Lord Sneddon any more harm, mind, otherwise you'll be out on your ear.'

'Yes, Mr Crabtree, thank you Mr Crabtree.'

While the other servants went their various ways to complete chores before they called it a night, the young footman remained seated at the table, looking at the dregs of tea in his teacup. He had given the butler his word but he had no qualms about breaking it. His eyes took on a steely glare and his hands gripped his cup so tightly that he almost broke the china. He wondered whether or not he had the nerve to carry it through; he wondered if he had the nerve to kill Lord Sneddon.

Chapter Six

'Come in.'

'Oh, Josephine, it's you,' said Isabella in a resigned voice, glancing over her shoulder as her sister came into her room. She had been studying her face critically in her dressing table mirror.

'Who were you expecting?' asked Josephine coldly, hovering by the door for a moment before she closed it quietly behind her. 'Hugh?'

'Oh, you, I suppose,' replied her sister in a bored sort of voice. 'I might have known you'd take the first available opportunity to come and berate me. Well, let's get it over with then; it's late, I'm very tired and I want to go to bed.'

'What on earth were you thinking of, Isabella, bringing Hugh here?' Josephine enquired flopping herself down on the bed and glaring at her sister's reflection in the mirror.

Isabella swung around in her seat, angrily. 'It's not all about you, you know. This is my home too. I can bring whoever I want here. I don't have to ask your permission even if you do pretend to be the mistress of the house. Father doesn't mind I brought Hugh, he's delighted, you saw him tonight.'

'Yes, I did. That was a clever move on your part. Was it your idea or Hugh's to send him in to Father's study to announce your engagement? You knew you'd get short shrift from us all otherwise.'

'Well, I still did, didn't I? Hallam made a complete fool of himself, and in front of Cedric and his shop girl too.'

'Her name's Rose, not that you'd bother to find out. Is she beneath you?' Josephine put a hand to her forehead, as if she had the beginnings of a headache. She suddenly looked very tired. 'Let's not argue, Issy. I just want to understand why you're doing what you're doing. And anyway, I wasn't thinking about me, I was thinking about Hallam.' Not that you'd care about my feelings anyway, she was tempted to add, but didn't. It would only lead to a row and it just wasn't worth it. 'Didn't you think how he'd feel at you bringing that man down here after everything that's happened?'

'It was just idle gossip, that's all.'

'It was a lot more than that, Isabella,' snapped Josephine, becoming angry despite her good intentions. 'What about the girl? He as good as murdered her!'

'Don't say that, don't you dare!' snapped Isabella rising angrily from her seat and looking furious. Josephine put her hand to her face and looked alarmed. The gesture seemed to calm her sister for she sat back down again, slowly. 'Don't say that, Jo. He didn't mean to, you know it was —'

'Oh, my goodness, he doesn't know, does he?' Realisation dawned on Josephine's face. 'Oh, but I don't suppose he'd care, anyway, knowing the sort of man he is. But even so, you must tell him, you must tell him what he's done.'

'No, and you won't tell him either.' Isabella said firmly. 'And anyway, it was only a servant.'

'How can you be so callous?' asked Josephine, angrily. 'Honestly, Isabella, I wish you'd grow up and stop being so selfish. She may only have been a servant, as you put it, but she mattered, of course she mattered. And besides, what about the other servants? How do you think they feel? It's not fair on them. You don't think it was an accident, do you, Robert spilling hot soup on Hugh.'

'Oh, that was rather funny, wasn't it?' giggled Isabella, 'You should have seen Hugh's face, I thought he was going to explode.'

'Issy!' said Josephine, shocked. 'Of course it wasn't funny. Hugh could have been seriously hurt. And besides, Robert's lost his job because of it.'

'Oh well, I'm sure you'll talk Father round.'

'Well of course I'll try to. But Issy, why are you marrying Hugh? It's obvious you're not in love with him and even you wouldn't marry someone just for a title, not someone like him, anyway. Are you in some sort of trouble? You're not —'

'No! Please, Josephine, don't try to interfere. I'm marrying him and that's all there is to it.' She looked at her sister, anxiously. 'Look, I do love him in my own way. Well as much as I'll ever love anyone.'

'I don't believe you.'

'Well, we can't all be like you, can we?'

'What's that supposed to mean?' demanded Josephine.

'Having romantic notions about marriage. And we can't all be the dutiful little daughter staying at home looking after Father. I couldn't bear to be cooped up here in the wilderness with absolutely no society to speak of unless you count the vicar and the country doctor and solicitor. I'd simply go mad. I want to see the world; I want to experience everything. Oh, it's all right for you,' she added dismissively, 'it's exactly what you want, to be shut up here.'

'How do you know that's what I want, or what I'm like come to that?' asked Josephine. There was a strange note to her voice which made her sister look at her curiously. 'Have you ever bothered to ask or try to find out? How do you really know that I like being shut away here, as you put it?'

'But you love living here, you're always saying how much you do.' Isabella looked surprised.

'Yes, of course, I do but …' Josephine faltered, suddenly looking dejected.

'What is it?' Isabella felt a surge of curiosity, all her interest was transferred to her sister now.

'Oh, it's nothing, really. I'm just being silly, just ignore me.' She thought, haven't I already said those words before this evening? I'm going to go mad if I don't tell someone soon, but I can't tell Issy and I can't tell Hallam. They'd never understand. They'll find out soon enough and then they'll hate me for what I've done. They'll never have anything to do with me, they'll …

'Oh, don't cry, Josephine, I can't bear it.' Isabella came over to the bed, sat down and put her arm around her older sister's shoulders. 'Don't cry old thing, there's no need. I know I've been rather beastly. I admit I've behaved badly, but I thought you were over him. I never really thought that you were ever that keen on him anyway. But please don't cry.'

'There's every need for me to cry, if only you knew. And it's got nothing to do with Hugh, I'm quite over him. But I'm scared, Isabella, I'm scared about what's going to happen.'

'So am I,' said Isabella, slowly and with feeling, 'so am I.'

Chapter Seven

When Rose went down to breakfast the next morning she found only Josephine seated there eating a slice of toast.

'I do hope you slept well, Rose,' said Josephine, pleasantly. 'Do help yourself to breakfast. There's bacon, eggs and devilled kidneys in the chafing dishes on the sideboard and Sidney will serve you coffee and hot toast.' She turned her attention to the footman. 'I do hope you're feeling better, Sidney. Crabtree said that you were laid up in bed yesterday quite ill. I suppose we are rather short staffed now that poor Robert's gone. I do hope I can get Father to reconsider his dismissal. He has a mother and two small brothers to support, hasn't he?'

'Yes, miss,' said the footman and hurried off to the kitchen as soon as he had served Rose, eager to break the good news to Robert that the mistress intended to speak on his behalf. While Sidney understood why Robert had done what he had done, he had not appreciated being roused from his sick bed to undertake both his and Robert's duties which were onerous even when he was feeling on top form, which he most definitely was not today.

There was a companionable silence for a time as each girl indulged in eating her breakfast.

'I'm sorry we're a bit light on the ground,' Josephine said, turning her attention back to Rose, 'Isabella's insisted on taking breakfast in her room and Father always breakfasts early. He's bending poor Cedric's ear in his study while we speak. About Hallam, of course. He wants Cedric to keep him occupied. I think he's afraid that otherwise he might challenge Hugh to a duel or something equally idiotic.'

'Your brother certainly seems very upset by Lord Sneddon's arrival,' Rose said carefully, not wishing to be accused of prying.

'Yes, it really is most unfortunate. I can't imagine what Isabella was thinking bringing him here; she might have known how Hallam would react. I suppose I ought to explain it all to you, although I'm afraid it's all rather sordid. You see, there was a bit of a scandal earlier this year when –' Josephine broke off speaking suddenly at the arrival of Sidney with fresh coffee and more slices of hot toast. 'I say, do you fancy having a walk in the gardens in say three quarters of an hour? I've got a few chores to do first and then I'll tell you all about it.'

Rose finished her coffee and left the room quickly, not long after Josephine. No mention had been made as to whether or not Lord Sneddon had breakfasted and she did not wish to find herself suddenly alone with him over bacon and eggs. She walked swiftly out into the hall in time to catch the end of a conversation Josephine was having with the butler.

'Are you sure that this is all the post that's come this morning, Crabtree?' she was asking, flicking through some envelopes.

'Quite sure, madam,' confirmed the butler. 'There are just the two letters for you, miss, and five for the master.'

'Oh, but I was expecting another one. Why hasn't it come?' Josephine sounded clearly agitated. 'Crabtree, are you sure this is everything? I'm waiting on a very important letter. I must get it today. Send the boot boy down to the post office, will you, and check whether it's there.'

'This is all the post, miss.'

'I don't care, Crabtree, I want the boy to check. I was expecting the letter yesterday, it's obviously been mislaid somewhere at the post office; get the boy to go over there and get them to check thoroughly.'

'Very good, madam,' said the butler in a resigned manner, sure of the outcome but carrying out his orders nevertheless.

'Oh, there you are, Rose,' said Josephine suddenly catching sight of her. 'I didn't know you were there.' Was it Rose's imagination or had Josephine blushed slightly as if she had been caught out in something of a dubious nature? 'You must have thought I was making rather a song and dance about that letter. It was just that I'm expecting a note from a shop about an outfit I'm having made to wear to a party. The invitation was so very grand, and now I'm having second thoughts about having my dress made locally. I should really have gone up to London to organise my costume. The shop said they'd get back to me with some ideas. And normally they're so reliable, which makes me feel sure that they've lost the letter somewhere at the post office. We are always having dreadful problems with post going astray.' With that she made her way hurriedly upstairs, and again Rose may have been mistaken, but she had the feeling that the girl was close to tears.

Rose wondered idly what the letter was that Josephine was waiting on so impatiently. Not for a moment did she believe the story of a fancy dress party. It was clear to her that this had been the first thing that had come into Josephine's mind in a clumsy attempt to explain her agitation. Besides anything, Rose could not imagine Josephine attending a fancy dress ball; it seemed to her much more the sort of thing her sister, Isabella, would do. Before she could dwell on the matter further, she almost collided with Cedric who was coming out of Baron Atherton's study, a rather serious and resigned expression on his face.

'Oh, there you are, Rose. I am glad to see you. I'm sorry I missed you at breakfast. The baron was very keen to have a word with me about Hallam. He's got it into his head that the boy means to do Lord Sneddon harm and he wants to take all necessary precautions to ensure that Isabella's marriage to Hugh takes place.' He took her hand and led her into the drawing room in order that they might continue their conversation in private. 'Between you and me, Rose, I'm having difficulty reasoning with the man. I've tried to explain what a cad Sneddon is, and how Isabella would be much better off not marrying him, but he simply won't listen. He's got his heart set on his daughter becoming a duchess. Really the man's intolerable; he seems to have very little regard for his daughter's future happiness. Having said that, I'm sure Isabella can look after herself. I have never known her do anything that she doesn't want to do. My mother used to think her even more headstrong than Lavinia, and that's saying something.'

'Josephine mentioned something about a scandal that happened earlier this year involving Sneddon. She's going to tell me all about it later when we go for a walk in the gardens.'

'Good. I know I said last night that I didn't want us to get involved in all this, but I think now the sooner we get to the bottom of it, the sooner we can sort everything out and enjoy this weekend. I'm off to have a word with Hallam to get his side of the story. I'm pleased to see that Hugh's keeping a low profile this morning.' With that, he mounted the staircase and, taking the stairs two at a time, soon disappeared from view.

Rose looked at her wristwatch. She still had twenty minutes or so before she was due to meet Josephine for a walk in the gardens and she wondered how she should occupy herself until then. She glanced around the hall and her eye rested on the door to the library. No doubt it would be full of some interesting books that she could browse through to while away the time until she met up with Josephine; certainly it seemed a waste of time and energy to go back upstairs.

She opened the door to the library and went in. For a moment she did nothing but take in the splendour of the room, the pale yellow walls with vast Victorian mahogany brass-trimmed bookcases, completely filled with books bound in calf leather, and which covered large areas of the walls almost up to the ceiling. The bookcases in turn were divided by Corinthian columns and surmounted on the occasional plinth around the room were a number of marble busts. A pair of late nineteenth century, high backed, tufted leather wing chairs had been drawn up to the great marble fireplace at the end of the room, which remained unlit.

Rose selected a book from the shelves at random and went and sat on one of the leather wing chairs. Due to the height of the back and the way the chair was positioned, it amused her to think that if she tucked up her legs beneath her on the seat, which was easily done given that the chair was so large, then any servant happening to open the door would assume that the room was empty for she would be completely hidden from view by the chair back. She leaned back into the leather, finding the chair surprisingly comfortable and this, coupled with the act of reading, began to make her feel drowsy. Afterwards, she realised that she must have fallen asleep, even if only for a few minutes, for she did not hear the door open until it was too late.

'Hallam, your father has asked me to come and speak with you,' Cedric began, walking into the young man's bedroom.

'Don't bother,' replied Hallam listlessly. He was lying out-stretched and fully clothed on his bed which, together with the dark rings under his eyes, indicated that he had been up for hours. As far as Cedric could tell, he had been throwing balls of rolled up paper at the ceiling, seemingly having abandoned attempts to get them into the wickerwork waste paper basket situated at the other end of the room.

'Come on, old man,' said Cedric, sitting down on the bed beside him, 'you'd better tell me what's going on. You'll feel better for it and you never know, perhaps I can help.'

'It's no use, Cedric, my father won't listen to me. I went to see him first thing this morning to have my say, but he's adamant that Isabella's going to marry Sneddon. There's nothing I can do to change his mind.'

'If you feel so strongly about it, then perhaps you should try and change Isabella's mind; after all she's the one who'll be marrying the fellow. Come on. You can't just lie there doing nothing but giving the servants additional work. I know it's early, but I'll give you a game of billiards in the game's room. You can tell me what you've got against Sneddon marrying your sister while we're playing.'

The door was flung open and then shut again loudly and Rose awoke with a start, realising that she was no longer alone in the library. But before she could make her presence known a heated argument broke out, so that she was left to sit where she was, concealed from view, a reluctant eavesdropper.

'Hugh, I don't think I can go through with it; please don't make me.' Rose had not heard the aloof Isabella sound so wretched.

'Pull yourself together, Isabella.' Rose recognised Lord Sneddon's voice which sounded cold, harsh and unrelenting. 'We had an agreement, my dear, don't you remember? I'll keep quiet about certain of your escapades if you honour your side of the bargain.'

'But it's too much, Hugh, too much to ask of anyone. I can't do it,' she sobbed, 'I simply can't do it.'

'Well, in that case I'll hand these letters over to a newspaper or perhaps distribute them all over London.' Rose heard the rustle of paper as Lord Sneddon took a bundle of papers from his pocket. 'Is that what you really want, Isabella? I'm sure the baron will be delighted to find out what his darling daughter really gets up to in London. I'm sure he'd love to know that the illicit affair between the Honourable Isabella Atherton and her penniless French tutor is common gossip among high society.'

'No, Hugh, please.' Rose could hear what she supposed was Isabella attempting to snatch the letters from Sneddon's grasp.

'Not so quick, my dear. Besides, don't take me for a fool. I'm not so stupid as to keep all your letters with me. What I have here are only a few. Still, they make very interesting reading, now let's see: "My darling Claude. I cannot wait until I am in your arms and your lips are on mine; to feel our bodies entwined as one ..." Really, my dear, how very risqué. I only hope that his letters to you were equally passionate.'

'Please, Hugh, don't ...' There was a silence as if each were contemplating their next move.

'Tell me that you haven't read all my letters to Claude. I couldn't bear it,' Isabella said at last.

'No need to fret, my dear. I've only glanced through one or two just to get the general gist of things, so to speak. Believe me, my dear Isabella, I get no thrill out of reading your impassioned words to another man. Now, if such words were addressed to me, well that would be another matter altogether.'

'If I do go through with it, do you give me your word as a gentleman that you'll return every single one of my letters to me?'

'I do. At our wedding breakfast if you so desire. We can stand side by side as you count them and then we'll throw them into the fire.'

'I don't understand why you want to marry me in the first place. Surely you'd prefer a willing bride rather than one blackmailed into marrying you against her will.'

'I've explained before, Isabella. I need money, and lots of it. I haven't time to woo an heiress. I wasted enough time on Lavinia and a number before her as it is. My creditors won't wait. You're not quite as rich as I would have liked, but you'll have to do; beggars can't be choosers. Still, it needn't be too awful. You are very lovely, my dear; it needn't be such a sacrifice if you don't want it to be. And it's not as if you're not getting anything out of it other than the return of your letters. You'll be a duchess in due course and many women consider me more than tolerably handsome.'

There was a silence as neither spoke for a moment.

'If I do agree to go through with it,' Rose heard Isabella say finally, 'do you promise me faithfully that you won't read any more of my letters?'

'I do, you have my word.'

'Very well then, so be it.' A noise suggested that Isabella was stifling a sob.

'Cheer up, my dear. You'll need to put a brave face on it, if only to convince your darling siblings that this is what you want. I don't really want to be forced to run your brother through with a sword.' Lord Sneddon laughed, as if he were attempting a joke, but the sound was not pleasant.

'So you see,' Hallam was saying as he paused to take a particularly difficult shot, 'why I'm far from keen that Isabella should marry that scoundrel. He did nothing but bring scandal on this household last time he was here, to say nothing of breaking poor Josephine's heart. She really fell for him, you know, and to see them together you'd have thought that he was just as keen on her when all the time ...' His voice faltered as he thought over again what Sneddon had done.

'I can see why you feel as you do towards him,' said Cedric, 'but are you sure that Josephine was as fond of him as you imagine? I grant you she looked rather shocked when he turned up last night, but I wouldn't have gone so far as to say she looked devastated.'

'Well, it did happen about a year ago,' admitted Hallam, 'but even so she took it very badly at the time. She's become very secretive and withdrawn. There was a time when we told each other everything, but now she hardly says a word about how she's really feeling. She always puts on a bit of an act for Father, you know, pretends everything's fine, but sometimes when she thinks no one is looking at her she has such a sad look on her face.'

'And you think that's to do with Sneddon?'

'Yes, I'm sure of it. The man's an absolute rotter. I mean, pretending on the one hand that he's mad about her when all the while he's cavorting with one of the ... Oh, bother!' Hallam broke off as he missed his shot and Cedric took his go.

'I take it that Isabella knew all about this?'

'Yes she did and that's why I can't understand it. She was in London at the time, but she knew what effect Sneddon's behaviour had on Josephine, she saw it for herself when she came back at weekends. Why, we even stayed up half the night talking about it once.' Hallam suddenly looked dejected. 'That's what I don't understand, Cedric. I know Isabella's never been the sympathetic kind, but she was genuinely upset for Josephine and then when we found out that awful business with the maid, why, I'm surprised she even spoke to Sneddon in London let alone became engaged to him.'

'Well, I've just told you what happened at Ashgrove, so what you've told me hardly surprises me, although the situation with the maid is very tragic. But I'm afraid you've got to face up to it, old chap. Whether you like it or not, Isabella's set on marrying the man.'

'That's just it, Cedric. Although I can't stand the chap after everything he's done, I suppose I could have made a bit of an effort to get along with him, if only for Isabella's sake. But it's just that I don't think she's very happy about it all; I don't think it's what she really wants.'

'I think you may be right,' Cedric admitted slowly and reluctantly, knowing as he did so that his saying so would only act to encourage Hallam in his speculation. 'She certainly looked pretty miserable about it all last night. Of course, it could have been because of your outburst.'

'Yes, but why didn't she tell me just to be quiet? It wasn't like her at all just to stand there and say nothing. You know what she's like. I would have expected her to be over the moon at the prospect of marrying a man who'll inherit a dukedom one day. Don't get me wrong, she would have been sad about how Josephine might take the news, but she would have been pretty delighted about the prospect all the same.'

'Yes, and their arrival at the last minute before dinner was rather strange,' said Cedric thinking. 'I say, Hallam, concentrate a bit on the game, won't you, that was a very easy shot, you could have won.'

'Sorry,' Hallam said, sheepishly. 'I can understand though why Isabella was elusive about who her guest was going to be. She knew I'd kick up a fuss about it. And I'm not surprised Sneddon insisted on seeing Father straightaway; he knew that Father would have been minded to have him thrown out. Of course, Sneddon knew that dangling the fact that he had asked Isabella to marry him was enough to get Father's support behind him. Father's always been desperate for at least one of his daughters to marry well and he's always been rather worried about Isabella.'

'Hallam,' began Cedric, slowly, choosing his words carefully, 'you don't think Isabella's being coerced into accepting Sneddon's proposal, do you?'

'You mean being blackmailed?' Hallam dropped his cue with a thud on the floor. 'Why, that would explain everything! That's why Isabella looked so miserable last night and didn't seem to care a jot when the footman dropped boiling hot soup over Sneddon at dinner. I say, I could have cheered when he did. Father was jolly rotten to give Robert his marching orders.'

'If Isabella's being coerced into this marriage, we're going to have to do something about it, Hallam.'

'Too right, we are,' agreed Hallam gleefully. 'I've a good mind to challenge the man to a duel. I'm jolly good at fencing, you know. Although knowing Sneddon, I bet he'd insist that we use pistols.'

'Do talk sense, Hallam. What I'm proposing is that we try and talk to Isabella, find out exactly what's going on.'

'Oh, I am talking sense, Cedric. If I find out that Sneddon's been blackmailing my sister into marrying him, I'm going to kill him.' There was a certain look of determination on his face and bitterness in his voice which suggested to Cedric that he was being serious. It occurred to Cedric then that he might be forced to take matters into his own hands.

Rose heard the door open and the sound of movement as both Sneddon and Isabella walked through it and shut the door behind them.

As soon as the door had closed and she knew that she was alone again, Rose uncurled her legs from under her and stood up trembling slightly. It was not so much because of what she had heard for, if she were truthful, it hardly surprised her given the way Isabella had behaved towards Sneddon the previous evening. No, it was more the distraught state that Isabella had been in, and Sneddon's coldness towards her and total disregard of her feelings. She knew that both parties would have been appalled had they known that their conversation had been overheard, yet she felt that she must do something. She could not let Isabella go through with a marriage to Lord Sneddon, not when it was so obviously against her wishes. She hardly knew Isabella, but even so she resolved there and then that she would do whatever it took to ensure that Isabella did not have to go through with her side of the bargain.

Chapter Eight

Rose wandered out into the hall, still in a bit of a daze, going over and over in her mind what she had just heard.

'Oh, there you are, Rose, I've been looking for you everywhere,' said Josephine, suddenly appearing. 'Shall we go for our walk now? It's pretty warm outside. I thought we might wander down to the lake.'

The two girls set off, Rose still deep in her own thoughts. Josephine did not appear to notice because she chatted on endlessly, apparently without expectation of any response. It was only afterwards that Rose wondered whether her incessant chatter had been contrived, hiding other deeper emotions.

'I expect I'd better tell you all about it, this business with Hugh. As I said earlier, I'm afraid it's all rather unpleasant, but it'll help explain why Hallam is acting the way he is. He is behaving rather childishly, but justifiably, I would say. It's a great pity Hugh's here. Hallam had great plans for all the things we were going to do together this weekend, but now I expect most of the time will be taken in keeping him and Hugh apart.'

'I got the impression last night that he thought you'd be very upset by Lord Sneddon's unexpected arrival,' began Rose, tentatively.

'Yes, well, I was of course.' Josephine stopped abruptly. 'I might as well tell you, Rose. It's all rather embarrassing but there was a time when I thought Hugh was rather keen on me. It was about this time last year; perhaps a month or two later. He made an awful fuss of me and I was rather taken by him, myself. He is awfully handsome and can be quite charming when he wants to be. And of course Father was delighted, as you can imagine. He's always wanted either Isabella or myself to marry well. Everyone thought it would be Isabella, of course, what with her being much prettier than me and loving high society. Father just assumed that I'd be content staying here at Dareswick and of course I would have been if only …'

'… it hadn't been for Hugh.' Rose finished Josephine's sentence for her because the girl seemed to hesitate.

'Hugh? Yes, of course, Hugh.' Josephine's hand went sharply up to the side of her face. At the same moment a breath of wind happened to sweep a strand of hair aside and Rose could not help herself from letting out a gasp. For, not far from her left eye was an ugly scar the length of a lipstick, quite white as if it had been made years before.

'Oh, my scar,' said Josephine, looking at the horror on Rose's face and covering her scar instinctively with her hand. 'I'm afraid I'm rather sensitive about anyone seeing it, it's usually covered by my hair.'

'I'm sorry, I didn't mean to stare at it.'

'It's all right, really it is. I know I'm silly about it. Hallam is always telling me that it doesn't look that awful. It's just the result of a silly little sibling argument that got out of hand when we were children.'

'Hallam gave you that scar?'

Josephine hesitated slightly before nodding. 'Yes, but don't say anything about noticing it to him, will you? He's awfully ashamed about it, poor dear. It's one of the reasons I keep it covered up by my hair so as not to remind him of it. We were both only young children when it happened, she didn't mean anything by it.'

Rose wasn't so sure. It seemed to her that it would have taken some considerable effort to cause such a wound, which led her to think that it might have been deliberate rather than an accident. She thought of Hallam's outburst the night before, how he had worked himself up into such a state. She shivered slightly despite the warmth of the day. For the first time that morning she was glad that Cedric was keeping him occupied and wondered whether Hallam was seriously intending to do Lord Sneddon harm. In her mind's eye, she could see him raising his hand and slashing Hugh's face with a knife as he must have done all those years before to Josephine's.

'Anyway, what was I saying?' continued Josephine hurriedly, her hair safely put back in place with a realigned hairpin. 'Oh yes, Hugh's behaviour. Well, unbeknown to us all, at the same time that he was supposedly courting me, he was also paying his respects to one of the housemaids. The under housemaid at the time, a young girl called Mabel. A pretty little thing she was but very naive, I'm afraid, certainly insofar as men were concerned.'

'What happened?'

'Well, perhaps not surprisingly, he got her into trouble. The whole household knew Lord Sneddon was responsible, but somehow word went around the village that Hallam was to blame, when anyone who knows him at all would know that he wouldn't have dreamed of doing such a thing.'

'How awful.'

'Yes, thankfully our own servants knew he wasn't at fault, but I'm afraid that's not all. I'm afraid it was much worse than that you see –'

'Lord Sneddon's blackmailing Isabella to marry him!' Rose blurted out suddenly, before she even had time to reconsider her words. Afterwards she realised things may have turned out differently if only she had kept quiet. But all the while Josephine had been talking, alluding to sordid and unsavoury acts on Sneddon's part, Rose had felt the need to confide in her the awful course Sneddon had chosen to adopt with regard to her sister's future. She heard again in her mind Isabella's pleading voice and Sneddon's merciless response. She had felt she must tell someone, she must. She had imagined that the person she would tell would be Cedric, but here was Isabella's sister, kind and sensible Josephine, standing with her in the gardens far from the house and the possibility of being overheard. Who better to tell but Isabella's older sister? Who better to rescue Isabella from her fate? Even so, as the words tumbled from her mouth, she wondered even then whether she had made a mistake. Even then it occurred to her that she should have kept silent until she had had the opportunity to speak things over with Cedric. But it was too late; the words were out now and could not be retracted.

'What!' Josephine was aghast. 'Whatever do you mean? How do you know he's blackmailing her? Did Isabella tell you he was?'

'No, she didn't have to. You see ...' Rose hesitated. She was beginning to regret her outburst, not least because she would have to admit that she had listened in, however unintentionally, to a conversation not meant for others' ears. 'I was in the library this morning after breakfast, sitting in one of those great wing chairs by the fireplace, reading a book. I was trying to kill time before meeting up with you to go for this walk.' Rose could feel her face burning. 'There didn't seem much point –'

'Yes?' interrupted Josephine impatiently.

'I must have fallen asleep for a couple of minutes because I didn't hear the door open. Lord Sneddon and your sister came in. They couldn't have seen me sitting by the fireplace. I was hidden by the chair back. Anyway, before I knew what was happening, they were having an argument. I didn't know what to do. Whether I should make my presence known or not. So I'm afraid I just sat there and listened until they left.'

'I see.' Josephine said slowly. 'That would explain Isabella's mood last night. It's funny but I'm almost glad in a way. Not that she's being blackmailed, of course, but that she isn't intentionally hurting Hallam and me. But what I don't understand is what could Hugh possibly have to blackmail her over? I daresay she's a bit reckless when she's in London, probably drinks a little too much and that sort of thing, but I can't imagine that he could have such a hold over her as to force her into marrying him against her will.'

'He's got hold of some letters somehow.'

'Letters? What sort of letters?'

'About a love affair, I think. With someone unsuitable. And I'm afraid they were rather incriminating.'

'In what way?' Josephine's eyes had gone wide. She was staring at Rose so intently that Rose began to squirm under such scrutiny.

'"I cannot wait until I am in your arms again and your lips are on mine", that sort of thing,' Rose said looking at the ground, embarrassed.

'Oh, my God!' said Josephine sitting down slowly on a nearby bench. 'And do you know who these letters were addressed to, who Isabella's lover was?'

'Yes, Lord Sneddon mentioned his name,' said Rose, racking her brains. 'Claude something, I think. I don't remember his surname, I'm afraid. I'm not even sure he mentioned it, but he said something about him having been Isabella's French tutor.'

'Claude Lambert,' said Josephine slowly. 'So I was right all along. Oh my God, I was right!' She covered her face with her hands.

'You knew about it?'

'I had my suspicions, yes. I just hoped that they would prove unfounded.'

'Did you ever meet him?'

'Yes, I met him a few times when I was up visiting Isabella in London.' She groaned. 'How could she have been so stupid?'

Rose studied Josephine closely. She had expected her to be upset by the news, but the girl appeared absolutely distraught; she was positively shaking.

'Would it be so disastrous if those letters became public?'

'What? Oh … yes, it would. My father has quite a temper as you have seen first-hand by the way he treated the poor footman last night for spilling the soup on Lord Sneddon. If he found out about those letters I've no doubt he'd disinherit her. And if the content of those letters became public, it would be even worse. Any chance Isabella had of a good marriage would be gone.'

'But we can't let Lord Sneddon get away with it,' pleaded Rose. 'We can't let him force your sister into marrying him. You should have heard Isabella this morning. She was desperate and he didn't care one bit; he was completely heartless.'

'No, we can't let him blackmail her into marrying him,' agreed Josephine slowly. She looked preoccupied as if she was trying to work out the best course of action. 'Rose, I want you to leave this with me. I don't want you to tell anyone else about this, not even Cedric. Will you promise me that you won't tell anyone, nobody at all?' There was an urgency in Josephine's manner that Rose found unnerving. She felt a sense of foreboding, as if something was very wrong, worse even than Isabella being blackmailed.

'Yes, all right,' Rose agreed reluctantly for now more than ever she desperately wanted to tell Cedric, 'if that's what you want. But what are you going to do? Are you going to reason with him? Do you think he will listen to you?'

'Leave it with me, Rose,' Josephine said firmly. 'Now, I'm going back to my room to think what to do.' For the first time she seemed aware of the concern on Rose's face. 'You needn't look so worried, Rose, it'll be all right, I'll think of something. But you must promise me that you won't breathe a word about this to anyone.' With that, Josephine walked quickly back to the house; indeed, she was almost running.

Rose looked after the retreating figure feeling anything but reassured. She had made a mistake, she was sure of it now. If only she could take back her words. She and Josephine could still be talking now about the scandal involving Lord Sneddon that had taken place at Dareswick earlier in the year. He had got one of the servant girls into trouble, Josephine had said, but she had hinted also that that was not the worst thing that he had done. What could be worse, Rose wondered, than ruining a young girl's life? And it was only now after Josephine was gone and Rose was left to wander the gardens alone, to survey the work beginning to be done by the gardeners in preparation for the winter to come, that it occurred to her that not once had Josephine asked why Lord Sneddon should wish to marry her sister.

Chapter Nine

Rose did not hurry back indoors. She felt sure that Josephine would be closeted in her bedroom, or perhaps a sitting room or morning room, deep in thought as she tried to formulate a solution to Isabella's dilemma. Cedric no doubt was ensconced with Hallam in some room trying to persuade the young man not to do anything rash. Isabella, she hazarded a guess, had returned to her room and the baron was no doubt holed up in his study. The only person she was likely to come across if she returned to the house now, other than the servants, was Lord Sneddon. Such a prospect was not only unpleasant and unwelcome, but she felt sure that, despite the promise she had made to Josephine, she would find it very hard to hold her tongue and make small talk with the blackmailer. Besides, it was still warm and the gardens seemed to beckon her, a haven from the tensions in the house that stifled the atmosphere like heat and dust.

In the end it was Cedric that came for her, and she could tell, even from a distance, that he was agitated.

'I had the whole story from Hallam as to why he hates Sneddon so, and I have to say I don't blame him in the slightest for wanting to give Sneddon his marching orders. Why, I did the same thing myself not so long ago, if you remember?'

'I do,' smiled Rose, and a surge of love filled her heart for Cedric.

'Still, I was mindful of the promise I had made the baron to keep Hallam out of trouble, or at least prevent him from doing anything to jeopardise the engagement. So I made up my mind to have it out with Sneddon, find out exactly what he's playing at. I almost wondered whether he saw it as some sort of game.'

'And does he?' asked Rose inquisitively, curious to find out if Sneddon would reveal his hand or keep his act of intimidation firmly hidden.

'The man has upped and gone to London, damn him!' cursed Cedric. 'Feigned some important family business he had to attend to that wouldn't wait. He won't be back until just before dinner.'

'Oh, that's good, isn't it?' exclaimed Rose. 'We can relax now in the knowledge that we won't come across him loitering in the grounds and be forced to be polite to him. And you won't have to keep an eye on Hallam.'

'There is that,' admitted Cedric, grudgingly, 'but I'd rather get it all over and done with, you know, have my say. I can't help thinking that the longer I leave it, and the more all this is allowed to drag on, the worse it will be. Don't you feel it, Rose, that something awful is going to happen? Or is it just me, am I just being fanciful?'

'It's just you, silly,' said Rose and kissed him. She did not want to admit even to herself that she felt the same. It was like a waiting game. They were all sat there waiting for something to happen, or was she just imagining things like Cedric? She must think on the positives. With Sneddon gone, albeit only temporarily, Josephine could plan how to extract Isabella from her precarious situation and Hallam had time to calm down. And best of all she could spend time with Cedric. They could have the weekend that they had longed for, even if just for a few hours.

But at the back of her mind her thoughts were with Isabella. She wondered idly whether she would keep to her rooms feeling ostracised. She did not like to think of her alone pacing the floor like a caged tiger feeling miserable and wretched, forced into an intolerable situation. She longed to tell her that she knew her secret, knew why she was intending to marry a man she despised. She wanted to tell her that Josephine knew, that her sister would rescue her. For Rose put great faith in Josephine. There was something about the way that she had said that she would see to it which made Rose feel sure that she would. She remembered the determined look on Josephine's face, the look of resolve in her eyes. She would take whatever measures she considered necessary to ensure that her sister was not forced to marry Sneddon against her will. With a shiver, Rose wondered what those measures would be.

'Course I could always tell his lordship that that footman is still here, the one he dismissed for spilling soup on old Sneddon,' said Ricketts, sidling into the butler's pantry where the butler had just managed to down a sobering shot of whisky.

'It's Lord Sneddon to you,' Crabtree retorted stiffly. 'And you'd do well to keep your nose out of things that don't concern you.'

'Well I'd say this does. It was my man got scolded after all. What's it worth to you for me to keep quiet like?' The valet lounged against the Belfast sink, sucking his teeth. 'I doubt whether your master will be too pleased that you've disobeyed his orders. You might lose your own job.'

'You may be used to blackmailing people where you've come from, but it won't work here,' Crabtree said firmly, the whisky having given him the additional courage he needed to stand up to the man. 'And I'd think twice if I were you before you go running to his lordship. Because I've got half a mind to look into where you've come from. You're no valet or I'll eat my hat. You've never even been in service before. And I'll have you know that I've got contacts in loads of places; who knows what I may find out?'

It was decided that the morning at least should be spent wandering into the village of Dareswick and having a look around before returning for a late lunch. Dareswick was located some three miles from Dareswick Hall and the journey involved trudging over fields and muddy farm tracks. This together with the continued warm weather and fresh air had a positive effect on the party, lifting everyone's spirits, with Hallam chatting happily to Cedric about how he was finding Oxford and Josephine filling Rose in on the village's history. Isabella had declined to join them on their expedition citing tiredness and having letters to write. The absence of Isabella and Sneddon helped to lighten the atmosphere and Rose had a glimpse of how the weekend might have gone if it had not been for the arrival of the unwelcome visitor.

The village of Dareswick was picturesque with its narrow lanes and tiny streets populated by old stone houses and cottages, many of them thatched. Rose and Josephine wandered around the ancient church, which had some Norman work remaining in its north and south doorways, and Josephine pointed out to Rose its seventeenth century canopied pulpit and medieval stained glass windows. Cedric and Hallam meanwhile, having both been in the church on numerous occasions, loitered in the churchyard until the girls had finished their visit. They retired to one of Dareswick's many tearooms on the pretext of having coffee, but the smell of freshly baked loaves, thick golden farm butter and other appetising aromas enticed them to stay for lunch.

It was therefore mid-afternoon before they returned to Dareswick Hall. Rose thought that it was probably just her fancy but it seemed to her that, with each step nearer they got to the Hall, the mood became more subdued until the happy chat dwindled to a stop with each of them apparently lost in their own thoughts. Rose found that she herself was dreading encountering Isabella, for it occurred to her that Josephine's first course of action on being told about the blackmail would have been to go to her sister to demand the full story. Rose did not see how Josephine could tell Isabella how she knew what was happening without disclosing that she, Rose, however unintentionally, had overheard Isabella's intensely private conversation with Sneddon in the library. Rose felt her cheeks burning at the thought.

As it happened, her fears appeared unfounded, for when she encountered Isabella later in the day in the drawing room she gave no indication that she viewed Rose any differently than she had the night before. Just as puzzlingly, Rose had the distinct impression that Josephine had said nothing to Isabella about the blackmail. How odd, she thought. It occurred to her then that Josephine's intention might be to bypass Isabella altogether and tackle Sneddon head on. The thought made her tremble as she could easily imagine Sneddon's wrath at the discovery of his plans. He was also likely to turn his anger towards her as the person who had let the cat out of the bag. Rose had no doubt that he would feel vindictive and would want some form of retribution. How she longed to tell Cedric, but she had been sworn to secrecy by Josephine and she was not one to go back on her word. Besides, she was afraid of what Cedric might do if he were to know the truth. If the time came, she would have to rely on herself.

The day dragged on into a waiting game for Lord Sneddon's return, the sense of foreboding Rose felt growing stronger with each passing hour. Cedric roamed the gardens with Hallam, as if to tire him out, and Rose remained in the drawing room with Josephine, flicking idly through a copy of a *Woman's Weekly* magazine, perusing *The London Girl's Dress Gossip* article and reading the questions and advice given in the *Mrs Marryat Advises* column. She tried to imagine what Mrs Marryat's advice would be to their dilemma, something along the lines of "My dear readers, one of the most senseless things a girl can do is to marry a man because she is being coerced to do so." Oh, if only she had been aware of the problem before, then perhaps she could have sent a stamped and addressed envelope to Mrs Marryat for a private reply.

Following a fleeting appearance when Cedric and Hallam were safely ensconced in the vegetable garden, Isabella had retired again to her room, but not before Rose had taken in how deathly pale and listless she was. Josephine, she noticed with surprise, hardly acknowledged her sister's presence and yet there was a pleading look in Isabella's eyes as if she was desperate to impart something to Josephine or ask her for advice. Josephine appeared oblivious to this and Rose felt that her own presence in the room was proving a hindrance. It occurred to her that the most diplomatic course of action would be to leave, but before she could do so, Isabella had disappeared.

During the course of the afternoon, Josephine had gone into the garden and returned with a bunch of soft apricot coloured roses, together with some old newspaper and a vase provided to her by one of the maids.

'Oh, I do love roses, don't you? And isn't it wonderful how some are repeat-flowering? First they bloom in June or July and then again in autumn when you think they are all gone and winter is approaching,' said Josephine, removing some wilted chrysanthemums from another vase and discarding them on the open newspaper which she had laid out on the floor in front of her. 'They're your namesake, roses. Does your mother especially like them?'

'Yes,' said Rose, glancing up from her magazine. 'They're her favourite flower. She loves the old varieties that have hundreds of petals, and she likes the tea roses, of course.'

'Yes, we have loads of those in the rose garden,' Josephine agreed, busying herself with her flower arranging. 'There, how do those look? Certainly brightened up the room, don't you think?' She stood back to admire her work. 'Right, I'll just clear this mess up and take it out into the kitchen and … oh!' She let out a sharp gasp.

'What's the matter?' Rose asked, looking up, concerned.

'Oh, nothing. It's nothing. I've just pricked my finger on a thorn, that's all. That's the trouble with roses, isn't it?' With that, she rushed from the room to see to her injured finger and rid herself of the newspaper and dead chrysanthemums.

It was only much later, after the murders, that Rose wondered at the significance of this incident.

Chapter Ten

Isabella did not appear again until they all came down to dinner that evening. While Rose was dressing for dinner, she was aware of someone arriving and marching up the stairs, a number of servants in his wake, no doubt to run a steaming bath and lay out dinner clothes. So Lord Sneddon has left it to the very last minute to return, she thought. It was probably a sensible course of action on his part, as it gave Hallam little opportunity to accost him. Unfortunately, Rose thought, it also meant that Josephine would have no opportunity to speak with him before dinner, so the blackmail matter was unlikely to be resolved until the next day. Isabella would be faced with yet another night of torment.

Oh well, it was unfortunate, but it couldn't be helped. Now where did she put her mother's pearls? She had worn them last night with her black velvet dress, but she couldn't find them on the dressing table where she was sure she had left them. Perhaps the maid had packed them away in her case, it was the sort of thing they probably did. She couldn't remember, it was such a very long time since her family had had servants of their own. Well, it didn't really matter, Rose thought. Her blue and silver dress was quite dressy enough without the need for jewellery to accentuate the effect. Besides, she didn't want to be down late to dinner, which a search of her things would surely result in; she would go down as she was.

Isabella left it to the very last minute to come down, escorted by Sneddon. Both looked apprehensive and, in Isabella's case, very pale despite the liberal application of foundation creams and rouge. Rose was shocked by her changed appearance from that of the woman who had arrived the previous evening. Even in comparison with earlier that afternoon, Isabella's countenance had deteriorated to an alarming degree. Her eyes were red rimmed and swollen and there were dark shadows underneath them betraying a sleepless night. Rose glanced at Hallam apprehensively, afraid that he would be spurred into action by the wretched state of his sister. But, while she saw him gasp and clench his fists until she could see the whiteness of his knuckles, he remained silent. Cedric, she noticed, was watching him intently as if anxious as to whether or not he would adhere to the course of action that they had presumably agreed to take. She caught Cedric's eye. It appeared that he, like Josephine, intended to have a word with Sneddon at the first available opportunity.

Only the baron, Rose thought, appeared unaware of the misery of his youngest daughter. If he noticed her altered appearance, he gave no sign, but instead beamed at the gathering as if it were a joyful occasion and the atmosphere was easy and light. Everyone else, Rose felt sure, was aware of the tension in the room. Conversation was strained and formal, and focused on discussing matters of a trivial nature. No mention was made of the engagement and forthcoming marriage. It was almost, Rose thought, that by not mentioning it everyone hoped that it would go away.

She realised that she was fortunate in where she was seated in that the baron was determined to keep conversation flowing at his end of the table and kept up a continuous dialogue on the history of the village and its church. Rose readily nodded and murmured words of encouragement at appropriate intervals or lapses in the conversation, painfully aware that there was often silence at the other end of the table broken only by the odd word or unenthusiastically asked question, the answer to which was more often than not a monosyllable.

Cedric, she noticed, was trying to engage Josephine in a pretence at least of some sort of conversation. But it was as if Josephine could not hear his words because she seemed wrapped up in her own world, oblivious to all around her except for every now and then throwing the odd anxious glance at Isabella, as if she could not quite comprehend that her sister was even contemplating the possibility of entering into marriage with a man such as Sneddon. Sneddon himself, Josephine barely cast a look at, as if he was beneath consideration.

Sneddon hardly said a word to anyone, staring straight ahead above Isabella's head as if the answer to his thoughts lay through the wall and outside the room. Every now and then his eyes darted towards the servants as if he was searching for one in particular who was not there. He flinched each time a servant stood beside him to serve him dishes or replenish his wine. The whole table looked on in excited apprehension when the still poorly Sid came to serve him soup, but there were no further mishaps.

Both Hallam and Isabella stared sullenly at the tablecloth, the former playing idly with his cutlery, the latter toying with her glass. Both looked equally dejected.

The prospect of having to try and make small talk in the drawing room after dinner was almost too awful to comprehend. Rose wondered how long she would have to wait until she could reasonably be excused and retire to bed. Perhaps she could feign a headache straightaway.

As it happened, both Josephine and Isabella made their excuses and retired to bed as soon as the coffee and liqueurs were served. With the departure of her hostess, Rose was now free to leave herself. She cast a final look over her shoulder before closing the drawing room door behind her and retreating to her room. Cedric and Hallam were at one end of the room deep in conversation. By the way they spoke earnestly together, their heads bent, Rose had the impression that Cedric was imploring Hallam not to have a confrontation with Lord Sneddon in front of his father, but to wait until morning. Meanwhile the baron and the heir to the dukedom were in the opposite corner of the room. They appeared to be deep in friendly conversation, with the baron every now and then giving a hearty laugh as if Hugh had said something amusing. Each time the baron laughed, Hallam looked daggers at his father as if he felt betrayed.

It had been a trying day from the servants' perspective, but at last Crabtree had been able to send them all off to bed, so that he could relax uninterrupted in his pantry and partake of his favourite tipple for a few snatched minutes before he himself retired for the night.

Little consideration was given to servants nowadays, he thought secretly to himself, and sighed for he would never have admitted this thought aloud, even to Mrs Hodges. Mrs Gooden and her kitchen maid had spent much of their time and effort on the luncheon only to find that all the young people, with the exception of Miss Isabella, who hardly ate a morsel even at the best of times and this certainly was not one of them, had decided to dine out in the village. So he had been forced to spend time that he could ill afford consoling the cook about the wasted efforts of herself and her minions, not that the fare had gone to waste because at least the servants had enjoyed a good spread today. Yes, that was one consolation and he was pleased to note that all the servants had been profuse in their compliments regarding Mrs

Gooden's cooking, so that her ruffled feathers had been smoothed and she had quite basked in the adoration.

Well, at least the household and guests had retired early. Even the baron and Lord Sneddon had not stayed up much later than the others chatting. Crabtree had already been around all the doors and windows ensuring that they were safely locked and barred. The house was ready for the night. He sighed, and poured himself another generous measure of whisky and settled back in his chair, savouring the taste of the golden liquid in his mouth. His final glass before he turned in for the night, the final ...

He had just closed his eyes when his quiet contemplations were rudely interrupted by the shrill and persistent ringing of one of the servants' bells in the servants' hall. He leapt from his seat, almost spilling the contents of his glass, and hurried into the servants' hall, afraid lest the noise should wake the whole house. He saw at once, from glancing at the servants' bell board, that it was the library servants' bell pull that was being pulled so vigorously. Who could be requiring the servants' services at this hour? Had not the whole household retired to bed a good half an hour or so ago?

He hurried to the library, rather regretting partaking of that last glass of whisky. He was ready for his bed, not to carry out some duty or other. He opened the library door and was greeted by the sight of Lord Sneddon, swaying slightly, an empty whisky decanter in his hand.

'Oh, there you are, Crabtree, that's your name isn't it? I've been ringing and ringing on this damn bell pull. Thought nobody was coming, afraid everyone had gone to bed. Suppose you don't keep late hours in the country, not like we do in town.'

'What can I do for you, my lord?' The whisky had taken the edge off the butler's impeccable manners, a touch of exasperation clearly audible in his voice. But if Sneddon was aware of it he gave no indication, the alcohol he himself had consumed no doubt having dulled his senses.

'There's no more whisky in this decanter. Get me another one, will you.'

Crabtree went and soon reappeared with a fresh decanter, inwardly fuming that his master's fine single malt whisky should be wasted on such a man. It was this, and more probably the amount of whisky that he himself had consumed, that resulted in him being more outspoken in the conversation that followed with his lordship than he would otherwise have been, unruffled and sober.

Sneddon grabbed the decanter from him and immediately poured himself a generous measure. He raised his glass. 'To my betrothed', he slurred, 'the beautiful Miss Atherton; the Honourable Isabella Atherton, no less. What think you, Crabtree? Has she the makings of a duchess?'

The butler remained silent.

'Quite right, Crabtree, old man,' said Sneddon, 'ignore me, I would, I spoke disrespectfully of your betters, and that really will not do.'

'If that's all, your lordship', Crabtree turned to leave.

'Just a moment,' said Sneddon hastily, seemingly sobering up somewhat, 'before you go, can you tell me what's happened to a housemaid that worked here. Is she still here?'

'We have a number of housemaids in this establishment, my lord. To which one in particular are you referring?'

'To one that was here when last I visited Dareswick. I think her name was Mavis or Mary, or something like that. It definitely began with an 'M'.'

'Ah, that would have been young Mabel, an under housemaid, my lord,' said Crabtree. It was as if the world stood still. Could it be that she had meant so little to him that his lordship could not remember her name, this man that had ruined her? Aloud he said more gruffly than he had intended: 'She doesn't work here anymore, my lord.'

There must have been something in the way he said the words that caught Sneddon's attention, for he left off drinking his whisky and looked at the butler curiously.

'Why not? Why doesn't she work here anymore?' There was fear in his voice, Crabtree felt sure, as well there might be. The whisky he had consumed would loosen his tongue, he knew even before he opened his mouth to respond. All those pent up months of guilt and anguish that he and Mrs Hodges had endured, wondering whether there was anything that they could have done differently to have prevented what had happened, that awful tragic and desperate act on a cold and bleak winter's day.

'She got into trouble. A young man who should have known better got her into trouble.' The butler almost spat out the words as he glared at Sneddon. 'A despicable, heartless young man who took advantage of her naivety. A young man who held a station in society high above her own and prayed on her innocence and kindly nature and the fact that she would be in awe of him. A young –'

'All right, all right,' interrupted Sneddon abruptly, averting his gaze to study the floor, 'I get the picture about the young man. But what happened to her? I take it she was dismissed because of her condition. Where is she now? With family? In the workhouse, although those are being abolished are they not, thank God. But there's still poor relief, isn't there?' He swung around suddenly, as an awful thought suddenly struck him. 'Tell me she's not on the streets, tell me ...' His voice trailed off until it came to a complete and awkward stop.

'None of those fates befell her,' answered Crabtree, speaking slowly. 'As I said, she was an innocent girl before she was ruined. She had a shy and trusting nature but few friends and no family to turn to, having grown up in the local orphanage. Her parentage was uncertain. Before she came to Dareswick she had been in service as maid to an old woman who had died. She hadn't been here long, six months at most. She was still learning the ways of being in service in a great house like this. I daresay Mrs Hodges and I were a little hard on her. We have to be, you see, with new servants to ensure that they know their place. Anyway, she was a quiet girl, diligent in her work. But I realise now she probably felt daunted and lonely. So it was easy for the first cad that showed a bit of interest in her to take advantage of her.' Whether it was the whisky or his memories, or a mixture of the two, the butler was close to tears.

'What happened to her?' Sneddon asked quietly, clutching his glass so tightly in his hand that there was a very real possibility that it would break. The butler looked on unmoved. He wanted the glass to shatter. He wanted the man before him to feel some pain.

'She was in awe of us, Mrs Hodges and myself, too afraid of us to tell us the truth. And she was ashamed of what she'd done. She knew she would bring shame on the household. She didn't know what to do. She didn't know who to turn to. She should have turned to us, of course, Mrs Hodges and me. We would have helped her, made sure that she and the babe didn't starve. She should have known that our bark was worse than our bite, she should have –'

'Damn it, man, just tell me what happened to her!' Sneddon almost shouted the words in his impatience. His face was now a ghastly shade of white and he was perspiring profusely, as if he had a fever. He turned and looked beseechingly at the butler and lowered his voice to just above a whisper. 'Please, just tell me what happened to her.'

'She took the only course of action that lay open to her, as she saw it, my lord,' Crabtree said slowly. 'One morning early this year, a cold and frosty morning if I recollect, she got up at dawn and stole out of the house. She went down to the lake, filled her pockets with stones and drowned herself.'

'Oh, my God!' Sneddon let out a cry and began to sob. 'But I didn't know, I didn't know. If only she'd come to me for help.'

'And what would you have done, my lord, if she had?' demanded Crabtree, giving full vent to his fury. 'Would you have helped her or sent her packing? If it hadn't been for you she could have been happy here. Who knows, she may have risen to the station of housekeeper here one day. Or she might have had a chance of marriage. That young footman who spilt the soup on you, and has lost his position as a consequence, he was sweet on the girl but painfully shy. He'd have made her a good husband, he'd have done right by her.'

'Is that why Hallam hates me so? Because of the girl? I thought it was because of Josephine, I thought –'

'Mabel's death brought scandal to this house. We all knew, the servants I should say, who'd done her wrong, but inevitably there was gossip in the village and the general view held was that Mr Hallam had got Mabel into trouble. We tried to put them straight, the other servants and I, but to no avail. Mud sticks as they say. No smoke without fire. Young Mr Hallam, he's had an awful time of it. And Mrs Hodges and I, we are that upset by what has happened and always will be. We see it that we let her down, you see. We will always feel that we could have done more to help the girl if only she had felt that she could confide in us.'

'I want to be left alone now, please,' Sneddon said, pouring himself another glass of whisky, his eyes still filled with tears.

Crabtree withdrew, closing the door quietly behind him. Suddenly he felt quite sober as he made his way back to the servants' quarters. He had overstepped the mark, he knew. He had berated Lord Sneddon as if he had been a delinquent junior servant in his charge, not a guest and a member of the British aristocracy at that. He had little doubt that in the morning, in the cold light of day, Lord Sneddon would see things differently. He would look back and consider the butler's behaviour towards him as having been impertinent. He would be vindictive, Crabtree felt sure, particularly as the butler had seen him at his worst, blubbering like a child. Would he insist that the butler be dismissed from his position? Would he make it a prerequisite to his marrying Miss Isabella? The baron, he knew, would acquiesce however reluctantly, for he was desperate that at least one of his daughters marry well. And he could do no better than have his daughter marry a man destined to become a duke.

Crabtree trembled. He had let his emotions get the better of him. If only he had not drunk that last glass of whisky. If only Lord Sneddon had retired to bed at the same time as the others. It might be the last night, he thought, that he lay beneath the roof of Dareswick Hall in the employ of his master. What would he do? He had nowhere else to go, this was his home. Things could not get much worse than this. He must take matters into his own hands. He must go and speak to Lord Sneddon first thing in the morning, apologise for his outburst. With that last thought, he turned over in his bed and fell into a fitful sleep.

Had he but known that things were to get very much worse, he would not have slept. But he was not to know that the bright light of day was to take the thought of apologising completely from his mind and that instead he would be faced with something altogether more shocking. Dareswick Hall had had its share of scandal and been the subject of much gossip. But it had never before had a murder in its midst.

Chapter Eleven

Rose slept for a couple of hours at most before she woke up with a start. Why exactly she had woken she did not know, but she knew, even without turning restlessly in her bed, plumping up her pillow and pulling the bedclothes up to her neck, that she would not be able to go back to sleep again. Despite this knowledge, she spent fifteen minutes or so sighing and tossing and turning but sleep eluded her. She switched on her bedside light and her wristwatch showed her that it was only just gone midnight. She thought of the long hours that stretched out before her until the morning. If she did not go back to sleep now she would be tired and irritable tomorrow and it would spoil the precious time she had to spend with Cedric. There was only one thing to do. She must find something that would send her to sleep. She had no sleeping powders with her, but she had always found that reading in bed made her drowsy, particularly if the book was not very engaging. She would go down to the library and choose a book.

A dressing gown thrown on and tied hurriedly around her, she stole out of her room, across the landing, and groped her way down the stairs in the darkness, afraid that turning a light on might awaken the whole house. She opened the library door and was surprised to find that, although empty, the room was not in darkness. A lamp burned brightly on a table near one of the wing chairs by the fireplace and embers from the dying fire still glowed. She went over to the nearest bookcase and quickly scanned the titles on the spines. She must find something vaguely interesting, but not too absorbing that it would prevent her from drifting off to sleep …

A noise in the room stopped her in her tracks, her hand hovering over a book. She looked around anxiously. A great form was emerging from the wing chair. In the half light of the room it took on an almost ghostly presence as if it were not human. Rose's hand went instinctively to her heart and she could not prevent herself from emitting a stifled scream.

'Don't be alarmed, Miss Simpson.'

'Lord Sneddon, you startled me. I just came in for a book,' Rose said hurriedly, grabbing the first book that came to hand. 'And now I must go, goodnight.'

In what seemed to Rose no more than one bound, Sneddon was beside her and had taken the book from her grasp.

'*The History of the Decline and Fall of the Roman Empire*,' read Sneddon. 'I say, Miss Simpson, that's hardly light reading for last thing at night. Although I have to say it may well send you to sleep. But don't go, please, I should like to talk to you. I should like to ask your advice.'

Memories of her last encounter with Sneddon on the stairs at Ashgrove came back to her. This moment here at Dareswick, shut in a library a distance away from any other living soul, she felt more vulnerable still. There was no chance of escape, Sneddon had seen to that because he was now standing between her and the door.

'Please …'

'I give you my word that you have no reason to be frightened, Rose,' Sneddon said gently, seeing the fear in her eyes. 'Look I am going to go back to the chair by the fireplace and turn it around so that I am facing you. You can remain standing by the door if you so wish, so that you can leave whenever you want to, I won't stop you. Although, of course, I'd prefer it if you pulled up the other wing chair and sat with me beside the fire, you'll catch your death in that attire.'

Rose looked at him apprehensively. He held an empty glass in his hand and that, together with a part empty decanter of whisky on the table by his chair, indicated that he may well be in drink, and yet the way he held her gaze suggested that he was quite sober. She longed to go and sit in the other wing chair by the dying fire and enjoy the last moments of its warmth, for her feet were quite frozen. But she did not trust him so instead stood with the closed door behind her back, the door knob clutched awkwardly in her clenched hand, ready to make a quick escape should the circumstances so dictate.

Sneddon shrugged his shoulders and walked over to the fireplace, turned his chair around so that it was facing her, and sat down heavily.

'Thank you. Can I at least offer you a drink?'

'No, and I think you have probably had enough.'

'Ha! You are quite right, Miss Simpson, but I'm afraid I shall require another glass if I am to bare my soul to you and ask for your advice.'

'I don't know why you would. What advice could I possibly give you and why would you want to take it?'

'Because I like you.' Sneddon held up a hand as she was about to protest. 'I know you don't like me and, believe me, I do not blame you. Why would someone like you, so honest and good, see anything but the bad in me? I have behaved in the most appalling way towards you in the past, and yet I ask you to overlook that and hear me out. Will you do that for me, Rose?'

Rose looked at him keenly for signs that he was mocking her. But he was in all seriousness she suddenly had no doubt. There was no sign of his habitual arrogance about him, instead he looked in earnest. Indeed, now that she looked at him more closely, she wondered if he were ill. Despite his good looks, he looked haggard. He was pale and his eyes were red and swollen as if he had recently been weeping.

'Please help me, Rose,' he implored. 'You must tell me what I can do to put it right. Will you?'

'Yes,' she said slowly, after a slight hesitation, 'if I can.' He was clearly in a desperate and pathetic state. Despite her reservations she moved forward slightly, as if to give substance to her words. For a moment she even wished that the old self-assured and patronising Lord Sneddon would return and replace the broken man before her. She moved further into the room, she was no longer afraid.

'Bless you. I have done so many dreadful things, Rose, hurt so many people. I don't really care about the likes of Isabella and Lavinia, of course, they can look after themselves. It's the others that I hurt that I can't live with. And it's all too late,' his shoulders drooped and he buried his head in his hands. 'I've only just realised how very much I cared for them, and now it's too late. It's too late to do anything about it.'

'Is there really nothing you can do?' asked Rose, alarmed by his anguish.

'I suppose you don't know, well, why would you? There was a young housemaid here last time I came to stay. A pretty, timid little thing, wouldn't say boo to a goose. A friendless orphan who nobody cared very much about. I remember she was so desperate to believe my attentions towards her meant something. I swear I didn't know that I had ruined her. But the awful thing is that, even if I had, I probably wouldn't have done anything to help her ...'

'Yes, Josephine told me something of it. The villagers thought Hallam was to blame.' Rose now looked at him contemptuously, her heart hardening somewhat towards him.

'But that isn't the half of it, Rose. She was so ashamed and friendless. She felt she had no one to turn to for help. So she drowned herself in the lake here at Dareswick. One cold winter morning, she filled her pockets with stones and walked out into the lake.'

Rose gasped with horror as what he was saying sunk in. It was the only sound in the room besides the ticking of the clock on the mantelpiece. In her mind's eye a vision of the girl rose up before her, young and desperate, tripping and stumbling towards the lake, half blinded by tears as she made her way on her last journey to her awful fate. Rose looked at the pathetic creature before her, crumpled and bent over with remorse. She could not bring herself to feel pity towards him, did not want to even, for such feelings would be misplaced.

'You are right, there is nothing you can do. She is beyond help now.' She turned to leave with a heavy heart, her book quite forgotten.

'No, I can't help her. But there must be something that I can do, if not for her, then for the others that I have hurt. Tell me, Rose, do you think I can change? Do you think that I can become a better person?'

'No,' Rose said honestly, the single word springing from her lips unchecked before she could soften it with other words. 'But you must try.' And then she left.

Afterwards, in the days and months that followed, she regretted what she had said. She should have shown more compassion. He had indicated a wish to change and she should have given him encouragement, not cast doubt on his ability to do so. She would remember too the way he had looked that night, desperate and distraught, a shadow of the man he usually showed the world. She could not get this last image of him out of her head; it would haunt her. If only she had realised at the time, as she left him to his sorrow, that by the morning he would be dead.

Chapter Twelve

'Mr Crabtree, Mr Crabtree, wake up, something terrible has happened!'

The butler reluctantly began to rouse himself from his sleep, his head still heavy from the effects of the whisky he had drunk the night before. As he opened his eyes and became fully conscious, he was alarmed to find that the person who was waking him so rudely from his slumber, tearing at his sheets and blanket, was none other than the housekeeper.

'Mrs Hodges!' he shot up into a sitting position, checking that his pyjama jacket was properly done up and that he was quite decent. 'Whatever are you doing?' A sudden thought struck him, unforgivable in a butler of standing like himself. 'Have I overslept?' Quickly he looked at the clock on his bedside table to reassure himself that this was not the case, but no, he still had half an hour or so before he had to rise. He breathed a sigh of relief and hoped Mrs Hodges could not smell alcohol on his breath. It was then that he recollected his actions of the night before, most particularly the way he had been so outspoken in his condemnation of Lord Sneddon's conduct. Of course, it had been the whisky talking, he would never have spoken to a guest of the baron's like that, and a peer to boot, if he had been sober. There could be no other explanation for why the housekeeper saw fit to wake him herself at this hour. Lord Sneddon must have already been to see the master to complain about his butler's impertinence.

Meanwhile, Mrs Hodges was almost sobbing in her distress.

'Mr Crabtree, Mr Crabtree, it's awful, so it is. Young Doris went to open the shutters and curtains in the downstairs rooms as usual and such, and she was just emptying the grate in the library when she said an awful feeling came over her as if she were not alone but being watched by some evil spirit. You know what she's like, a fanciful girl even at the best of times. But this time she was right! She said as how she looked up from where she was crouched dusting the grate and there he was, seated at that old library table that Miss Josephine uses as a writing desk. He was seated facing her, or he would have been if his body weren't slouched over the desk, his head buried on the table. It gave her such a fright, it did, not least because she must have walked right past him in the dark when she went to open the shutters and curtains. Always complaining to me, she is, that the room's so dark that she's always tripping and stumbling over things –'

'Yes, but I still don't understand –' began the butler, confused.

'He's dead, Mr Crabtree, Doris has just found him dead in the library!'

Despite her disturbed night, Rose woke early. At first she thought it was because of the unease she felt in respect of her last conversation with Lord Sneddon. With the clarifying light of day, when concerns and worries become less, she realised that she had been too hard on him. That he felt genuine distress and responsibility for the young housemaid's death could not be doubted and, instead of encouraging him to make amends as best he could, she had damned him and abandoned him to his feelings of hopelessness. She should have sat down with him and heard him out. She should have used the opportunity at least to persuade Sneddon to return Isabella's letters and release her from her promise.

There was considerable noise coming from downstairs, she realised, doors banging, the hurrying of feet, whispered voices being shushed, even the sound of weeping. Perhaps this is what had woken her, rather than her feelings of unease. Something was definitely afoot. The servants at Dareswick usually undertook their chores quietly so that the household and guests were almost unaware of their presence. She wondered what the matter was. For the second time in what was only a few hours, she donned her peach and cream brocade dressing gown and ventured out on to the landing where she intended to peer over the banisters into the hall below, or to detain a passing servant to find out what was amiss. Instead, she saw Cedric running up the stairs, his face pale, obviously in shock.

'Oh, Rose, how glad I am to see you. I've just been down in the library with Crabtree. Something awful has happened and so he and Mrs Hodges came to get me. Hallam's too young to deal with it and the baron hates being disturbed at this hour even at a time like this, so the butler and housekeeper came to me.'

'What's happened, Cedric?' asked Rose, apprehensively. Even though she asked the question, she didn't want to know, not really, but at the same time she did not wish to be left in ignorance, fearing the worst.

'It's Sneddon, Rose. I'm afraid he's dead. It's all rather awful, you see he's been …' He broke off as Rose began to sob. 'Oh, I say, please don't cry.

I'm no good at this. I should have broken it to you more gently. I'm afraid I just didn't think. I just came out with the first thing in my head. I was so relieved to see you, you see. Say you forgive me. I know it must have been an awful shock and –'

'It's not that,' Rose said, clinging on to him, leaning her head on his shoulder and sobbing bitterly, only vaguely aware of what a mess she must look. They stood there entwined for some moments, neither saying a word, with Cedric cursing himself for having broken the news so abruptly. Rose was clearly in shock. He should have led up to it, at least made sure that Rose was sitting down and perhaps a glass of water to hand and –

'Cedric, you see, it was me,' said Rose, finally breaking away from his embrace and wiping away her tears clumsily with the back of her hand, 'I killed him, I killed Lord Sneddon.'

'Don't say anything,' instructed Cedric as he half led, half dragged her out of the house and across the lawn, 'not until we're definitely out of earshot of anyone in the house. I'm afraid our voices will carry. We'll walk on through these first couple of formal gardens out into the rose garden; they've got a traditional one here, been here some three hundred years I believe, almost as old as Sedgwick's.'

It was some twenty minutes or so since Rose had made her devastating announcement. The colour had drained immediately from Cedric's face and he had stared at her uncomprehendingly for a moment, before his expression had become grim. He had insisted that they get dressed and go as far away from the house as possible so that they could decide what to do. Rose had never known Cedric look so serious. She had followed him obediently and had made no protest even though he held her hand so tightly that it hurt.

They did not stop until they had come to the rose garden, where they collapsed onto an old wrought iron bench, which had been designed more for visual effect than for comfort. Cedric looked around hastily to reassure himself that the garden was indeed deserted while Rose sat there almost numb of emotion.

'Right, let me think,' said Cedric, clutching his forehead in his hand. A sudden thought seemed to strike him and he looked alarmed. 'He didn't try and attack you, did he, Rose? Tell me he didn't harm you; oh, my God, he didn't –'

'No, no, he did nothing like that,' Rose said hastily, clutching his hand. Was it her imagination or did he seem to draw it away from her as if he were recoiling from her touch?

'Well, we must think. We can say that he tried to attack you, that you had no other option but to ... But no, that won't work. He was seated at that damned desk with his back to the door. That won't wash. Rose. Why ever did you do it? I know that he was the most awful of men, but even so ...'

'But –'

'Of course, if it comes to it, I'll say I did it. I'll take the blame as any gentleman would, but –'

'Cedric, oh do be quiet for a moment, please,' implored Rose. 'What are you saying exactly? Wasn't it suicide?'

'No, of course not, he was murdered. But you know that. He was stabbed in the back with a knife, well a gold letter-opener, anyway. But of course you know that because you did it.'

'Oh, thank God!' Rose began to cry tears of relief while Cedric looked at her in disbelief. 'Oh, you needn't look at me like that, Cedric. I'm not mad. I didn't murder Lord Sneddon. I thought I'd driven him to suicide because I hadn't been sympathetic to his plight. He was so melancholy and depressed, you see, when I last saw him. He was full of remorse because a young housemaid he got into trouble had drowned herself in the lake here. He was clearly shocked and I did nothing to alleviate his guilt. I felt disgusted. I wanted him to suffer. I said there was nothing he could do to put it right, but that he must try. When you told me just now that he was dead, I just assumed that he had taken his own life, that he thought it was the only thing he could do to make amends.'

'Oh, Rose, darling Rose,' he drew her to him. 'How could I have possibly thought you could have killed Sneddon? I should have known you would never have done anything like that, do you forgive me?'

'Of course I do, silly. It's hardly surprising, after all I said I did it. But I feel so guilty. I should have been more sympathetic, I should –'

'Nonsense, Lord Sneddon brought it upon himself as I am sure he did his murder.'

'Would you really have gone to the gallows for me?'

'Yes, I like to think I would. But I'm afraid I would have felt differently towards you had you really killed Sneddon. I wouldn't have wanted to, of course, but I would have done. It all seems so underhand somehow, to creep up on a man when his back is turned and plunge a knife in his back when he is seated at a desk. Why, there's something awfully cowardly about it, isn't there?'

'Yes'. Rose shivered slightly as she conjured up the image in her mind. She remembered the distraught man she had left in the library. She wondered whether he had been planning how to make amends for his past unsavoury acts when the knife had struck. She would never know now whether he would have turned out good in the end; he hadn't been given the chance.

Chapter Thirteen

'The police are on their way, my lord, a detective inspector and sergeant from Scotland Yard, I believe.' Crabtree looked at the baron apprehensively. Surely Lord Sneddon wouldn't have had a chance to speak to his lordship about the butler's conduct before his untimely demise.

The baron hardly seemed to register his butler's existence. He was too busy mopping his brow with a crumpled handkerchief and fanning himself with a sheet taken from *The Times* newspaper. His butler looked at him with concern. His master was clearly overcome with emotion and he doubted whether he was in a fit state to be interviewed by the police. Crabtree himself felt singularly green about the gills. It had not escaped his notice that he must have been one of the last people to have seen Lord Sneddon alive, besides the murderer, of course. The thought made him shiver. If he had not been made of sterner stuff, he would have had half a mind to take to his bed. Goodness knows, his head was still throbbing from the amount of whisky he had drunk the night before and he felt quite sick with the worry of it all.

When he had hurriedly followed Mrs Hodges to the library, where she had stubbornly insisted on hovering in the doorway and looking out towards the hall, part of him had half expected to find Lord Sneddon unconscious in a deep, alcohol-induced sleep. Goodness knew Doris was not the brightest housemaid Dareswick had ever employed; she was just the sort of silly young girl to mistake a man asleep for dead. Sadly, however, she had been proved correct. The little gold dagger protruding from Sneddon's back removed all doubt that she was right in her thinking. The man was dead. And clearly had been murdered at that.

'How can this have happened, Crabtree?' demanded the baron. 'In Dareswick of all places, the safest place in all the world or so I thought.'

'Indeed so, my lord, it's most unfortunate.'

'It's a jolly deal more than that, Crabtree. The man was betrothed to my daughter. She was going to be a duchess. Poor Isabella. I suppose Josephine is with her now, trying to comfort her, dear girl.'

'I'm afraid not, my lord, you see –'

'I say, Crabtree, you must have forgotten to lock or bar a door or window last night. That's how the blighter must have got in. He must have sneaked up on Lord Sneddon and caught him unawares. Hopefully the poor fellow knew nothing about it, was dead before he knew what or who had stabbed him.'

'Indeed, my lord, I can assure you that I carried out all my checks as usual last night,' replied Crabtree somewhat indignant. 'The house was safely locked and barred by half past seven. As Sidney is my witness, he and I checked and double-checked each door and window, as is our habit, and all was secure.'

'Nonsense, man. How on earth did he get in then, this murderer? You're surely not telling me he's one of my guests or a member of the household, are you? You must have overlooked some door or window. The police won't go easy on you, I can tell you, and neither will I if I find you were to blame for letting the wretch get in.'

The baron stood and glowered at his butler. Crabtree returned his stare with a look of indignation. How long this standoff would have continued neither was to find out, for at that moment Sidney came into the study to announce that the gentlemen from Scotland Yard had arrived.

'Show them in, show them in.' Baron Atherton waved one arm impatiently in the air at the footman. 'I suppose you'd better stay, Crabtree. After all, you were one of the first to see the corpse, the first if you discount that silly young housemaid of yours. Doris, is that her name? No doubt crying her eyes out now and drinking all the best sherry in the house, is she?'

'She's in the servants' hall with Mrs Gooden, my lord, and drinking nothing stronger than very weak tea with a good deal of sugar in it for the shock.'

'Detective Inspector Deacon and Sergeant Lane from Scotland Yard, my lord,' announced Sidney, ushering in a tall, dark-haired young man accompanied by a man of similar age but who, in the baron's opinion, looked nothing as he imagined a detective sergeant should look. There was a slight cockiness in his look and manner that the baron found displeasing, although he approved of the way he seemed to defer to the detective inspector, who he appeared to hold in high esteem.

The baron appraised the inspector. Well dressed and handsome, he should say, probably a favourite with the ladies. Still, he had a courteous air about him, knew his place, and his suit was well cut, if not expensive. He supposed he'd do. And he'd come from Scotland Yard so no doubt he knew his job. He looked a discreet sort of chap too, hopefully he'd sort out this mess as quickly as possible, lay his hands on the reprobate who'd done this dreadful deed and leave them in peace to weather the scandal as best they could. It wouldn't be easy, of course. Lord Sneddon had been the only surviving son of the Duke of Haywater. He could visualise the gathering of pressmen. In a day or two he would have to get his gardeners and gamekeeper to patrol the perimeter of his land to keep them out lest the place become overrun with them. He recalled that Cedric had been obliged to do the same at Sedgwick Court. He could not bear it if his beloved Dareswick Hall was for evermore associated in people's minds with violent death.

He shuddered and beckoned them to sit down while he himself half flopped into his favourite Charles II winged armchair. There was something soothing and comforting about its high back, as it supported him and held him up in a sitting position lest he collapse. The inspector seated himself on the edge of a burgundy buttoned leather sofa, where he was able to sit facing the baron diagonally. Meanwhile, the sergeant chose a chair which was a little away from the baron, outside his direct line of vision.

'I hardly need tell you, Inspector, what a very great shock this has been to us all. One minute we're celebrating my daughter's engagement to the fellow and the next minute he's dead. And killed in my own house to boot. My daughter's absolutely distraught, as you can imagine. She's being comforted now by my other daughter.' He was prevented from continuing for a moment by a cough from the butler, which distracted him, making him lose his train of thought. 'Crabtree, I was talking to the inspector, don't interrupt. No doubt you should have a word with my butler in a moment, Crabtree was one of the first on the scene, so to speak.'

'Indeed?' Inspector Deacon eyed the butler with interest. He turned slightly in his seat and caught his sergeant's eye. Yes. He had not been mistaken, Lane had picked up on it too. The butler was clearly disagreeing with something that the baron had said, but what? He had said so very little, only what you would expect a man to say who found himself in such unpleasant circumstances.

'I appreciate this must be a very difficult time for you and your family, my lord,' the inspector said soothingly. 'But as I am sure you understand, we need to get to work as soon as possible, and I'm afraid that will mean interviewing everyone in this house including your daughters. The police constables are busy now scouring the grounds, but it's just possible that one of your household or guests may have some vital piece of information that may help us catch the murderer.

'Perhaps we could start with you telling us who was here this weekend. Let's start with the members of your family. I understand all your children were present?'

'Yes, Inspector. My son, Hallam, is here. He splits his time between Dareswick and Oxford, don't you know. Isabella, she's my youngest daughter, she lives in a service flat in London. Rarely see her. Can't say I really approve, but you know what young girls are like nowadays. Since the war they've become independent and know their own minds. Likes the bright lights and the bustle of London, does my Isabella. She finds Dareswick a trifle quiet, whereas my eldest daughter, Josephine, quite loves the place. Keeps house for me since my wife died and a very good job of it she does. Don't think I would ever be able to tear her from this place, she lives and breathes it. Not that I'd want her to leave, of course, the current arrangement suits us both very well.'

'I see. And it was Miss Isabella who was betrothed to the deceased?'

'Yes, indeed,' said the baron, sadly. 'Tragic, quite tragic, Inspector. I say, I really must go and see how my daughter's getting on. Haven't seen her yet since this awful business happened. Don't know how badly she's taken it. Don't even know if the doctor's given her a sedative. Has he, Crabtree?'

'No, my lord. A sedative was offered but Miss Isabella declined.'

'She's a chip off the old block, Inspector. Made of stern stuff, that girl of mine. Still, I'd better go and see her. Where is she, Crabtree, in the drawing room?'

'No, my lord,' said the butler looking rather appalled at the suggestion. 'Mrs Hodges and I thought the drawing room was located a little too near to the library. She's in the upstairs sitting room.'

'If you'll excuse me, Inspector, I'd like to go and see my daughter now. I feel I've been rather remiss', the baron said, rising from his chair. It was clear to all those present that he intended what he said to be a statement rather than a question.

'Yes, indeed, my lord. We can talk to you later about your guests. In the meantime, I'd like to ask your butler here a few questions and I would like to have another look at the murder scene. We glanced in on it on our way through the hall to make our introductions. Our men should be almost finished with the room by now, although I hardly need to tell you that we'll need to keep it locked.'

As the baron left the room, the inspector got up and started slowly pacing the room, going first to the mantelpiece and idly picking up an ornament, looking at it for a moment and then replacing it and then going over to the baron's winged chair where he paused, stood behind it and rested his arms on the back. He leaned forward slightly, shifting some of his weight to the chair, and looked keenly at the butler. Crabtree in turn seemed to flinch under such scrutiny and made as if to avert his gaze.

'Well, what is it man, out with it,' demanded the inspector, not unkindly, but rather abruptly.

'I don't know what you mean, sir,' stammered the butler, clearly flustered.

'Just now you didn't agree with something that his lordship said. Your cough gave you away. You wanted to contradict what he said, but you thought better of it.'

'I'm sorry, sir, I'd rather not –'

'I don't care what you'd rather not. This is no time for discretion or to hold things back. This is a murder investigation. My sergeant here and I need to know everything, do you hear me, no matter how irrelevant you may think it is, or,' Deacon's eyes seemed to bore into the butler, 'or incriminating. Is that it, man? You're afraid of incriminating someone in this house?'

For a moment Crabtree said nothing, as if he was trying to make up his mind what to do and then he nodded, miserably.

'Miss Josephine,' he mumbled, so softly that Deacon was not sure whether he had heard him correctly. However, a quick glance over at his sergeant showed him by the surprised expression on Lane's face that he had not misheard.

'Miss Josephine? The baron's eldest daughter, the one that was not engaged to Lord Sneddon?'

But before the butler had a chance to nod or say any more, the door of the study burst open and an irate Baron Atherton came rushing in, the look on his face that of a man about to explode, quelling the butler into silence.

'Where is she? Where is Miss Josephine? You said she was comforting Miss Isabella. But the poor girl's all alone in her room and she says she's not seen her sister all morning. I met Mrs Hodges on the landing and the woman was damned evasive, I can tell you. Wouldn't answer my questions at all. Why, she wouldn't even look me in the eye, she just kept going on about how I should speak to you. Well, I'm waiting, Crabtree. Why did you lie to me? Why did you tell me that Miss Josephine was looking after Miss Isabella if she wasn't?'

The baron glared at the butler, his face thunderous.

'M-my, l-lord I –' began the poor man stammering.

'Actually, my lord, I think you will find that your butler did not lie to you,' said Deacon, coming to Crabtree's rescue. He held up a hand as the baron tried to protest. 'I think, my lord, that you quite naturally and understandably assumed that Miss Josephine was looking after her sister, because it was the sort of thing she would do.' He turned to the butler. 'Do you know where she is?'

'No, sir.'

'But there is something that you're keeping from us, isn't there? Out with it, man.'

'Yes, spit it out, Crabtree,' demanded the baron. 'Where is my daughter?'

'I don't know where Miss Josephine is, sir, as God is my witness. But there is something else.' Crabtree took a deep breath, in anticipation of the storm which was surely about to erupt. 'When the maid took a cup of tea to Miss Josephine this morning, as is her habit, only it was a bit later than usual because of all the fuss about –'

'Get on with it, man,' demanded the baron, rudely.

'She found Miss Josephine's room empty and she said her bed had not been slept in. She immediately got Mrs Hodges and they went through her wardrobe. Some of Miss Josephine's everyday clothes had gone, together with her jewellery box. I sent young Robert to go and see Brimshaw in his quarters over the garage. He's the chauffeur, sir,' Crabtree explained to the inspector, 'to see if Miss Josephine had asked him to drive her somewhere.'

'Robert? Robert!' bellowed the baron. 'What's he still doing here? I dismissed the fellow and demanded that he leave by first light yesterday. So what's he still doing here, Crabtree?'

'Never mind about that now,' said Deacon firmly, 'we'll come to that later. What had Brimshaw to say?'

'He wasn't there, sir, neither him nor the Rolls-Royce. No one's had sight or sound of either him or Miss Josephine since last night. They've both disappeared.'

Chapter Fourteen

'Well, what do you make of that, Lane?' Inspector Deacon asked his sergeant when they at last had the study to themselves.

'The same as the baron, sir. That they've eloped. While the baron was in here tearing his hair out and after I'd rung the station to put calls out to the stations and air and sea ports, I took the liberty of going down to the servants' hall and having a word with a couple of the maids.' He broke off as he blushed slightly at Deacon's raised eyebrows and knowing smile. 'Purely business, of course sir, although Mrs Gooden, she's the cook, sir, did press upon me a nice hot cup of tea. Nice and strong too, it was, just like my mother makes. But anyway,' he continued, seeing the look of exasperation on his inspector's face, 'the maids, Doris and Pearl, they said how Brimshaw was an awfully good looking young man and how jealous they were of Miss Josephine for running off with him and that, given half the chance, they'd have done the same.'

'I see, so it's possible that they've just eloped.'

'*Just*, sir?' queried Lane. 'I don't think the baron sees it like that. I think he thinks that it is the worst possible thing that can have happened to his daughter.'

'Well, then the man lacks imagination,' said Deacon, somewhat dismissively. 'A peer of the realm is found murdered in his house and his daughter is found to be missing. It seems to me that there are two far more awful alternatives with regard to her possible fate.'

'You think that she may have been murdered too?' queried Lane, looking alarmed. 'You think this Brimshaw fellow bumped her off as well as Lord Sneddon? The constables are busy searching the grounds so they'll discover her body if it's been dumped in the woods or the garden. I'll just go and get a couple of them to do a quick search of all the rooms in the Hall, before we start the thorough search, just to make sure that she's not in the house.'

Deacon went and seated himself on the leather sofa while he awaited his sergeant's return. Lane found him deep in thought when he came back into the room.

'Right, that's all organised. You said there was another awful possibility regarding Miss Josephine's fate, sir,' he reminded the inspector.

'Yes, I did, the gallows. Does it not strike you as strange, Lane, that Lord Sneddon should be murdered on the very same night that Josephine Atherton and this chap Brimshaw decide to elope?'

'You think then that the two things are connected, sir?'

'I do. It's too much of a coincidence that they are not. I don't want us to jump to any conclusions just yet, but the obvious one is that Sneddon disturbed them as they were making preparations to leave. I'm sure that they stole out of the house at the dead of night when they could be quite certain that all the household had retired to bed.

'Brimshaw had his room over the garage, that old converted stable block that we saw earlier when we first arrived, but no doubt he came into the house to help Josephine Atherton down the stairs with her suitcase. I hardly see her doing that herself. Perhaps they went into the library for Josephine to write her father a farewell note. That desk that Sneddon was found slumped over looks like the sort often used by ladies as a writing desk. Perhaps Sneddon came in to get himself a whisky, there was a half empty decanter of the stuff and a glass on the table near the armchair by the fire if you remember, and he discovered them. We both know the sort of man Sneddon was, we saw that for ourselves at Ashgrove. It's quite an advantage for us, I think, having already had some dealings with the victim before he was murdered. Anyway, Sneddon could have threatened to alert the baron. There could have been a scuffle and he was killed. Either Josephine Atherton or Brimshaw could have struck the fatal blow. I can certainly envisage Sneddon fighting with Brimshaw, particularly if he was in drink and Josephine panicking, fearing that the house would be roused and their plan uncovered, or perhaps that Brimshaw would be hurt. Then, without quite realising what she was doing, picking up the letter opener and stabbing Sneddon in the back. I am sure that they would have regretted their actions immediately, especially once they realised that Sneddon was dead and not just incapacitated. And then fearing the consequences of their actions, they decided to make a run for it.'

'You think that's what happened, sir?' asked the sergeant, looking appalled. 'That Josephine Atherton murdered Lord Sneddon?'

'No, not necessarily. All I'm saying is that it is possible and so shouldn't be ruled out. And that, instead of raging and cursing as he did earlier, the baron should be praying that eloping with the chauffeur is the only thing Josephine Atherton was guilty of last night.'

Both men pondered on this theory for a while, before Deacon roused himself from his musings.

'Ring the bell pull, Lane, will you. I'd like to have another word with that Crabtree fellow. I'd like to find out who exactly is staying here at Dareswick this weekend besides the family. I would ask the baron, but I have a feeling we won't get much sense out of him between him fuming about the elopement of his daughter and trying to get up the courage to inform the Duke of Haywater of the unfortunate demise of his only surviving son. Why he doesn't leave it to us to do, I can't imagine.'

'I think he sees it as his responsibility, sir,' replied the sergeant, 'you know, what with Lord Sneddon being a guest in his house, so to speak. Do you want me to stay and take notes while you speak to the butler?'

'Actually, I'd rather you went back to the servants' hall and chatted some more with the servants. I have a feeling they'll be more forthcoming with Crabtree out of the way talking to me and not breathing down their necks. And you always seem to have a particular way with the maids. I'd like you to have a word with this Robert fellow too. Find out the story there. The baron almost had a fit when he realised that he was still in the house. Find out what exactly this Robert chap did to incur the baron's wrath and get dismissed.'

'Yes, sir.' The sergeant left and the inspector was left to contemplate how he might be able to penetrate Crabtree's natural reserve. The fact that no one would be taking down the butler's words verbatim would hopefully give a more informal air to the proceedings and encourage the butler to speak more openly.

'Is your master all right?' enquired Deacon, when the butler appeared.

'He is very distressed about Miss Josephine, sir, and of course also about Lord Sneddon's death.'

'Yes, of course. It must have been an awful shock for all the servants as well.'

'Yes, indeed, sir, it was. Young Doris is beside herself, she is. It was she who found Lord Sneddon this morning. She walked straight past him and didn't see him until she had opened the curtains and begun to empty and sweep the grate. Gave her an awful fright it did, seeing the corpse like that.'

'I can imagine,' said the inspector, sympathetically.

'She's talking about leaving Dareswick for good. She was talking about running home to her parents' house today. It was all Mrs Hodges could do to make her stop and have a cup of tea.'

'Well, don't .let her go until she's spoken to my sergeant,' warned Deacon. 'We'll need to talk to her, see if she saw anything. And if she does go I'd rather one of my constables saw her home. For all we know there's a murderer still in the grounds, although I have to say the constables have seen no sign of him so far and they have been combing the area for a fair few hours now. Talking of which, we could find no sign of a forced entry. What time were the doors and windows locked last night? Is there a possibility that a door or window could have been left unlocked unintentionally so to speak?'

'No, sir. We follow a special routine here at Dareswick, his lordship's most particular. A lot of houses around here don't lock their doors and windows until ten o'clock, but his lordship insists that all doors and windows are locked by half past seven sharp. Most insistent about it, he is. And Sidney, he's the first footman, he and I do it together to make sure the job is done properly.'

'So one of you locks the window or door and the other one checks that it is secured properly?'

'Yes, sir.'

'And that's what happened last night?'

'Yes, sir,' confirmed the butler. Deacon looked at him keenly. He did not strike him as a man who would lie to protect himself or a man who did not undertake a job thoroughly.

'In which case,' said the inspector slowly, 'unless Lord Sneddon let in his murderer himself, say by one of the French windows in the library, the murderer did not come in from outside.'

'He couldn't have let him in by the library, sir. The locks on the French windows have seized up. Those windows haven't been open for years. There's some valuable books on the bookshelves. We keep the curtains drawn when there's strong sunlight to keep the bindings from fading. And on no account are we to open the windows. So ...'

'… the murderer must have been someone from within the house, yes, it certainly looks like it, doesn't it?'

Chapter Fifteen

'Is it true?' Hallam asked Cedric, entering the room clenching and unclenching his hands in his agitation. They were in the garden room, a room rarely used except in the heat of summer, and as such it had a disused feel about it, notwithstanding that the grate had been hastily swept and a fire laid. The warmth coming from the hearth, however, did not seem to have penetrated the room for the other occupants huddled in their seats as if they felt the cold. However, the garden room was located far enough away from both the library and the study, to make those present feel somewhat protected from the awful events that had occurred and were unfolding in the rest of the house.

'About Josephine? Yes, apparently so,' sighed Cedric. 'Crabtree and Mrs Hodges sought me out not long after the servants had discovered Sneddon's body. The two of them were beside themselves, they didn't know what to do. They were afraid to tell your father because they knew he'd blow a gasket, especially when he found out about your chauffeur's disappearance.'

'I just can't believe it. Josephine would never elope with *Brimshaw.*' Hallam gave a look of disgust. 'I mean, there's nothing wrong with the chap, of course, but there is nothing for her to see in him either. Rose, you'd agree with me, wouldn't you? Brimshaw is a nice enough chap but really nothing to write home about, is he? He's not the sort of man to make you girls go weak at the knees, is he?'

Rose, being put on the spot, fidgeted uncomfortably in her seat. She herself had not felt any particular attraction to the chauffeur, but then all her attention and feelings had been focused on Cedric who she had known would be awaiting her at Dareswick. At the time, it was true, if she remembered correctly, she had idly thought Brimshaw rather a handsome young man in a pleasant sort of way, and his character had been perfectly agreeable. But what of Josephine, stuck out at Dareswick in the middle of nowhere, with very little company to speak of? She imagined her entertaining the aged vicar and his wife and arranging village bazaars and suchlike. In such circumstances, starved of eligible young men, might she not be attracted to a good looking servant with a pleasant manner? There would have been plenty of opportunity for a fledgling romance to grow. Brimshaw would have driven Josephine about the place probably every day with Dareswick being so out in the sticks. It would have been necessary to travel by car to go anywhere and surely they would have passed the time of day. Josephine, Rose felt sure, would have chatted to the chauffeur, she would not have just sat there in silence. Also, of course, Brimshaw had his own private quarters above the garage where they would have been able to meet secretly, unobserved by the other servants.

There was something else too, niggling at the back of her mind. Josephine had been visibly agitated, or at the very least distracted. She had clearly had something on her mind. Rose remembered vividly their walk in the gardens following her arrival at Dareswick Hall. Josephine had said something about the flowers which suggested that she would not be there to see if the gardener had been right in his choice of home grown bulbs over imported ones. And she had become very flustered when Rose had picked her up on it and asked if she would be going away. She had vehemently denied that she would be; with hindsight, perhaps she had protested too much. But Josephine loved Dareswick with all her heart, she had said as much. Would she really give it all up to run away with her father's chauffeur? Once she had gone there would be no turning back. Rose did not know the baron well but, from what little she had seen of him, he did not strike her as the sort of man to forgive such an act of abandonment. He would cut Josephine off completely, she felt sure. He would disown her and insist that her name never be mentioned in the house, as if she had never been. Rose shivered. Poor Josephine. Was Brimshaw really worth all that?

Out loud she said slowly: 'Brimshaw is quite handsome in a pleasant sort of way, but I can't quite believe Josephine would be so unwise as to lose her head over him.'

'Of course she wouldn't,' agreed Hallam. 'It's preposterous to even think that she would.'

'Well, in which case,' said Cedric, sounding less convinced than the other two, 'where is she? Mrs Hodges says that Josephine has taken some of her clothes with her. Just the simple practical ones that she'd get to wear if she was going off for a life with someone like Brimshaw. She's left all her evening gowns but taken most of her jewellery. She could pawn that. And, if she only meant Brimshaw to drive her somewhere, why hasn't he come back yet?'

No one answered but, as if one, their thoughts went to Lord Sneddon. Only Cedric had seen his body, but their minds still conjured up the vision of a man seated in a chair at the little writing desk, his upper body slouched over the table, his once handsome face half buried in his arms, hidden by his hair which spread out over his features like a fan. And protruding from his back, from a patch crimson with blood, a delicate gold dagger which looked almost too beautiful and slight to have done such an awful deed.

'You don't think …' Hallam began asking and then faltered, the idea too awful to put into words.

'I'm sure her disappearance has absolutely nothing to do with Sneddon's murder, old chap,' said Cedric, giving Hallam a reassuring pat on the back. 'Don't give it another thought. We all know the kind of chap Sneddon was. I don't like speaking ill of the dead but there must have been loads of people who would have liked to see him out of the way. Someone must have followed him down from London and waited until everyone had retired to bed and then done him in. It was just fortunate that he was still downstairs in the library and they didn't have to try all the bedrooms looking for him. I say,' he broke off as a sudden thought struck him, 'it *was* awfully convenient for the murderer that Sneddon was downstairs; you don't think he had arranged to meet someone there, in the library, do you? Pre-arranged it, I mean? Old Crabtree's a stickler for locking up the place at night, I know, but Sneddon could have let the murderer in by the French windows and then Sneddon could have –'

Cedric had broken off at the sight of the door opening. All eyes turned towards it, wondering no doubt whether it was the baron or the policemen and considering that it might not be wise to be caught speculating as to who the murderer was or why Josephine had disappeared. The reality was much worse, for the figure that came into the room was that of Isabella, her face ashen. She still looked very beautiful, Rose thought, but in a frail sort of way, as if she would blow away if a gust of wind should happen to catch her. She's in shock, Rose thought, and who could blame her? She may have hated Sneddon, he may have been blackmailing her into marrying him, but even so …

Both men had jumped up at her entrance and were looking rather sheepish, hoping that she had not overheard them discussing Sneddon's failings. Rather ineffectually they tried to express their condolences and escort Isabella to the sofa. But she would have none of it, and stood firm in the entrance, brushing them away with her hand as if they had been crumbs on the tablecloth. Rose herself had not ventured forward, although she had got up from the sofa. Now she hovered to one side of it feeling awkward. With Josephine gone, she felt that she should have offered to sit with Isabella, but the girl always had such a cool, aloof air about her that Rose had been discouraged from doing so. Besides, when she had spoken earlier with Mrs Hodges, she had been advised that Isabella had said she wanted to be left alone. From the look the housekeeper gave her when she said it, Rose had got the distinct impression that when Isabella said something she meant it, and woe betide anyone who went against her wishes, particularly a servant, or a shop girl, she added to herself, as an afterthought.

'Oh, do sit down, Isabella, it's been an awful shock for us all, but to you in particular, of course,' said Cedric, kindly. Would you like a glass of brandy? I really do think you could do with a glass, you look as if you're about to faint any minute.'

'I'll have a small glass.' But she remained standing in the doorway and looked around the room suspiciously. 'I suppose you're all glad he's dead. None of you liked him very much, did you, even you,' she added looking at Rose. 'I saw the way you spoke to him at dinner each night, you could hardly bear to look at him, and you were casting daggers at him all the time, Cedric.' She laughed a shrill little laugh. 'Ha, a pun I believe, I must be on top form. But whatever did he do at Ashgrove to have made you hate him so much? You used to be best friends with him, didn't you, Cedric? What very strange tastes men have in friends.'

'Do sit down, Issy, there's a girl, you're being hysterical,' said her brother, looking rather embarrassed.

'Very well I will, if you're all going to treat me like a child. But first I want to know if it's true. Has Josephine really eloped with Brimshaw? I realise she's rather starved of suitable company down here, but I say, the chauffeur! You would have thought she could have done better than that.'

'You needn't look so pleased or be so beastly,' Hallam said angrily. 'It's preposterous to think she'd do such a thing. I'm sure there's some innocent explanation for why she's not here.'

'Are you really sure?' Isabella asked, coldly. 'Honestly, you men do tend to put her on a bit of a pedestal. Butter wouldn't melt and all that. I know I said what I did about Brimshaw, but really I wouldn't blame her. It must be so very dull being stuck here, no one to talk to most of the time but the servants. Daddy away in town, staying at his club. She must have been very bored.'

'Nonsense, Josephine loves it here at Dareswick, you know she does,' Hallam replied crossly, but Rose thought she detected a slight hesitation, as if he suddenly did not feel so sure.

'*I'm* not so certain.' Isabella made her way over to the vacated sofa and sat on the edge of one side, her glass clutched in her hand. She gulped down its contents in one go and made a face. 'Arh, I've never liked the taste of brandy. But I suppose it's medicinal.' She put the empty glass down on an occasional table and looked at them all slowly.

'Josephine came to see me in my room the night I arrived with Hugh. She was in a very strange mood, quite unhappy in herself, not like her at all. And she was quite short with me when I said she loved living here. She asked me how I knew how she felt. And, you know, she was right. I had no idea how she felt, I've never really had an idea about what goes on inside her mind. We're just very different, I suppose. But what I'm really saying is she clearly had something on her mind. She was definitely upset about something because she started crying and I think she said something about there being every need for her to cry, if only I knew. That would fit in with her leaving Dareswick, wouldn't it? It would be a bit of a wrench for her to leave here, even if she was going off to be with the man she loved. And Daddy would never allow her to come back, you know he wouldn't. He'd disown her for eloping with a servant. He'd feel as if she'd made him into a laughing stock. The news would be all around his club. It would cause a scandal, you know it would.'

Hallam all of a sudden looked uncomfortable and paced the room for a while before sinking into an armchair. He passed a hand through his hair clearly agitated. Rose was reminded of how very young he was.

'Now that you mention it,' he confessed, 'I remember Josephine saying something similar to me before you all came down this weekend. She wasn't her usual self at all now that I come to think of it. I think she may have been worried about something, only I didn't see it at the time.'

'You wouldn't,' Isabella said rather spitefully. Hallam ignored her and continued.

'She was very interested to hear about who you were bringing down with you, Isabella. Do you think she had an inkling that it might be Sneddon? She went on and on about it, wouldn't leave me alone. I say,' Hallam suddenly looked at them all, alarmed. 'I've suddenly remembered something she did say. She said something along the lines of she hoped I would always think of her fondly no matter what happened in the future. And that she never meant to hurt any of us ...' his voice trailed off. 'So it's true. She has eloped with Brimshaw!'

'Steady on, old man,' said Cedric. 'Perhaps we're all jumping too readily to conclusions. It was the first time he had spoken for some time and both brother and sister turned to look at him as if seeking reassurance. 'We'll know in good time what Josephine's done. She's sure to write and tell you. She wouldn't just vanish off the face of the earth, she's not that type of girl.'

Rose had sat quietly during these various exchanges. She did not think it her place to say anything or comment on Josephine's behaviour. What appeared to her most strange, however, was that everyone seemed far more concerned by Josephine's disappearance than by Sneddon's murder. The police, she knew, were unlikely to take that view.

As if he could read her very thoughts, Cedric continued:

'But I think we're all worrying about the wrong thing here. I know what I said just now to you Hallam about not giving it another thought. But whether Josephine has, or has not, run off with the chauffeur, to put it rather bluntly, is beside the point. What is far more worrying is that she disappeared on the same night that Sneddon was murdered.'

There was a few moment's silence, which was broken by an indignant Isabella.

'Surely you're not suggesting that my sister had a hand in Hugh's death? Oh, that's absolutely ridiculous. She can't possibly have done. You know that, Cedric, how beastly of you to even suggest it.' For the first time since her arrival in the garden room, Isabella appeared close to tears.

'There, there, Isabella,' said Cedric, soothingly, going to sit on the arm of the sofa beside her where he patted her arm reassuringly. 'Of course I don't think that Josephine murdered Hugh, none of us who know her would ever think that. But we must be prepared for the fact that the police are bound to think it is a little too much of a coincidence. We will just have to assure them that Josephine had absolutely no motive for wishing Sneddon dead.'

Cedric raised his head and caught Rose's eye. She gave him a weak smile and then immediately dropped her gaze to study the carpet. She could not share in Cedric's optimism, which she thought anyway was a little forced and mostly for the benefit of Isabella and Hallam. It seemed to her that everyone was conveniently forgetting that last year Josephine had been very much in love with Sneddon and that, even if she had now found solace in Brimshaw, she may not have been prepared to accept that Hugh marry her sister. She would surely have felt, and quite rightly in Rose's opinion, betrayed by both Hugh and Isabella. Who knew what feelings of resentment and possibly even hatred she had kept bottled up inside? At the very least it would have been a considerable shock to discover that her sister was to marry a man she had once had feelings for. If only it was just that.

For Rose could not help but remember how distraught Josephine had been to find out that Lord Sneddon was blackmailing Isabella into marrying him. Rose remembered too Josephine's determination that she should be the one to rescue Isabella and put things right. Rose shivered, remembering the sense of foreboding that had engulfed her in the garden. As soon as the words had sprung unbidden from her lips, she had regretted telling Josephine about Sneddon's antics, had known all along that nothing good could come of it. Josephine no doubt thought that Sneddon had some affection for her still, that she could appeal to his better nature. But Rose knew that Lord Sneddon had not been a man to be trifled with or one to listen to reason. She was sure that, had Josephine approached him before his fit of remorse, he would sooner have laughed in her face rather than relinquish the letters. And how would Josephine have taken that? Rose thought it unlikely that she would readily admit defeat where the future happiness of her younger sister was concerned. No, Rose felt sure that it was far more likely that Josephine would have seen it as her responsibility, her duty even, to free her sister from an awful fate by whatever means she deemed necessary. The question was, did that include murder?

Chapter Sixteen

'Right,' said Deacon, 'I'll ask you about the other guests in a minute but before I do I want you to tell me about this Robert fellow. Who exactly is he?'

'The second footman, sir, or at least he was until his lordship dismissed him.'

'And when was that?'

'Friday night, sir, at dinner.'

'Indeed, it seems a strange time to decide to dismiss a servant, in the middle of entertaining guests when you are no doubt rather short-staffed. What had this Robert done to merit such treatment?'

'He spilt some boiling hot soup over Lord Sneddon, sir.'

'Did he indeed?' Had they not been investigating the man's murder and had Lane been present, the inspector was sure his sergeant would have been smirking in the corner at such news. As it was, the inspector was more interested in the butler's obvious discomfort in being forced to disclose such information. 'Most unfortunate, I give you, but it seems rather harsh of his lordship to dismiss the man for an accident,' he said, watching Crabtree closely. 'Or perhaps it was not an accident? Do you think he did it deliberately?'

'I don't know, sir. I'm afraid you'll have to ask him that.'

'I intend to. Or at least my sergeant will, he's down with the servants as we speak. I expect he's talking to young Robert right now.'

The butler visibly paled, but said nothing. Deacon decided not to push him, confident that Lane would get to the bottom of whatever Crabtree was trying to hide.

'Why is Robert still here if the baron dismissed him? His lordship doesn't strike me as a man who likes to be defied.'

'No, he isn't,' Crabtree agreed. 'Confiding in you, sir, and not meaning to speak out of turn, his lordship on occasion does have rather a temper and is apt to say things that he doesn't really mean. Robert supports his mother and little brothers, sir. He needs to keep his position here otherwise they'll be destitute, particularly if he has no references. I knew his lordship was particularly upset because of who it was he spilt soup over. You know, sir, the heir to a dukedom and the man who'd just asked for his daughter's hand in marriage. I knew that the whole thing would probably blow over in a day or so and that his lordship would then look on things more leniently. Particularly as Lord Sneddon didn't make much fuss about it.'

'Didn't he?' The inspector raised an eyebrow. 'That doesn't sound like the Lord Sneddon I've met. Just the sort of man to make a song and dance about something like that I'd have thought.'

'Yes, but you see he had an inkling that it was …' The butler faltered and then reddened.

'It would be much better to tell me it all, you know, Crabtree. It's bound to come out in the end, it always does.'

'I'm sorry, sir, but I don't think it's my place to do so. If you don't mind, I'd like to get back to my duties now. I need to check on young Doris and the other servants. They've all taken it very badly, as you can imagine, a murder in the house. I'll send Mr Hallam in. He can tell you all you need to know about his lordship's guests.'

And before the inspector had a chance to utter a word of protest, Crabtree was gone.

'I've told you, sergeant, I wanted to kill him, believe me I did, but I didn't do it. Someone got to him first.' The young footman stared the sergeant straight in the eye as if challenging him to question the sincerity of his words.

Lane in turn looked at him steadily. That Robert meant what he said about wanting to kill Sneddon he had little doubt but, according to Mrs Gooden, the young man had been a nervous wreck after the incident with the soup. The sergeant wondered then whether the footman had sufficient courage to kill a man in cold blood. Perhaps if Sneddon had provoked him verbally he might have done it. He could certainly picture the man going to see Sneddon in the library after the rest of the house had retired to bed. Likewise he could imagine Sneddon laughing at him, calling him a fool, perhaps saying something derogatory about little Mabel or questioning the young man's abilities as a suitor. Yes, he could easily see Lord Sneddon doing that. It would have caused him amusement to rile a servant and he would have had no reservations about turning his back on him. The weapon would have been to hand. According to Crabtree and the maids the gold letter opener was always kept on the writing table; Josephine Atherton used it to open her correspondence. So, almost without thinking, Robert could have picked it up and plunged it into Sneddon's back. It would have been the work of mere moments.

'Robert, go and finish polishing the silver.' The entrance of the newcomer had been unobserved by both Robert and Lane who jumped up from their seats at the servants' table. There was a sternness in Crabtree's voice that indicated that it was a command and that his instructions were to be immediately adhered to. With an apologetic look at the sergeant, Robert disappeared and the butler turned a face red with indignation on the sergeant.

'I don't know what the boy's been telling you but he didn't kill Lord Sneddon.'

'Well, he certainly denied doing so,' began Lane. He felt at a distinct disadvantage being in the servants' hall. This was Crabtree's domain where he ruled supreme. The sergeant's presence was unwelcome here. Even the young maids who had giggled when they first saw him, impressed by his good looks and easy charm, had turned their backs on him at the butler's entrance. Only old Mrs Gooden had stubbornly ignored Crabtree's outburst and poured Lane another cup of tea.

'Well he couldn't have done it even if he had wanted to,' said the butler. 'Besides myself, all the servants' bedrooms are in the attic. The male and female servants' corridors are separated by a door which is kept locked at all times and to which only Mrs Hodges has a key. As a consequence of what happened to poor Mabel while Lord Sneddon was visiting, Mrs Hodges also took the precaution of locking the door to the attic at the top of the stairs on the women's side. Likewise I did the same on the men's side to prevent Robert doing anything stupid at night or Ricketts pilfering the silver or anything else of value. So you see, sergeant, Robert, together with the rest of the staff, was effectively locked in.'

'I see. And who is this Ricketts fellow, the one that you don't trust? I'm somewhat surprised you keep someone in your employ who you consider untrustworthy.'

'He is not an employee of Dareswick. He came with Lord Sneddon as his valet.'

'*Came* as his valet rather than *is*, or rather *was*, his valet?'

'I do not think that he knows the first thing about what the role of being a valet entails.'

'I see, most intriguing, I'm sure the inspector will want to have a word with him in due course.' With one last look around, Lane left the servants to their duties. The thing that struck him most, as he made his way through the green baize door, was how afraid they all were.

'So it looks as if they're ruled out,' said Deacon, once Lane had returned to the study and filled him in on his various conversations with the servants.

'Yes, they were locked in for the night, so unless that old stick Crabtree or the housekeeper did it, they're in the clear. And I don't mind telling you, sir, I'm relieved. That boy Robert's a loose cannon to be sure, highly strung. Just the sort of lad, in fact, to do something stupid like bump off Sneddon and then think about the consequences later. He's definitely one to act in haste and repent at leisure, that boy.'

'Can't say I'd blame him on this occasion,' said the inspector, getting up from the table to stretch his legs. 'He was the poor girl's young man, you say.'

'Not as such, no, sir,' the sergeant said, sadly. 'They hadn't got as far as courting or walking out together, or whatever you want to call it. In fact I'm not sure Mabel knew how Robert felt about her, he was awfully shy around her, Mrs Hodges, the housekeeper, told me when he wasn't there. Trying to pluck up the courage to ask her out on her next day off, I think he was. And then of course it was too late. What is a crying shame though, sir, is that he would probably have been quite happy to take both her and the baby on, you know, made an honest woman of her and brought up the baby as his own. But she wasn't to know that, was she? All the servants feel that they let her down somehow but they weren't to know, were they? She never let on, see.'

'A tragic story indeed, Sergeant', agreed Deacon. 'And it certainly gives us a motive as to why the servants may have wanted him dead even if they couldn't have done the deed themselves.'

'That's not all, sir. It was a great shock to them Sneddon turning up when he did. None of the servants had any inkling that he would be Miss Isabella's mysterious guest. Mrs Hodges said she thought even the baron and the children didn't know who Isabella was bringing with her. Didn't know even if it was going to be one of her girlfriends or a gentleman. Josephine

Atherton insisted that two bedrooms be got ready just to be on the safe side, one in the women's corridor and one in the men's.'

'I see, so it was likely to have been just as much of a shock for the Athertons as it was for their servants,' the inspector said thoughtfully, pausing to look at the picture above the fireplace, an oil painting of a pheasant.

'You could say that,' agreed Lane. 'Apparently Mr Hallam was right livid when he discovered who his sister's guest was, made rather a scene about it he did. His father demanded that he behave himself. There was also talk in the servants' hall that Miss Josephine had had rather a soft spot for Sneddon. There had been some speculation as to whether there would be a wedding.'

'In which case the servants weren't the only ones to have had ill feelings towards Sneddon. I'm beginning to wonder whether anyone liked him. Rather insensitive of Isabella Atherton to have brought him to the house, I'd have said. Shows a certain disregard for the feelings of her sister and her father's servants. Still, she at least must have seen something in the man to get engaged to him.'

'Either that or she just wanted to be a duchess,' said Lane, cynically. 'If I remember rightly, Lord Sneddon was the Duke of Haywater's only surviving son, wasn't he?'

'He was indeed. The duke's two older sons both died in the war and now his youngest one has been murdered. It just goes to show, Lane, you can have all the riches and titles in the world but still it all boils down to luck, which the poor duke appears to have had very little of.'

'Do you think that could have been a motive for his murder, sir? Should we be looking to see who's next in line to the dukedom?'

'Possibly, and yes, of course we should look into that. But I have a feeling the murderer's closer to home than that. You heard what old Crabtree said. The French windows in the library are stuck, so it's unlikely Sneddon let his murderer in. Also, it looks as if Sneddon's decision to come to Dareswick this weekend was rather last minute, although of course we'll have to check with Isabella Atherton, so it's unlikely that anyone else knew he'd be here.'

'Oh, sir, there's something else that I almost forgot to mention.'

'And what is that, Lane?' enquired Deacon, looking interested.

However, as it happened, the inspector had to wait a while for an answer. For just at that minute there was a loud knock on the door and an eager young constable entered hardly waiting to be admitted.

'Well, what is it, Constable?' Deacon said rather offhand, resenting the disturbance.

'Sir, Walsh and I were just making a thorough search of the deceased's room like you told us to, before you joined us, like –'

'Yes?' Deacon said, irritably.

'Well, we've found something, sir, me and Walsh. He said as how you'd better come and see for yourself, how you wouldn't want us to move anything without showing you first.'

'Right, Constable, lead the way …'

Chapter Seventeen

'Mrs Gooden told me what happened,' said Mrs Hodges, as she and the butler relaxed for a few minutes in the housekeeper's sitting room to enjoy their mid-morning cup of tea. 'How the sergeant came down here and found out all about what had happened to poor little Mabel and the grudge Robert held against Lord Sneddon.'

'Yes, I came as soon as I realised what was going on. That inspector's a clever fellow. He'd kept me out of the way in the study answering his questions. I had stupidly let slip in front of his lordship that I'd sent Robert to see if Brimshaw had driven Miss Josephine anywhere, you know, when we found out she'd disappeared. His lordship hit the roof about it and, of course, the inspector wanted to know why Robert had been dismissed so suddenly.'

'Ah, well, no harm done,' said the housekeeper, taking a sip of tea. 'They now know that Robert can't have killed Lord Sneddon, not with us having kept all of the doors to the attic locked at night.'

'But that's just it, Mrs Hodges,' said Crabtree, his face at last showing the worry that he had kept bottled up inside all morning, 'and I'd only say this to you. I locked the door last night, I know I did because I distinctly remember doing so. But this morning when I went to open it, slightly later than usual I grant you because of all the to-do with Lord Sneddon, I found it was open.'

'Open?'

'Yes. Well, what I mean is that it was closed but unlocked.'

'So …'

'So Robert could have done it. He could have crept out in the night and killed him, and no one would have been any the wiser.'

'Ah, the poor boy,' wailed Mrs Hodges, clutching at her teacup, the tea within it now lukewarm and quite forgotten.

'Well, that was rather unexpected, sir,' said Lane as both he and Deacon came back into the study and closed the door behind them.

'It certainly puts a different complexion on things,' agreed the inspector settling himself down on the sofa while the sergeant took out his notebook and started scribbling down some notes on their discovery. 'It opens up another motive, certainly. If he was doing that, it makes me wonder what else he may have been doing. We never did think very much of his moral character, did we, Sergeant, but even we didn't think he would stoop so low.'

'Do you think someone may have found out what he was doing?' enquired the sergeant. 'You know, caught him in the act. Even the baron might have thought twice about letting his daughter marry such a rogue. Talking of the baron, he's got quite a temper on him, hasn't he? Look at the way he laid into that poor butler of his for not sending the footman away. I'd say he's not a man to cross. I reckon even Sneddon would have come out the worst in a fight with him.'

'So do I, Lane, so do I. I say, this makes me keen to meet this so called valet of his, Ricketts, didn't you say the chap's name was? I wonder whether they were in it together. It would make more sense if they were. I can't see old Sneddon carrying out the deed himself, can you? He wouldn't have had the opportunity to snoop around for a start. Whoever did that would have had to do it while everyone else was busy downstairs, the baron and his family and guests in the dining and drawing rooms, and the servants occupied with waiting on them.'

'It would still have taken some nerve, sir. If this Ricketts fellow had been caught coming out of one of the women's rooms he'd have found it hard to come up with a decent excuse. More likely as not they would have called us in.'

'Well, he must have been very good at it because as far as we know he wasn't caught. Unless the murderer caught him, of course, but no, that doesn't make sense, otherwise it would be Ricketts we would have found dead draped over the desk in the library, not Lord Sneddon.'

'Shall I get the fellow in now, sir, see what he has to say for himself?'

'Yes … no, on second thoughts let's leave him for a bit. He's not going anywhere so let's leave him to fret for a while wondering what we know. Then maybe he'll be more cooperative when we do speak to him. You had better get one of the constables to keep an eye on him, though. We don't want him to scarper before we've had a chance to interrogate him.' Deacon moved over to the fireplace to study the picture of the bird again. 'You know, Lane, this painting really is jolly fine. Quite the thing for a country squire to have in his study. Now let me see, I think we'll have the Honourable Hallam Atherton in next. We'll give the Honourable Isabella

Atherton a little more time to compose herself, I think. And we never did find out from their father the identity of the guests staying here. We'll ask this Hallam fellow and also find out what he really thought of Sneddon.'

Deacon sat down on the leather settee to collect his thoughts. There would be a short delay before the sergeant returned. Not only did Lane have to brief one of the constables stationed in the hall to keep an eye on the whereabouts of Lord Sneddon's valet, but the guests and members of the household were still holed up in the garden room, which was located a little distance from the study.

Deacon decided to put the time to good use. Now, what were his first impressions of the murder scene? Thinking it over, as he did now, he found the location of Sneddon's body worried him. If the man had come across Josephine and Brimshaw as they had prepared for flight and had as a consequence become embroiled in a fight with the chauffeur, a theory he himself had put forward to Lane, then surely there would have been signs of the furniture having been knocked out of place or even overturned in the ensuing struggle. And Sneddon's body would have been found lying on the floor not seated in a chair drawn up to the desk. It was a nonsense to suppose that Brimshaw and Josephine would have taken the time to drag Sneddon's body over the carpet and position him in the chair. What was the point of it? They would have been much better to arrange his body in one of the wing chairs by the fire where its presence would have been hidden from anyone passing the door or going into the library for a book. It could not even be argued that they had tried to disguise the murder as a suicide. The little gold letter opener had been left protruding from Sneddon's back for all to see the cause of death.

So what had Sneddon been doing at the desk? An empty glass and half empty whisky decanter had been found on the occasional table beside one of the armchairs near the fire. Sneddon had obviously sat there drinking. What had made him move away from the warmth of the dying fire to the writing desk? He sighed. It was yet something else that he and Lane would need to find out if they were to solve this case. There was something else niggling him too. It had struck him as soon as he had laid eyes on Lord Sneddon's body. He had meant to mention it to Lane at the time but he had been distracted by other things. Oh well, it would have to wait now. They needed to get on with interviewing the household and guests, find out where everyone was, and who the last person was to see Lord Sneddon alive.

Rose paced the garden room wondering what to do. The police had spoken to the baron and now she supposed they would want to speak to Hallam and Isabella. It would be a little while before they asked to speak to her surely, so plenty of time for her to decide what to say and do. She looked over to where Isabella was sitting on the settee, her face pale and white. It would have made another woman look faded and drawn. On Isabella it only accentuated her beauty, making her look fragile and vulnerable. Perhaps the police would take pity on her. Oh, how she hoped so. Then it wouldn't be so awful what she had to tell them. They may be reluctant to jump to the obvious conclusion if Isabella looked delicate. They would think she was distraught by her fiancé's death rather than merely shocked. They would want to help her and lessen the ordeal of being interviewed. They would not see the hidden steeliness of her character or think that a woman such as Isabella could be quite ruthless when it came to self-preservation. A woman would see that, Rose felt, a woman such as herself who Isabella was not trying to impress. Perhaps things would be all right after all. Perhaps she wouldn't be faced with having to make a choice as to whether or not to tell the police what she knew.

But wouldn't she then be guilty of withholding evidence? She knew it was her duty to tell the police what she knew of Isabella being blackmailed by Sneddon. But if she did she would be giving Isabella a clear motive for wishing him dead. She remembered her promise to Josephine to say nothing to anyone of the blackmail business. But Josephine hadn't known then that Sneddon was going to be murdered. She had promised to sort it out, but where was she now? She had abandoned her sister and, anyway, Isabella had not known that Josephine had undertaken to rescue her from her awful predicament. What if Isabella considered a future with Sneddon too awful to endure? What if she had thought that death was the only way out; either her own, or Sneddon's? And, once she had decided on that course of action, she had carried it through? Whichever way she looked at it, Rose felt that she could not just hand Isabella over to the police on a plate. They might not bother to search for another motive for Sneddon's murder, and how would she feel then? But on the other hand she did not wish to be guilty of withholding evidence or of obstructing the police from their enquiries or whatever it was called. So really there was only one thing for it, she must forewarn Isabella.

She walked unhurriedly over to the sofa as casually as she could and sat down next to Isabella. She leaned towards her slightly and hoped that to a casual observer it would appear only that she was trying to express her condolences. Isabella did not help. If anything she looked annoyed by Rose's unexpected appearance beside her, and made to shift her seat and move a little away to the other end of the sofa. Rose put out her hand and touched her lightly on the forearm both to get her attention and to prevent her from moving. Isabella flinched slightly and looked furious, but at least her eyes were now turned to look at Rose.

'Listen, I know Lord Sneddon was blackmailing you,' Rose said in a hurried whisper. 'And I'm afraid I'm going to have to tell the police.' Isabella's eyes grew wide at this and she looked positively scared. 'I have to, don't you see?' Rose carried on urgently. 'They're bound to find out. They'll find your letters in Sneddon's possessions if nothing else, and it will look bad for you. But if you tell them about it first, then perhaps it won't look so awful. Do you understand what I'm saying?' No word escaped Isabella's lips, but Rose thought she could just about make out the barest of nods. It would have to do, she had done her best. It was now up to Isabella whether she followed her advice. She did not look up, afraid that Cedric's or Hallam's eyes would be on her, staring at her curiously. Unless they were blind, they must be wondering what she was talking so urgently to Isabella about; unless they were too wrapped up in their own thoughts, of course.

But before she could think about it all any further, the door opened, a constable appeared and Hallam was called for interview.

Chapter Eighteen

'Ah, Lane, back already? I thought it would take a while for you to get the son and bring him back with you.' Deacon got up reluctantly from the sofa.

'I decided to send one of the constables to get him, sir. I thought it would be better if I got myself positioned, so to speak. You know, seated in that chair behind the settee so he hardly knows I'm there taking notes of everything he says. I'll just blend into the background, become part of the wallpaper. It does mean, though, that I didn't get a look at the guests. Not that I would have recognised any of them as they're bound to be toffs.'

'Well, you're here now, Sergeant, so better get seated and let's put your theory into practice. Because, unless I am very much mistaken, I hear his footsteps approaching now, along with those of that constable you sent to fetch him.'

Deacon's first impression of the Honourable Hallam Atherton was how very young he looked. His second impression was that the boy was clearly scared. The inspector looked up and caught his sergeant's eye; good, Lane was obviously of the same opinion, which was somewhat strengthened by Hallam's refusal to sit down. Instead the young man began pacing the room, his manner restive. The inspector noticed that he clenched and unclenched his hands as if he did not know what to do with them, and every now and then he passed his fingers through his hair as if they were a comb. The boy was clearly agitated about something.

'She had nothing to do with it, you know.'

'Who didn't?' Deacon asked, at once interested.

'Josephine, of course, my sister. She had absolutely nothing to do with Sneddon's death.'

'I'm not aware that I had suggested she had,' Deacon replied, speaking slowly. The boy scowled at him, a red blush spreading across his face. He went to bite his nails and then thought better of it.

'Yes, but you were about to. Cedric said you were bound to suspect her because she disappeared on the same night that Sneddon was murdered. But she couldn't have done it, do you hear me? Josephine wouldn't hurt a fly.'

'I'm glad to hear it,' the inspector said, gently. 'And if what you say is true, then she has nothing to be afraid of.'

At once the boy looked relieved. He stopped his pacing and flung himself down inelegantly on the sofa. 'I thought you'd decide it must be her and not investigate properly.'

'That's not how we operate, sir,' answered Lane from where he was sitting behind the sofa, clearly offended. Hallam jumped involuntarily as if unaware of Lane's presence in the room.

'I'm glad to hear it,' the boy said, turning around to face Lane. 'Of course, I appreciate it looks a bit odd, but I think Josephine's just taken herself away for a few days.'

'So you don't think she's eloped with Brimshaw?' Deacon asked, trying hard to hide his surprise.

'Of course not, the idea's preposterous.' Hallam turned his attention back to the inspector. 'My sister would never consider eloping with a servant. I'm afraid you are barking up the wrong tree there, inspector.'

'Indeed, and yet she is not here, is she, sir? You don't find it a little strange that your sister should choose both this weekend and at such an unearthly hour to decide to up and leave. She must have felt something was very important not to wait until morning. So she left in the dead of night with no explanation and has not returned to explain herself. You have guests staying here this weekend, don't you? Would she usually disappear in the middle of entertaining? Is it the way she normally behaves?'

'Of course not.' Hallam frowned and glared at the carpet. 'She's a jolly good hostess, everyone says so.'

'And yet she has gone, and you don't think she's eloped with the chauffeur. Don't you think that would be the logical explanation for her disappearance?'

'No … yes … I don't know, you're confusing me.' The boy looked close to tears. 'I don't think she would elope with Brimshaw, no,' he said slowly, as if he was trying to work it out for himself as he said the words. 'I know she would never have killed Sneddon. And, God forbid, if she had she would have stayed and faced the music, not run away. But if you are asking me where she is or why she felt the need to vanish as she has then I'm afraid I don't know.' He looked up at the inspector, clearly anxious. 'You think she's all right, don't you? You don't think anything's happened to her?'

'No, I'm sure she's fine. We'll find her, don't you worry. Now, first things first, did you know Lord Sneddon was coming to stay here this weekend.'

'No, I jolly well didn't.' The boy now sounded indignant. 'I'd jolly well have prevented it, if I'd known he was coming down, I can tell you. But Isabella was very cloak and dagger about it all. She wouldn't let on who she was bringing down with her. Why, we didn't even know if it was going to be a man or a woman. Josephine was in quite a state about it. She didn't know which bedroom to ask Mrs Hodges to get ready.'

'I see. So your sister Josephine didn't know either?'

'That's what I've just said. She had no idea and it was all jolly inconvenient, I can tell you. Not made any easier by them arriving so late. At one point we thought we were going to have to start dinner without them. But that's just like Isabella. She can be awfully inconsiderate at times.'

'So, just so we are absolutely clear, neither you nor your sister, Josephine, had any idea that Lord Sneddon would be coming to stay at Dareswick this weekend?'

No, only ...' Hallam hesitated and looked at his hands.

'Only what?' Deacon prompted him.

'Oh, it's probably nothing.'

'I'll be the judge of that if you don't mind. Only what?'

'Well, Josephine was awfully keen to know who Isabella was bringing down with her. I was curious too, of course, because she was being jolly secretive about it. But Josephine *really* wanted to know. She kept pestering me about it, wouldn't leave off. It was driving me to distraction, I can tell you.'

'Do you think she may have had an inkling it would be Lord Sneddon?'

'No, I don't think so, Inspector. I suppose you know already that there was a time when she and Sneddon were rather sweet on each other. Father was imagining wedding bells and all that. But it didn't come to anything. No doubt the servants have filled you in on that awful business with the little maid. Anyway, I was very anxious when Sneddon appeared. I was afraid it would be an awful shock for Josephine, and of course it was. She went very pale and looked as if she was about to faint.'

'I see.' Deacon looked thoughtful.

114

'The funny thing is, Inspector, that when my father went and gave that awful toast, you know, wishing the happy couple all the best and all that, well I could have sworn that Josephine looked relieved. Doesn't make sense, does it, not if she was still fond of the blighter?'

'It wouldn't appear to, no,' agreed Deacon.

'Even so, it was awfully thoughtless of Isabella to spring it on us like that. If she hadn't got Sneddon to speak to Father before dinner and ask his permission for Isabella's hand in marriage, well then I think he'd have been out on his ear.'

'I understand you didn't take Lord Sneddon's appearance on the scene that well,' said Deacon, carefully.

'You bet I didn't,' Hallam said, his voice rising. 'I wanted to give him what for, I can tell you. How the man had the nerve to show his face here after what he'd done, I don't know. And Father expected us just to sit there and pretend that nothing was wrong, that he would be a welcome addition to our family. While all the time I just wanted to ...' He banged his fist on to the sofa cushion.

'Yes? What did you want to do, Mr Atherton?'

'Nothing,' Hallam mumbled. He got up from the sofa, hovered for a moment uncertainly, and then lowered himself back down again, defeated. 'Sorry, I got a bit carried away.'

'Did you kill Lord Sneddon, Mr Atherton?'

'No, of course I didn't. How can you suspect such a thing? I was jolly annoyed with the chap, of course, who wouldn't be in my position? But I didn't murder him.'

Deacon found that he felt pity towards the young man. He watched as Hallam sat squirming in his seat, his eyes averted. He feels he's made a bit of a fool of himself, thought the inspector, and of course he has. But more importantly for us, he has shown that he can work himself up and then who knows what he may be capable of? Yes, he's highly strung, that lad. Aloud, as much to change the subject and encourage Hallam to talk as anything else, he said:

'We are trying to determine Lord Sneddon's movements on the night that he died, or it might have been in the early hours of this morning. And we need to know the movements of everyone else, of course; just routine, you understand. When did you last see Lord Sneddon?'

'Well, it was last night, of course. Let me see, about half past ten I would imagine. Cedric and I decided to call it a night and go up to bed early. We left Sneddon deep in conversation with my father. To tell you the truth, it had been an awful evening and I couldn't wait for it to be over. We'd had a jolly nice day wandering over to the village. Sneddon had disappeared off to London so we didn't have to worry about him being there to spoil things. But then he came back. He cut it a bit sharp, almost missed dinner again. Anyway, it was awful. No one felt inclined to talk. Only Father put a brave face on everything. Everyone else was miserable, even Isabella. I was trying to be on my best behaviour, you know, not saying anything. Father had put the fear of God in me that morning, said if I did anything to try and stop Isabella from marrying the fellow he'd disinherit me and all that.'

'I see. And that was the last time you saw Lord Sneddon?'

'It was. I feel jolly rotten now, to tell the truth. If I'd realised at the time he only had a couple more hours on this earth I daresay I'd have been a bit nicer to him.'

'Right, now who's this Cedric chap? You've mentioned him a couple of times. Is he one of the guests staying here?'

'Yes, Cedric, or Ceddie as his sister Lavinia will call him.' Hallam laughed, unaware that both the inspector and sergeant had looked up sharply on hearing this. 'I still want to keep calling him Lord Sedgwick, but he's come into the earldom now. He's the Earl of Belvedere.' This time Hallam caught the exchange of glances between inspector and sergeant. 'I say, do you know him, have you come across Cedric before?'

'We have indeed, sir, a couple of months or so ago. Our paths crossed when we were investigating an incident at Ashgrove House.'

'Oh, were you the police chappies who looked into all that?' Hallam asked, excitedly. 'Jolly good. Cedric spoke very highly of you, you know.' With that Hallam bounded to the door looking relieved but also anxious to be gone.

'Just a moment, Mr Atherton, before you go. Can you tell us please who else is staying here? Have you any other guests staying apart from the Lord Belvedere?'

'Oh yes, Miss Simpson. Miss Rose Simpson. She's ... oh, but of course you already know her, don't you, because she was at Ashgrove as well, wasn't she?'

116

Chapter Nineteen

'Well, well, well, Lane, what do you make of that?' Deacon moved over to the fireplace and looked into the fire. It seemed to him that one could never tell what the weather would do this time of year, it was so changeable. Sometimes it was hot and sunny almost like a summer's day as it had been yesterday, and at other times, like today, it had an almost wintry feel to it, even though it was only part way through autumn.

'It will be jolly nice, sir, seeing Miss Simpson again. A nice young lady she is and very helpful she was too in helping us solve that case at Ashgrove. I expect she can tell us a thing or two about what's been going on here.'

'I don't doubt it, Sergeant,' agreed Deacon, a smile creeping across his face. 'But actually I was referring to the Honourable Hallam Atherton. What did you make of him?'

'A nervy type I would say, sir, you know, highly strung. I could well imagine him lashing out at Lord Sneddon after working himself up into a bit of a fit of temper and then being racked by remorse afterwards.'

'I agree with you, Lane. He's just the sort of chap who would act first and think later. He seems pretty close to his sisters; his oldest one, at least. As soon as he came into the room, he kept going on and on about how Josephine Atherton couldn't have killed Sneddon, even before we'd had a chance to say anything to suggest that we were of the view that she might have done.'

'Yes, strange that. I suppose he just wanted to get his pennyworth in first,' Lane replied, putting away his notebook and pencil and taking the opportunity to stretch his legs. 'He admitted himself that it looked rather suspicious her vanishing like that in the middle of the night without so much as a by your leave.'

'I was wondering myself whether "the man doth protest too much" to misquote the great Bard.'

'I'm sorry, sir, I don't think I quite follow,' A look of utter confusion had appeared on Lane's face.

'Shakespeare, Sergeant. The actual line is: "The lady doth protest too much, methinks". It comes from the play, *Hamlet*. By vehemently trying to convince us that Josephine had nothing to do with Sneddon's murder, I wonder if our Mr Hallam is in fact afraid that the opposite is true.'

'You mean he thinks his sister *did* do it?'

'I think the thought has crossed his mind and that he may be trying to convince himself as much as us that she can't possibly have done it.'

'Inspector Deacon, jolly good to see you again, although I would have preferred for it to have been under different circumstances,' Cedric said, coming into the study and extending his hand to the inspector. Deacon on his part was slightly taken aback by the gesture, but nevertheless shook the new earl's hand warmly. 'Had rather hoped that murder was not going to cross my path again, I can tell you,' Cedric continued, seating himself down on the sofa, 'but jolly glad it's you and Sergeant Lane here who'll be undertaking the investigation. A nasty business this, what? No love lost between me and Sneddon as you well know, but I wouldn't have wished this fate on him, poor blighter.'

'Yes, it's most unfortunate, my lord. As you will appreciate, we're anxious to clear up this business as soon as possible. We have the advantage this time of having met the victim and knowing the sort of man he was.'

'Yes, indeed, Inspector. A man who'd have made a number of enemies, I'd imagine. Can't say I envy your task in trying to find out who murdered him.'

'We're pretty certain that Lord Sneddon was murdered by someone in this house.'

'Good Lord, what makes you think that?' Cedric almost leapt from his seat. 'Surely it's more likely that someone followed him down from London? No doubt Sneddon arranged some dubious assignation in the library and let the man in by the French windows.'

'Highly unlikely, my lord. The butler informed us that the French windows in the library had seized up some time ago and won't open now. And we didn't just take his word for it, of course. My men have tried to open them and failed to do so.'

'Well, perhaps the murderer came in by some other door or window. You've seen how many doors and windows this house has. The servants probably forgot to lock a couple.'

'The butler has assured me that he is always very thorough in ensuring that the house is secured for the night and that last night was no exception,' said the inspector firmly. 'Baron Atherton is most particular about it, I understand. Has a bit of a bee in his bonnet about it so the butler told us. He is most insistent that all the doors and windows are locked by seven thirty sharp and Crabtree and one of the footman undertake the task together so that they can double check that it's done properly.'

'I see.' Cedric had turned pale. 'But why are you telling me this, Inspector? Surely it would be better for you to keep such information to yourself, at least for the time being.'

'Because the temptation for everyone in this house is to assume, or try and convince themselves, that the murderer was someone from outside. Lane and I will be made to hear no end of stories of how it must have been a burglary gone wrong or the work of a passing tramp. But the evidence speaks for itself. It must have been someone in this house. You know the Athertons and the servants in this house well, my lord. They'll trust you and believe what you tell them. They need to be told the truth and made to face up to the facts. They need to be persuaded to help us with our enquiries, not hinder them. It doesn't much help that Lord Sneddon was universally so disliked.'

'I see.' Cedric held his head in his hand for a moment and then looked up. 'So you think one of the Athertons killed him?'

'Either that or one of their servants, yes,' confirmed Deacon.

'What about me? I could have killed him, you know. I despised the fellow.'

Deacon chose not to comment directly on this statement. It was obvious that the young earl was badly affected by what he had just been told. Far better to concentrate on facts.

'Did you know that Isabella Atherton would be bringing Lord Sneddon down with her to Dareswick this weekend?'

'No, of course not. Otherwise Rose and I would never have come. The Athertons are old friends of my family. My father and the baron went back a long way. Lavinia and I practically grew up with Josephine, Isabella and Hallam. I've always loved this place, that it's so remote, in the middle of nowhere. We used to run almost wild here as children, it was our Utopia, our escape from everything. I thought it would be the perfect place to come for the weekend. God knows, after what I've been through the last couple of months, I needed some respite.'

'I'm sorry you've had such a rum old time of it with the pressmen, my lord.'

'If it hadn't been for your efforts, it would have been an awful lot worse,' Cedric acknowledged gratefully. 'Now what was I saying? Yes … I had no idea that Sneddon would be here this weekend, I don't think anyone had, apart from Isabella, of course. It was an awful shock to us all, to tell the truth. Embarrassingly so, I'm afraid. When he walked into the drawing room with the baron, we all just stopped talking and stared. You could have heard a pin drop. You've probably already heard all about what happened last time Sneddon visited?' The inspector nodded and Cedric continued. 'Good, I'm glad I don't have to go into all the unsavoury details. It was a most tragic business, that's for certain, simply awful, and the household is still recovering from the aftermath, both the Athertons and their servants.'

'So Lord Sneddon's arrival was unwelcome?'

'You can say that again,' Cedric said with conviction. 'Hallam made rather a scene, begged his sister not to marry the man. It was awful. And one of the servants dropped boiling hot soup in his lap. Sneddon could have been badly scolded but, thankfully, he was relatively unharmed …' Cedric did not finish his sentence because the vision came unbidden into his mind of Sneddon slumped lifelessly over the writing table, a gold dagger protruding from his back, as melodramatic a scene as if it had been performed before him on a stage. Sneddon had escaped being badly burned, but he had not escaped death.

'So Hallam Atherton was upset to see Lord Sneddon?' Deacon asked carefully.

'I say he was, and who could blame him?' Cedric asked, indignantly. 'At one point I thought they might come to blows, that's to say Hallam might punch him because, to give Sneddon his due, he didn't seem to bear any animosity towards Hallam, even after his outburst. It was jolly awkward for the rest of us, of course. We didn't know where to look or what to do.' Cedric sighed. 'You have to give it to Hallam, he only voiced out loud what the rest of us thought in private.'

'How serious was this outburst, my lord? Did Hallam Atherton need to be restrained to avoid harming Lord Sneddon?'

'I'm not sure, that's to say, when I say Hallam was hell bent on hitting Sneddon, I may have been a bit hasty,' Cedric said, looking uncomfortable. 'In the heat of the moment he might have done it, it's true. But he wouldn't have come down in the middle of the night and stabbed Sneddon in the back, if that's what you're thinking. I don't think Hallam's the type of chap to do that. That wouldn't have been sporting at all, Inspector, definitely not cricket. If he was going to fight Sneddon he would have let him know about it. He wouldn't have sneaked up behind him and killed him. Besides,' continued Cedric, warming to his subject, 'on recollection I think all he wanted to do was to let off steam a bit. He wanted to tell him what he thought of his conduct and perhaps give him a bloody nose, nothing more.'

'You don't think he might have set about planning how to kill Lord Sneddon and get away with it?' Deacon asked, quietly.

'Of course not, Inspector, the idea's preposterous. Whoever killed Sneddon did it in a cowardly, underhand manner. Hallam's not your man.' Cedric glared at Deacon.

'Very well, what about the Honourable Josephine Atherton?'

'No, certainly not. She's a respectable, properly brought up young lady, Inspector, not the sort to get herself mixed up in murder. And she has a sensible head on her shoulders. Not one to give way to hysteria or doing something on impulse. And I don't believe that she's eloped with that chauffeur fellow either, whatever anyone says. I'm sure there's some logical explanation for her disappearance, you see if I'm not right, Inspector.'

'It's Deacon,' Cedric said quietly to Rose on his return to the garden room. He had taken her by the arm and led her to the far end of the room where it was unlikely their conversation would be overheard by Hallam or Isabella. 'He and Sergeant Lane are carrying out the investigation into Sneddon's murder.'

'That's good, isn't it?' said Rose, looking relieved. 'They won't jump to any silly conclusions or try and build a case against someone when there isn't any evidence.'

'I don't know,' replied Cedric, thoughtfully. 'Deacon's a clever chap, but I think he's got it into his head that either Hallam or Josephine are involved somehow in Sneddon's death. It didn't help me telling him about Hallam's outburst on Friday night. I wish I'd kept quiet about that now. It doesn't put the boy in a good light. Deacon probably thinks Hallam's a loose cannon. He's suspicious of Josephine too, which is hardly surprising. Goodness knows what she was thinking of just disappearing like that. Oh, if only he knew her like we do, he'd realise how ludicrous it is to suspect her of anything underhand, let alone murder.'

It was on the tip of Rose's tongue to say that she hardly knew Josephine herself, and that she wasn't sure how the girl usually acted, but thought it best to remain quiet. Instead she said: 'Doesn't he think that it's far more likely that the murderer broke into the house or was just let in by Sneddon himself?'

'No, the place is thoroughly locked at night and apparently the French windows in the library don't open, although I find that hard to believe. So unless Sneddon trotted along to another room to let someone into the house, the police think his murderer must be someone from within.'

'Sneddon looked pretty engrossed in the library when I left him,' mused Rose, thinking back to her last sight of him, a broken and distraught man. She shivered. She should have stayed with him. If she had, then perhaps he would not be dead now. At the very least she should have shown pity or given encouragement. He had told her that he wished to make amends and now she would never know whether he would have followed through on his words. He had reached out to her for help and she had turned her back on him. It was that, she realised when she looked back over the events that followed, that made her feel that his death could not go unpunished and, if nothing else, she owed it to him to find his murderer and bring him to justice.

'Miss Simpson? Come with me please, the Inspector wants to interview you next.' The constable had already turned on his heel and set off up the corridor before Rose had caught up with him. Before she could stop herself, she found herself tugging at his sleeve in an attempt to make him stop. He turned around impatiently, clearly unamused by such seemingly childish tactics.

'Please, stop,' said Rose quickly, before he could protest. 'Surely there must be some mistake? The inspector will want to see Isabella first, he's bound to. She was the deceased's fiancée after all, he'll have simply loads of questions to ask her, I'm sure. He'll want to interview her first.'

122

'No, miss, the inspector was very specific. He said that he wanted to interview you next.'

'Oh.' What should she do, she didn't know. What *could* she do? There was nothing she could do without drawing more attention to herself and Isabella. She glanced back helplessly into the garden room. Through the open doorway her eyes rested on Isabella, sitting upright on the very edge of the sofa, her eyes cast down to the floor and her hands clutched demurely in her lap as if she were ushering up a prayer, as well she might under the circumstances, Rose thought.

Well, Isabella was enduring this setback well. She had not raised her eyes to Rose and given her an imploring look to remain silent about the blackmail. It appeared instead that she was deliberately not catching Rose's eye and Rose wondered if, in all conscience, she could remain quiet.

Rose took a deep breath. There was nothing for it; she must make the best of it. She must give the impression that Isabella meant to tell the police about the blackmail. Yet, as she looked back now to catch one last glimpse of the girl who sat so resolutely on the sofa, the girl who refused to lift her head and appeal to her with a look, Rose knew instinctively that Isabella had no intention of volunteering the information to the police. If Rose herself did not mention the blackmail business, then she knew, as surely as if Isabella had told her so herself, that Isabella would not.

Chapter Twenty

'Oh, what shall we do?' asked Mrs Hodges, wringing her hands in her lap. The teacup lay discarded on the table beside her. For once, when her eyes stole around the room in search of the whisky bottle it was so she herself could take a sip. But Crabtree had obviously already purloined it and hidden it in his own quarters. Really, the man was too bad. At a time like this when a good, honest, hardworking, law-abiding person like herself really did need to take a sip for medicinal purposes. Instead she gave the butler a steely look.

'Whatever we do, we mustn't be hasty, Mr Crabtree,' she said firmly.

'It's our duty to inform the police of what we know, Mrs Hodges,' said the butler, drawing himself up to his full height and pulling in his stomach as he did so. Mrs Hodges would have laughed if things had not been so serious.

'But if we do tell the police they'll have young Robert arrested for murder before we know it, you know they will. Far easier and more convenient for them to arrest a servant than one of the family or, God forbid, one of the guests. And there will be pressure on them to make a quick arrest, you mark my words. What with Lord Sneddon's father being the Duke of Haywater and all. He's probably got the police in his pocket. And no one will want any scandal, will they? Who knows what secrets will come tumbling out of the woodwork the longer they delay in making an arrest. The papers will have a field day. They'll be rife with speculation.'

'I share your concerns, Mrs Hodges, but even so, we must inform the police of what we know. It is our duty.'

'Damn duty, Mr Crabtree!' cried the housekeeper, banging her fist down upon the table, making the cup and saucer rattle. 'Do you want to be responsible for sending young Robert to the gallows? Do you want to see him swing?' She turned a contemptuous look upon the butler who gulped and looked pale. His eyes darted around the room as if he himself this time were trying to locate the whisky bottle. 'I'll tell you what we'll do, we'll do nothing, absolutely nothing. Those policemen are from Scotland Yard, aren't they?' Crabtree merely nodded. 'Well then, they'll be the best of the best, won't they? They'll only take the most clever detectives in Scotland Yard, it stands to reason. Well, let them find out about it for themselves.'

'But, Mrs Hodges –'

'No "buts", Mr Crabtree, that's what we'll do,' said the housekeeper, nodding her head with conviction.

'But, Mrs Hodges,' and this time the butler held up his hand to stop her from interrupting or trying to contradict him, 'it's not just Robert we have to consider.'

'Whatever do you mean, Mr Crabtree?'

'Robert isn't the only suspect who could have let himself out of the servants' quarters and gone downstairs and murdered Lord Sneddon?'

'Surely you're not suggesting that Sidney did it? Really, Mr Crabtree, have you gone –'

'No, I was thinking of a much more likely candidate,'

'Ah!' Daylight dawned on the housekeeper's troubled brain. 'You mean –
'

'Exactly, Mrs Hodges, I was referring to Lord Sneddon's dubious so-called valet, Ricketts.'

'Miss Simpson.' Both Inspector Deacon and Sergeant Lane had risen from their seats as soon as the study door was opened and she was ushered in by the constable. Somewhat inexplicably, she felt as she had done when summoned once to her headmistress's room; a feeling of apprehension at what lay ahead. How absurd really, she thought, to feel like this, particularly as she suddenly realised how very pleased she was to see them.

'Inspector Deacon, Sergeant Lane. Oh, I'm so frightfully glad it's you who are investigating this awful murder. Cedric just told me. We're jolly pleased, I can tell you. I can't quite believe it's happened again. Another murder, I mean. I can't take it in. What are the odds of it happening to someone more than once, I wonder. You know, being involved in more than one murder?'

'Quite a lot if you happen to be a policeman,' Deacon smiled.

I'm behaving like a complete idiot, thought Rose. I'm talking a lot of old rot, what must they think of me? They'll realise straightaway that I'm nervous, that I've something to hide. Why don't I just keep quiet?

'I'm sorry,' said Rose. 'It's because I've just been sitting there quietly in the garden room listening to everyone speculating. I thought I was going to go mad. I didn't think it was my place to say anything about what's happened, you know, offer an opinion in front of Isabella and Hallam. They're so frightfully confused, you see. Well we all are rather. And we're all terribly worried about Josephine. Do you know where she is? Have you found her yet?'

'We're still looking for Miss Atherton,' said the inspector. He studied her closely. 'How are the others taking her sudden disappearance? Do they think it out of character for her to just vanish like this?'

'Well, yes they do, although they're trying hard to convince themselves that nothing is amiss. Of course, I hardly knew Josephine. I only met her for the first time on Friday, but she seemed the steady, dependable sort, the kind of person who holds the family together. I can imagine everyone coming to her if they were in trouble or worried about something. Oh dear, it makes her sound very boring, but really she isn't. She is very pleasant actually. I liked her as soon as we were introduced. I can't think why she would leave like she has, not in the middle of entertaining guests and everything. It seems so very odd to leave in the middle of the night unless ...'

'Yes, Miss Simpson, unless what?' Deacon prompted, visibly sitting forward in his seat. The move unnerved Rose who dropped her gaze to her skirt where she fidgeted with the fabric between her fingers.

'I ... I don't know, I can't really think ...'

'Perhaps you were thinking it was very odd unless she had just killed a man?'

'Oh my goodness, no! You can't possibly think Josephine had anything to do with Lord Sneddon's death.' How very stupid she was being. She had been concentrating so much on shielding Isabella that she had been rather careless in what she had said about Josephine.

'You have to admit, Miss Simpson, that it is rather a coincidence that Josephine Atherton disappeared on the same night a murder took place in this house. She probably even vanished around the very time Sneddon was being murdered.' There was a silence interrupted only by the irritating ticking of the clock on the mantelpiece. The noise became almost unbearable and everyone was restive, she noticed, even Lane, who fiddled with the pages in his notebook. But no one spoke. Eventually Deacon decided to change tack.

'Tell me, Miss Simpson, Rose, do you think it likely that Miss Atherton has eloped with the chauffeur?'

'With Brimshaw? If you want my honest opinion, Inspector, no I don't,' Rose said frankly, 'And I'm not just trying to preserve her reputation. Brimshaw is a nice enough chap, very pleasant and rather good-looking in a way, but I can't see Josephine losing her head over him to such an extent that she would just up and leave. If nothing else, she would consider it frightfully bad manners to leave like that. I am assuming she didn't leave a note?' Rose looked up expectantly at Deacon who shook his head. 'But I'm also convinced she had nothing to do with Lord Sneddon's death. I just can't understand it. The baron has something of a temper. She'd know that he would be bound to be livid. If she has eloped with the chauffeur the baron will never let her set foot in Dareswick again. Why, I think he'd sooner disown her than lay eyes on her if she's eloped with a servant. But she simply can't have done that, it's not something she would do. And besides, she loves Dareswick too much. You should have heard her go on about the gardens. She had obviously spent a lot of time talking with the gardener about what bulbs they were going to plant and where they were going to get them from and … oh …'

'What is it?' Deacon asked sharply. Even Sergeant Lane had looked up from his notebook in anticipation, his pencil poised in his hand.

'Oh, it's probably nothing and I can't quite remember what she said exactly,' Rose said, wishing now she'd kept quiet. But it was too late. There was nothing she could do but tell the truth. 'She seemed awfully nice, as I've said, but rather distracted, as if she had something on her mind. And then she said something about it being a pity that she wouldn't be there to see the flowers. I thought it was rather odd at the time. I remember I asked whether she was going away and then she got rather flustered and told me to ignore her, that she was just talking a lot of nonsense.'

'So you think she may have been planning to go away all along? It still seems rather a strange time to choose, doesn't it, in the middle of having her family and guests to stay. I understand that the baron often stays in town and sleeps at his club. It would seem to make more sense for her to leave on one of those occasions when he was absent from the house and her sister was in London and her brother in Oxford.'

'Yes,' agreed Rose, 'as I have already said, I can't understand what would have made her leave so suddenly.' Other than murdering Lord Sneddon, she thought. She looked up. Deacon obviously was of the same opinion but had thought better of pursuing the subject with her again.

'You helped us a great deal with that business at Ashgrove,' the inspector said, smiling. 'If it hadn't been for you, I'm not sure the case would have been solved. So I'd be interested to have your impressions of the other members of the household. Let's start with Hallam Atherton shall we. What are your impressions of him?'

'He's jolly nice, a very affable young man, the little I have seen of him. Cedric's very fond of him, regards him a bit like a younger brother, I think. If I were being honest,' Rose paused, reluctant to say anything that could be seen as detrimental, 'I'd probably say that he is a little immature, you know, a bit young for his age. He's still very much a boy really, although he's trying very hard to appear a man. I think he has probably been a bit spoilt and over indulged by his older sisters, but it hasn't gone to his head, he's very pleasant.'

'Thank you, most comprehensive. I understand from both him and Lord Belvedere that Lord Sneddon's arrival at Dareswick came as something of an unpleasant surprise to everyone here?'

'Yes. We all knew Isabella would be bringing a guest with her, but no one was quite sure who it was going to be; there was even some confusion as to whether it would be a man or woman. It was something of a shock, I can tell you, to see Lord Sneddon. I never thought to see him again, certainly not here.'

'Quite so. Now, tell me your impressions of the baron. I take it he alone was pleased by the news of the engagement?'

'Yes, I think he was quite determined that at least one of his daughters should marry well. I daresay things like that matter very much to people like him. And, as you know, Lord Sneddon was due to come into a dukedom on the death of his father. The poor man, to lose all your sons to violent deaths before their time.' Rose paused for a few moments, as she thought of the old duke. He had had to endure his two older sons being killed in the war, and now his youngest son had been murdered. 'I've seen very little of the baron really, certainly not much on which to base an opinion as to his character. I've only really spoken to him at dinner and then only to pass the time of day. He seemed loud and jovial then, certainly when things were going his way. But he has quite a temper. I wouldn't be at all surprised to learn that his

128

children are quite scared of him. He was jolly angry when Hallam spoke out about Lord Sneddon being there. He looked as if he was about to burst a blood vessel. I can't say I blame him altogether, though. Hallam really shouldn't have said what he did in front of Lord Sneddon. It was very embarrassing for all concerned.'

'Do you think, if provoked, Hallam might have been violent towards Lord Sneddon?'

'If you are asking me whether I think Hallam would kill him in cold blood, then my answer to your question is definitely not,' Rose said with feeling. 'He's a sweet boy, Inspector. He was concerned about his sisters. He was worried Josephine would be upset by Sneddon's arrival and he couldn't understand why Isabella would want to marry the fellow. Hallam's a romantic by nature. If he was intent on fighting Lord Sneddon, then he would have challenged him to a duel, not sneaked up behind him and plunged a knife into his back when he wasn't looking.'

'You sound rather like Lord Belvedere.'

'Do I?' Rose's eyes sparkled and, quite unreasonably in Deacon's opinion, he felt a spark of jealousy.

'So you do not see Hallam Atherton as having a tendency towards violence?'

'No.' She might have said more if she could have been sure that by so doing she wouldn't betray the sudden feeling of uncertainty she now felt in the utterance of that word. For a picture had floated unbidden before her eyes. Josephine's scar, not as it was now, half covered by Josephine's hair, but as it must have looked when just made, large and angry and ugly. She imagined the force that must have been used to create such a wound. And she saw Hallam's childish face, screwed up and distorted in anger, a knife or some such sharp object gripped in his hand. Her mind drifted inevitably to a picture of Sneddon slumped on the desk, a small gold dagger protruding from his back. It didn't mean anything, she told herself. Hallam had only been a child when he attacked his sister and all children, when very young, had a tendency to lash out when they could not get their own way. It had just been unfortunate that he had injured Josephine as he had. And he deeply regretted it, Josephine had said so herself. He was ashamed of what he had done, hated to be reminded of it, which was one of the reasons Josephine kept it covered by her hairstyle.

'What about the Honourable Miss Isabella Atherton?' Deacon enquired. 'What do you make of her?' It could have been his imagination, but he could have sworn that he saw Rose stiffen slightly at mention of Isabella's name, certainly she turned her gaze to the floor as if she were trying to choose her words carefully. He could see that Lane too was looking at her fixedly and, as if aware of both gentlemen staring at her intently, colour began to spread across her cheeks and she seemed flustered.

'I've hardly spoken to Isabella since I've been here. She's rather aloof and seems to keep herself very much to herself. She and Lord Sneddon arrived just before dinner on Friday, and yesterday, when we made an excursion to the village she gave her apologies. She went to bed early last night too. Both she and Josephine went upstairs as soon as the coffee and liqueurs were served. I retired myself, a few minutes after. So you see, I've hardly had a chance to speak to her. Not that I think she is particularly interested in making my acquaintance.' Rose sighed. 'I don't think she really approves of my being here, she thinks I am rather beneath them all.'

'I see.' Deacon looked thoughtful. 'So you can't explain why she decided to bring Lord Sneddon down with her this weekend in particular, other than for him to ask her father for her hand in marriage?'

He got up from his chair and walked over to the fireplace, picked up an ornament, looked at it briefly and then put it back. It seemed an age to Rose before he turned and gave her his full attention. The silence that had arisen from his getting up and moving to the fireplace had caused her to look up from the carpet. When he turned to look at her, she met his gaze and though she reprimanded herself for it being a totally inopportune time to think such a thing, being questioned about a murder as she was, she was reminded how handsome he was; in a very different way from Cedric's good looks, of course.

'It just strikes me, you see, Miss Simpson, as a very odd thing for her to have done. She was aware that Lord Sneddon was likely to receive a very frosty reception from her brother and sister. Indeed, it does not involve much of a stretch of the imagination to believe that Hallam might have punched him. He also led me to believe that there was a time not so long ago when Josephine had hoped to marry Lord Sneddon herself. So her sister must have assumed that Josephine would be distressed at Sneddon's sudden appearance, especially on being informed that he had switched his attentions and now intended to marry her sister.'

'I'm not so sure that Josephine really was so very fond of him,' Rose said, stubbornly. 'Certainly, when she spoke of him to me in the garden yesterday, she gave the impression that she had been merely flattered by his attentions, nothing more. I don't think she was ever seriously in love with him. It was just that everyone else thought she was or wanted her to be.'

'Even so, it seems a very tactless thing for Isabella Atherton to have done. Mean and rather cruel, I'd say, but most of all, completely unnecessary.'

'What do you mean?' asked Rose, curious despite everything.

'Why bring Sneddon here this weekend? Why not choose a weekend when she knew her brother would be safely away in Oxford? She might have chosen a weekend when her sister was also away. I understand she visits London not infrequently. Why make it so very unpleasant for everyone when she didn't need to?'

Rose said nothing. It occurred to her that Isabella had had no choice in the matter. Or perhaps, on second thoughts, she had chosen this weekend on purpose because she didn't want to make it easy for Sneddon. She might have felt that she had no option but to submit to his blackmail demands, but Rose doubted that she would have done it willingly. Making him feel uncomfortable was the one act of defiance left open to her. She remembered suddenly how she had been struck by Isabella's seemingly odd behaviour when Sneddon had been doused in boiling hot soup by the footman. She had been remarkably unmoved by the incident. No, worse than that, she had even smiled a secret, half hidden smile that had confused Rose at the time. Then she had been unaware of the blackmail business. Now she realised that Isabella must have been half hoping that Sneddon had been badly burned by the mishap. She shuddered involuntarily and shifted in her seat to try and disguise the fact.

'You don't think it strange?' Deacon was looking at her closely.

'No,' said Rose, reluctantly. She took a deep breath. 'You see she was being blackmailed.'

'Blackmailed!' It was the sergeant who exclaimed the word and dropped his pencil onto the floor. He scrabbled on the ground on his hands and knees after it.

'Who was blackmailing her, Miss Simpson?' asked the inspector, quietly, pointedly ignoring the mishap.

'Lord Sneddon, of course,' Rose said, angry with herself for not being able to keep quiet. 'Who else?'

And before Deacon could question her further she had recounted every single excruciating detail of the episode she had unintentionally overheard between Lord Sneddon and Isabella in the library, while she had sat hidden in the chair. She felt herself squirming in her seat as she did so. What must they think of her, these policemen? Anyone else, she thought, would have coughed or sneezed or made some such noise to alert Sneddon and Isabella to their presence before they had embarked too far on their discussion, why hadn't she?

'I'd fallen asleep,' said Rose, scrabbling around for an excuse. 'Reading often makes me feel drowsy and so I'm afraid I nodded off. And it took me a while to wake up fully, and when I did, well it was too late to do anything without making everyone feel awkward. So I thought the best thing for all concerned was for me just to pretend I wasn't there.'

'Interesting, this blackmail business I mean. It certainly gives us another avenue to explore.'

'Isabella was going to tell you all about it herself,' Rose said, hurriedly. 'She still will, of course. Naturally we assumed that you'd interview her first, what with her being Lord Sneddon's fiancée.'

'We had assumed that Isabella Atherton would be upset at the death of the man she was to marry and were allowing her as much time as possible to compose herself for our interview,' Deacon said, sounding somewhat annoyed. 'Now I see we were under something of a misapprehension. I imagine that the death of a man who was about to force her to marry him will not have caused her too much grief. Indeed, I would go so far as to say that she may very well be relieved by the situation, if not absolutely delighted.'

'I think that's rather unfair,' objected Rose. 'She's awfully upset, as we all are.'

'I find it somewhat strange that a woman, who by your own admission has gone out of her way to have as little to do with you as possible, should take it upon herself to confide in you that she intends to tell us about the deceased's blackmailing activities. Particularly when as far as she was aware, you knew nothing about the business.'

Rose bit her lip and said nothing. How she wished that she had had the same self-control ten minutes earlier.

'I take it from your silence that you were the one to broach the subject.' Deacon did not pause to wait for an answer. 'You informed her what you had overheard and advised her you considered it your duty to inform us. No doubt you suggested that it would be better for her if she was seen to volunteer the information to us first. Is that right?'

'I am certain that she was going to tell you all about it anyway.'

'Even though it gives her a splendid motive for wanting to have done away with the victim?' The inspector looked at her somewhat sceptically and sighed. 'Well, one thing's for sure, we'll never know now, will we?'

Rose could tell he was thoroughly annoyed by her interference, but trying very hard not to show it. She imagined he felt that she had let him down and she couldn't blame him. She had been instrumental in helping to solve the case at Ashgrove and he had probably hoped that she might do the same here at Dareswick. Instead she had held back information, indeed, she was still doing so even now. She felt wretched. Any moment now the inspector would ask her who else knew about the blackmail business and she would have to …

'You can go now, Miss Simpson.' Deacon's voice broke into her musings. 'But don't go far because I'll want to speak to you again just as soon as I've spoken to Isabella Atherton.'

'Sir, excuse me for interrupting you but I thought I would catch you between interviews, so to speak. I've just caught sight of Miss Simpson leaving. But I feel it my duty to speak to you on a matter of some delicacy.'

Deacon looked up from where he was sitting and glared at the butler.

'Can't this wait, Crabtree?' he said, irritated. 'I've just asked my sergeant to go and get Isabella Atherton.'

'It won't take a minute, sir,' the butler assured him, although the way in which he took a deep breath and puffed up his chest seemed to suggest otherwise.

Chapter Twenty-one

It was something akin to relief that Rose felt when she left the study. As she was leaving she had caught Sergeant Lane's eye and he had smiled at her sympathetically. Deacon had pointedly ignored her, staring down at the sheets of paper spread out on the desk. She had felt like a naughty child. Now, as she walked slowly back to the garden room, or rather dawdled, as her mother would have said, she was reluctant to meet Isabella's eye, too aware that she had made things worse for her notwithstanding her efforts to make things better. She felt now that she should have kept quiet both in respect of warning Isabella and in telling the police what she had overheard. She could imagine all too vividly the inspector and sergeant standing now, huddled together, deciding that Isabella was their chief murder suspect.

As it happened, not looking where she was going, she had bumped into one of the housemaids, upsetting her bundle of crisp white sheets. Despite protestations on the part of the maid, she had stopped to help gather up the bedclothes. The task had taken longer than anticipated as some of the sheets needed to be refolded, and so it was that she missed Isabella being collected and shown into the study. Instead she had caught a glimpse only of the back of her head, from where she sat on the hall floor by the staircase bundles of bed sheets in her arms. Even so she had marvelled at how the girl had seemed so composed, knowing as she did that the police would be aware that she had a very good motive for having wished Sneddon dead.

'Let me get this straight,' Deacon said, glaring at the butler who in turn was looking rather sheepish. 'Are you telling me you were drunk when you answered the bell to Lord Sneddon?'

'Oh, no, no, not at all sir,' said Crabtree hurriedly, looking clearly horrified. 'A man in my position can never allow himself to become drunk. That would never do at all. What would the master say? I'd be out on my ear, I can tell you, to say nothing of setting a bad example to the junior servants. They look up to me. Why, some of them see me as a bit of a father figure, others as a teacher imparting his wisdom –'

'Yes, yes,' said the inspector abruptly, 'I get the picture man. You were not so much in drink as to fall over and make a fool of yourself, but the stuff may have loosened your tongue somewhat. So what time was this, that Lord Sneddon summoned you to the library?'

'About half past eleven, sir. I thought everyone had retired to bed and that my services would not be required again for the night, notwithstanding that it was rather early. Otherwise I would never have partaken of that glass of whisky, not if I'd known I would be called upon again. Not the done thing at all to have the smell of alcohol on one's breath when one is attending to the needs of guests or –'

'All right, all right,' the inspector interrupted rudely. 'Let's put your drinking, or,' he added hurriedly seeing that the butler was about to protest, 'not drinking aside for the moment, shall we? You answered the bell. Lord Sneddon requested another decanter of whisky, which you brought him. Now tell me again what happened next.'

'He asked about the housemaid, Mabel, sir.'

'The maid he got into trouble and who then drowned herself in the lake?'

'Yes, sir.' Deacon noticed that the colour appeared to have drained from the man's face and that he was trembling slightly with emotion.

'A tragic business, indeed,' the inspector said more gently. 'It must have been very upsetting for you all.'

'We felt we'd let her down, you see, sir,' Crabtree said, bowing his head slightly. 'Mrs Hodges, she's the housekeeper, she and I, well, we took it very badly. We blamed ourselves, you see. We should have been there for the girl. She should have felt that she could come to us. We'd have helped her, Mrs Hodges and me, we'd have seen that she was all right. There was no need for her to drown herself in the lake. It brings tears to my eyes just thinking about it, sir, it does. The water, it must have been icy cold at that time of year. Oh, the poor little mite.'

Deacon looked beseechingly at Lane who hurried over and helped the butler into a chair, ignoring his protests that he must remain standing.

'I'm sorry, sir, making such a show of myself. You won't tell his lordship, will you? He expects his servants to be beyond reproach. But every time I think of little Mabel and how desperate she must have been to do what she did, well, I'm quite overcome.'

'So how did you feel, Crabtree, when Lord Sneddon asked after Mabel?' the inspector asked gently, as soon as the butler had regained some composure.

'Angry, sir, and flabbergasted, to tell the truth.'

'Why flabbergasted?' pressed Deacon, trying at the same time to hide his interest.

'He didn't know what had happened to her. He didn't know that she had killed herself because of him. But it was the rage that loosened my tongue, sir. She had meant so little to him that he had even forgotten her name. He thought it was Mavis or Mary. All he could remember was that it began with an 'M'.'

'I can imagine how you must have felt.'

'Can you, sir? I wanted him to know everything. I wanted him to experience some of the pain that we had gone through. I wanted him to be sorry. I was frank, sir, brutal and cruel now I look back on it. It wasn't more than he deserved, I don't regret it. He was upset when I left him, sir, and I thought that was right, that he should be. He even shed a tear or two, you know, sobbed a bit. He wanted me to leave him alone so he could think and weep and no doubt drink himself senseless. I hadn't held anything back, sir, he could hear the disgust in my voice and I felt it was a weight off my shoulders. Only, as I was walking back to the servants' quarters, I was afraid that he might complain to the master, and then I'd be dismissed because his lordship wouldn't have let anything stand in the way of his daughter marrying a man destined to become a duke, no matter how bad he was.'

'So what did you do?' asked Deacon, suddenly becoming alarmed. 'Tell me you didn't go back and kill the man.' Looking across at his sergeant, the inspector saw that Lane too was looking equally appalled at the possibility.

'No, sir, I didn't kill him. Although I'm not sure I don't condone the actions of the person who did. It's just ...' Crabtree looked up and stared the inspector straight in the face. 'It's just that he was that upset. I didn't expect it to affect him so, truth be told. But, the more I think about it, the more I think that his being so distraught had a bearing on his death. I'm probably being silly but I can't get the thought out of my mind.'

'I wonder,' said the inspector and to the sergeant, who knew his actions well, he looked thoughtful.

'Rose, there you are. Inspector Deacon kept you a long time, whatever did you have to talk about?' Cedric descended on Rose as soon as she entered the garden room. She looked around anxiously and saw that the only other inhabitant was Hallam, who was himself pacing the room in a restive manner. The room felt oppressive and she wished that a fire had not been lit in the grate. The thought of having to sit in this room for another hour or so until the police had finished their initial investigations and searched their rooms was unbearable. As if reading her thoughts, Cedric moved to the French windows and started to open them.

'Cedric, you mustn't do that, we can't go out. Inspector Deacon wants to speak to me again in a moment after he's finished interviewing Isabella.'

'He can go to the devil,' Cedric said, crossly. 'I can't stay in this room a moment longer. I feel like a caged animal. We need to get some fresh air and talk. The police will be able to see us from the windows and they can send one of the constables after us if they need to speak with us.'

With some misgivings, for she did not want to do anything that might antagonise the inspector further, Rose followed Cedric out into the formal gardens. As soon as she stepped outside the windows she breathed in the fresh air. They had not stopped to don hats and coats and the cold air made her feel suddenly invigorated. If only she were here with Cedric under different circumstances she would enjoy this walk.

'I say, Rose, I'm awfully sorry about all this.' Cedric paused and took her hands in his. 'It's an awfully bad show, I know. It never occurred to me that anything like this might happen. Sneddon be damned! I know one shouldn't speak ill of the dead but really that man's brought nothing but trouble. You've heard that story about the maid, no doubt? What can I say? You'll never want to see me again after this weekend. I bring nothing but murder.'

'You could just as easily say the same about me,' and Rose found herself laughing despite everything. 'Until you laid eyes on me your life hadn't been littered with murders and deaths, had it?'

'No, of course not. But even so I feel jolly bad about all this. Your mother will never let you see me again. She'll consider me a bad influence and I can't say I blame her. But I'm so jolly glad you're here. It's awfully good to see you again. I really don't know what I'd have done without you. Fall to pieces, I expect, you're the only thing that's keeping me sane. I once considered Sneddon a friend and now he's been brutally murdered, it's unbelievable.'

'It is,' agreed Rose, 'the whole thing's jolly strange.'

'Between you and me, I'm awfully afraid that Hallam might have killed him.'

'Whatever makes you think that?'

'Well, the boy can be awfully hot headed at times. I've tried to keep an eye on him as much as possible, you know, kept him occupied and tried to make sure that he wasn't by himself in the same room with Sneddon, that sort of thing. But I wouldn't put it past him to have challenged Sneddon to some sort of duel. Still, I don't think a gold letter opener really cuts it, do you? Not the sort of weapon that I can imagine him using even as a last resort. I say, Rose, I did something jolly silly the other night.'

'What? What did you do?' Rose tightened her hold on Cedric's hand making him wince. A picture came before her of Cedric plunging the little gold dagger into Sneddon's back in a misguided attempt to prevent Hallam from doing likewise. That he would do whatever it took to protect the boy, she had no doubt. And Hallam was certainly a loose cannon. She had been witness to his enraged outburst and seen the fury in his eyes every time he glanced at Sneddon. She had known that Cedric was worried about the boy, was afraid what he might do. But surely Cedric, darling Cedric, wouldn't take it upon himself to do away with Sneddon?

'I put the idea into the boy's head that Isabella might be being coerced into marrying Sneddon,' Cedric admitted. 'Hallam jumped at the idea; he thought it explained everything. We agreed that we should have it out with her before we did anything, but knowing Hallam he might have acted first.'

'Cedric,' Rose chose her words carefully. 'Sneddon *was* blackmailing Isabella into marrying him. I overheard them arguing about it.'

'Oh, yes, I know,' said Cedric, rather matter-of-factly. 'Those damned love letters to her French tutor. Whatever can the girl have been thinking of?'

138

Chapter Twenty-two

The inspector and sergeant were struck in equal measures by both the Honourable Isabella Atherton's beauty and the composed manner in which she entered the room. She held herself very upright even when she sat down on the chair offered her, apparently not tempted to slump or slouch as some would have done finding themselves in similar circumstances. She certainly is a lovely creature, Deacon thought, as he surveyed her covertly. Apart from the dark smudges under her eyes and a paleness of skin which he admitted was probably as much due to powder as to grief, the girl looked calm and collected. There was a certain frailty about her that Deacon thought some men would find appealing, Lane for one, he thought. He himself however was not so easily deceived. He saw the way she eyed him warily and, unless he was much mistaken, there was a glint in her eye as if she were issuing him with a challenge to penetrate her armour. It was not lost on him either that, when she entered the study and cast a sweeping glance over the room, while acknowledging his presence with a graceful tilt of her head and the shadow of a smile, she had looked straight through his sergeant as if Lane was not there. A slight furrowing of the brow showed that Lane was aware of this slight and that she had gone down in his estimations because of it.

'First, I should like to express my condolences at your loss and assure you that −' Deacon broke off from what he was saying as the woman seated before him raised a well-manicured hand and smiled at him sweetly.

'Please, please Inspector, let us not pretend. You and I are both a little old for nursery games. I am sure that you have been made fully aware by now that my engagement to Lord Sneddon had not been entered into voluntarily. I am sure that that Simpson girl told you that.'

Deacon saw his sergeant visibly flinch at the way she spoke of Rose. He himself felt indignant on her behalf.

'Miss Simpson told us that she had inadvertently overheard a conversation between yourself and the deceased, yes,' Deacon said, looking at Isabella a little coldly, 'in which it was apparent that you were being pressured into entering into marriage with him in exchange for the return of some love letters to a French tutor.' Was it his imagination or had Isabella blushed at the mention of her lover's profession? Certainly she looked annoyed, although he could tell she was trying hard to disguise the fact.

'Oh, Inspector. How I wish I hadn't written those ridiculous letters. They were written on a girlish whim and how I have regretted putting pen to paper ever since. But yes, Lord Sneddon used them to blackmail me, into agreeing to marry him. There I've said it, such an ugly, hateful word, isn't it, "blackmail"? And that blasted girl overheard me imploring him to release me from our bargain. Why she could not have made her presence known, although I suppose those sort of girls are always on the lookout for scandal and gossip. No doubt it enlivens the rather dull, drab little lives they lead. It can't be much fun can it, working in a dress shop, probably waiting hand and foot on the most ghastly people.'

There was a gleam in Isabella's eye and an upward turn of her lip, and Deacon was left with the strange impression that she was almost trying to provoke him. How very odd, he thought. Usually suspects bent over backwards to try and persuade him of their innocence, and yet here was this woman willing him to dislike her even though she was in the vulnerable position of having had a very strong motive for wishing the victim dead. It did not make sense and he found it unnerving. It was as if she were playing a game with him despite her fine speech about not playing nursery tricks. She was of the view, he thought, that she held all the cards and at the last minute he was afraid that she might produce something out of the hat. Right now, he felt that he would get some pleasure in arresting her for the murder of Lord Sneddon albeit the evidence at this stage was only circumstantial. And because he knew she was bringing out the very worst in him he tried to curb his feelings and hide his distaste.

Lane, fortunate in being concealed from Isabella's view where he sat, was not obliged to disguise what he felt. A frown had crossed his face and his mouth was set in a straight line. Every now and then he looked up from his scribbling and glared at the back of Isabella's head. Deacon wondered whether she could feel his eyes boring into her. As a child he had always been sure that a person must be aware when they were being stared at, that the stare must in some way be physically penetrating so that the person felt compelled to spin around to see who was spying on them. Isabella Atherton, however, appeared blissfully unaware of the looks of animosity being cast her way by his sergeant.

'I understand that Miss Simpson gave you the very sensible piece of advice to tell us about your being blackmailed?'

'She did indeed,' Isabella said, looking distinctly bored. 'I knew the girl wouldn't be able to hold her tongue; that sort never can. But as it happens, Inspector, I had every intention of telling you all about those awful letters myself.'

'Did you indeed?' Deacon said, not sounding particularly convinced.

'Yes I did as a matter of fact.' Isabella smiled sweetly, clearly amused. Deacon felt uncomfortable, as if he was being laughed at. He found it a very odd sensation and decided to change tack.

'Right now, Miss Atherton, suppose you tell us when exactly you decided that Lord Sneddon should accompany you to Dareswick this weekend. Was it a longstanding arrangement? I ask because it appears no one was aware of the identity of your guest until he arrived.'

'Quite right, Inspector. I kept them guessing, you see. I was rather hoping not to have to bring Hugh down with me even up to the last half hour or so before we set off. I was going to bring my girlfriend, Celia, but Hugh would insist that I bring him instead. It really was very tiresome of him. I'm afraid I really rather despised the fellow, Inspector. Not very kind of me to say so considering he's dead and all that, but there it is.'

'Understandable I would have thought, given the circumstances. I take it Lord Sneddon wanted to marry you for your money?' As soon as the words had escaped his lips, Deacon regretted being so abrupt.

''How very nicely put, Inspector,' Isabella said sarcastically, all the while smiling at him sweetly. 'But, yes, you're right. He wanted to marry me for my money, not for my wonderful good looks or my sparkling wit. And to make matters worse I wasn't his first choice. I believe he had tried his hand with others before me, my own sister for one before he bored of her and got that housemaid into trouble. And then, of course, I rather think he had his eye on Lavinia, but of course that came to nothing because of all that business at Ashgrove.'

'Suppose we stop playing games, you and I, Miss Atherton,' said Deacon, suddenly sounding serious. If truth were told he was getting tired of her and had decided it was high time to cut to the chase. 'You said yourself we are too old to play childish games and really this matter is far too serious. A man has been brutally and cold-bloodedly murdered, a man who you had good reason to want dead. I understand you were beside yourself at the prospect of marrying Lord Sneddon. You were a desperate woman and desperate people do desperate things. I do not think that there is a court in this land who would not understand if you were to admit that in a moment of madness, you felt provoked into killing your blackmailer. I am sure you would be treated with some leniency.'

There was complete silence as the words seemed to fill the room, reverberating off the furniture. The mood of the room had suddenly become sombre and the inspector felt the tension could have been cut with a knife, it was so tangible. He felt himself on tenterhooks lest Isabella should confess; he could almost imagine that it was on the tip of her tongue to do so. Certainly she was no longer smiling; she appeared to cease to find the situation amusing. Instead, she clenched her hands together and bit at her lip as if she were trying to pluck up courage to say something. To the policemen who waited, it seemed a very long time before she lifted her head and spoke, although it was probably in reality only a few minutes, if that. When she at last lifted her beautiful face, Deacon thought he could detect tears in her eyes and a tremble about her lips. For the first time he felt pity towards her for the predicament that she found herself in.

'You know about Isabella's love letters to her French tutor?' Rose stared at Cedric in disbelief. 'You knew that Sneddon was blackmailing her? She told you? Oh, Cedric, my darling, you mustn't tell the inspector about it, promise me. It'll give you a motive, don't you see, for wishing him dead.'

'Hardly,' said Cedric, 'but I say, Rose, do keep on calling me darling. It makes me believe that you can't think too badly of me for bringing you into all this.'

'I don't, of course I don't,' said Rose, alarming herself by finding that she was close to tears. 'But Cedric, promise me you won't say anything to the inspector about it. I couldn't bear it if —'

'Rose,' Cedric said, drawing her to him. 'Don't fret so. There's nothing to worry about really there isn't. I didn't know anything about this blackmail business until just now, certainly not before Sneddon was killed. Isabella's just told Hallam and me about it. You know, while you were in with the inspector.'

A wave of relief immediately flooded over Rose. He hadn't had a motive for doing away with Sneddon after all, other than just not liking the man, in common with everyone else. But this feeling was almost at once replaced by another of anxiety. What was Isabella up to? Why had she told Cedric and her brother about the letters? There had been no need. The police were hardly likely to broadcast their existence and Isabella could not think that she, herself, would discuss them with anyone other than the police, not when she had taken such pains to make sure that no one overheard their conversation. It made no sense at all. Isabella had been prepared to marry a man she did not love, no, worse than that, despised, in order to keep the existence and contents of the letters secret. And yet at the first opportunity she had told the others about them. Instinctively Rose felt that something was wrong. Things were certainly not as they had first appeared.

Chapter Twenty-three

'You're right, Inspector, of course. I did hate Lord Sneddon,' Isabella said slowly, appearing resigned now to telling the truth. 'I hated Hugh for stooping so low as to blackmail me into marrying him against my wishes. If nothing else, it's common knowledge that he has a gambling habit; I knew within a year of marriage he would have gone through my dowry and I'd have become destitute, reduced to living on hand-outs from friends and family. It would have been demeaning even if I was a duchess. I couldn't go through with it and I couldn't see a way out. Death seemed the only way although, if truth be told, I thought more of my own than his. I could not bear the humiliation, you see, if those letters ever became public. He threatened to show one or two to my father. He would have disowned me, Inspector, as no doubt he will disown poor Josephine for running off with the chauffeur.'

'Miss Atherton, perhaps you would like a solicitor present before you say anything further.' He didn't want to stop her flow now that she had opened up and finally resolved to talk seriously, but out of the corner of his eye he could see Lane scribbling furiously in his notebook to catch her every word.

'No, Inspector, thank you. It's all right. I know my words are being taken down. But I want you to understand how I felt, it's important to me. Silly really, I know, but there you have it. I don't want a solicitor here telling me to nod my head or say nothing.'

'I would advise you not to proceed any further without a solicitor being present to protect your interests, Miss Atherton.'

'That's very good of you, I'm sure, but I've already told you I wish to proceed without one.' Isabella said, speaking firmly while all the time smiling a sad little smile. 'Now, where was I? Oh, yes, I wished Hugh dead. I visualised killing him a thousand times in my head. I even thought about the different methods I might use. Sometimes I thought that it would be absurdly easy to do away with him. The man didn't see me as a threat you see. And at other times I worried about how I'd get away with it until I was left to think that the only option was to poison myself, while perhaps making it look like Hugh had done it, so I could get my own back, you understand.'

144

The inspector and sergeant exchanged glances, both clearly appalled. It occurred to Deacon that Isabella might not be quite right in the head. That she could talk so matter-of-factly about the process she had arrived at to dispose of Sneddon, quite sickened him.

'Perhaps, if you will, you could tell us about last night and the events leading up to the ... eh ... incident,' said Deacon. 'I understand you women all retired early to bed?'

'Yes, we did, rather. None of us were feeling particularly in the party mood, which was a shame. I walked up with Josephine. I had rather a headache and I couldn't bear the way that my father kept sidling up to Sneddon. Really, Daddy is dreadful. I could see him almost rubbing his hands with glee. He's always found me rather trying, you see. He thinks I'm rather rebellious and headstrong, not at all like Josephine who's always been rather a Daddy's girl, well-behaved and dutiful. Well, up until now of course. Eloping with the chauffeur rather takes the biscuit, don't you think?'

'You were saying about last night,' prompted Deacon.

'Ah, well, Hallam was looking daggers at me all night. Oh, how clever of me, excuse the pun!' Isabella paused to emit a shrill little laugh. 'So I thought it best to just go and leave them all to it. Only, of course, I went to bed far too early so I couldn't sleep. When I'm in town I'm never in bed before midnight. So there it was, I couldn't sleep. I kept fretting, you see, about Hugh. I decided once and for all that I really couldn't go through with it. I decided to throw myself on his mercy. I had nothing to lose after all but my pride. So I listened out for the others to come upstairs. I knew Hugh was unlikely to go to bed early. He keeps later hours in town than I do. So all I had to do was lie there and wait.'

'And then you came down when the coast was clear?'

'Yes, I almost collided with that Simpson girl. She was coming up the stairs as I was about to venture down. I caught sight of her just in time and nipped back into my room and closed the door. I doubt very much whether she saw me.'

'Indeed.' The inspector looked interested. Rose had made no mention of going back downstairs during their interview. It occurred to him that there had been rather a few things that she had kept to herself. They would have to ask her about it when they spoke with her again later. He caught Lane's eye and signalled to him to be sure to make a note.

'Yes, well, I checked that the coast was clear again. I was afraid that there might be someone else roaming around, but it was quite quiet, so I decided to take the chance.'

'What time was this?'

'About a quarter to one this morning, I think. Strange to think that it was today. I suppose that means he hasn't been dead so very long, has he?' She shuddered at the thought before continuing. 'Anyway, I tried the drawing room first and found it empty. So I tried the library next. I thought he'd be there. It's smaller and cosier than the drawing room, you see, and stays warmer. I thought he and Daddy had probably retired there to take their whisky or brandy or what not and talk and that Daddy had probably retired to bed leaving Hugh. Anyway, as I thought, Hugh was there alone.'

'How did he take your sudden appearance?' asked Deacon, leaning forward.

'Well that was what was so strange,' said Isabella, savouring the moment. 'He was delighted to see me. It rather took me aback, I can tell you. I thought I was going to have to start crying and pulling my hair out before I had any effect on him. But not a bit of it. He took me in his arms and said how sorry he was for his behaviour, that he released me from my promise to marry him and how he wanted to make amends. To tell you the truth, I thought he was rather drunk, but I wasn't going to waste the moment. I thought I'd better make the most of his change of heart in case he changed his mind again in the morning when he was sober.'

'So what did you do?'

'I asked for the letters back.'

'And what did he say to that?' It seemed to Deacon that he was waiting for Isabella's answer with bated breath. Even Lane had stopped his writing and was staring fixedly at the back of her head.

'He said that his manservant, Ricketts, would be down in a moment and that he would ask him to fetch them as he was not sure where they had been hidden.'

'And did this man appear.'

'Yes, only a few moments later as it happened. And a more disreputable fellow one couldn't imagine. He passes himself off for a valet, but one would never guess. I don't think he knows the first thing about dress. Certainly, if he did, he did not apply the knowledge to his own appearance.'

146

'Yes, yes,' said Deacon, impatiently. 'And what happened next? Did Sneddon send this man to fetch the letters?'

'He did.'

'And?'

'He returned with the letters, Inspector, and gave them to me,' Isabella said with a triumphant glint in her eye as she proceeded to produce from her handbag, which only now Deacon noticed was oversized, a great bundle of letters tied together roughly with string. 'So you see, Inspector, I had no reason to kill Lord Sneddon because he no longer had a hold over me. He had released me from our engagement and returned my letters.'

It seemed to Deacon that a long time had elapsed between Isabella uttering those earth shattering words and his brain taking in the full implication of them. She had had no reason to kill Sneddon! He, Deacon, had been about to arrest her for murder. He had believed that he was hearing her heart-felt confession when all the time she had been toying with them for her own amusement. She had set the scene and built up the suspense and now she looked at him jubilantly, elated with her success. Initially he had felt relief that she was innocent of the murder, now he felt only anger at having been treated as a fool. She had enjoyed the deception, the illusion she was creating. What kind of person was she, he wondered?

She was starting to gather up the letters on her lap, no doubt with the intention of restoring them to her bag. The inspector sprang up and almost snatched them from her. She looked at him and, for the first time, he saw a look of terror in her eyes. She half got up from her seat, as if tempted to snatch back the letters, and then seemed to think better of it and sat back down.

'Just a moment, Miss Atherton. I want to just double-check that these are indeed what you purport them to be. Let me see.' He glanced at an envelope and then at one of the letters. "Monsieur C. Lambert". He took out the first letter and read aloud: "My darling Claude. I cannot wait until I am in your arms and your lips are on mine, to feel –'

'Enough!' Isabella almost shouted, her face quite crimson. She put her hand to her face and began to sob. 'Must you humiliate and embarrass me so and in front of your sergeant too.' She turned and scowled at Lane as if it were his fault. 'Haven't I endured enough with Hugh reading out snippets and laughing at my wretchedness? I would have thought better of you, Inspector. You can see the letters are what I claim them to be. You can have no reason to read them aloud other than for your own amusement and my discomfort. Please don't read them all, I couldn't bear it.' She put her hand to her chest and took a deep breath. 'Please give them back to me, I beg you. I want to get rid of them once and for all. I never want to set eyes on them again, I want them destroyed. Claude was a fool to keep them. He should have thrown them on the fire as soon as he had read them.'

'Is that what you did with his letters?'

'What?' For a moment Isabella looked bewildered. 'Yes ... yes, of course. I threw them on the fire as soon as it was all over.'

'Which was not so very long ago,' said the inspector, 'looking at some of the dates on these letters.'

'Please,' implored Isabella, 'let me have them back so I can get rid of them.' She stretched out her hand to take them.

'I am afraid, Miss Atherton, we must retain them for a while longer,' said Deacon, not unkindly. 'They are evidence of a sort. Although I must warn you we will be checking with Lord Sneddon's valet that his account of events corroborates yours.'

He had put down the bundle of letters on the edge of the desk and turned away. It had not occurred to him for one moment that she would not accept what he had told her. Consequently his reactions were delayed. In a moment she had sprung from her seat, caught up the letters in her grasp and hurled them all into the fire where the flames engulfed them. She then threw herself beside the fire lest one of the policemen be tempted to try and retrieve some of the letters from the flames. So closely did she kneel beside the fireplace that there was a distinct possibility that her hair would get singed. Sergeant Lane had flung down his notebook and rather roughly took her by the arm and hauled her from her position by the hearth. By the time she had been pulled away, and the inspector had crouched by the hearth and surveyed the fire, there was nothing left of the letters, not even charred remains.

'That was a very foolish thing to do, Miss Atherton,' said Deacon, coldly. 'Not only have you just destroyed some evidence, but you could have got badly burned in the process.'

'I'm sorry, Inspector, really I am,' sobbed Isabella. 'But you see I had to get rid of them. I couldn't bear the idea of anyone getting hold of them again.

You don't know what it's been like for me with Sneddon blackmailing me. I've been in absolute torment. I don't want to give anyone else the opportunity to blackmail me again.'

'They would have been quite safe with us, Miss Atherton. Ah, well,' sighed Deacon, 'it's no use crying over spilt milk, as my mother would say. You're free to go, Miss Atherton, as long as you don't leave Dareswick. We may well need to speak to you again. In the meantime can you ask Miss Simpson to join us? I should like another word with her.'

Isabella gave a fleeting smile of triumph and was gone.

'Quick, Lane,' Deacon said in an urgent whisper as soon as the door had closed behind her. 'I want you to go and get Ricketts and bring him here before she has a chance to find him and bribe him to back up her story of events.'

'You think she's lying, sir?' Lane sounded surprised.

'I don't know, but it seems to me that something is not quite right. Of course I could be imagining it. But I didn't like the way she played us along. I'm not sure I'd put anything past that young lady.'

'You don't think she may have spoken with Ricketts already?'

'No, I don't. For one thing, I don't think she has had the opportunity, and for another, she had no reason to. If the opinion that I'm forming of this Ricketts character is correct, he is not the sort of man to go out of his way to help the police with their enquiries, the opposite in fact would be true, I'd say. No, I doubt the Honourable Isabella Atherton had any intention of mentioning the blackmail business to us; until, that is, Miss Simpson told her what she knew and that she intended to tell us herself. But go quickly, man. I don't want her to get to him first.'

Chapter Twenty-four

Rose entered the room tentatively, unsure of her reception. She found Inspector Deacon alone in the study. He nodded at her, frowned slightly and indicated she should sit down, while he himself carried on his reading of Sergeant Lane's notebook, flicking between the various pages. Rose in turn fidgeted with the folds in her skirt and then turned her attention to study a crack in the ceiling. Every now and then she furtively stole a glance around the room to see if she could see the sergeant lurking in the shadows. At length, not being able to bear the silence any longer and Deacon showing no sign of finishing his study of the notebook, she said:

'Did Isabella tell you about the blackmail business?'

'Yes, indeed, she was most informative.'

'She told the boys all about it too, while I was in here earlier. So you see she had no intention of being secretive about it.'

'This is after you had told her what you knew and what you intended to tell us?'

'Yes,' she admitted.

'You didn't mention when last we spoke that you were probably one of the last people to see Lord Sneddon alive.' The Inspector cast her a reproving glance.

'Well, you hardly gave me the chance to do so, did you?' Rose retorted, indignantly. 'You were more interested to hear my thoughts on the Athertons and then you sent me out with a flea in my ear when I mentioned Lord Sneddon had been blackmailing Isabella.'

Deacon attempted to conceal a smile.

'Well, now you may tell me all, Miss Simpson. When did you last see Lord Sneddon?'

'I suppose it must have been about twenty past twelve, perhaps a little earlier. It could even have been a bit later. I did look at my watch at the time but I can't remember what it said. I couldn't sleep. Josephine, Isabella and I all retired to bed quite early last night. The atmosphere was somewhat tense and strained. I think everyone felt it, except for the baron perhaps. I don't know what time the men went up, I wouldn't have thought they'd have stayed up talking and drinking for long. Anyway, I'd fallen asleep and then woken up and couldn't get back to sleep again. So I decided to go down to the library and get a book. Reading in bed always makes me feel rather drowsy. And when I went into the library I found Lord Sneddon there. I didn't see him at first, he had been sitting in one of those infamous wing chairs by the fire. I was rather alarmed to see him, I can tell you, particularly when I saw that he had been drinking. But he was most adamant that I stay and talk to him. Or rather he wanted to talk to me.'

'What sort of a mood was he in?'

'A melancholy one, I should say. I wouldn't have been surprised if he had been sitting brooding in front of the fire for some time. You know, reflecting on his life and not liking what he saw. He certainly seemed very depressed. To tell you the truth, I felt sorry for him, he seemed so pathetic really.'

'Did he say why he felt as he did?'

'Yes, I think it was because of the maid who drowned herself in the lake. You've heard all about that already, I expect?'

'Yes, and it would fit with what Crabtree told us,' said Deacon. 'Sneddon summoned him around half past eleven to request another decanter of whisky. The butler had had a glass or two of the stuff himself by then and it helped loosen his tongue. Sneddon made the mistake of asking after the maid in question and Crabtree told him in no uncertain terms what had happened to her and whose fault it was. Up until then I think he had been in ignorance about her death. Crabtree acknowledged, albeit rather grudgingly, that Sneddon was devastated by the news. He pretty much broke down, I think.'

'Then I was right, he had been brooding on things,' said Rose, thinking over her last conversation with Sneddon. 'He wanted to make amends. He asked me whether I thought he could become a better person and I told him no, but that he must try. Oh,' Rose's eyes filled with tears, how I wish now that I had said yes. I should have given him hope, I should have been more charitable, I should –'

'You weren't to know,' Deacon said quickly. 'No one was. It was no bad thing for him to be made to think for once about what he had done and those he had hurt. Now, I take it you stayed talking with Sneddon for some time. For how long exactly do you think? Does twenty minutes to half an hour, give or take five minutes or so, sound about right to you?' Rose nodded.

'After which I take it you returned upstairs to your room?' Again Rose nodded.

'Good. That fits in nicely with what Isabella Atherton told us. She almost collided with you on the stairs as you were coming up and she was going down.'

'I never saw her,' said Rose, sounding surprised.

'You wouldn't have done. She nipped back into her room pretty promptly and closed the door behind her. Then she waited until the coast was clear before venturing out again.'

'Are you saying she went downstairs to confront Lord Sneddon?' Rose could feel the muscles in her chest tighten.

'Yes, and being in the mood he was in, seeing it as an opportunity to make amends so to speak, he gave her back her letters.'

'What!'

'Yes, exactly, Miss Simpson. You see you needn't have been so concerned about incriminating Isabella Atherton. Sneddon gave her back her letters before he was murdered.'

'Are you sure?'

'Yes, she showed them to us. They were addressed to Claude Lambert. At least I think that was his name. I read out a bit of one of them and Lane jotted it down. And very flowery stuff it was too. Let me see.' He picked up the sergeant's notebook and flicked through a couple of pages. 'Ah, yes, here we are: "My darling Claude. I cannot wait until I am in your arms and your lips are on mine, to feel ..." Ah, yes, I remember, I was forced to stop midsentence in my reading out because Miss Atherton was very embarrassed. She implored me to stop.'

'I don't blame her. It was rather cruel of you,' Rose said, giving him a reproachful stare.

'She'd been playing games with us. She was leading us up the garden path making us think she was about to confess to Sneddon's murder. But as it happens she got her own back. She threw the letters onto the fire before I could read any more of them out to her.'

'Are you sure Sneddon gave the letters back to her?' asked Rose, suddenly.

'You mean as opposed to her killing Sneddon and then going and rifling through the papers in his room to find them? What a suspicious mind you do

152

have, Miss Simpson, you'd make a good detective. The very same thought did cross my mind but, as it happens, we have a witness, the man's so-called valet. He was sent to fetch the letters and handed them back to her. Lane's gone to get the man now to see if he will corroborate Miss Atherton's story.'

'Why do you refer to him as Sneddon's so-called valet? Surely he is or he isn't?'

'I rather think that our Lord Sneddon may have been employing him for other purposes and that his purporting to be a valet was just a façade. Apparently the man hasn't the first idea about what the job of being a gentleman's valet entails.'

'Well, that would help explain something that I thought rather odd that happened on Friday night.'

'What was that?' Deacon was intrigued.

'It was after the footman had spilt the soup all over Sneddon. There was much ado about it, as you can imagine. The baron demanded that the footman get Lord Sneddon's valet to see to him straight away. But Sneddon asked for the baron's valet instead because he said his man wouldn't be any good at dealing with it. It just seemed to me strange at the time, that's all.'

'Interesting,' agreed the inspector. He thought for a moment as if trying to decide about something and then said; 'Let me show you something, Rose. A couple of the constables discovered this at the back of Sneddon's wardrobe while they were making a search of his room.' He produced an ornate, paisley-patterned man's handkerchief from his breast pocket and proceeded to unfold it and empty its contents onto the desk revealing various pieces of expensive looking jewellery.

'Why, it's my mother's pearl necklace!' exclaimed Rose, holding up a string of pearls. 'I wore them to dinner on the Friday night but I couldn't find them last night when I was dressing for dinner. I was sure that I had left them on the dressing table and just assumed that the maid had packed them away in my case. I was in a bit of a rush so I didn't have time to look, and then later I forgot all about it. Oh!' Her face clouded as an awful thought struck her. 'Are you saying that Lord Sneddon was rummaging about in my things and stole them? Surely not!'

'I think it's much more likely to have been his valet, but he'd certainly have had to have been in on the act. They were found in his wardrobe after all. Do you recognise anything else?'

'This looks a bit like the gold necklace that Josephine wore at dinner last night, although I wouldn't swear to it being the same one,' said Rose, peering closely at the trinkets.

It was on the tip of her tongue to suggest that he ask Josephine to take a look, and then she remembered just in time that Josephine had inexplicably disappeared. Her conscience pricked her. Now that they were sharing information, and the inspector had even gone so far as to call her by her Christian name, it seemed as good a time as any to disclose to him that Josephine knew about her sister being blackmailed; worse, that she had said she would tackle Sneddon on the matter herself. However, Rose told herself, surely if she had done Sneddon would have informed her that he had returned the letters to Isabella's safekeeping. There would have been no need for her to kill him, although the very thought that she might have done such a thing was preposterous. But it worried her that Sneddon had been found with his back to the door slumped over the desk. It was just possible that Josephine had not bothered to ask him for the letters, had assumed that he would refuse to give them up. If it had not been for the distress of the news of the maid's death leading him to re-evaluate his life, then Sneddon would surely have laughed in her face and refused to hand the letters over.

How awful, thought Rose, if Josephine had killed Sneddon needlessly. She looked up. Had Deacon met her gaze at that moment, she might have been tempted to tell him her fears. As it was he appeared deeply absorbed in looking at the jewellery, turning each piece over looking for the hallmark.

Further consideration of or discussion on the matter was not possible as they both became aware of a kerfuffle in the hall followed by various sets of men's footsteps. There appeared to be a scuffle going on, this impression further heightened by the utterance of an oath and a man shouting.

'That'll be Lane now with the infamous Mr Ricketts who appears to be kicking up a bit of a fuss. No doubt we'll speak again, Miss Simpson.'

It seemed to Rose as she left the room, looking with interest as she passed through the hall at the disreputable and restrained figure of Ricketts, that Deacon had given her sufficient food for thought. But something in particular was niggling at the back of her mind. It was only when she was approaching the garden room that she realised what it was. Something told her that there had been another reason for Isabella throwing the letters onto the fire than the one she had given, but she couldn't for the life of her think what it could be.

Chapter Twenty-five

'Well, well, Mr Ricketts, do come in. I've been rather curious to meet you, I must admit.' Deacon held open the study door and Lane deposited the man, still struggling, onto the nearest chair.

'He tried to make a run for it, sir,' explained the sergeant. 'He might've got away with it too if greed hadn't got the better of him. He stopped off on the way to go into Lord Sneddon's room and rummage through his things.'

'Ah, indeed Ricketts, no doubt you were looking for this.' Deacon held up the jewellery. The man cursed and spat onto the floor.

'Really, Sergeant, what is the world coming to?' enquired the inspector. 'They certainly don't make valets like they used to. I'd have expected better manners from one, wouldn't you?'

'Particularly one who was valet to the British aristocracy,' replied Lane, grinning.

'And what's that whiff? When did you last have a wash, Ricketts? And that's a very interesting way to button a waistcoat. It's new to me, no doubt it must be the latest fashion.'

'You've got nothing on me,' protested the valet. 'That stuff weren't found in my room, were it?'

'It wasn't,' agreed Deacon. 'But you knew it was in your master's room because you put it there.'

'How do you know I did?' said Ricketts, sullenly. 'How do you know as he didn't put it there himself?'

'Even I don't think that Sneddon would stoop so low as to actually pilfer himself. No, he'd leave that for you to do. You know the saying, no use having a dog if you've got to bark yourself, well, no use having a tealeaf if you've got to steal yourself.'

'Who are you calling a tealeaf? I'm no thief,' wailed Ricketts.

'I beg to differ,' said Deacon, holding up his hand as the man made a move to protest further. 'Look Ricketts, I'm not interested in your stealing, well, not so far as it has nothing to do with Lord Sneddon's death that is. Of course, you will be thoroughly searched before you leave these premises. So if you've a mind to take anything with you that doesn't belong to you, think again.'

'It ain't got nothing to do with his murder,' Ricketts replied, scowling at the carpet.

'I'm glad to hear it, although forgive me if I don't just take your word for it. Now, listen to me.' Deacon became serious. 'We know Sneddon was short of money, what with his gambling and suchlike, and I understand his father's estate is heavily mortgaged to the bank. So let's just suppose he decides that the answer to his immediate problems is to marry a rich woman. However, unfortunately for him, despite his good looks and the charming manner he can effect when the mood takes him, his reputation goes before him and there is a severe shortage of suitable women prepared to tie the knot with him. He, on the other hand, is particularly desperate to hurry things along. That's where you came in, I think. I think the two of you entered into a sort of partnership. You stole to order, jewellery and other such items that could be easily hidden by Sneddon in his room and also material which could be used by him for the purposes of blackmail. Am I right?'

'Might be,' the inspector thought he heard the man mumble under his breath. He chose to interpret it as confirmation.

'Right, now I want you to tell me all about last night. I assume that you had some sort of arrangement whereby you would show Sneddon what items you had taken during the day and he would then hide them in his room?' There was silence. 'Come on, man, cooperate, otherwise you might just find this murder pinned on you,' said the inspector, losing patience and raising his voice. 'I think we could put a good case together for you two having had a disagreement which got out of hand over how to split your spoils, don't you, Sergeant?'

'I do, sir,' agreed Lane. 'It would certainly make life easier for us. An open and shut case. We could go back to London right now. We might even be home in time for tea.'

'All right, all right,' said Ricketts, admitting defeat. 'I'd arranged to meet him in the library at one o'clock this morning. We usually met around that time 'cause all the household are normally in bed by then, even that damned butler who keeps insisting on doing the rounds before he retires for the night.'

'How did you get out?'

'What do you mean?'

'The doors to the servants' quarters were kept locked at night. Crabtree told us so himself.'

Ricketts made a face. 'It didn't take much effort to pick the lock, I can tell you. It was child's play, that's what it was. The silly old fool thought he was being so clever.'

'So what happened last night when you met up with Sneddon?'

'Well, I found her there, didn't I? You know, the woman he was all set to marry. Gave me quite a turn it did, seeing her there, because of course I wasn't expecting to.'

'And then what happened?' prompted the inspector.

'He asked me bold as brass to return her letters to her. You could have knocked me down with a feather.'

'And?' said Deacon, impatiently.

'Well, I went out and got them, of course, and gave them back to her.'

'That can't have made you very happy. You must have been annoyed, furious in fact, I would have thought. I take it you had arranged to take a cut of the blackmail proceeds?'

'As it happens, Lord Sneddon had already paid me for that particular service when I first gave him the letters. But I was a bit miffed, yes, I admit it. I went to a great deal of effort to get those letters. I didn't know what he was playing at giving them back to her. I weren't afraid that he'd turned over a new leaf, if that's what you're getting at. He needed the money too much for that. Nah, I just thought that he might have been going a bit soft as far as she was concerned. But then it occurred to me that he might have his eyes set on bigger pickings, you know, a richer wife.'

'You must have been curious, though. Weren't you tempted to return to the library once Isabella Atherton had left in order to have it out with him?'

'No, it were late by that time and he told me we would be leaving first thing in the morning, or should I say today. So I thought I'd just wait and speak to him then. It were obvious he had a plan of some sort. He wouldn't have just upped and left, now would he?'

'He might have done if he'd had a change of heart about the whole blackmail and stealing business. Now, just one more question. And think carefully, Ricketts, before you answer this one. Was Lord Sneddon blackmailing anyone else in this house besides Miss Atherton? And I would recommend that you tell me the truth. If he was blackmailing someone else then that person would have had a very good motive for wishing him dead.'

Ricketts gave him a sly look and grinned, revealing one or two rotten teeth. Deacon sighed. He could tell at once that the man was not going to play ball. He supposed that it had been a bit of a long shot that Ricketts would tell them the truth. For a man like him, lying was a way of life. The man's next words confirmed his fears.

'No, he weren't blackmailing anyone else.'

'I suppose you do realise that you yourself may well be in danger? It would be far better for you if you told us who it was and handed over whatever you had on them.'

'I told you already, he weren't blackmailing anyone else,' Ricketts said stubbornly.

The inspector threw up his hands in frustration and glanced at his sergeant. They both knew Ricketts was lying, but that they would get no more out of him no matter how long they persisted. The man was playing with fire and Deacon hoped he knew that. But there was very little they could do about it.

With a sigh Deacon let the valet go with a strict warning not to try and leave Dareswick unless he wanted to see the inside of a prison cell, of which the inspector was sure he was already well acquainted.

'Do you think that wise, sir?' asked Lane, as soon as the door had closed after the retreating Rickets. 'He's just the sort of slippery individual who'd get away and who we'd never find again. I bet he's got loads of bolt holes where he can lie low until all the fuss has died down.'

'You're probably right, Lane,' agreed Deacon, 'but that's what I'm after in a way. I want him to try and make a run for it, as long as we're there to catch him of course.'

'Can I ask why, sir?' asked the sergeant looking confused.

'We need to find out who else Sneddon was blackmailing. We'll never get the information out of Ricketts just by asking him. But he's sure to take any incriminating material with him when he makes a run for it. There are rich pickings to be made now that the stakes have become so much higher. We're not talking about indiscretions now, we're talking about murder. I'm sure this blackmail business is tied up with Sneddon's death somehow. Did you see how that fellow Ricketts smirked when I asked him about it? He won't be able to resist trying to do a bit of blackmail himself.'

'Then the man's a fool and that's for sure. Doesn't he realise the danger he's in? If he's not careful he'll end up with a dagger in his back himself.'

'That sort are driven by greed and to hell with the risks. I take it the constables have searched his room and found nothing?' Lane nodded and Deacon continued. 'He's not clever, that one, but he is sneaky. He'd have realised that, if there was a search, his would be one of the first rooms turned over. He's probably buried the stuff in the garden or behind a fireplace or in the larder, or somewhere. Somewhere we'd never find it anyway, not without a great deal of effort and resources. Far better for him to take us to it, and he'll only do that when he scarpers. We'll have to be discreet though, he'll do nothing if he thinks he's being watched. He's probably got eyes in the back of his head, that one.'

'So what are you proposing to do?'

'I doubt he'll risk making a run for it before it's dark and he thinks we're away from here. I'm going to post a couple of men at the entrance to Dareswick, a couple on the road leading out of the village and a couple at the back of the house, down by the lake, where there's a path off to the woods. He's bound to try and leave by one of those ways. We'll catch him then.'

'You don't think he could have done in Sneddon himself, do you, sir? It seems to me that he could easily have got into an argument with him over the splitting of the proceeds like you suggested, especially if Sneddon told him that he wasn't going to be involved in that sort of thing anymore as a consequence of his change of heart. They probably had quite a lucrative thing going on. I can't see Ricketts being happy about just giving it up.'

'That's as may be, and he'd be annoyed, I grant you, but I've come across fellows like him before. They're sneaky and conniving but basically they're cowardly and tend to run from any sign of violence. I think he'd have just upped and left, probably taking the stolen jewellery with him. So no, I don't reckon Ricketts has got it in him to kill a man in cold blood, but I could be wrong.'

'He could just decide to stay put until we've finished our investigation.'

'He could do, but I don't think he will. He won't want to have the police breathing down his neck. Now, tell me, Lane, what do you think about the others? Is there a murderer amongst them? Who shall we start with? What about the baron, let's start with him.'

Chapter Twenty-six

'There you are Rose,' Cedric said as soon as she re-entered the garden room, 'I wanted to wait until you'd got back before I went. The baron wants me to go up and help him. Hallam's with him now. Apparently he is having some difficulty getting hold of the duke. He's very ill, at death's door himself, according to his secretary, a chap called Harding. He's at a clinic in Switzerland and they're having difficulty getting through to him. And this fellow Harding, he's not being much help. He's reluctant to have anyone break the news to the duke about his son. He thinks it will finish him off. Says there's a chance that he won't see out the day as it is, so why distress him unnecessarily? He has a point but it's dashed difficult for the baron, of course, puts him in a jolly awkward spot, what. He doesn't know what to do for the best. That's why he wants to talk it over with Hallam and me.'

He cast a glance at Isabella who was the only other occupant of the room besides themselves and lowered his voice. 'You know, Rose, you don't have to stay here, in this room I mean. One of the constables has just told me that we're free to move around the house now as long as we don't leave the premises. I suppose it's because they've now interviewed everyone and searched all our rooms. I wonder if they found anything incriminating. I fancy a bit of a stroll in the garden later. I feel as if I've been cooped up in here all day and it isn't even lunchtime.'

Rose wondered whether to mention the jewellery that had been discovered in Lord Sneddon's room but, on balance, decided against it. It was not that Inspector Deacon had asked her specifically to keep the information to herself but on the other hand she did not feel that he would want the matter widely broadcast. But then Cedric wasn't just anyone, was he? But right now he was needed elsewhere and if she were to tell him about it, then she would want them to have time to discuss the implications. Instead, feeling somewhat dejected, she watched him go to attend to the concerns of their host.

But how she longed that he would stay with her, that they could wander in the grounds alone, oblivious to the cares around them. Oh, why did Lord Sneddon have to go and get himself murdered, how very inconsiderate of him! If only she and Cedric could be allowed to enjoy their brief time together, this short respite before Madame Renard's shop claimed her and the affairs of Sedgwick Court required his attentions. She realised now, perhaps too late, that she had been pinning so very much on this weekend. She wondered what would happen now. Would their fledgling romance just fizzle out or was it strong enough to hold the course, despite the murders that seemed to surround them? She knew what she wanted. The question was, did Cedric feel the same?

But before she would allow herself to spend any more time dwelling on the matter and making herself feel miserable, for she had an unbearable, overpowering feeling that the outcome of their relationship was inevitably doomed, she must solve Lord Sneddon's murder. Only then could things return to normal. Only then could she think about their future. Inspector Deacon's belief in her ability to help the police investigation had buoyed her spirits in that area at least and she realised now, as she stood hesitantly in the doorway to the garden room, that she had an overwhelming wish to redeem herself in his eyes. With the best of intentions she had held things back from him and he had been disappointed in her. Rose remembered the look on his face. She was determined to restore his good opinion of her. For some reason that she could not quite fathom it mattered very much to her.

There was something else nagging at her conscience that made her feel that she must see that justice was done. Irrational though it might be, she could not shake the feeling that she had in some way contributed to Sneddon's death. True, she had not snatched the little golden dagger and plunged it into his back, but she had encouraged his change of heart, shamed him into making amends. Had this in some way led to his death? Had he not been feeling so distraught and guilty would he be alive now, a patronising sneer on his arrogant face, a cutting remark falling from his lips? In life she had disliked him very much. In death she had resolved to seek out the person who had brought about his violent end.

This renewed purpose lifted her spirits somewhat. She cast a glance at Isabella but the girl was purposely ignoring her. No doubt she had felt compelled to tell Cedric and Hallam about the wretched blackmail business lest Rose did so. Inwardly Rose cursed herself. She should have told Isabella that she had no intention of mentioning anything about it to the boys. No wonder Isabella did not like her. She could not blame her any more than she could bring herself to sit in this room and endure an uncomfortable and inevitable silence. But where could she go? To her room seemed the obvious answer but she did not want to shut herself away and feel isolated. Without Cedric beside her she suddenly felt very alone and unwelcome in this house. How she wished Josephine were here talking about comforting, inane, trivial matters. Why, she wouldn't even mind now if she went on endlessly about bulbs and flowers ... flowers! There was something significant about flowers and Josephine but she could not at this minute think quite what it was. She had wandered in the gardens on two occasions with Josephine when the girl had been nattering on pleasantly about everyday things. And Josephine had arranged some flowers in a vase. Flowers and Josephine, always flowers and Josephine and something of importance, if only she could think what it was.

The association with flowers made her decide to venture outside in the grounds. Her head ached, as much from her lack of sleep the night before as from the shock of Sneddon's murder, and fresh air would surely do some good. Although Cedric had said that the police wanted everyone to stay on the premises, she assumed that this included the gardens and not just the house. Certainly Cedric was of that opinion if he were considering taking a stroll with her later.

With one last look at Isabella, who was trying hard to appear oblivious to Rose's very existence, she sighed and fetched her cloche hat and tweed coat and let herself out into the garden.

The fresh air whipped around her face and Rose drank it in, savouring the moment. She had not realised until then how claustrophobic and stifling the house had become and how much she had felt trapped and shut up in it like some prisoner. Inside she had not been able to think. It had been as if the very air inside the Hall had fuddled her brain, but outside in the fresh air her mind became active again, awoken from its forced hibernation. Now that she had emerged into the gardens she felt a certain clarity, and perhaps more importantly, confidence. She had been instrumental in solving the case at Ashgrove, she reminded herself; she could be the same here. All she needed to do was to think through things logically, piece together the bits of the puzzle, and she would arrive at the answer as she had done before. It would give her a sense of purpose, something to focus on, so that she was not forced to sit there and just play a sort of waiting game. And she would restore her standing in Deacon's eyes, a little voice said, but she chose to ignore it for that was secondary after all.

Having made a decision on how to proceed she wondered why it had taken her so long to do so. It was only when her eye caught sight of the rosebush that she realised why. She had known all along who the most likely murderer of Lord Sneddon was, although she had been reluctant to admit it to herself. Certainly she had no wish to send that person to the gallows.

'Well, sir, I can't see that the baron would have had a motive for wishing old Sneddon dead,' said Sergeant Lane, standing before the fireplace and holding his hands out before him to catch the warmth from the flames. He flexed his fingers which ached from all his note taking. 'The exact opposite's the case, I'd say. He's the only one who was pleased by his daughter's engagement to the fellow. Bit of a snob, I'd say. Couldn't believe his luck that his daughter was going to marry a duke's son. He'd be beside himself when she became a duchess and all. Something to brag about at his club.'

'Yes', agreed Inspector Deacon, 'he certainly appears to be that type of a fellow. One to be happy to have his daughters enter into marriages of convenience whether or not they happened to like the chaps in question. And if what everyone is saying is true, about there being a time when Sneddon and Josephine were close, then he doesn't seem to have had any qualms about upsetting his eldest daughter. One would expect any father who cared for his daughter would want to break the news to her gently himself, if only to gauge if it would upset her because she still had some feelings for the man.'

'Whereas in this case,' said Lane, 'the baron didn't seem to give a damn. Was in an untimely rush to announce the engagement as well, if you ask me. He could have waited until yesterday to have made the announcement. Seen how the land lay, so to speak.'

'I wonder whether he was worried Isabella Atherton might change her mind,' pondered Deacon. 'It made it dashed more difficult for the girl to break it off if everyone knew about it.'

'Which would explain, sir, why he was so angry with Hallam regarding his outburst,' said the sergeant. He paused to flick through his notes. 'According to Lord Belvedere, young Hallam begged his sister not to marry

Sneddon, in front of everyone too, even the servants. The baron must have been afraid Sneddon would take offence and walk out.'

'Yes, he wasn't to know how strapped for money he was. I'm beginning to think Sneddon chose Isabella to marry as a bit of a last resort. He can't have imagined that the marriage would ever have been a happy one.'

'Not given that he'd blackmailed her into it rather than turned on the charm and persuaded her to marry him of her own free will.'

'The man was desperate, Lane, we've got to remember that. He hadn't sufficient time to charm the girl. He was involved in blackmail and theft, for goodness sake, and who knows what else.' Deacon sighed. 'Anyway, getting back to the baron who was happily oblivious to all this. He was probably the only person in this house who wanted Lord Sneddon present and for him to marry his youngest daughter. Although ...' he paused and sat for a few moments in contemplation.

'Although?' prompted the sergeant, eagerly, after a few moments had elapsed.

'Well, I was just wondering, Lane. We say that the baron was keen for his daughter to marry Sneddon, but I'm just wondering if he would have been so keen if he'd found out just some of the truth about the man.'

'What do you mean, sir? Are you talking about the blackmail and the stealing?'

'I was actually thinking more along the lines of finding out our Sneddon was hard up and had a list of creditors as long as his arm. Even the baron would have reservations about his daughter becoming destitute. He wouldn't want to see Sneddon waste her dowry on paying off gambling debts no matter if she was able to put "duchess" in front of her name in a few years' time. No, that could definitely have soured his mood towards Lord Sneddon.'

He began pacing the room. 'But you're right, Lane, he could have got wind of the blackmail business or the thefts, or both come to that. And he wouldn't have taken too kindly to either of those, would he? Even he would resent his daughter being blackmailed into marriage, and he'd hardly just stand by and let his guests be robbed in his own house, now would he? And we know he's got a temper. Loud and jovial when things are going his own way, didn't Miss Simpson say? But prepared to fly into a temper when things don't. Look how angry he was with Hallam Atherton when he spoke out of turn about Sneddon being there. And that poor footman. He dismissed the man on the spot.'

'You don't think Sneddon could have been blackmailing the baron too, do you, sir?'

'All things are possible, Sergeant. I could well imagine a man like the baron having a few murky secrets in his past or a mistress in town that he doesn't want his daughters to know about.'

'So the baron might have had reason to wish Sneddon dead after all?'

'It's certainly possible. We shouldn't rule him out as a suspect quite yet. But, moving away from suspects for a moment, Lane, there's something that's been bothering me about the murder itself that I've been meaning to talk over with you …'

She must go through the list of suspects logically. That was the only way to do things. She would find a bench and sit and think with the cool air blowing on her face. Thank goodness it was only cold and not raining. She could not bear the idea of going back into the house just yet. Cedric, she felt sure, would still be with the baron. No doubt trying to stop Hallam from arguing with his father or else offering a comforting shoulder, because who really knew how Hallam was feeling about it all? He had been jolly rotten to Sneddon, of course, not that the man hadn't deserved it given what he had put the whole family through. The way he'd treated Josephine and the young maid with the village thinking that Hallam had been to blame. But Sneddon was dead, had been brutally murdered, cut down in his youth as his brothers had been. Who was to say that Hallam didn't feel a sense of guilt or shame now? He might even this very moment be wishing that he had behaved differently.

Unless of course he was the murderer, said a little voice inside her head. It was tempting to dismiss the idea but Rose had set herself the task of finding the murderer and Hallam was a credible suspect even if the idea of him killing Sneddon was unpalatable, given how very young he was.

She opted for a wooden bench beside one of the gravel drives that edged the formal gardens and gave a good view of the Hall and consequently anyone who happened to venture outside, should Cedric come out to find her, or Inspector Deacon, she thought as an afterthought.

She didn't want to think for one moment that the murderer might be Hallam, but he was young and impulsive and she could easily imagine him convincing himself that it was the right thing to do to protect his sisters. Cedric had admitted that he had put the idea into the boy's head that Isabella was being coerced into marrying Sneddon. She would have said that he was not the violent type, certainly not the sort of fellow to kill a man in a cowardly, cold-blooded way. But he had once attacked Josephine, she reminded herself, attacked her badly enough for the scar to still be visible all these years later. But he had bitterly regretted it ever since, Josephine had said so. He could not bear to be reminded of what he had done so she made sure to keep the scar hidden. Hallam could have done it, Rose eventually admitted to herself, in a fit of anger he could have struck Sneddon, as he had done his sister all those years before, but he would have regretted it instantly. She could imagine him standing over Sneddon shaking, his face white and his lips trembling. If he had done it, she thought, he would have stayed at the scene and taken responsibility for his actions. He wouldn't have slipped away to escape the consequences. Besides, he would have been in shock, he would have been unable to move even had he wanted to.

But, said the little voice in her head, it was probably hours between the time Sneddon was killed and when he was discovered by Doris, the maid. Even someone in deep shock might have recovered his wits sufficiently by then and crept away from the scene. Yes, said another voice, but would he have been able to keep to himself what he had done? Hallam was just the sort of young man who would go to pieces and confess or show some other sign that gave the game away. She thought back to how he had appeared to her in the garden room. He had been distressed by the murder as they all had been and, now she thought back on it, she remembered that he had appeared particularly agitated, clenching and unclenching his fists. He had been particularly concerned too about Josephine and whether her sudden vanishing act could be interpreted as her having had a hand in Sneddon's death, she remembered. Exactly as he would act and feel, she realised, if he were afraid that his sister would be blamed for his crime.

And who was to say that he had not confessed to what he had done? Certainly he had not confessed to the police but that did not mean that he had not confessed to someone else. Who was to say that he had not confessed to his father and Cedric and that was the reason they were all holed up so long together? Perhaps the tale of trying to get hold of the Duke of Haywater and deciding exactly what to tell him was just a ruse to give them time together to decide what to do to save Hallam from the gallows. Even now they might be planning to stow him away in the dirty laundry sent out to be washed. A fast car might be ready to take him to the coast so that he could set sail for America or India, or anywhere else where he might be able to lose himself, until the hue and cry had died down and the police had lost interest in the case.

But surely Cedric would have told her or, even if he had been sworn to secrecy, he would have given some tell-tale sign that would have given the game away. But then she had seen so little of him this weekend. And what time they had spent together, they had rarely been alone. She stifled a sob. Please, she prayed, don't let it fizzle out before it's even really started, I couldn't bear it.

Chapter Twenty-seven

'But I've already told you, Mr Crabtree, I didn't do it!' wailed Robert. He had been summoned to the housekeeper's sitting room and been alarmed to find, as soon as he had crossed the threshold, both the butler and Mrs Hodges bearing down on him and interrogating him about every aspect of his movements the night before. They had eyed him suspiciously as he had answered each question and he was left with the distinct impression that they only half believed what he was telling them. The housekeeper in particular was looking at him very strangely, he felt himself flinch under her penetrating stare. His mouth went dry and suddenly he found that his collar was too tight and was beginning to rub the back of his neck, as if too much starch had been used.

'It's very important you tell us the truth lad,' said Mrs Hodges, 'Mr Crabtree and me, we only want to help you but we can only do that if you tells us the truth. Isn't that right, Mr Crabtree?'

'It is, indeed,' agreed the butler, taking over. 'Now, Robert, you're quite sure you didn't go back downstairs for anything after everyone had retired to bed. Nothing that you'd forgotten? A book perhaps, or a pencil, something insignificant like that that you may have gone back down for?'

'I've already told you, I didn't, Mr Crabtree. I went to bed as soon as you sent me up. Do you remember you sent me up rather early on account of your not wanting me to run into the master? You said as he would more likely than not have me thrown off the grounds if he caught a glimpse of me. And I knew you were keen to lock 'em doors to the attic and get to your bed yourself, and who wouldn't after the day we'd had? All the fetching and carrying and cleaning and polishing and them upstairs, they have no idea of all the work we do to make sure everything goes like clockwork like.'

'Which it certainly didn't do last night when you doused Lord Sneddon with boiling soup,' admonished Crabtree sternly, feeling obliged to make some form of retort as Robert had criticised their betters and, perhaps more importantly, their paymasters.

'I did have half a mind to go down and kill the man, I admit,' said Robert, sullenly. Mrs Hodges put a hand to her heart and looked as if she were about to faint. 'But I didn't mind you,' he added hastily, seeing the effect of his words. 'Not that he didn't deserve it after what he made poor Mabel do. But I was afraid to when I thought about it. Not the killing part, I'd have had no problem doing that, it was the consequences that I was afraid of, you know, getting caught and letting you and Mrs Hodges down, Mr Crabtree, after all you've done for me and all.'

'If the police happen to interview you again, for goodness sake keep that bit about wanting to kill Lord Sneddon to yourself, Robert,' said the housekeeper somewhat recovered from her fright. 'They'll be looking for a scapegoat, someone to pin the murder on, you mark my words if they're not.'

The footman decided not to tell her that he had already confessed as much to Sergeant Lane.

'Robert, did you know that the door to the attic was unlocked last night?' Crabtree said, carefully. 'I must have forgotten to lock it which was very remiss of me, although I could have sworn I had.'

'You did, Mr Crabtree,' the boy said eagerly, ''cause I saw you do it. And I heard you do it too.'

'I thought I had!' The butler sounded as if he had scored a point. In truth he had been wondering whether he was becoming rather forgetful with age. It was a relief to know that he was not declining with the years. 'I will be that glad when we get back to normal and I don't have to go about locking doors and the such,' said the butler with feeling. 'But this morning the door was open when I tried it, I can't explain it.'

'I reckon it was that Ricketts chap,' said Robert, earnestly. 'That's why you started locking the door in the first place, wasn't it? I wouldn't trust him as far as I could throw him. He's the look of a prison about him, I bet he can pick a lock or two.'

'By Jove, you're right, lad.' Crabtree sounded ecstatic. 'Mrs Hodges and I were only saying how he could be the murderer. And of course you're right. A fellow like him would know just how to pick a lock. No doubt he and his master had a falling out and he took a knife to him. It would make far more sense that, than the murderer being a member of the household or one of the guests.'

'It also explains why the police have been watching him so closely,' said the housekeeper, herself warming to the suggestion. 'Have you noticed that they're not letting him out of their sights?'

'They're afraid he'll do a runner, I reckon,' agreed the footman.

'Oh, Mrs Hodges, Robert, I cannot tell you how relieved I am,' said Crabtree collapsing into one of the armchairs, dabbing at his forehead with a handkerchief. 'I have been that afraid about who the murderer might be it has been making me quite ill with worry, I can tell you. But you are quite right, Robert. The murderer more likely as not is this Ricketts scoundrel and the police already have him in their sights, so to speak. Yes, they are on to him. Mark my words, Mrs Hodges, before long we'll be back to normal. Peace and order will be restored to Dareswick. It will be as if this tragic event never happened. Right, now we've put the world to rights I think we deserve a nice cup of tea, don't you, Mrs Hodges?'

Ten minutes later butler and housekeeper were sitting contentedly sipping tea grateful in the knowledge that the trying events of the last couple of days would soon be over. It did not occur to either of them as they relaxed, sharing a welcome respite of a few brief minutes from their many duties and chores, that matters were about to take a turn for the worse.

'I think I know what's bothering you about the murder scene, sir,' said Lane. 'I was thinking myself it all looked rather neat, you know, no chairs or tables knocked over in a struggle as you might have expected if there had been a bit of a scuffle. I know whoever had a fight with Lord Sneddon would have wanted to keep the noise down in case they awoke the house, but even so it made me wonder if things had been tidied up a bit by the servants. But Crabtree swears no one touched a thing. The little maid, Doris, almost died of fright by all accounts when she saw the body. She dropped her dustpan and brush and fled like a mad thing from the room. The housekeeper's most perturbed because she says the ash will be a devil to get out of the carpet. Anyway, the butler says he was summoned by Mrs Hodges as soon as the body was discovered and that, once he'd established that Sneddon was dead he locked the room and pocketed the key. Apparently he didn't even go over the threshold. Said it was obvious from where he stood in the doorway to the room that the man was dead and there was nothing he could do for him. If you ask me, sir, he was a bit squeamish as far as the body was concerned.'

'Well, he was right in that Sneddon was dead. He'd have been dead some hours at least when he was found. There'd have been nothing he could have done for him. And I don't think there ever was a scuffle, Lane, no fight of any sort, I'd say. I think it happened exactly as it looks like it happened. There were no defensive wounds discovered on the body, I've just found out from the police doctor, no scratches or skin under the fingernails or that sort of thing, as there would have been if there'd been a struggle of sorts. Sneddon was sitting at the writing desk, writing. Now we know about Miss Simpson's nocturnal visit to the library and what was discussed between her and Sneddon and his subsequent change of heart about blackmailing Isabella Atherton. I think it's fair to assume that Sneddon was compiling, or about to compile, a list of the people he had wronged.'

'In which case, sir, the murderer's name was probably on that list. And he more likely as not took the list away with him, don't you think?'

'I do. Although I think it just as likely that Sneddon might not even have got around to writing the list before he was killed. Anyway it's neither here nor there because the murderer would have been sure to have got rid of the list by now, it would have been far too incriminating. And he'd have had ample opportunity. No, Lane,' said Deacon, 'that's not what's worrying me.'

'What is it then, sir?'

'I think Sneddon was taken unawares. I think someone either sneaked up behind him and stuck the knife in his back and he never knew anything about it, or else that he did not feel threatened by the presence of his murderer and so turned his back on him and sat down at the desk.'

'Yes, sir,' agreed the sergeant, somewhat disappointed. He did not know what he had been expecting the inspector to say, but something more than this. He thought that they'd already established a scenario like this as a strong possibility.

'We know the murder was not premeditated, Lane, because the murderer grasped the first thing that came to hand, namely the letter opener which, by all accounts, would have been on the desk.'

'Or they might have known it would be there and decided to use it before they entered the room.'

'Possibly, but that would have been a bit risky. They weren't to know that Sneddon would be seated at the desk. For all they knew he could have been at the other end of the room. In which case he would see them pick up the letter opener and be on his guard or, at the very least, curious as to what they intended to do with it. No, Lane, that's not it. Don't you see what it is?'

'No, sir, quite frankly, I don't.'

'If there had been any form of struggle the murderer would have needed to have had some degree of physical strength. Sneddon was a fit young man with a strong physique. He wouldn't have been killed without a fight and we have just established that no tussle took place.'

'I still don't see what you're getting at, sir.'

'I think, Lane, that our Lord Sneddon was killed by a woman. I think she either crept up on him or Sneddon dismissed her and made the mistake of turning his back on her. Either way, it would have been easy enough for a woman to have plunged the knife in his back. She wouldn't have been faced with any resistance and, because she would have been leaning over him, she wouldn't have needed any strength to do the job. You know, Lane, there's another saying from Shakespeare along the lines of "there is no fury like a woman scorned."'

'So you think –'

'– the murderer's the Honourable Josephine Atherton,' said Deacon, finishing his sergeant's sentence. 'Yes I do, or at least I think it's a very strong possibility.'

Rose, with a slowing step and heavy heart, angry at her own lack of faith, had suddenly come to the very same conclusion. If she thought about it, she realised that she had always been afraid that the murderer was Josephine. It was the only solution that made any sense.

Josephine had been welcoming and shown her kindness, even if she had been a little distracted as if she had had something of significance preying on her mind. It was to be expected that Josephine might feel some bitterness towards Sneddon. He had led her to believe that he had feelings for her which might lead to marriage and then he had abruptly switched his attentions to her maid. How humiliating it must have been for her, particularly given that he had got the girl into trouble and then the girl had chosen such an awful resolution to her problems. And then to find that he was to marry her own sister who was being coerced into submitting to the arrangement. It must have been too awful for her to bear. She had too many motives for wishing Sneddon dead not to be the murderer or, at the very least, have had some hand in his death. Perhaps she had managed to bribe Brimshaw to do the deed himself rather than dirty her own hands with Sneddon's blood. Perhaps they had panicked, perhaps that's why they had fled. Or perhaps that had been the arrangement all along. Brimshaw might be at the other end of the world by now, and Josephine might have set off in the other direction or might return all innocent, claiming to have been kidnaped and in fear of her life.

Rose did not care for Isabella and because of that she had wished to think her guilty, if one was to accept the unpalatable notion that the murderer must have come from within Dareswick Hall. Isabella had looked down on her, if she even bothered to acknowledge her at all. When they had been introduced she had smiled at her mockingly, considered her a source of amusement, laughed at her expense. Rose's cheeks went crimson. She suddenly wondered if they all thought like Isabella did; the baron, Josephine and Hallam. They probably thought of her as they did Brimshaw, and look how horrified the baron and Hallam had been at the possibility that Josephine might have eloped with the chauffeur, almost as if it had been worse than her murdering Sneddon. She was making Cedric into a laughing stock. His friends were no doubt laughing behind his back, horrified in an amused sort of way that he had the nerve to flaunt her in public, saying that his mother would have sent her packing if she had still been alive. Perhaps even the servants laughed at her while they undertook their tasks in the shadows or before the house had fully awoken. Even now they might be sitting in the servants' hall having a gossip about her, wondering when Cedric would come to his senses and marry Josephine who, after all, would be far more suitable. Perhaps even her sister, although she thought Isabella would find Cedric too dull and he would find her too flighty.

She felt a surge of emotion well up inside her. She could not bear it. The thought of standing by and watching Cedric marry someone else was unbearable. Whatever happened, whoever the murderer turned out to be, she was determined to be with Cedric whatever obstacles were put in her way. And with this thought she hurried to the house, eager to lay eyes on him again. Perhaps he had felt something of the same for at that moment one of the French windows opened and out walked Cedric, tall and blonde and handsome, even from a distance. He was looking for her she could tell and, without a second thought for how it would look or what the servants would think, she was calling out his name and waving her arms lest he should not see her. He turned and looked in her direction. His face instantly lit up and he smiled and with a glowing feeling Rose thought, I am the cause of the look of joy on his face, it's my company he seeks above all others. And, before she quite knew what she was doing, she found herself half walking, half running and he was doing the same only his strides were longer so he was quicker and then they were laughing and collapsing into each other's arms, and Dareswick Hall and Sneddon's murder seemed very far away indeed.

'It's not so much a case of who was the last person to see Lord Sneddon in the hour or two before his death, more a case of who do not see him,' complained Deacon.

'I know what you mean, sir,' agreed the sergeant. 'It seems to me that it was a bit like Piccadilly Circus with all the comings and goings that went on here last night. If what everyone says is correct, then no sooner had one person been down and gone, another one would arrive.'

'You're right, sergeant. Now if I've got it straight, the baron leaves Sneddon in the library. Sneddon rings for Crabtree who comes and brings him another decanter of whisky. While he's drinking that, Miss Simpson comes down to the library in search of a book. After a time she leaves and Isabella Atherton comes down, followed later by the manservant who goes and fetches the letters. Then Isabella leaves and Ricketts stays with Sneddon a while before he too goes, leaving the way clear for the murderer to come down and kill Sneddon.'

'Sounds like the murderer was jolly lucky not to have bumped into someone while doing the deed,' said Lane.

'Yes, I think he or she would have had to leave it quite a while before coming down so that they could be sure that they weren't going to be disturbed.'

'That fits in with Josephine Atherton doing the deed,' said Lane, 'or at least witnessing the deed being done by the chauffeur, before setting off into the night.'

'It does. On the other hand …' Deacon broke off from what he was saying as the noise of running feet and general activity could be heard in the hall outside.

'Oh, lor,' sighed Lane, 'don't tell me Ricketts has tried to make a break for freedom again, won't the fellow ever learn?'

'Sir, sir, please sir.' A young constable burst unceremoniously into the room. 'Sorry sir, for not knocking and all, but they're back. We just caught sight of the car at the brow of the drive from the upstairs windows. They'll be at the door in a moment.'

'Who will be, Constable?'

'Why, Josephine Atherton and the chauffeur, sir. Well at least definitely the chauffeur. It was impossible to tell from this distance sir, whether there was anyone in the back seat.'

'Quick, Lane.' The Inspector bounded over to the door. 'You get out into the hall and head off any of the servants that come, or family or guests, come to that. I don't want any of them to have a chance to warn or speak to the couple before we've had an opportunity to interview them ourselves. We'll let Crabtree open the door to them but he's to stay by the front door. I don't want any of the footmen to go out. As soon as the chauffeur has got out of the car and so can't drive away, I want you, Lane, and one of the constables to appear and apprehend Brimshaw. You can take him to the garage and interview him there. Constable, you stay with me and we'll escort Josephine Atherton into the house and I'll interview her in here. Is that clear? Right, come on then!'

Chapter Twenty-eight

It seemed to Deacon, much to his annoyance, that the whole house had turned out to watch the wanderers come home. In reality it was only Sidney and Robert, who were soon sent packing back to the servants' hall, Crabtree, who remained, and Rose and Cedric who had just come in from the garden through the drawing room French windows and had ventured out into the hall to ascertain what all the commotion and excitement was about. The inspector gave them a quick look of reproach but refrained from saying anything as the car was fast approaching. Indeed, unless he was mistaken, the car had come to a stop in front of the house. He gave one final warning glance to Rose and Cedric to say nothing and nodded to the butler to open the door. His sergeant stood at his shoulder, biting at the bit, anxious to pounce on the chauffeur as soon as he had climbed out of the car.

It seemed to Rose that everyone was holding their breath to see what was going to happen. With a stab of something akin to pity, she heard Josephine's clear, pleasant voice float through the air.

'Oh, there you are, Crabtree. I wondered where everyone was. Will you send Robert and Sidney out please, there's a suitcase in the boot and a few other things for them to bring in so that Brimshaw can garage the car. I suppose Father's frightfully cross, isn't he, my up and leaving in the middle of the night like that, especially as we've got guests. I know it looks a little odd but I can explain everything, really I can. And you mustn't be angry with Brimshaw, he was only doing what I asked of him. Where's Father, in his study?' It appeared that Crabtree had seen fit to nod, incorrect though this answer was. Either way, Josephine had received sufficient encouragement to enter the house, apparently totally unaware of what was awaiting her within.

'Yes, I suppose I'd better get it over with. I expect Father's been behaving like a bear with a sore head all morning, hasn't he? He's no doubt been awfully worried about me, silly old thing, I … Oh, I say,' Josephine was taken aback slightly so as to lose her flow by Lane pushing past her rather rudely to apprehend Brimshaw before he had a chance of getting back in the car and driving away. 'I do hope that's not the new footman come to replace

Robert, Crabtree. He seems an awfully rude sort of a fellow and he's dressed rather badly. Wasn't there a uniform available that would fit him?'

Crabtree had stepped aside so that she could cross the threshold and it was only then that she caught sight of Deacon and the worried and anxious faces of Cedric and Rose. She must have realised instinctively that something was wrong, for she opened her mouth once or twice to say something but no sound came out. Deacon stepped forward so as not to prolong the confusion.

'Miss Atherton, my name's Detective Inspector Deacon. I'm from Scotland Yard. I'd like to have a few words with you in your father's study, if you don't mind. Just one or two questions that I would like to ask you.

'Detective Inspector? Why …?'

'This way if you would, please, miss,' Deacon had deftly opened the study door and was attempting to usher her inside. 'And you needn't worry about the young man who's just gone out. He's not your new footman, he's my sergeant. He's just gone to have a few words with your chauffeur.'

Josephine appeared taken aback by events. So much so that it appeared at first that she would allow herself to be herded into the study without making a fuss. But just as she was about to go through the door she turned and hesitated.

'I should like Rose to come in with me please, Inspector. Say you will, Rose. Father's less likely to be too angry with me in front of guests. He doesn't agree with washing one's dirty laundry in public. That's why he was so furious with Hallam when he said what he did to Lord Sneddon.'

For a moment no one spoke, as if confused or embarrassed as to what to say. Rose decided to seize her chance. She had to find out what Josephine told the police. She had to discover what had happened the night before and what had caused Josephine to flee in the way she had. And why had she come back? Surely she realised the danger she was putting herself in by returning? And if she were to confess to her part in the crime, well then Rose would be there to offer what little comfort she could, given the circumstances.

'Yes, of course,' Rose said, and she had sailed into the room before Deacon had the presence of mind to refuse her admittance or to correct Josephine's mistaken belief that her father was in the study waiting to admonish her.

179

Deacon closed the door behind the three of them. He glared at Rose but she pretended not to notice, refusing to meet his eye, and instead she wandered over to the window and looked out, as if fascinated by the view. She waited until Josephine and the inspector had chosen their seats and then deliberately chose a chair a little away from Deacon's, where she was outside his line of vision but where she could catch Josephine's eye if she found it necessary. If the inspector noticed this deliberate manoeuvre he made no sign and said nothing. Perhaps, thought Rose, he was impatient for the interview to get going. For him it had been a long day. He and his sergeant had barely stopped for lunch, snatching a few sandwiches hastily put together by the kitchen staff, washed down with a pot of tea. The family and guests had fared little better, no one having had much of an appetite and the servants being restive and unsettled. Unbeknown to her, Mrs Gooden had had to give the scullery and kitchen maids a stern talking to. They were now disinclined to work being torn as they were between crying their eyes out at the thought of being in a house where a murder had occurred and huddling in a corner speculating on who could have done such a thing.

'Really, Inspector, my father does tend to overreact somewhat. I mean to say, calling in Scotland Yard to investigate my disappearance. Well I never! I'm frightfully sorry to have caused you such inconvenience. I'm sure that you've got far better things to look into than my being gone for the night.'

Deacon studied her to see if she were being sincere. She was an ordinary, pleasant looking young woman, he thought. She had neither the fierce beauty nor strong temperament of her sister, he conjectured. A sensible sort of young woman, he supposed, one who would put the needs of others before herself, unlike Isabella Atherton.

'We are not here to investigate your disappearance, Miss Atherton, although having said that I am sure your father will be delighted to find that you have returned from wherever you've been safe and well,' Deacon said slowly, watching the reaction on her face closely as his words sunk in.

'You're not?' To Rose, Josephine both looked and sounded surprised. 'Well, I must say, that's a relief. I would have hated you to have wasted your time over me. I can imagine your time's jolly precious and all that.' She smiled and looked at him expectantly, waiting for him to explain why he was there. Then she looked around the room. 'I say, where's my father? I thought he'd be here to read me the riot act.'

'He's trying to make contact with the Duke of Haywater. Your brother and the Earl of Belvedere are with him now.' Deacon pulled himself up straight and looked her in the eye. 'I'm here, Miss Atherton, to investigate the murder of Lord Sneddon. His body was discovered this morning in the library by one of your maids.'

'Oh!' A stifled scream escaped from Josephine's lips and her hand flew to her face and she covered her eyes. Deacon, Rose saw, was watching her keenly. To Rose's eyes she was clearly distraught by the news and inwardly she cursed the inspector for breaking it to her so bluntly.

'He had been stabbed in the back with this.' Deacon took from the table the little gold dagger, which he held at one end, a handkerchief wrapped around the handle. It looked such a beautiful, inoffensive sort of thing. It was almost incomprehensible, Rose thought, that such an item could be a murder weapon. 'Do you recognise it, Miss Atherton? Do you recognise the murder weapon?'

Josephine's face filled with a look of horror as she nodded her head very slowly before replying. 'It's my letter opener, Inspector. I keep it on my writing desk in the library. I use it nearly every day.' She laughed a high pitched little laugh and then shuddered involuntarily. 'I shall never use it again, of course. It is quite ruined, contaminated. I want you to take it away; I never want to lay eyes on it again.'

'We shall certainly be taking it away with us for the time being,' agreed the inspector. 'It is evidence. You look shocked, Miss Atherton, if I may say so. Can I take it you were unaware of Lord Sneddon's death until now?'

'Well, yes, of course, Inspector, I would hardly have just disappeared if I had known about it, would I?'

'Well, you might have if you'd had anything to do with his death,' replied Deacon, his face taking on a serious look.

'Are you suggesting that I murdered Hugh?' exclaimed Josephine, looking at him incredulously. 'Surely you can't believe *I* killed him?'

'Perhaps not you personally,' agreed Deacon. 'Perhaps you got the chauffeur to do the deed for you.'

'Brimshaw?' Josephine paled visibly. 'Are you suggesting that our chauffeur had a hand in murdering Lord Sneddon?'

'It is a possibility, Miss Atherton, and certainly something we will be looking into.'

'Oh, this is ridiculous, Inspector. What possible reason could I, or our servant, have had to wish the man dead?'

'You must look at it from our perspective, Miss Atherton. On the very same night, probably at the very same time, that Lord Sneddon was being murdered, you took it upon yourself to up and leave in the middle of the night leaving no note or explanation for your sudden absence. That seems to me very strange behaviour, Miss Atherton, particularly as you had guests in the house. Tell me, were you intending on coming back or was there a sudden change of plan?'

'Of course I was coming back. Why, I would have been there and come back again and no one would have been any the wiser,' Josephine said, desperately.

'"Would have" I think you said, Miss Atherton,' said Deacon, looking at her sternly. 'Do I take it that you set off later than you were intending to?'

'Much later, yes. I had wanted to set off considerably earlier but people were still up and about. Everyone had retired to bed quite early but then they all seemed to start getting up and moving around again.'

'Give me a few examples if you will, Miss Atherton.'

'Well, the first time I was pretty sure that the whole household had gone to bed including the servants but, when I crept down the stairs to make sure, I heard Crabtree talking to Hugh. The library door was slightly ajar. I didn't stop and listen to what they were saying but Hugh sounded rather upset. Well, then I went upstairs and waited some more and was just about to go downstairs again when I heard Rose's door open and her go downstairs. I'm afraid I was rather annoyed with you, Rose,' Josephine said looking up. 'Particularly as you didn't return straightaway. Well I waited some more, heard you come back and go into your room and then was just about to come out again when I heard Isabella's door open. Her room is next to mine. Well, I waited an age for her to come back, I can tell you, and then when she did I pretty well ran down the stairs and went out of the house.'

'What time was this?'

'About two o'clock, I think. But it could have been earlier. I remember thinking it was jolly late. I almost thought about not going at all.'

'I'll come on to that later. Now, did you happen to go past the library when you left the house?'

'Yes.'

'And was Sneddon there alone or was someone with him?'

'I don't know, the door was shut. Someone might have been in there with him but I'm afraid I didn't hear anything.'

'You didn't happen to go into the room yourself by any chance?'

'And pick up my letter opener and plunge it into his back?' asked Josephine. 'No, I didn't Inspector. The last time I laid eyes on Lord Sneddon was when I left the drawing room after dinner to go to bed, and he was very much alive then.'

'What about Brimshaw?'

'What about him?'

'Didn't you let him in to help you carry your suitcase down the stairs?'

'No, I managed that myself, Inspector. I would have liked him to have carried it for me, of course, but it was too risky. If he'd been caught, he couldn't have explained why he was there. His living quarters are above the garage, you see.'

'Yes, I see that. So you staggered with your suitcase down the stairs and then what did you do?'

'I let myself out of one of the little side doors. Crabtree's a bit of a stickler for locks and bolts and things, and it is one of the only doors that's not bolted. I didn't want to make any unnecessary noise, you see, pulling back the bolts and all that.'

'So you just unlocked the side door with a key, I assume?'

'Yes, and I locked it behind me too. I knew Crabtree would be annoyed in the morning if he found the door unlocked.'

'You're sure you locked it?'

'Absolutely, Inspector. I tried the handle a couple of times just to make sure.'

'I see. What did you do with the key, Miss Atherton?'

'It's here, Inspector.' With that, she produced it from her handbag.

'Did you lend it to anyone while you were away from here?'

'No, I've had it with me all the time in my bag.'

'So, what happened after you let yourself out and locked the door behind you?'

'Brimshaw was waiting for me on the other side of the door. The poor man had been waiting for me for ages. I was rather surprised to see him still there, to tell you the truth. I half thought he might have given up waiting for me and gone back to the garage. But he was still there.'

'And then what?'

'Why, he took the suitcase from me and we walked over to the garage, of course, loaded up the car and set off on our journey.'

'And where exactly was this journey to?' enquired Deacon.

There was silence. For the first time during the interview Josephine refused to answer.

'Come, come, Miss Atherton, you'd do well to tell me. You said a few minutes ago that you had hoped to have returned before anyone was aware that you were missing. And yet you took a suitcase with you which we know from your maid was filled with a number of your clothes and jewels. That seems to indicate that there was a possibility at least that you intended to go for a very long time. In fact, perhaps you intended never to come back. Your brother and Miss Simpson here were certainly of that opinion.'

Josephine looked at the floor and still said nothing.

'When you came in just now, before you knew we were here, you said you were going to go and explain to your father where you'd been,' said Deacon becoming exasperated. 'Explain to me now, Miss Atherton, if you will.'

'Yes, but that was before …'

'Before what, Miss Atherton?'

'Before …'

'Before you'd heard about the murder.'

'Yes.' Josephine bit her lip and looked pale.

'And now that you have, you won't tell me where you were?'

'I'm sorry, Inspector, but no I won't.'

'Miss Atherton. May I remind you that this is not some game? A man was brutally murdered in this house at the same time that you were, at the very least, passing the door. By what you are saying, or not saying, to be more precise, your very journey or destination seems to have had some bearing or connection with this man's death. I need to know where you went and why you set off at such an unusual hour when your house was full of guests.'

'I'm very sorry, Inspector. I'm not meaning to be awkward, really I'm not, but I'm afraid I can't say anything yet. I need to think things through first.'

184

'Miss Atherton –'

The conversation was interrupted by the constable knocking on the door and coming in somewhat apologetically, requesting that the Inspector come out of the room at once so that he might have a few words with him in private. The Inspector gave a quick glance at Josephine. It appeared to Rose that for a moment he had forgotten her own presence in the room. Later she wondered whether things would have happened any differently if he had demanded that she leave the room with him, rather than leaving her to converse with Josephine in his absence.

'Stay where you are, if you will, Miss Atherton,' Deacon said and, without giving a backward glance at Rose, he left the room.

'Rose, what should I do?' Josephine cried desperately, as soon as the door had closed behind the policeman. 'Is it really true? Is Hugh really dead? Murdered! I just can't believe it, there must be some mistake. Are they absolutely sure he was killed with my letter opener? Couldn't he have just tripped and hit his head against the fireplace or some such thing? It's the sort of thing men do all the time, isn't it, particularly when they've been drinking which I assume Hugh had been.' She put her hand to her face. To Rose's alarm, she saw the girl was shaking.

'No, Josephine, there's no mistake.' Rose walked over to her and took her hand. 'He was found slumped over the desk with your letter opener in his back. But what do you mean by asking what you should do? You must tell the inspector the truth, of course. You must tell him where you went and the reason for your leaving so abruptly. I'm afraid, you see, that it all looks so very suspicious. It makes it look as if you've got something to hide.'

'Perhaps I have,' said Josephine rather ominously. Rose found herself shrinking back from her slightly. Josephine noticed her reaction and clung to her hand tightly, almost making the girl wince. 'Please, Rose, you have nothing to be afraid of. It's just that I've got to think very carefully about things, that's all, before I say anything to that inspector. Everything's such a muddle. I don't know what's important and what isn't. But what I do know is that I have got to sort everything out in my mind first before I say anything. I know I'm not being very fair on you, by not telling you what this is all about, but you must help me, please. You must tell me what I can say to the inspector to make him leave me alone, if only for a little while. He's trying to force the truth out of me and I can't tell him, I can't, at least not now. I want to be left alone. I need to make sense of everything.' She looked up beseechingly at Rose clearly at her wits end. Rose felt a certain pity towards her and was somewhat alarmed at her pathetic state. This was not the same Josephine who had welcomed her to Dareswick. 'Please, Rose, I'm desperate. I think I'll go mad otherwise, quite mad.'

'Well,' said Rose, hesitating slightly, 'there is one thing that you could do although I think you may find it rather embarrassing. But if you stick to your story I think Inspector Deacon may leave you alone, at least for the time being.'

'And what's that?' Josephine asked eagerly, clinging at the sleeve of Rose's dress. 'I'll say anything so long as it means I'll be left alone to think.'

'When it was realised that you had gone missing, there was some idle speculation that you might have eloped with the chauffeur,' Rose said, colouring a little.

'Eloped with Brimshaw?' Josephine looked appalled at the suggestion and went crimson. 'I mean, he's a jolly decent fellow and all that, he's quite handsome, but I'd –'

'I don't believe anyone seriously believed that you'd eloped with him,' Rose said, quickly. 'But you could pretend you had to Inspector Deacon, just for a little while. It would buy you some time to think what to do. But, Josephine, I beg you to tell the inspector the truth. He's very reasonable, you know, for a policeman I mean. Cedric and I have had dealings with him before. He investigated that awful business at Ashgrove. He's jolly decent. Anyway, you'll have to decide quickly what you're going to do because, unless I'm mistaken, I can hear him coming back.'

Rose hurried back to her chair while the door opened and Deacon came in.

'Ah, Miss Simpson, I had forgotten you were here. How very remiss of me.' He stared at her suspiciously and Rose had the decency to blush. 'Now where were we, Miss Atherton? Ah, yes, you were about to tell me what was so urgent that you had to set off at the dead of night and where exactly you have been.'

Josephine took a deep breath and blushed.

'Rose has just been telling me that I must tell you the truth, Inspector, no matter how embarrassing I might find it. She insisted that it was essential to your investigation that I tell you everything and, what is more, that it was my duty to do so.'

'Very good,' Deacon said slowly, turning to stare at Rose for a moment. To Rose, he did not look or sound completely convinced by what Josephine was saying but had obviously decided to let it pass.

'It's all rather embarrassing, I'm afraid,' said Josephine quickly, as if she were afraid that she would change her mind. She put her hand up to the side of her face. 'I do hope that you will keep this to yourself, Inspector. I should so hate my father to find out. It's not the sort of thing he'd understand at all.' Deacon said nothing, he did not even give a slight nod of the head or mutter of encouragement. Josephine, having bitten the bullet, decided to plough on regardless. 'It all sounds rather sordid but really it's not. You see, Brimshaw ... eh, that's to say James, and I, well, we've sort of fallen for each other.'

'Indeed?'

'Yes, awfully inappropriate I know, and Father will be frightfully cross if he finds out, but there you are, one can't really help who one falls in love with, can one?'

'I suppose not.'

'Well, there you have it, Inspector. Brim ... James and I, we just couldn't bear it any longer, all the secrecy and everything, you know, making do with snatched moments and all that. We decided that we had to be together properly. I knew Father would never stand for my marrying the chauffeur, he's awfully old-fashioned about that sort of thing, almost Edwardian in fact. So there really was nothing for it. If we wanted a life together, and we did, really we did, well there was only one thing we could do. We just had to elope. You do see that, don't you?'

'But what I don't understand, Miss Atherton, supposing your story to be true, and I must admit that I do have certain reservations in believing what you are telling me,' Deacon paused and turned to raise his eyebrows at Rose before turning back to Josephine, 'is why you chose to elope this weekend of all weekends, when your house was full of guests and all the family were here. Why didn't you choose a weekend when your father and sister were in town and your brother in Oxford? You wouldn't have had to leave at the dead of night then.'

'You make a jolly good point, Inspector, and what you say is very true,' agreed Josephine, looking rather desperate, 'And of course that's what we were planning to do, only our plans were a bit upset by the arrival of Lord Sneddon.'

'Ah,' said Deacon, sounding interested for the first time since he had re-entered the room. 'Now I think we may be getting somewhere.'

'Yes, you see I'm afraid I got terribly upset by it all. I couldn't believe that Hugh was engaged to be married to my sister. It was all rather a shock. There was a time, you see, Inspector, when I thought he was rather keen on me and I had feelings for him myself and I, well, hoped that one day … well, you can imagine what I hoped for. And then to discover that he was going to marry my sister and to know I was going to be forced to spend the whole weekend being nice to them, pretending that I didn't mind at all, when really I minded a great deal. To have to wish them well and pretend that it was the greatest news ever. I just couldn't bear it. So I told James that if his feelings for me were genuine then I wanted us to elope immediately, and so we did.'

'That's all very well, Miss Atherton, but if that's the case, what made you come back to Dareswick? Why aren't you in Manchester or Dublin or on board a ship heading somewhere further afield?'

'Well …' Josephine began, not at all sure how to continue, her imagination now completely having run dry.

'They had second thoughts,' Rose said, helpfully. 'Josephine's just been telling me all about it. When it came to the crunch, they just couldn't go through with it. Josephine found she didn't want to leave Dareswick and her family forever, which is what it would have meant, of course. And Brimshaw found that he rather liked being a chauffeur and didn't really want the responsibility yet of providing for a wife.'

'Yes, Inspector,' Josephine agreed, readily. 'We found that we had made the most awful mistake. So Brimshaw is going to continue working here until he gets another position and we're just both going to pretend that nothing of this sort ever happened. You won't tell anyone, will you, Inspector, especially not my father? He won't take it at all well. It's just so embarrassing, I just don't want to think about it.'

'Miss Atherton, if you do know anything about what happened here last night, or are connected with Lord Sneddon's death in any way, then I must advise you that it would be in your best interests to tell me everything you know this moment. Not only is it withholding evidence but, more importantly from your perspective, it may place you in considerable danger. I do not want to find that we have another murder on our hands.'

He was not to know then that his fears were to prove quite founded.

Chapter Twenty-nine

'Well, Lane, what did you find out from the chauffeur?' enquired the inspector, as soon as Lane had come back into the study. He had let Josephine and Rose go shortly before, his dire warning ringing in their ears. 'A deal more than I found out from Miss Atherton, I hope.'

'So she wasn't very cooperative?' asked his sergeant, 'or was the reason for her going all rather mundane and not connected with the murder at all?'

'I'm pretty sure there is a connection between Sneddon's murder and her sudden departure, but for the life of me I can't think what it can be. She seemed genuinely shocked to hear about Sneddon's death. I'm sure she didn't know about it before she left. It's possible I suppose, that she sent Brimshaw back into the house to get something for her and wonders whether he might have done Sneddon in, but I don't think so.'

'Did she tell you why she had left so suddenly or where she went, sir?'

'Not really, Lane. She gave me some cock and bull story about eloping with this Brimshaw fellow and choosing to go when she did because her nose was put out of joint by Sneddon getting engaged to her sister after he'd been dallying with her affections some months before. To tell you the truth, I didn't believe a word of it. I think our Miss Simpson suggested she gave us that story.'

'Do you think Miss Simpson suspects she is guilty and is trying to protect her?'

'Yes, I do. Certainly she seemed very worried about her friend. If I'm honest, I forgot for a moment that Rose was in the room.' Lane looked up and raised his eyebrows, slightly taken aback by the inspector's use of Miss Simpson's Christian name. Deacon, it appeared, was oblivious to having done such a thing. 'I reckon the inspector's got a soft spot for her,' the sergeant would later tell his girl when they returned to London, 'you mark my words if he hasn't.' Now, though, he said nothing and the inspector continued. 'It was damned stupid of me, of course. One of the constables called me out of the room to show me quite a vast sum of money that they had discovered in Miss Atherton's luggage. So the two of them had the opportunity to get together and concoct the story of her eloping with the chauffeur.'

'Still, it looks as if she was going away somewhere, doesn't it?'

'Yes, going away and not coming back by the looks of it. I wonder where she was going and what made her change her mind. Was that Brimshaw chap able to tell you anything?'

'Not much. He said Miss Atherton called on him shortly before dinner at the garage. It gave him quite a turn to see her there, he said. She was all dressed up for dinner in a long velvet gown, he told me, and there he was looking a right mess with his shirtsleeves rolled up and wiping his hand on a greasy rag having been tinkering with the car. He was that afraid, he said, that she'd get oil or grease on her nice dress.'

'Yes, well, never mind about all that,' said Deacon, impatiently. 'What did she say?'

'She wanted him to drive her up to London as soon as the house had retired to bed. He tried to suggest that they go up first thing in the morning instead, but she was having none of it. She said that it was very urgent that she made the journey that night, and anyway she wouldn't have the opportunity to get away the next day, not with the guests and her brother and sister being here. She said that they would be back before the house rose for the day, so no one would be any the wiser and she was quite happy for him to have a lie in today.'

'I gather then from what you are saying that there never was any intention of their eloping?'

'None whatsoever, sir. I put that very question to the man and he denied it emphatically, he did. I'm sure he wasn't lying either. He looked very shocked at the suggestion and was worried in case Mr Crabtree was of the same view and he'd lose his job.'

'What did he tell you happened?'

'He said as how Miss Josephine told him to wait by the side door and that she would come out to him as soon as the coast was clear. He had to wait so long for her to appear that he thought she'd changed her mind. He was about to return to the garage when she appeared. He said it gave him a bit of a fright to see her carrying a suitcase, given that it was only supposed to be a flying visit, but she reassured him that it was unlikely that she'd be staying in town. But that if she was she'd give him a message to take back to her father.'

'I see, interesting. So it was by no means certain that Miss Atherton would be running away, so to speak, just a possibility. It's beginning to sound to me, Lane, that the girl had been jilted or was beginning to feel that she had been jilted. Anyway, when she appeared at the door, did he say whether she appeared agitated or in shock as she would have been if she had just killed Sneddon.'

'No, sir, he didn't think so. I put that very question to him and he said that she was anxious and excited, as one would expect given the circumstances, but nothing else. And he assured me that he himself never had any occasion to go into the house. He just waited for her outside the door.'

'Well, what happened when they got to London, Lane? Where did she go?'

'Well that's just it, sir, he doesn't rightly know. As soon as they arrived she got him to stop the car and hail a cab for her. She gave him some money and told him to wait for her at a hotel. He was to snatch a few hours' sleep and she'd meet him in three or four hours' time to either take her back to Dareswick with him, or to take back a note to her father. He says he was very apprehensive about letting her go out into the night by herself, but that she had been most insistent.'

'Did she turn up as arranged?'

'Yes. Brimshaw said she was in a dreadful state. Her eyes were red and swollen and she was sniffing and dabbing her nose and her eyes with a handkerchief. It was obvious that she'd been crying. She was dreadfully pale too, as if she had received something of a shock. The chauffeur says his heart went out to her, but that he said nothing and pretended that he hadn't noticed anything was amiss. He said she sobbed quietly in the back of the car all the way back to Dareswick.'

'And yet, when she arrived, she gave no indication that she was in so much distress,' Deacon said, thoughtfully, crossing to look out of the window. 'It is very lovely here. I can imagine that anyone would have reservations about leaving this place. But it does look as if she was planning to run away. However, for some reason or other, she didn't see it through. And goodness knows how but I am absolutely certain it's all connected with Sneddon's death in some way.'

As soon as they had left the study, Josephine made her excuses and said she was going upstairs to her room. She asked Rose to make it clear to everyone, with perhaps the exception of her father, that she did not wish to be disturbed. Rose, who had no wish to encounter the baron in a bad temper due to the various antics of his daughter, was relieved to find that he was still holed up with Cedric and Hallam, trying to get hold of the elusive duke. She was glad that she was not with them, for she understood from snatches of conversation she overheard between Crabtree and Mrs Hodges that the baron was getting very agitated and concerned that the duke would hear the news about his son's sad demise first from the papers rather than from himself.

With time to herself, she tried to make sense of Josephine's position regarding the murder. She could not help but remember that shortly before Josephine's arrival she had decided that she was the most likely person to have killed Sneddon. But she was sure that Josephine had been genuinely shocked to hear the news about Sneddon's death. She was equally certain that his murder had also made her less forthcoming about where she had been and why she had felt the need to set off as she had in the middle of the night. There must be some connection, only what was it? The girl was scared. It seemed to Rose, that Josephine had feared the worse and then discovered that her fears had been realised.

Rose was conscious that she had still not disclosed to Inspector Deacon that Josephine had known that Sneddon was blackmailing her sister into marrying him and that she had advised her that she would deal with the matter. What was more, and Rose blushed the more she thought of it, she had deliberately provided Josephine with an excuse as to why there had been a need for her to run away as she had done. Deacon had not been fooled. He had seen through the ruse immediately and no doubt she had fallen even further in his eyes. But Josephine had been desperate, had cried out to her for help. What was she to do? Josephine was involved in it all, she felt sure, but was she really responsible for Sneddon's death?

'I don't think there's any more we can do today,' said Deacon, stretching his arms behind his head, stifling a yawn. It seemed to him that he had been sitting at a desk pretty well all day. He resolved to go for a walk when he got home. If nothing else, it would be an opportunity to think over the case. 'It's been a long day for everyone. Let's leave the Athertons and their guests to their dinner, and we'll come back here bright and early tomorrow. Hopefully that Ricketts chap will be caught trying to leave and we'll discover who else he and Sneddon were blackmailing. If we find that out then I think we'll find our murderer. Right, have you got the men stationed and waiting?'

'Yes, sir, there's no way he'll be able to leave Dareswick without being caught.'

'Good, well let's get on and tomorrow we can see what the new day brings.'

Unfortunately, although neither policeman knew it at the time, it was to bring another death.

'I don't know what we're going to do about serving dinner tonight, Mrs Hodges,' Crabtree said, looking about the room in search of the whisky bottle as if its physical presence would be enough to steady his nerves without him even having to take a sip. Although he did promise himself that he would pour himself a very small measure as soon as the housekeeper's back was turned, for medicinal purposes only, of course, for he was still reeling from the shock of a murder having occurred in a house where he was butler.

'Oh, what's the matter now, Mr Crabtree?' Mrs Hodges sighed, 'Haven't we got enough to worry about without something else cropping up?'

'Sidney's come down with his cold again. Sneezing something rotten he was just now,' said the butler. 'I packed him straight off to bed. We can't have him spluttering into the food tonight while he's serving. But I daren't have young Robert do it. The baron's sure to notice and I'm afraid that he's in rather a foul mood about this tragic business.'

'Can't say I blame him. Hardly likely to encourage a flurry of guests, is it, not if one gets himself murdered in your house, even if he does bring it on himself what with all his shenanigans and –'

'Thank you, Mrs Hodges,' said Crabtree quickly, suddenly aware that Sneddon's manservant was lurking in the shadows. 'The problem we have is that there is no one to help serve dinner. I suppose one of your housemaids might do but –'

'I'll do it, Mr Crabtree.'

'*You!*' Ricketts had appeared at his shoulder so suddenly that it was all the butler could do not to jump into the air with fright. He looked disparagingly at the man and his attire. 'What do you know about waiting on table? And look at yourself, man! You look completely dishevelled, not to say dirty. You'd be enough to put the master and his guests off their food and I'd hazard a guess that you're a clumsy fellow. You'd probably end up ladling the soup into their laps.'

'Like the other fellow did, Robert's his name isn't it, and that's his normal job too,' retorted Ricketts with a sneer. 'Ah, give us a chance, Mr Crabtree. I'm sure you've got a nice suit of clothes I could change into and I'll go and have a wash now and comb my hair. I'm telling you, you won't recognise me. I scrub up very well when I want to, I can tell you. And I've helped out at my cousin's public house once or twice, waited at tables, collected glasses and the like.'

'Waiting at table in a public house is hardly the same as waiting at table in a grand house like this,' Crabtree said huffily. 'It's not the same thing at all.'

'Ah, go on, Mr Crabtree. I'm a quick learner, I am. You just go through with me now what I've got to do. I won't let you down, I promise. And to tell you the truth, I'm awful bored, what with my master being dead and all, I've had nothing to do all day.'

'Other than being interviewed by the policemen.'

'Oh, give him a chance, Mr Crabtree,' said Mrs Hodges, who had been watching the exchange with interest. 'It's not as if you've got much choice after all, is it? And there's no soup on the menu tonight. Mrs Gooden didn't want to risk it after what happened last night. You needn't decide right now. See how the fellow scrubs up first. If he looks halfway presentable and can master the basics when you go through it with him, well, as I say, you've nothing to lose.'

'Well,' said Crabtree, visibly wavering, but still looking at Ricketts rather doubtfully. 'I think we have a spare suit of livery that might fit this fellow. But make sure you wash yourself thoroughly, young man, I don't want it ruined. And then we'll see if you're the quick learner you claim to be.'

'Ah, thank you Mr Crabtree, you won't regret it,' Ricketts said, with an insolent grin on his face.

Crabtree sighed. He had a feeling that he was going to regret it very much indeed.

Dinner was an uncomfortable meal for all concerned. Josephine had come down for it but just sat there picking at her bread roll, eating very little, and saying even less. It transpired that she had given her father a half-hearted explanation for her disappearance. She had told him that she had left to attend a party in town that she had thought he might not wholly approve of and that, in order to disguise what she was doing, she had delayed setting off until everyone had gone to bed, including the servants, with the intention of returning before the house was up. No one would have been any the wiser had they not had the misfortune to encounter a nail or some other such bit of metal in the road, which had resulted in one of the tyres getting a puncture. This mishap had considerably delayed their return. That no one, probably not even the baron, believed this explanation seemed immaterial. It had been given and, to all intents and purposes, accepted. Only Isabella, Rose noticed, glanced at her sister suspiciously every now and then as if trying to work out from her expression what had really happened. Hallam and Cedric, Rose supposed, were just grateful that Josephine had returned safely and that the baron had not made too much of a fuss about it all.

Rose was somewhat surprised to see Sneddon's valet, Ricketts, enter the room in a rather ill-fitting livery. The man looked slightly more presentable than he had done the last time she had seen him, although his hair was still unruly and he appeared on edge. It brought back memories of Robert's behaviour on the night she had arrived and she noticed that the butler was watching him like a hawk, as he had done the other young footman. She looked around at the others seated at the table. If they had noticed that they were being attended to by a different footman than usual then they gave no sign. Clearly they had not noticed that the man was in an excited state or that Crabtree was watching his every move with a look of barely concealed anxiety. Instinctively, Rose knew that something was going to happen.

At first it looked as if her fears had been unfounded. The first course of fried whiting was served without incident, as was the entrée of veal cutlets. Rose saw the butler visibly relax, for indeed Ricketts appeared an able footman despite his scruffy appearance and insolent manner. Rose found herself breathing a sigh of relief. But she had acted prematurely. The second course of a haunch of mutton had just been served and Ricketts had moved to Isabella with the dish of vegetables for her to help herself when catastrophe struck. Whether it was his fault or hers was unclear to the observers, for one moment everything seemed all right and the next the dish had become dislodged from Ricketts' grasp and buttered carrots and green beans fell onto the tablecloth and a few onto Isabella's lap. The girl let out a shriek and leapt up from her seat. A contrite and humiliated Ricketts passed her a dinner-napkin to dab at her soiled dress. Isabella grabbed the napkin, looked at it with disgust, and threw it onto the table before hurrying out of the room. The gentlemen, who had risen from their seats when she had, sat down and looked about them awkwardly.

'Shouldn't someone go after her, Josephine?' asked Cedric. 'Shouldn't you?'

'Oh, she'll be fine,' snapped Josephine unkindly. 'You men do make the greatest fuss about the littlest things. It was only some vegetables, for goodness sake. Her dress is hardly ruined. Her maid will see to her and she will be back in no time, you'll see, wearing another wonderful creation.'

Rose looked at her with surprise but said nothing. Meanwhile the baron was berating poor Crabtree, who was looking utterly dejected and being very apologetic as if the mishap had in some way been all his fault.

'I say,' said Cedric, when he had managed to snatch a few words with Rose in the dining room as they were having coffee, 'have you heard the explanation that Josephine gave her father for disappearing from the house like she did? It's a lot of old rot if you ask me. Josephine's never been one for parties, at least not the sort that the baron wouldn't approve of, that's more Isabella's game. Did she tell the police where she'd really gone? Have you been sworn to secrecy?'

'No,' answered Rose. 'She didn't want to tell them, especially when she heard about what happened to Lord Sneddon. Inspector Deacon was called out of the room for a few moments by one of the constables, and she took the opportunity to ask me what she should say. I suggested she tell them that she had eloped with Brimshaw and then thought better of it.'

'You never did!' Cedric looked shocked. 'Let's hope that the baron doesn't get wind of that story or he'll throw her out and the chauffeur too. Although,' he looked over at the baron, who was being comforted by his eldest daughter, 'perhaps he has decided to let bygones be bygones. You know, because she came back of her own accord. Perhaps he'd rather pretend that it didn't happen. He's dreadfully worried, you know, that we'll have crowds of pressmen here tomorrow. We never did get hold of the duke to tell him about his son. His secretary was right, he was at death's door. He died this afternoon without hearing the news. Perhaps it was a blessing. I say, I wonder who will inherit the title now. I wonder if he's a suspect, you know, in Sneddon's murder?'

Chapter Thirty

'Mr Crabtree, Mr Crabtree!' Robert came running into the servants' hall, narrowly missing bumping into Doris in his haste. The maid, having rather an eye for the young man, secretly wished that they had collided so that she'd have been given an excuse to clutch on to him. Instead, she contented herself with giving him a coy smile, of which he was, at that moment, totally oblivious.

'Steady on, lad, you'll be bumping into the table and having my pots and pans over in a moment,' Mrs Gooden said. 'And then where'll all those breakfasts be? And they'll be hungry too, 'em upstairs. 'Ardly ate anything last night, they did, on account of the murder I reckon. Well, they'll be wanting to make up for it today now that it's all sunk in, you mark my words if they don't. They'll have empty stomachs the lot of 'em. They won't take too kindly having to wait for their breakfasts on account of it being on the floor.'

'Have you seen Mr Crabtree, Mrs Gooden? I've got to speak with him, it's urgent.'

'He's in his pantry. But don't you run, I don't want you upsetting anything or breaking anything and he won't neither.' But her words disappeared into thin air for Robert was already gone. She sighed and decided to take her frustration out on the unfortunate Doris. 'And you, miss, you can stop going all gooey eyed over that fellow. I'm sure you've got work to do. You don't want to have Mrs Hodges on your back again, now do you?'

'Mr Crabtree, Mr Crabtree.'

'What is it, Robert?' asked the butler, looking up from his self-appointed task. 'I'm counting the silver if you wonder what I'm doing. I want to make sure nothing's gone missing. I don't trust that Ricketts fellow as far as I can throw him, I don't mind telling you. Light fingered I'd say he is, and no mistake.'

'That's just it, Mr Crabtree –'

'What! Catch the blighter pinching, did you? Wait until I get my hands on him, I'll give him a piece of my mind.'

'Mr Crabtree, he's gone missing. He ain't here, not in his room, that is. I looked around his door just as I were coming downstairs. He's not there and his bed's not been slept in.'

'He's scarpered! Well, that doesn't surprise me at all. Right, you'd better give me a hand. We've even more reason to count the silver now.'

'Hadn't we better call the police? They were keeping ever such a close eye on him yesterday. Seems strange they just let him go like that.'

'Oh, I suppose so,' sighed Crabtree. 'Though they'll be back here soon enough anyway. I was just hoping that we might have had a couple of hours when we could have at least pretended that everything was back to normal, but apparently not.'

'Sir,' said Lane shurriedly as soon as Deacon had walked into Dareswick police station. 'I've just taken a call from the butler at Dareswick Hall. It seems that Ricketts fellow has gone missing. His bed hadn't been slept in, so old Crabtree told me.'

'Well, that's hardly a surprise, Sergeant,' replied the inspector, sounding relatively unconcerned. 'He'll have been picked up by one of our lot trying to make his escape. Hopefully they've discovered the blackmail stuff on him by now.'

'But that's just it, sir. They've all telephoned in and none of them have seen anything of him. He must have slipped through our fingers, sir.'

'What!' He had Deacon's full attention now. 'Get more men over there now. I want all the attics and outbuildings, follies and boatsheds searched with a fine tooth comb. No stone unturned, do you hear me, Lane?'

'Yes, sir. I reckon he's still on the premises though. He must be hiding from us. There's no way he could have got away from Dareswick without our men knowing about it, of that I'm sure.'

'He's a slippery toad, all right. It's possible that I may have underestimated him. But let's get to Dareswick and see, shall we?'

'Have you found him yet?' Deacon asked the first constable he came to at Dareswick Hall.

'No, sir, we've checked all the rooms in the house, even the ones that have been shut up, as well as the basement and the attics. There's no sign of him. One man's even been onto the roof to see if he's hiding up there. We've spread out and are searching the grounds now. Wherever he is, he can't have gone far. He's here somewhere.'

'Lane, I don't like this,' the inspector said, turning to his sergeant. 'I've got a feeling something's wrong. The sooner we find this fellow the better. Go and help them with the search, will you, I'd feel better if I knew you had your ear to the ground and were making sure they're doing it thoroughly. I don't want the man to make a run for it as soon as their backs are turned.'

Deacon wandered into the study, rang the old bell pull and requested coffee. He then proceeded to flick through the notes of the interviews Lane had made in his notebook, pausing every now and then to scribble down a salient point on a separate sheet of paper. How long he was engaged in this task, he did not know, but the noise of a disturbance in the hall made him look up at the same moment that a wild looking Lane crashed into the room, his face white.

'Good God, man, what is it?' Deacon had leapt up from his seat. 'You look as if you've seen a ghost.'

'We've found him, sir. We've found Ricketts. He was in the little boatshed by the lake.'

'Good stuff. Well, bring him in here and we'll see what he has to say for himself. Did you find anything on him? Any blackmail material?'

'I'm afraid I can't do that, sir. He won't be telling us anything. You see, when I said that we'd found him, I suppose it would have been more accurate to say that we'd found his body. He's dead, sir. He's been murdered!'

Chapter Thirty-one

'Rose, from now on I am not going to leave you for one moment by yourself,' Cedric said, holding her hand. They were sitting on a bench in the rose garden, the day surprisingly warm after the cold of the day before. 'It's quite one thing to have one murder at Dareswick but to have two! We can't cling to the notion that it could have been some strange madman who just happened to be in the vicinity, however much we might want to. Although I have to admit that my money was on that Ricketts fellow, which just goes to show how wrong I was. Your mother's never going to let you see me again. She'll think I'm a terribly bad influence or that my friends and family are the worst sort. They do seem to have a tendency to get themselves messed up in this sort of thing. You know, I bumped into that sergeant fellow, Lane, in the hall. He says there's absolutely no doubt in the police's mind now that the murderer came from within, so to speak. Apparently they had been watching Dareswick last night and no one from outside could have sneaked in without them having known about it. They were afraid Ricketts would try and make a run for it and they wanted to find out who else he and Sneddon had been blackmailing. It's a pity they weren't watching in the house rather than patrolling the various lanes and entrances to Dareswick. They might have caught the murderer in the act then.'

'So they think he was killed last night, this Ricketts fellow?' asked Rose.

'Yes, either very late last night or in the early hours of this morning, just like Sneddon the night before. They're busy doing tests and suchlike to try and narrow down the timeframe. Apparently they think he had most likely arranged to meet the murderer after everyone had gone to bed. Obviously he had in mind to do his own bit of blackmail.' Cedric paused to sigh at the man's stupidity. 'His bed hadn't been slept in. The police think that he'd arranged to meet the murderer in the old boatshed down by the lake because he was afraid they'd be disturbed if they met in the house, I suppose. Fancy being daft enough to try and blackmail the fellow. A jolly risky and foolhardy thing to do, I'd say. The man had already killed once.'

'Or woman,' said Rose, thoughtfully. 'Did you find out all this from Sergeant Lane? He seems to have been awfully forthcoming.'

'Well, from him and Crabtree. I rather got the impression from the sergeant that he was hoping that you would give them a hand like you did at Ashgrove.' He held her hand more tightly. 'I say, Rose, why don't we do it together, solve the murders, I mean. Oh, I know I won't be much good but I'll be able to keep you safe while you investigate. I'll be Watson to your Holmes.'

'You're right, Cedric. I've been putting it off rather, having a go at solving this case I mean. It's because I think the truth might prove rather unpalatable. I'm afraid the murderer is going to turn out to be someone I rather like. But I've an awful feeling that there might be more deaths unless they are caught.'

'That's a girl. Right, so where do we start, Sherlock?' Cedric asked enthusiastically.

'You know, just because I managed to work things out at Ashgrove doesn't mean that I will here. It could have just been a fluke. I'm not sure I've got a knack for it.'

'Well, I have every confidence in you and your abilities, Rose, I really do. And Sergeant Lane does too. It sounds to me like they're pretty stumped by the whole thing.'

'I suppose,' said Rose, 'that we should just go through everything that's happened since we first arrived and what our impressions have been. I must say, I think the key to all this is Josephine. I'm not saying she's the murderer, of course,' she added hastily, catching the look on Cedric's face. 'All I'm saying is that I think she knows more about this business than she's letting on. I think she may even have a very good idea who the murderer is. But it's no use trying to ask her about it, she won't say anything.'

'You're right. Hallam has been trying to get out of her what she was up to in London, and so has Isabella, I think. But she's refusing to say anything. She's shut herself up in her room and won't come out. They're both awfully worried about her.'

'Surely the police managed to speak with her about Ricketts' death?'

'Yes, I think she spoke to them briefly, but probably she just told them exactly what we all said. I mean, we all retired to bed rather early last night, didn't we? I think we were all feeling rather drained what with the shock of Sneddon's murder and everything. I assume everyone took the precaution of locking their doors and went straight to bed, I know I did. I'd be jolly surprised if anyone took part in any midnight wanderings last night, wouldn't you?'

'All except the murderer and Ricketts, of course,' Rose agreed. 'I assume Ricketts had arranged to hand over the letters, or whatever they were, for a tidy sum.'

'But why go to the trouble of killing the chap?' asked Cedric. 'Do you think Ricketts refused to hand over all the stuff or asked for more money, or something like that?'

'No, I think the murderer probably always intended to kill him. Think about it, Cedric. If the murderer killed Lord Sneddon because of this blackmail business then he probably wouldn't think twice about killing a servant. And the stakes were much higher this time, weren't they? It wasn't just that Ricketts had got hold of some information that could embarrass or humiliate them. No, he had in his possession a motive for the murder of Lord Sneddon. The murderer couldn't risk leaving him alive. Even if Ricketts did hand over all the incriminating evidence, there was nothing to stop him from telling the police all about it afterwards, was there, especially if he thought he might get a reward. Or he might have decided to tell them about it next time he was arrested for something. Did I tell you that Inspector Deacon thought he was some sort of petty criminal? No, while he lived he was always going to be a threat to our murderer.'

'Gosh, Rose, you're right. I hadn't thought about it like that.'

'I doubt whether Lord Sneddon's valet had either, otherwise he would never have agreed to meet the murderer in the boatshed, no, he'd have chosen somewhere much safer to make the exchange. He probably asked for a ridiculous amount of money or jewellery or whatever, and when he had received that he was happy to hand everything over and think no more about it. He can't have seen the danger he was putting himself in.'

'And so all the murderer had to do was just wait until Ricketts turned his back and then stab him?'

'We'll get nothing out of them, sir,' said Lane, as soon as all the interviews were over. 'Josephine Atherton refuses to tell us what she knows and none of the others have seen anything. I doubt anyone slept very well last night but, even so, they are sure to have locked themselves in. They won't have ventured out so they won't have seen anyone else creeping about when they shouldn't have been.'

'You're right, Sergeant, I think it's Sneddon's murder we'll have to concentrate on if we want to catch the murderer. I just wonder who else in this house Ricketts could have been blackmailing.'

'And apparently he was stabbed from behind again, wasn't he, sir?' said Lane, 'So it definitely looks like the same chap killed both Sneddon and his servant.'

'It does indeed. In fact, the murderer was jolly clever. Ricketts was not only stabbed in the back but he was also crouching on the floor when he was killed, so the police surgeon thinks. The fellow was stupid enough to place himself in a very vulnerable position. Do you know what I think, Lane? I think our murderer dropped some of the money or trinkets that he had taken with him to pay off Ricketts. I think he did it on purpose to make the task of killing Ricketts that much easier.'

'And of course Ricketts fell for it because he was exactly that sort of greedy, money grasping sort of scoundrel. His first instinct would have been to scurry around on the ground scooping the stuff up rather than putting his own safety first. Our murderer must have banked on that.'

'Exactly,' agreed Deacon. 'And do you know what else that tells us, Lane?'

'Oh, I think I'm right up there with you this time, sir,' laughed the sergeant. 'It means that not only was Ricketts killed in exactly the same manner as Sneddon but, just like last time, it wouldn't have required much force if Ricketts was scrabbling about on his hands and knees. So what you're thinking, sir, is that it could just as easily have been a woman who killed him, as a man?'

'You know, Cedric, I think something was worrying Josephine even before we arrived,' said Rose, as they wandered through the grounds. 'She seemed awfully nice, but dreadfully preoccupied a lot of the time. Something was definitely distracting her.'

'Hallam said she was awfully interested to find out who Isabella was bringing down with her. He didn't give it much thought at the time. I say, do you think she was afraid that it might be Sneddon? Perhaps she still had some feelings for the blighter after all.'

'Or perhaps he was blackmailing *her* too, you know as well as Isabella. Perhaps she had written letters to him that were compromising. Finding out that he was also blackmailing her sister could have been the final straw.' Rose walked in silence for a while, deep in thought. 'No,' she said at last, 'that simply will not do. When Sneddon first arrived she was just as shocked as everyone else to see him. In fact probably more so. I remember that she went very pale and looked as if she might faint. Hallam was most concerned about her if I recall. But do you know what? Something quite strange happened.'

'What was it?' Cedric stopped walking and was looking at her intently.

'I know it sounds silly, given the circumstances, and perhaps I was just imagining it. But after Josephine had got over the initial shock of seeing Sneddon again I could have sworn that she looked relieved.'

'Relieved?' Cedric sounded incredulous.

'Yes, I know it doesn't make any sense, but I'm sure for a moment she looked very relieved. Perhaps she was afraid that Isabella was bringing someone else down with her. And then almost immediately she looked worried again, but I think that was more to do with being concerned about how Hallam might react than anything else.' They carried on with their stroll. 'You know, Cedric, I don't think Josephine was nearly as fond of Sneddon as everyone's made out. Yes, I think she was flattered by his attentions, but nothing more. Why, she said almost as much to me on Saturday morning. In fact I have been rather wondering whether it might not have been the other way around.'

'You mean Sneddon was more fond of her than she was of him? Do you think, then, that she was the one to give him the brush off?'

'Yes, that's exactly what I mean. It would help explain why he went and had a dalliance with that unfortunate maid. He was put out when his advances were rejected, unrequited love and all that. That's why, I think, Sneddon felt so badly about the maid when he found out what had happened to her. He knew he had used her very ill. But it also explains something else he said to me on Saturday night, when he was being all melancholy in the library.'

'And what was that?'

'He talked about hurting the people he cared for and only realising how very much he cared for *them* when it was too late. He rather dismissed

Isabella and your sister, Lavinia, I'm afraid as being able to look after themselves. I thought at the time he was just talking about the maid but he definitely said *them,* so I think he was also referring to Josephine.'

'But, in which case, it could just as easily have meant that he had let Josephine down and now regretted it. It was the sort of thing he'd do, after all.'

'It could, yes, but I don't think so. I mean, I think he let her down to the extent that she realised the sort of fellow he was before it was too late. But I still think she broke it off. Either way, I don't think Josephine ever held deep feelings for him.'

'Then why did everyone think she did? Hallam said she became quite withdrawn after the business with Sneddon.'

'I think she felt guilty about the maid. I think she felt that had she not spurned Sneddon's advances he wouldn't have got the maid into trouble. But there's something else.' Rose stopped and looked at Cedric earnestly. 'I think she deliberately let everyone think that she had been fonder of Lord Sneddon than she had been and that he had let her down and not the other way around.'

'Why on earth would she do that? She knew how upset Hallam was about it all. I can't believe she'd be so unkind as to distress him unnecessarily.'

'She wouldn't have wanted to, of course, but I think she felt she had to. You see, Cedric, I think she had a secret of her own to hide and that it suited her purposes very well for people to think she was in love with Lord Sneddon.'

'But why?'

'Because then they wouldn't think she was in love with someone else.'

Chapter Thirty-two

'You realise, sir,' said Lane pondering, 'that we've never really thought about the Earl of Belvedere as a possible suspect, have we? And yet he could easily be one, couldn't he? I mean, we could put together a decent motive, couldn't we, if we had to? Sneddon could have been blackmailing him over revealing what really happened at Ashgrove. Or perhaps Sneddon found out that he had got a girl into trouble and threatened to tell Miss Simpson.'

'Or he decided to kill Sneddon to protect the Athertons,' suggested Deacon. 'He definitely seemed a bit worried about the Hallam boy to me. It's just the sort of misguided act he might do out of a sense of chivalry. Having said that, I can't see him stabbing Sneddon in the back in cold blood, can you? As he said when we suggested to him that Hallam Atherton might have murdered Sneddon, it wasn't a very sporting way to kill him. The man's not a coward. He'd have confronted Sneddon face to face.'

'Even so, sir, he might easily have had a motive.'

'Quite right. We won't discount him quite yet.'

'Someone else? You mean she was in love with that chauffeur fellow all along?' Cedric looked appalled. 'So they really were running away together. Goodness, I hope the baron never finds out, he'd be absolutely furious. Still, the girl obviously came to her senses before it was too late. They must have had second thoughts about the whole escapade.'

'I don't think so. I don't think Josephine has ever been in love with Brimshaw. I think she is in love with someone else.'

'Oh, crikey.' Cedric, Rose noticed, had gone rather pink. 'I suppose I ought to tell you, Rose, that there was a time, a good few years ago now, when Josephine and I were rather fond of each other. To be honest, I thought more of her as a sister than anything else. She was a jolly lot easier to get along with than Lavinia, I can tell you, and she found Isabella a little trying. The Athertons are old family friends, as I told you before, and we spent a great deal of time together. I'm just wondering whether she might have thought about me in a somewhat more romantic light. I'm not saying I'm anything to write home about, but she doesn't get to meet very many eligible young men stuck out here in the sticks, so it's just possible that –'

'I don't want to hurt your feelings, darling,' laughed Rose, 'but I'm afraid that I don't think it's you she's in love with.'

'Well that's a relief,' said Cedric, with feeling, 'especially as –'

'Yes,' said Rose quickly, going crimson. 'But I do think there is someone, or was someone. Oh, it's hard to know for sure with Josephine. But she was definitely intending to go away never to return to Dareswick, I'm sure of it, and I can only think that an unsuitable match is the only explanation. According to the maid who brought me my cup of tea this morning, Josephine took her everyday clothes together with her jewellery box. They've all been unpacked now of course. The poor girl was grumbling about the extra work. But anyway, that proves at the very least that Josephine was going to be living a different sort of life to the one she was used to. She had no need for fancy gowns and the like and obviously took her jewellery with her so that she could pawn or sell pieces when she needed to.'

'But she came back?'

'Yes, things obviously did not turn out as she had hoped they would. And what's more, I don't think she intended to leave here this weekend, not with all her family at home and guests as well. No, I think she was intending to slip away quietly. Something forced her to go when she did. I wonder what it was.'

'Hello, you two, what are you doing hiding away here? Hope I'm not intruding and all that but I'm sick and tired of being stuck in the house all day. Thought I'd come out for a bit of fresh air.' Hallam's sudden appearance made both of them jump. Rose wondered how much of their conversation he had heard. He must have heard them talking about Josephine. She felt her cheeks going red just thinking about it. Hallam must have noticed.

'Sorry, I am intruding on you two lovebirds, aren't I? I say, this hasn't been much of a weekend for you, has it?'

'It hasn't been much of a weekend for anyone, old man,' said Cedric, sympathetically.

'No it hasn't. Damn Sneddon, why did he have to get himself killed here? Why couldn't he have got himself murdered in London? Oh, I know I sound heartily callous and all that, but it's not as if any of us liked him, is it? It's terribly hard to be sad when one couldn't stand the man. The servants didn't think too much of his valet either, from what Sidney told me. Old Crabtree didn't trust him with the silver and they generally seem to have thought that he was up to no good.'

'Even so,' said Cedric, 'It's a jolly rum old thing to have happened.'

Cedric, Rose thought, looked taken aback and slightly appalled at the blasé way in which the young man was treating the murders. Rose herself thought that it was a coping mechanism. But then again, was it? Cedric knew Hallam better than she did and he was visibly disturbed by what he had just heard the boy say. And she remembered how she had put together quite a case in her head for how the boy might have been the murderer, might in a fit of anger have killed Sneddon to protect his sisters, as he would have seen it. Of course, it all boiled down to that scar of Josephine's, she thought. The evidence of a vicious, impulsive streak. It would have taken a great deal of force and anger to cause such a wound, especially considering it had been done by a child. She remembered how Josephine had spoken about it, how embarrassed and ashamed she had been, particularly on behalf of her brother.

She remembered the very words Josephine had said as she tried to dismiss the event as insignificant, as childish high spirits that had got out of hand. She remembered … that was it! She remembered suddenly what Josephine had actually said and not what she had thought she meant because, of course, they were two completely different things! Oh how stupid she had been. It was significant, she knew it was. And in that moment, as she stopped walking abruptly, much to the surprise of both Cedric and Hallam who almost walked into her, she knew she was going to solve this case because she had suddenly recognised the first clue. She had something to latch on to.

It all focused around Josephine, Rose felt sure now. Sneddon and his servant were only indirectly involved. If she concentrated her efforts on finding out what Josephine was hiding then she would discover the truth and the identity of the person who had carried out the murders, she was sure of it. She sighed. She was sitting in a chair in the billiard room, appearing outwardly to the casual observer to be engrossed in her copy of the *Woman's Weekly* magazine. Inwardly, however, her mind was whirring. Oh, how she wished Cedric wasn't being so over protective as to insist that she not be out of his sight for a moment. And so, while she was trying to concentrate on working everything out, she was constantly being put off by the noise of one or other of Cedric or Hallam either hitting the cue balls or exclaiming when they missed a shot.

But how wonderful that Cedric should be so concerned about her safety. The knowledge gave her hope that, after this was all over, there was still the possibility of a future together, there was still … But no, she must not think about that now. Her priority was to find out the murderer before he or she struck again. She shivered. This murderer was particularly dangerous, she thought. In the claustrophobic, stifling air in the house she could feel it. He would think nothing of killing again. Perhaps he had even developed a taste for death, after all one read of such things.

As far as she was concerned everything had happened on the Saturday. Indeed, so much had happened yesterday that it was hard to believe that today was only Sunday. And of course there had even been another murder. Now how had Saturday started …? She had had breakfast and arranged to meet Josephine in the gardens later so that she might fill her in on Sneddon's exploits with the maid which had had such tragic consequences. Then of course there had been the business in the library. But no, something else had happened before then, something she had completely forgotten about.

She looked up. Cedric and Hallam appeared engrossed in their game of billiards. She wondered if they would notice if she slipped out of the room for a moment. She must find Crabtree. She must ask him. She looked around desperately, trying to think up an excuse that would enable her to leave without them insisting on following her.

It seemed then, just as she was quite sure that she could not think of anything, that her very wish to see the butler had been so strong as to draw him to her, as if she had summoned him by ringing the bell. For suddenly he was standing before her informing them that, due to the interviews having run on, it was the master's intention that a late luncheon-cum-early afternoon tea be taken in the dining room in half an hour or so. Crabtree turned as if about to go but before he could vacate the room she was upon him. Part of her even was desperate enough to want to tug at his sleeve to get his attention.

'Crabtree, Mr Crabtree, please. May I have a quick word with you before you go?'

'Of course, miss, how may I be of service?' If he was surprised by the eagerness in her voice, he did not show it.

'Yesterday morning Miss Josephine was quite anxious about a letter that she was expecting but which hadn't come. I believe she asked you to send a boy over to the post office to check that it had not been mislaid?'

'Yes, miss.'

'Did he find it there? Did he have any luck?'

'No, miss. The letter was not at the post office.'

'Had she been waiting on the letter long?'

'Yes, miss. She was always sure it would arrive the next day, but it never did.' Rose noticed that he was beginning to eye her rather curiously. Likewise, when she looked up she found that both Cedric and Hallam were interested to know why she had detained the butler.

'You must think this awfully strange, all my questions about Miss Josephine's letter I mean,' she said quickly, lowering her voice slightly to avoid being overheard. 'It's just that she mentioned that she was awaiting a letter about some fancy dress outfit she had ordered. She recommended the place to me and I'm awfully afraid that I have quite forgotten its name. I don't like to trouble her at a time like this. I understand she is feeling a little unwell. I was hoping she might have mentioned its name to you.'

'No, miss,' Crabtree said, relaxing. 'All she said to me, miss, was that she was awaiting an important letter from London. I'm glad it was only about a fancy dress costume. She seemed terribly anxious about it, not like her at all, miss.'

A letter from London, so Josephine had been lying to her! She had told her she was awaiting a letter from a local shop. And yes, Crabtree was right, she had been very upset, frantic even. She had even insisted that the boot boy be sent to the post office to check for the letter. She had been most insistent on the matter, if Rose recalled correctly. How very out of character it had been. It was more the sort of thing Isabella would have done. And she remembered even at the time she had not believed the letter to be just about a fancy dress costume, as Josephine had claimed it to be. It had been the first excuse Josephine could think of, she was sure, being caught on the spot as she had been with Rose's sudden appearance in the hall while she was interrogating the butler. Josephine had been embarrassed and flustered and had realised at once that she came across as such. Indeed, she had made reference to her agitated state, said that Rose must be thinking she was making a silly song and dance about it. And she had tried to explain it away, pretended that the letter had only been about a trivial matter when really it had been about something important, something so important that its failure to arrive had left her on the verge of tears.

Crabtree, deciding his presence was no longer required, had left the room. Rose meanwhile was thinking furiously. Josephine had been waiting anxiously for a letter, the contents of which were so important to her that she had refused to accept that the letter had not been sent, preferring to believe that it had been lost in the post rather than never written. And she had deliberately tried to hide from Rose what it was about and that it had come from London. The eagerly awaited letter from London had never arrived and, on the very same day that Josephine had been questioning Crabtree as to its possible whereabouts and the action to be taken to try and retrieve it, she had run off to London in the dead of night. The two things must be connected. It was too much of a coincidence if they were not. But there must be something else, Rose decided, to make her act so impulsively and irrationally, traits that one did not usually associate with Josephine. So it had certainly been a contributory factor in Josephine's sudden departure, but not the overriding one, Rose decided on reflection. There must have been something else that had made her decide to up and leave when she did, the house being full of her family and guests as it was. And she mustn't forget that Josephine had been prepared to forsake Dareswick forever, to steal out into the night, never to return. For she had taken with her a suitcase of practical clothes and jewellery that could be sold or pawned when times were bad.

And yet she had come back to Dareswick. Why *had* she come back? Had she known when she set off that there was a possibility that she would come back, that she would not see through what she was determined to do? And had it been her decision or had the decision to return been forced on her? It seemed most likely that she had been depending on someone else and that person had let her down.

It was no use dwelling for the time being on who that other person could be, Rose decided. What she must do instead was ascertain the other factors that had persuaded Josephine to take flight when she did. Well, that shouldn't be too difficult for Josephine had spent most of the day with her, one way or another.

Rose was roused from her contemplations by the clatter of cues on the billiard table. The game and match were over and Cedric was patting Hallam on the back and congratulating him. Rose wondered idly whether Cedric had let the boy win. Hallam then said that he had some letters to write and left to go to his room.

'I say, Rose,' Cedric said, coming over to her. 'Hallam going off to write letters has reminded me that I've got some to do as well. I was going to put them off until tomorrow but I'd rather get them over and done with now, I think. But I have no intention of leaving you by yourself. I expect the library's still locked, don't you, and even if it isn't I don't think either of us would much fancy using it after what's happened. I think there's a little sitting room that Hallam's mother used to use sometimes to sew in and do embroidery. Perhaps we could find that and you can finish reading your magazine while I write my letters.' He smiled and drew her towards him, holding her hands in his. Rose felt a tingle run up her spine. If only there had not been these murders, if only …

'More to the point,' Cedric was continuing, 'are you having any luck, Sherlock, in solving these murders? I looked up once or twice during our game of billiards to catch your eye and make sure you weren't getting too bored just sitting there. But you didn't see me at all. You were deep in thought and then you accosted poor old Crabtree. I could tell you had your detective hat on and wondered if you had decided who the murderer was and were going to make a pronouncement or something there and then.'

'You may mock me,' said Rose, laughing despite everything, 'but I admit I was thinking about it all, you know, turning it all over in my mind and trying to make some sense out of some of it. I think I may be getting somewhere with the mystery of the disappearing Josephine element but I have a way to go. So, yes, I'll carry on trying to do that while you write your ever so important letters. Lead on Watson.'

The moment of frivolity, however, was soon over as they walked out of the room, along the corridor and into the hall. Death seemed to hang in the air here, heavy and sombre. Rose cast a glance at the closed library door and thought of the horror that had taken place behind it. She remembered too the distraught, broken figure of the man she had left to repent and face his demons. They couldn't go on pretending it was some sort of game. It was far too serious and tragic for all that. She owed it to Lord Sneddon to find his murderer. She looked up at Cedric and saw that he too had been affected by the atmosphere for he had gone pale and there was no trace of a smile on his face.

He led the way off the hall and they walked in silence down a short corridor that Rose had not noticed before. Cedric was going to write letters and she was going to try and think. Letters … letters seemed to have featured a great deal this weekend, she thought. First, Josephine had been waiting desperately for a letter that had never arrived, and then Isabella had been blackmailed by letters that she must have heartily wished she had never written. Passionate letters, if one went by the extract that Sneddon had read aloud in the library. It seemed an age ago now and yet, unbelievably, it was only yesterday. She remembered how distraught Isabella had been on hearing such words spoken by a person whose sole purpose had been to embarrass her and ensure that she did his bidding. How had the extract gone again? Now that she was trying so hard to, she could not for the life of her remember the words. And yet something was niggling at the back of her mind. She had a feeling that something had not sounded quite right when the passage had been read aloud. It had been almost right, but not quite.

Chapter Thirty-three

'Miss Simpson, Lord Belvedere.' Inspector Deacon had looked startled, springing up from his chair as soon as Rose and Cedric had burst into the study in a somewhat ungainly fashion, failing even to knock. In his surprise, Lane had dropped his notebook and Rose, without hesitating, had snatched it from the floor and thrust it back into his hands.

'Sergeant Lane, you jotted down a bit from one of Isabella's letters to Claude Lambert, didn't you? It was the same bit that I overheard Lord Sneddon reading out to Isabella in the library. Can you find it for me, please?'

The sergeant glanced at Deacon and, receiving a nod, thumbed through a few pages of his notebook until he came across what he was seeking. There then followed an uncomfortable pause with Lane turning crimson and refusing to open his mouth. It was evident to all present that he did not relish the prospect of reading out the words in question. Rose gave a sigh of impatience and snatched the book from him.

'"My darling Claude. I cannot wait until I am in your arms and your lips are on mine, to feel ..."' read Rose, much to the amusement of Cedric. 'Yes, I was right. It's overdone. It doesn't sound real. You agree with me, Cedric, don't you? It doesn't read quite right, does it? It sounds too contrived, as if it was made-up somehow, more how a person might imagine a love letter should read. I'm not making myself clear I know and you all probably think I'm being jolly silly and pedantic. But I'm sure I'm right. What's more, it seems to me to be missing a word.

'I am not quite sure I follow,' said Deacon, looking confused but also, to Rose's relief, interested.

'I think it should read: "My darling Claude. I cannot wait until I am in your arms *again* and your lips are on mine, to feel ..." It's missing the word "again". Oh, don't you see?' she asked, looking at their blank faces with exasperation. 'Otherwise it implies that Isabella has never laid in Claude Lambert's arms before.'

'She may have written the letter hurriedly and missed out the word by mistake,' suggested Deacon, looking disappointed as if he had been

216

expecting more. 'I don't think the omission of the word "again" proves anything one way or the other. What are you suggesting? That there never was a love affair?' he said, looking sceptical. 'Are you proposing that these letters are just the result of a girl's overactive imagination?'

'No,' said Rose, slowly. 'I think there was a love affair but that there is more to it than meets the eye. I don't think the situation is quite as simple and straightforward as it seems.'

The inspector frowned but said nothing. Sergeant Lane averted his gaze to his shoes, which he suddenly seemed to find interesting, and Cedric gave her a small, sympathetic smile.

She could tell that they all thought she was making something out of nothing, that she was seeing things where there was nothing to see. She didn't really blame them. There were more pieces of the puzzle to get, she knew, before she could rearrange them and try and piece them together. But she was on to something, she was sure. It was all beginning to come together, whatever they might think. And then she would show them that her instincts had been right all along. She shivered. It would be nice to be proved right, but she was apprehensive as to how it would all end.

'You think I made rather a fool of myself in front of the policemen, don't you?'

'No … not exactly,' replied Cedric, choosing his words carefully. They were aimlessly wandering the grounds again, not sure what else to do given the circumstances.

'Oh, I know I sounded ridiculous. Why, what I was saying even sounded ridiculous to me, but I know I'm right. Now I've just got to figure out what to do now.'

'You've always said that you think Josephine holds the key. We've got to find out what made her run off to London when she did.'

'We know that the missing letter contributed to her departure, but what else I wonder. I've been thinking over the talk I had with her in the garden yesterday morning, just after I had overheard Lord Sneddon blackmailing Isabella in the library. She was preoccupied about something then, I'm sure of it. She didn't really give me her full attention until I told her what I had overheard.'

'Wait a minute, Rose. Are you telling me that you told Josephine about Sneddon blackmailing her sister into marrying him?'

'Yes, I —'

'Then she knew about the blackmail business before Sneddon was killed?'

'Yes, she made me promise I wouldn't tell anyone. She said she'd sort it out. That's why I didn't tell you about it. I wanted to of course but I —'

'Oh, my God, Rose, do you know what this means?' Cedric put his head in his hands.

'Yes, it gives her a very strong motive for killing Lord Sneddon, I know. But I'm sure she didn't do it, at least I hope she didn't. I so very much want her not to be guilty.'

'Do the police know?'

'No, I haven't told them. I know I should have but somehow I couldn't bring myself to do so.'

'Well, that's something, I suppose. I say, Rose, you don't think she could have done it, do you? I mean to protect Isabella and all that?'

'I did wonder. You know it was all rather odd come to think about it.'

'What was?'

'Well,' said Rose, 'she never once asked why Lord Sneddon was blackmailing Isabella into marrying him.'

'She must have realised it was for her money. Sneddon was jolly hard up, you know.'

'Yes, but Josephine wasn't to know that, was she? It wasn't something Sneddon liked to broadcast, was it?'

'I suppose not,' said Cedric, pondering. 'She may have thought Sneddon wanted to marry her sister because she's considered quite a beauty, although I have to admit I've never seen it myself. I've always found her rather trying which has probably clouded my judgement on her looks. But she does come from a good family. That sort of thing would matter to a fellow like Sneddon.'

Rose could not help smiling. Dear Cedric. Thank goodness that neither of those attributes mattered so very much to him, considering that she was somewhat lacking in both departments. For a moment she thought of Isabella's strong, almost fierce, beauty and her own rather pleasant plainness.

'Even so, Cedric, it seems to me a little odd, that's all. Oh, I know what you're going to say,' she added, catching his eye, 'that I am finding everything a bit strange. But even so, surely it would have been the first thing she would have asked. It's funny, you know, she seemed more interested in Isabella's letters to that Claude Lambert chap. She was visibly shocked by that. She had to sit herself down on a bench.'

'I'm not surprised, particularly if you told her some of the rot Isabella had written.'

'Yes, I did, and now I remember that Josephine said that she'd had suspicions about there being some sort of romance between her sister and this man, but that she had hoped they would prove unfounded. She was jolly upset by it all, you know. Why, she was even shaking at one point.'

'Well, the baron would have kicked up a right stink about it if he'd found out. He'd probably have disowned Isabella. Josephine was right to feel alarmed. If those letters were to fall into the wrong hands, why, all hell would have broken loose.'

'If the letters were to fall into the wrong hands … yes. You know, Cedric, perhaps that's the key to everything, the fear that the letters would fall into the wrong hands.'

'So that's it, then,' said Cedric, 'nothing else?'

'No, I don't think so.'

'It still doesn't explain why Josephine saw the need to forsake friends and family and dash off to London in the middle of the night, does it?'

'No, it doesn't, but I can't think of anything else. The rest of the day until my bumping into Lord Sneddon in the library later that night was rather uneventful.' Rose caught the look on Cedric's face. 'In the best possible way, of course,' she added. 'It was wonderful just wandering leisurely around the village. Absolutely divine. I wish the whole weekend could have been like that. It was nice Sneddon not being there to put a dampener on everything. And I know it sounds rather rotten but it made things less fraught and more relaxing Isabella being absent from the excursion. If she had been there, there would have been some tension, particularly between her and Hallam.'

'Yes, put like that, yesterday does sound rather uneventful as far as anything happening to spur Josephine to drop everything and rush off to London.'

'I doubt whether she even got the chance to confront Sneddon about the blackmail business when he came back. He didn't return until the very last minute, if you remember? He only just made it back in time for dinner.'

'So nothing else happened that you can think of?'

'No... Oh, I wonder ... but no, that was nothing. Or perhaps it was. Now that I come to think about it, perhaps something did happen, only I didn't realise the significance of it at the time. Or perhaps I'm just reading more into all this than there was.'

'I wish to goodness I knew what you were talking about. Tell me exactly what happened and then we'll be able to decide if it was significant or not.' Cedric was looking at her keenly.

'Well, Josephine decided to arrange some flowers in a vase.'

Chapter Thirty-four

'Josephine decided to replace the flowers in the drawing room. There were some rather wilted chrysanthemums in a vase that had clearly seen better days and needed throwing out. She picked some roses in the rose garden and one of the maids provided her with an old newspaper and a vase.'

'Yes?'

'Well, I was reading a magazine while she arranged the roses in the vase. She laid out the newspaper on the floor in front of her and put the dead chrysanthemums on it. I have to admit that I was only half listening to what she was saying, something about roses being one of her favourite flowers, I think. Anyway, she stood back from her arrangement to see how it looked from a distance and gave a bit of a gasp. It was loud enough to make me look up and ask her what the matter was.'

'And what was the matter?' Cedric looked torn between curiosity and wanting to yawn.

'She said that she had pricked her finger on a thorn, which she had done after she had finished examining the flower arrangement and was gathering up the wilted flowers. Then she picked up the newspaper with the dead chrysanthemums and hurried out of the room.'

'Is that all? I don't see –'

'I think that it was the first excuse she could think of. She had put all the roses in the vase and had stood back to admire them. She hadn't been holding any roses in her hands at the time, so there hadn't been a thorn on which to prick her finger. No, she'd just been gathering up the chrysanthemums in the newspaper, and chrysanthemums don't have thorns do they? And she'd been in a hurry to leave the room.'

'So what are you saying exactly?'

'I think, as she was clearing up, she suddenly caught sight of an article in the newspaper. I think it shocked her, or at the very least surprised her, and that she wanted to hurry off and read it somewhere where she could be alone.'

'And you think it was this newspaper article that made her decide to pack up her things and rush off to London as soon as she could?'

'Yes, I do. I know it probably seems a bit of a stretch of the imagination and all that, Cedric, but I think it's the only explanation for why Josephine did what she did.'

'That's all very well, but how do we find out if your theory is right?'

'We track down the newspaper and locate the article.'

Cedric was about to pull the bell pull when one of the housemaids entered the room, dustpan and brush in hand. She looked decidedly flustered when she saw them.

'Oh, I'm ever so sorry miss, my lord. I didn't think anyone would be in here. The morning room's not been used much since the mistress died. Miss Josephine and Miss Isabella prefer the drawing room and the library, they do, although I can't see either one of them ever wanting to go in the library again, not after what happened, like. I've told Mrs Hodges that I ain't ever going to set foot in there again, no fear. It was me as found him, you know –'

'Yes, yes,' said Cedric impatiently. 'It must have been awful for you, Doris, isn't it?'

'Yes, my lord.' The housemaid curtseyed rather belatedly.

'I wonder if you can help us, Doris. We're looking for a newspaper.'

'Oh, there are lots of those, Mr Crabtree keeps –'

'We're looking for a specific one,' said Rose, hurriedly, 'the one that Miss Josephine used when she was arranging the flowers to be exact. Do you know what became of it?'

'It'll have been put on one of the fires by now, miss. It wouldn't have been fit for reading, not after it had had water on it and been scrunched up with the dead flowers and whatnot.'

'I suppose that it would be too much to ask if you remember what newspaper it was and the precise edition?' asked Rose, rather hopelessly.

'Oh, of course I do, miss. It was an old copy of *The Daily,* it was. Mr Crabtree, he don't really like *The Daily*, he keeps going on about how inferior it is compared to the master's *Times*, so Pearl and me we have to sneak it in, we do, if we want to read it because he makes that much fuss about it. Anyway, I knows what edition it is 'cos it had an advertisement in it about Icilma face powder that I particularly wanted to keep. I was that cross with Pearl for giving that particular newspaper to Miss Josephine to use for her flowers without checking with me first that I'd finished with it.'

'That's all very interesting, Doris,' said Rose, 'but we really need to get a copy of that same newspaper as soon as possible. I don't suppose that there are any spares of it lying around, are there?'

'No, miss. But they get that newspaper in the house where my sister's in service. They might still have a copy of it because I know that young master Geoffrey likes to use the old newspapers for his papier-mâché, he does. He's always making model boats out of the stuff, he is.'

'Where is this place?'

'A couple of miles out of the village, miss. I tell you what, I'll send Cyril, the boot boy, if you want. He's always looking for an excuse to get out of the house and have a run about.'

'Good idea,' agreed Cedric. 'Tell him there's a half shilling in it for him if he brings back the right newspaper, and a full shilling if he's really quick.'

It was an agonising wait for Cyril, although in reality he managed to undertake the task in no time at all, the promise of a full shilling spurring him on. Cedric rewarded him handsomely on his return, especially as Doris had confirmed that he had brought back the right edition.

'What exactly are we looking for?' asked Cedric, as he and Rose pored over the pages of the newspaper.

'I'm not sure exactly,' admitted Rose, 'but I think I'll know when we find it. Let me see. The article would have needed to be big enough to have caught Josephine's eye because she wasn't looking for it. She would have been scooping up the dead flowers in it like this, and … oh, wait a minute, I think this could be it …'

'Let me see.' Cedric came over to her so that he could look at it over her shoulder as she held up the article. Rose read it aloud.

'"*London Murder Mystery*

The resources of Scotland Yard have been recruited in an attempt to solve the mysterious crime that occurred at a boarding house in Whitechapel last Thursday night, when the proprietress, a Mrs Higgins, discovered one of the boarders dead. The man, thought to be a foreigner, had been brutally stabbed. Despite extensive inquiries, the police have as yet been unable to narrow their investigations into any definite channel."'

'Oh, I say,' exclaimed Cedric, 'that sounds pretty grim. Are you sure that it was this article that caught her eye? What possible connection could Josephine have had with this crime?'

'I don't know. But it took place in London, which is where she went, and the headline would grab anyone's attention. I just have a feeling that it was this one that caught her eye.' Rose read it again. 'I wonder …' Her sentence remained unfinished as she became deep in thought.

'Yes, what do you wonder?'

'It's just an idea that I have. But I want to think about it some more before I run it past you.'

'Well, at the very least, we ought to try and find out who this murdered chap was, don't you think?'

They made their way to the study, where Inspector Deacon and Sergeant Lane looked up in surprise at the unexpected delegation. The policemen heard Rose out as she detailed her theory about the newspaper article being connected with Josephine's sudden departure to London. At the outset both appeared genuinely interested in what she had to say, although she was aware of Deacon's growing scepticism as the story progressed.

'And you surmised this all from Miss Atherton saying "Oh" and sounding surprised?' the inspector asked, raising one eyebrow incredulously. 'Did you even see her glance at the newspaper? For all you know, she just used it to put the dead flowers on and never even looked at it.'

'Oh, I know it sounds a bit far-fetched,' admitted Rose, suddenly feeling a little foolish.

'Just a bit,' agreed Deacon, rather curtly.

'Even so,' said Rose, quickly, 'you will find out who the murdered man was, won't you? You'll be able to do that easily enough. Scotland Yard are already looking into the murder. It'll probably only take you a couple of telephone calls to find out.' She stood before him excitedly, as if she expected him to make the telephone call there and then. And he probably would have done, he thought later, had not Cedric, who had remained silent during the exchange, decided to choose that moment to put his oar in.

'I say, old chap, you might as well. I mean, it's not as if you've got much else to go on, is it?'

Rose bit her lip in agitation. She knew that Cedric did not mean to sound unkind or to imply criticism, but she was awfully afraid that Deacon might take it that way. His next words confirmed her worst fears.

'That's as maybe,' Deacon said, wearily, 'but my sergeant and I have had a very long day, a couple of very long days in fact, and I'll kindly ask that you don't try and persuade us to prolong it any further.'

'But –' protested Rose.

'Don't worry, Miss Simpson, we will look into it, just not this evening. Lane, here, will telephone Scotland Yard first thing in the morning before we come here, won't you, Sergeant?' It was a decision he was later to regret.

Chapter Thirty-five

The late afternoon dragged on. There was little sign of Josephine or Isabella, who kept to their rooms, Josephine because something was obviously on her mind and Isabella, well, Rose was not quite sure why she did, other than that she did not wish to be interrogated by the others over the blackmail business. Or perhaps she just did not find the company very riveting. The baron was in a foul mood and best to be avoided. And Cedric spent most of his time with Hallam, trying to lift the boy's sagging spirits. Rose sat on the edge, a casual observer. The second murder, somewhat surprisingly she thought given that the victim was a relative stranger and not popular at that, had hit them all hard. It was difficult now for them not to acknowledge that the murderer must be one of them, although the baron at least was holding out hope that it might be one of the servants. The tension in the air was all consuming and oppressive and Rose suddenly found that she was very tired, as if she had not slept or her sleep had been fitful. She had decided to have a lie down in her room, having been escorted there by an insistent Cedric, who refused to go back downstairs until he was certain that she had securely locked her door behind him. For good measure and because Cedric had been so adamant about it, she also leaned a chair against the door lest the murderer should happen to have a key to her room.

She dozed and let her mind drift over the events of the last few days. Josephine, pleasant but preoccupied, Sneddon's unexpected arrival and the reaction that had caused, Hallam's concern that Josephine would be upset and then Josephine's own apparent indifference. Her mind wandered to the conversation she had overheard between Sneddon and Isabella concerning the blackmail, the girl's desperate, heartfelt plea that Sneddon not read the letters, and then Josephine's reaction to being told that Sneddon was blackmailing her sister into marriage and the interest she had displayed concerning the original recipient of the letters. Rose thought of Josephine's scar, ugly and hidden, and her sudden disappearance, and the newspaper article that she felt sure had in some way initiated it.

She considered Sneddon's change of heart and his wish to make amends, Isabella's general behaviour and how she had confessed to all and sundry about the blackmail, and then produced the blackmail letters triumphantly and thrown them onto the fire to prevent them being read or enabling anyone to have a hold over her again. Rose thought of the baron's temper and fury, of Hallam's hatred of Sneddon, of Isabella's wariness and downright contempt of her, and Josephine's abject misery. She considered the unfortunate Ricketts, sly and scheming, done up in his ill-fitting suit of livery that could not disguise the man he was. She remembered the inept way that he had tried to play at being a footman, and the manner in which Isabella had leapt up from the table to go and change, her dress as good as ruined as a result of the fellow's clumsiness.

It all merged together in her mind; the bits and pieces floating alongside and on top of each other until she found that it was all piecing together, as if of its own accord, until she knew what had happened and why it had happened. She sat up in her bed with a start, her hand clutching at the eiderdown. She knew. She knew with absolute certainty and clarity, as if the killer had stood before her and confessed. She knew why there had been two deaths at Dareswick, why the murderer had seen the need to kill not once but twice. But more importantly, above all else, she now knew who the murderer was.

Rose looked at her watch. She had not realised how late it was, or how long she must have dozed. The police had long departed for the day so there was no opportunity to talk to Inspector Deacon and tell him what she knew. Besides, it all sounded rather fanciful now that she went over it in her mind again to get it clear. Certainly it would involve a stretch of one's imagination. What she really needed was corroboration that her theory was correct or, better still, a confession. But first she must dress for dinner and go through the ordeal of the meal, knowing what she now knew. She must share the table with a murderer and engage in small talk and pretend that nothing was amiss.

She wondered for a moment whether to tell Cedric but she could well imagine his look of shocked disbelief. He would endeavour to keep the news to himself if she asked him to, but she doubted his ability not to betray what he knew by some small unwitting gesture. Certainly he would be quiet and reflective at dinner and the news would make him miserable. Rose bit her lip. She would keep the news from him until tomorrow then, when everyone would know. There was nothing to be gained by telling him any earlier, and yet she felt afraid to remain silent, knowing what she did. The murderer had developed a tendency towards killing, seemingly thought nothing of committing murder to remove an inconvenient obstruction, and would kill again, she felt sure, unless stopped. She was uncomfortably aware that, now she knew the truth she was potentially in danger. She must be on her guard.

The meal passed uneventfully and would have been in silence had not Cedric and the baron gallantly engaged in some forced conversation over some very trivial matter. Every now and then, Rose was called upon to contribute a few words to keep the conversation from dwindling. The baron's children, she noticed, hardly said a word or even looked up from the tablecloth, their faces pale and haggard looking, their mood restive. As if by unspoken agreement, no mention was made of the murders, although the memory of them was never far away and seemed to linger in the room like stale cigarette smoke.

Josephine came over to Rose in the drawing room after dinner, carrying her cup of coffee.

'Crabtree happened to mention that he saw you and Cedric going into the study this afternoon.' Josephine seemed anxious, fiddling with her cup and saucer to such a degree that she almost spilt the contents.

'Yes, we had something to tell Inspector Deacon,' said Rose, studying the girl closely who, in turn, was refusing to look her in the eye.

'Oh?' Josephine, Rose thought, was trying very hard not to appear too curious.

'Yes.' And before she could stop herself to consider for a moment whether or not what she was doing was wise, and because the situation was just so unbearable, Rose found herself blurting everything out to Josephine, as she had done in the garden the day before about the blackmail business. 'I know what made you go to London, Josephine. And that's what we told the police. It would be so much better if you come clean about it to the police yourself.'

'Oh!' Josephine's hand shot to the side of her face, as was her habit. 'I see. Did you tell them anything else?' She added hurriedly. Her eyes, Rose noticed, had gone very wide.

'Like who killed Lord Sneddon and his servant, you mean? No, we didn't tell them that. We didn't know, you see, not then. Only now I do. I suddenly realised just before dinner who did it and why. And I'm going to tell Inspector Deacon first thing in the morning. You'd –'

She broke off from what she was saying. Too late she realised that the whole room had gone silent. The gentle hum of conversation that had lulled her into a false sense of security had stopped abruptly a few moments earlier. Both Isabella and Hallam were regarding her with interest, and even the baron was looking at her curiously. Only Cedric seemed oblivious to what she had just said. Unless she was very much mistaken, everyone in the room except Cedric, even the servants pouring the coffee, had heard what she had just said to Josephine.

Chapter Thirty-six

'Did you find any?' asked Isabella, as soon as Josephine entered her bedroom later that night.

'My Veronal? Yes, here it is.'

'Will you be a dear and mix some in my glass of water for me while I take my necklace off. These jewels are very fine, but really this necklace is so jolly heavy.'

'I can't think why you decided to wear it in the first place. Here at Dareswick, I mean. It's not as if you have anyone to impress here, is it? Or have you set your sights on Cedric now Hugh is out of the way?'

Isabella stopped fiddling with the clip of her necklace and turned to look at Josephine. There was an uncomfortable silence where neither girl said anything.

'And you brought my cocoa too? It was sweet of you to bring it up to me. And you have brought a cup for yourself, I see. I didn't think you liked it, found it too bitter. Well, are you wanting us to sit down and have a nice sisterly little chat? I really do need to sleep you know, I've hardly slept a wink these last couple of nights, what with everything.'

'The cocoa is not for me, it's for Rose.'

'For Rose? Are you taking it to her now? Oh, do be a dear and pass me my hairbrush, will you? I think it's over there on my dressing table somewhere.'

'I'm not your servant, Isabella.' Even so, Josephine still went over to the dressing table in search of the hairbrush. 'It isn't here, you know. I say, Isabella, do you really need all these creams and potions?'

'It must be in one of the dressing table drawers, then. Yes, the top right hand one, I think. Do have a look.'

A few moments elapsed as Josephine rummaged through the contents of the drawer until she had located the elusive hairbrush.

'We are very different, you and I, aren't we?' said Isabella, as Josephine passed her the hairbrush. 'In character as well as looks, I mean. No one would take us for sisters, would they? You know, Josephine, I have always been rather frightened of you.'

'Have you?' Josephine said, slowly. 'Funny, I've always been rather frightened of *you*. Especially after …' her hand went up to her face.

'Don't!' Isabella exclaimed. 'Don't be so beastly as to remind me.'

'I'm sorry, I didn't mean to. It's just that I am frightened, Isabella, as much *for* you as *of* you.'

'How strange. You see, sister dear, I feel exactly the same way about you. Everyone thinks you are so kind, and good and reliable. They don't see what I see. Then they'd realise that you're nothing like that at all.'

'Oh, Isabella.' Josephine sat down on Isabella's bed and suddenly burst into tears, 'what am I to do; what am I to do?' She hid her head in her hands and sobbed. Isabella watched on, unmoved.

'Ah, Mrs Hodges,' said Josephine, coming out of Isabella's bedroom a few minutes later. 'Would you mind taking this cocoa along to Miss Simpson? I promised I'd bring her a cup. But I'm suddenly feeling jolly tired and she is sure to want me to stay for a bit of a chat, and I'm afraid I'm really not up to it. I feel quite done in.'

'Of course, Miss Josephine.'

'Oh, and there's just one other thing.'

'Yes, miss.'

'Miss Isabella is frightfully tired. Understandably she hasn't been sleeping well, what with what happened to Lord Sneddon and everything. I've given her some of my Veronal for her to use. I'd appreciate it if you'd make sure that she isn't disturbed tomorrow morning. I want her to have a bit of a lie in. I think it will do her the world of good, I really do.'

'Where is everyone?' asked Rose of Crabtree when she came down to breakfast the following morning. 'Am I the first one down? I know it's frightfully early but I just couldn't sleep.'

'The master's taken a stroll outside, miss. He often does first thing in the morning, believes it sets him up for the day, and the young gentlemen are still in bed. Miss Josephine's gone for a walk by the lake and Miss Isabella's sleeping in this morning. Her sister asked that she not be disturbed on account of her not sleeping well lately.'

'Miss Josephine said that?'

'Yes, miss, she told Mrs Hodges yesterday, last thing.'

'I see. And she's gone for a walk alone by the lake, you say?'

'Yes, miss. Beg pardon, miss, but the police inspector's just arrived with the sergeant. I need to see to them.'

'Yes, of course, I need to talk to them myself in a minute.'

It occurred to Rose that she should really eat something. Goodness knew when anyone would feel like eating when she told the police what she believed to be true. But her appetite had quite deserted her. She was worried about Josephine, she realised. Why had she gone for a walk by the lake? Was it possible that …

'Inspector Deacon.' She was so relieved to see him, it was all she could do not to throw herself in his arms. 'Please, it's Josephine, she's gone for a walk by the lake.'

'Good morning, Miss Simpson. And that worries you why?'

'I think she may be going to throw herself in. Please, you have to stop her. We might be too late as it is.' She found that she was clinging onto his sleeve in her desperation.

'Quick, Lane, take a couple of the constables with you. And when you get her, if she's in a fit state for questioning, I want her brought into the study. Miss Atherton is going to be answering questions this time, whether she likes it or not.'

'I'm sure she will,' said Rose, 'now that she knows it's all over.'

'Are you telling me that you know what happened and why it happened, Miss Simpson?' Deacon asked, leading the way to the study.

'Yes, I suppose I am. But first you must tell me about the man in the newspaper article, the one who has been murdered. Do you know who he was?'

'Yes, and you were right, you see he was –'

'Claude Lambert,' said Rose, hurriedly. 'I'm right. Aren't I?'

'You are indeed, Claude Lambert, erstwhile lover of Miss Isabella Atherton.'

'Oh, no, Inspector, you're quite wrong there. You see, he was never in love with Isabella Atherton. No, he was in love with her sister, Josephine. Don't you see? He was the man she was planning to elope with.'

Chapter Thirty-seven

'No, I don't see at all,' protested Deacon. 'This Claude Lambert chap must have been in love with Isabella Atherton at some point in time, otherwise why would she have sent him those letters, the ones that Sneddon used to blackmail her with? Surely you're not telling me they were forgeries? Or are you telling me they were written by Josephine Atherton not her sister? All this time has Isabella been trying to protect her sister?'

'No, I'm not trying to tell you anything of the sort, Inspector. You see, I said Claude Lambert was not in love with Isabella. I did not say she was not in love with him, or at least thought herself to be.'

'I'm afraid you're totally confusing me, Miss Simpson. You are going to have to explain yourself further,' Deacon said, sounding somewhat exasperated. 'I can't for the life of me understand what you're saying, I –' He broke off abruptly as the study door burst open. 'What on earth –'

'Sir.' Lane was standing there, his hair dishevelled and a look of disbelief on his face. 'Sir, she's dead.'

'Josephine?' Rose cried out, in distress. 'So we were too late. I should have known, I shouldn't –'

'No, miss, not Josephine Atherton. She's fine. We encountered her just now, just outside the house. She was on her way back from the lake. No, it's the other one. Isabella Atherton. Her maid's just found her in her bedroom. It looks like she's been poisoned.'

'Heaven help us, not another murder!' exclaimed the inspector, putting his head in his hands.

'No,' answered Rose, as Josephine Atherton was led into the room. 'It wasn't murder, Inspector. I think you will find it was suicide. She knew, you see, that I'd worked out the truth by something I said last night. She realised the game was up and took the only way out.'

'Are you telling me, Miss Simpson, that Isabella Atherton murdered two people?'

'No I'm not, Inspector. Because, in fact, she murdered three people. She murdered Claude Lambert too. Don't you see? That's what started it all.' Rose looked over at Josephine. The girl was pale and looked as if she was about to faint. Sergeant Lane was obviously of the same opinion and hastily pulled up a chair for her to sit in.

'You realised what she had done, didn't you?' Rose asked gently.

'Yes. Not at first of course, I was just as much in the dark as the rest of you. It was only after ...' She broke off to gulp back a generous measure of brandy which the diligent sergeant had also seen fit to pour her. Rose was pleased to see some colour returning to her cheeks.

'Suppose,' said Deacon, 'that, between the two of you, you tell us the whole story. Miss Atherton looks rather done in, so suppose you start, Miss Simpson, and then you just chip in, Miss Atherton, as you feel able.'

'Well,' said Rose. 'I suppose it all started when Josephine met Claude Lambert at her sister's. He was giving Isabella French lessons. I am assuming there was an instant attraction?'

'Yes,' agreed Josephine, 'I liked him enormously when I met him but didn't think anything of it. Then, purely by chance, we happened to bump into each other a week or two later when I was next in London for the day. We went to a little tea shop he knew and talked and talked for hours. I rather think he missed a couple of his lessons. After that we corresponded frequently and met up in London whenever we could, on the pretext of my going to visit Isabella.'

'And you kept your relationship secret,' prompted Rose.

'Yes. I knew Father would never accept Claude as a prospective husband. He doesn't like foreigners very much I'm afraid, and besides Claude was virtually penniless, eking out a meagre living giving French lessons to the wealthy. Father would have thought him totally beneath us, little more than a servant. He really wouldn't have viewed it as being any different to my eloping with Brimshaw.'

'And then Lord Sneddon came to stay at Dareswick,' said Rose.

'Yes. I thought it rather a blessing at first. You see I pretended to everyone that I was rather flattered by his attentions to me. I didn't think he really meant anything by them. But it was all jolly handy in helping disguise the fact that I was actually in love with someone else. So I just played along. Hugh had such a very bad reputation with women that it never occurred to me for a moment that he might actually fall in love with me, or that I would hurt his feelings or pride so when I rejected his advances.'

'But he did fall in love with you, didn't he? And, when he realised that his love for you was unrequited, he sought solace with your maid.'

'Yes,' said Josephine, sadly. 'I will never forgive myself for what happened to her, not as long as I live. If only I had known what he would do and to what lengths she would go to escape the shame.'

'You weren't to know, you mustn't blame yourself,' said Rose, with feeling. 'Everyone thought that he had got tired of you, not the other way around, didn't they?'

'Yes, you see I wasn't really his usual type. Not nearly pretty enough for one thing. It also meant that everyone left me alone for a bit to lick my wounds, so to speak. They didn't regard it as so very odd if I withdrew a bit from everyone. Which meant that I had all the time I needed to plan my escape with Claude so that we could be together. I knew I'd have to run away from Dareswick, never to return. Father would have disowned me for sure, I knew that. I would be saying goodbye to my family forever.'

'This is all very well,' said Deacon, who had remained silent up to now during the exchange between the two women. 'But what I'd really like to know, is how Isabella and the letters come in to all this.'

'I'm coming to that,' said Rose. 'The main thing is that Josephine and Claude had made plans to elope, to have taken effect in a few days' time, I would imagine. It explains why you were so preoccupied, Josephine, on Friday, and why you were sad about the idea of not being here to see the bulbs come into flower.'

'Yes, yes,' said Deacon, impatiently. 'But how does Isabella, and Sneddon for that matter, come into all this. What's the significance of the letters Sneddon used to blackmail your sister? Did Isabella write them to Claude Lambert, or didn't she?'

'Yes, she did. Correct me if I'm wrong, Josephine, but I think your sister became rather fixated on Claude Lambert, more so perhaps because her feelings weren't reciprocated. She was a beautiful and rich young woman. I am sure she was used to getting her own way and having men fall at her feet. I think she viewed Claude Lambert as something of a challenge.'

'Yes, Claude told me one of his students had become rather obsessed with him and was bombarding him with love letters. At first he laughed it off. I think he saw it as just a bit embarrassing to begin with, you know, what with Isabella being my sister and all that, although of course I didn't know that at the time because he didn't tell me that the letters were hers. But then I noticed a change in him. He seemed worried, and when I pressed him he said that the letters had started to get rather menacing and threatening. You can imagine the sort of thing. If she couldn't have him then nobody else would. He said he thought the girl was not quite right in the head. But he vehemently refused to show me the letters, no matter how hard I pleaded with him to do so, and he absolutely refused to go to the police about them. I realise now that he wanted to protect me from the truth.'

'Somehow,' said Rose, 'Lord Sneddon managed to get hold of the letters. I assume through the services of that Ricketts fellow of his. The irony was he didn't know their true value. He thought they were evidence of a love affair that would be damaging to a young woman's reputation if it became common knowledge. The truth was far more sinister. They were evidence of a decline into a fanatic obsession which led to murder.

'When I overheard the conversation between Lord Sneddon and Isabella in the library, I thought Isabella did not want him to read her letters to Claude out of embarrassment. But later I was struck by two things. One, that she was prepared to go through with the marriage if he promised to return every last letter to her; and second, when she produced them, that she insisted on throwing the letters onto the fire when Inspector Deacon advised that he would be keeping them as evidence. It was obvious then that there was something in them that she did not want known. I think she must have written in one or two of them her intention to kill your Claude, Josephine. The letters were too incriminating to remain to be read by anyone, because that is exactly what she did.' Rose shuddered. 'Although you didn't know Isabella had written the letters to Claude, I think you had a suspicion that she might be the author, didn't you, Josephine, which is why you looked relieved on Friday night when Isabella turned up with Lord Sneddon. You thought initially that she must be in love with him and so couldn't have written the letters to Claude.'

'But I knew something was wrong as soon as I saw them at dinner together and then later when I went to Isabella's room to find out what she was playing at. It was obvious she wasn't in love with Hugh. But it was still a shock to me the following morning when you told me about Hugh blackmailing Isabella over the letters. I realised then that she had written them after all, and that made me frightened. You see, I've always been a little afraid of Isabella. There was always something a little not quite right about her, even when we were children. She has always had these awful uncontrollable fits of violence.'

'She gave you that scar on your face, didn't she, not Hallam? I've noticed your hand often flies up to it when you're worried, or when you are anxious about Isabella.'

'Yes. I told you it was a sibling squabble that got out of hand. Because I said Hallam was always telling me that it didn't look so very awful you understandably assumed that he had given me the scar, not Isabella. And so I just agreed and played along. You see, I have always felt a little ashamed that Isabella could have done such a thing. Everyone assumed that it was an accident. But it wasn't, it was quite deliberate.'

'But you gave yourself away later in the conversation,' said Rose. 'I didn't realise it at the time, only later when I replayed our conversation in my mind. That was when I went for a lie down yesterday evening. You said: "We were both only young children when it happened, *she* didn't mean anything by it."'

'But whatever made you decide to run off to London in the middle of the night?' asked Deacon. 'What made you think that that man in the article could be Lambert?'

'Two things really,' answered Josephine. 'One, as I have explained, finding out that Isabella was the author of those awful letters to Claude and knowing that she would stop at nothing if she could not get her way. But secondly because Claude hadn't written to me. He wrote to me frequently and, of course, I was awaiting news from him as to when the arrangements were in place for us to elope. I hadn't received a letter from him for quite some time despite my writing to him every day begging him to tell me what was wrong. And all the time he was dead, oh ...' Josephine broke down in tears. It was probably the first time, thought Rose, that she had let herself grieve properly.

'You have been worried all this time about Isabella, haven't you?' said Rose. 'You didn't know whether you should hate her and give her up to the police, or whether as her older sister your first duty was to protect her.'

'Yes, and I loved her, you see.' Josephine said, mopping her eyes with a handkerchief. 'Oh, of course, I knew she was dangerous and had to be stopped. I just couldn't bring myself to be the one to give her up. I could never have lived with myself. And besides, you see, I wasn't absolutely sure she was the murderer until I found out Hugh had been murdered. Even then I thought it might have been his servant until he too was killed. I thought he might have had an argument with Hugh or something.'

'So you originally thought Lord Sneddon or Ricketts had killed Lambert?' asked Deacon. 'Because he, or more likely his servant, had stolen Isabella's letters from him, I assume?'

'Yes, I returned from London ready to confront Hugh. You can imagine what a shock it was for me to find out that he had been murdered. I didn't know quite what to think. I wanted it so much not to have been Isabella. But I suppose even then I thought it likely that she had murdered them both. I was relieved when I found out Crabtree and Mrs Hodges suspected Hugh's manservant.'

'But you were determined not to give her away, even though your sudden departure to London looked jolly suspicious,' said Rose.

'I just wanted some time by myself to try and work everything out and decide what to do.'

'What I can't quite understand,' said Deacon, 'is why your sister considered it necessary to kill Sneddon. From what you've said, Miss Simpson, it doesn't look as if Sneddon read more than one or two of the earlier letters. They may have been a bit over the top, contrived, I think you said, but relatively harmless in that she hadn't resorted to threats in them. And it appears he never had any serious intention or interest in reading them. Besides he returned them to her. So why did she see the need to kill him?'

'Because I don't think he returned them all to her,' said Rose slowly. 'I think he held one back, the last most damning one. When I say Lord Sneddon, I don't mean him, of course, I mean his servant. No, I think Lord Sneddon honestly thought that he had returned all the letters to Isabella.'

'Wait a minute,' said Deacon, holding up a hand. 'Let's go through this methodically. We'll start with Sneddon in the library. He summons Crabtree to get him another decanter of whisky. Crabtree, his own tongue loosened a bit by drink, tells him about the fate of the unfortunate housemaid, Mabel, laying the blame clearly at Sneddon's door. Sneddon, in turn, has a Damascan conversion and is filled with remorse. That's when you come on the scene, Miss Simpson, to get a book. Sneddon tells you about the maid and understandably, filled with disgust, you suggest that he try to make amends in whatever way he can. Whilst contemplating how he might do this, hot on your heels, Isabella appears. She pleads for him to return her letters. Much to her surprise, he agrees. A few minutes later, Sneddon's so-called servant, Ricketts, arrives and is dispatched to get the letters and hand them over to Isabella, which he does. Right, what happens next, Miss Simpson?'

'I would imagine that as soon as Isabella is given the letters she runs back to the safety of her room to go through them to make sure that she has all of them. To her horror, she finds that the last one, the most threatening and incriminating one in which she threatens to kill Claude Lambert, is missing.'

'And while Isabella is doing that,' said Deacon hurriedly, 'you, Miss Atherton, take the opportunity to rush downstairs with your suitcase and let yourself out of the house by a side door.'

'Meanwhile,' continued Rose, 'Isabella is panicking about the missing letter. Instinctively she thinks Lord Sneddon has tried to double cross her. In this I think she was mistaken. As I've already said, I think Lord Sneddon genuinely thought he had returned all her letters to her. I think the guilty party was in fact Ricketts who, seeing a source of income suddenly being whipped away from him, decided to keep a letter back for his own blackmail purposes.'

'So what happens next?' enquired Sergeant Lane, speaking for the first time.

'Well,' said Rose, 'Isabella's first reaction is to confront Lord Sneddon. Ricketts probably stayed with him a while so she has to wait for a few minutes to make sure he is alone, which would have done nothing to improve her temper. When she does at last confront him, he denies all knowledge of the missing letter. Unfortunately for him he does not see her as a danger and turns his back on her to sit down at the desk. His intention, I think, is to start writing a list of all the other people to whom he needs to make amends. Isabella, in a fit of anger, picks up the paper knife and stabs him in the back. She can't have been thinking straight because, of course, that gets her no nearer to getting the letter back.'

'She must have been tempted to search his room,' said Deacon. 'But presumably she was afraid of making a noise and waking the whole house.'

'I think she probably was also in shock,' said Rose. 'I don't think she intended to kill him. The next day she probably hoped to keep the blackmail business to herself, only I let slip what I had overheard. I think initially she panicked, but then she realised she could use it to her own advantage. By producing the letters it would seem then that she no longer had a motive for wishing Lord Sneddon dead. All she had to do was hope that Ricketts would hold his tongue about the missing letter. By then she must have been half expecting him to use it to blackmail her. And she knew he also had an additional hold over her now that Lord Sneddon was dead. It wasn't just a case of paying him to keep quiet about a romantic indiscretion. No, she would be paying him not to reveal that she was the murderer, or at the very least had a very strong motive for wanting Sneddon dead.'

'So Ricketts had to go,' said Deacon. 'You know, I've just thought of something that's explained now. When I asked Isabella whether she had thrown Lambert's letters to her on the fire, she looked utterly bewildered. My question threw her because, of course, Lambert never wrote her any letters so she had no need to throw them onto the fire.'

'And this all explains something else, sir,' chipped in Sergeant Lane. 'Do you remember how that Ricketts fellow looked awfully sly and gave us that crooked grin when we asked him who else Sneddon was blackmailing? He said how he wasn't blackmailing anyone else, and we didn't believe him one bit, do you remember, sir?'

'I do, Lane, and I see he thought he had one over on us, because he was telling the truth. They weren't blackmailing anyone else. What I don't understand though is how Ricketts managed to get a note to Isabella to inform her that he had the missing letter. He would have had to in order to arrange a time and place to meet for him to return it to her in exchange for money. The other servants were jolly suspicious of him. There's no way old Crabtree would have allowed him to roam around upstairs unchecked, and downstairs in the dining room or drawing room I imagine Isabella was always surrounded by people.'

'Oh, I think I know how he did that,' said Rose. 'Somehow he managed to arrange with Crabtree that he help wait at table last night. He dropped a dish of vegetables when he was serving Isabella and a few of the carrots and beans fell onto her lap. I think it was a deliberate act on his part. In the ensuing confusion, he passed her a napkin so that she could dab at the mess. I remember she looked strangely at the napkin for a moment and then fled from the room. I think Ricketts passed a note to her in the napkin.'

'And the silly fool went ahead and met her,' sighed Lane. 'Fellows like Ricketts never learn. That's why they more often than not find themselves behind bars ... or worse.'

Chapter Thirty-eight

'It must have been rather awful for you having to sit there and hear us talk like that about your sister,' said Rose, as she and Josephine strolled in the gardens a few hours later.

'Oh, it wasn't so very bad, really,' said Josephine languidly. She looked as if she hadn't slept properly for days and was still walking around in a trance. 'It was almost as if you were talking about someone else. I can't quite take it all in, any of it. Even now I can't believe what she did. How could she have killed Claude? I can't quite believe he's really dead. I can't believe she's dead, that I'll never see them again, I can't –' She broke down finally in a fit of sobbing and Rose put an arm around her shoulders and hugged her.

'It'll do you good to cry. I suppose it's only now that it's all over that you're beginning to take it all in. I say, I'm jolly glad, you know, that you didn't drown yourself in the lake.'

'What? W-why would I have done that?' Josephine glanced up at Rose nervously. She looked frightened.

'Because you killed your sister,' Rose said quietly.

'H-how do you know that? Are … are you going to tell the police?'

'To answer your first question, because I can't see Isabella killing herself. She would have gone down fighting. And, to answer your second question, no I'm not going to tell the police, and you mustn't either. I know you did it for her own sake, to save her from the public humiliation of a trial and ultimately the gallows. It was only a matter of time until the police worked it all out.'

'Even then, I'm not sure I would have given her away if … if.' Josephine faltered, and then continued, her voice quiet and strangely free of emotion. 'Last night, Isabella asked me if I had any Veronal that she could take as she had had trouble sleeping. I took some to her room and she told me to mix some in her glass of water for her. I thought then how easy it would be to give her an overdose. I thought about it, you know. But I couldn't bring myself to do it. It was only when …'

'Yes?' prompted Rose.

'It was only when she tried to kill you that I knew I had to do something.'

242

'Kill me? She tried to kill me?' Rose felt herself grow cold.

'I'd brought up her cocoa, and yours too. She was very interested when she heard that the second cup was for you. I was immediately suspicious, especially coming as it did after what you'd said about knowing who the murderer was and telling the police in the morning. She asked me to look for her hairbrush on her dressing table and, while I was looking for it, I caught sight of her reflection in the dressing table mirror. I saw her put Veronal into your cup of cocoa.'

'So what did you do?' Rose found that she could hardly breathe.

'I pretended that I hadn't noticed. Then, when her back was turned I switched the cups. When I walked out of her room that night, I knew that by morning she'd be dead.'

'Rose, I've been thinking,' said Cedric as they wandered down to the lake. The way he said the words filled Rose with a sense of dread. He never wants to see me again, she thought. He associates me with death. Two murders, no, three really if one counted poor Claude Lambert. It's too much. He wants to be able to visit his friends at weekends without being scared that a murder is suddenly going to crop up.

I can't say I blame him, she thought. I can't say that I blame him at all. Of course she'd be sad. No, she realised suddenly, she'd be far more than sad; she'd be devastated. The thought of never seeing Cedric again, why it would be unbearable. To know that he'd be living his life somewhere, while she was living her life somewhere else, as if they'd never met. It would be as if they'd never known each other, as if they were nothing more than strangers. She must make him change his mind, she must –

'I've been thinking, Rose, that next time we meet up it should just be you and me. What do you say? Oh, I know I'm not very exciting and that you might find it rather boring without some more company. I'm really rather a dull old thing and you're probably used to ...' He turned to look at her. 'Oh, I say, Rose, have you got something in your eye? It must be this wind. It's probably blown up a speck of dirt, shall I take a look?'

'Cedric,' said Rose, throwing herself into his arms. 'I can't think of anything nicer than it just being you and me. And don't worry, I'm absolutely sure there'll be no more murders ...'